I0564596

EVERMORE

AN INTRODUCTION

BREWIN

First published in Australia in 2001 by Infinite Spiral
Second edition published in Australia in 2003 by Brolga Publishing

This edition published in Great Britain in 2012 by Ignis
An imprint of Polybius Books

A CIP catalogue record for this book
is available from the British Library

ISBN 978-0-9565880-9-8

Cover Design by Arati Devasher, www.aratidevasher.com

Typeset by Elaine Sharples, www.typesetter.org.uk
Printed and bound in Great Britain by
MPG Biddles, King's Lynn, Norfolk, PE30 4LS

www.polybiusbooks.com

www.thebrewin.com

EVERMORE:

AN INTRODUCTION

Dear Readers,

It's sort of funny, I guess, that Brewin has asked me to write a profile of himself for a book which is, more than anything, a profile of himself. I seriously doubt whether I can top his efforts; and I think it is crazy to try. What I *do* think I can do, perhaps even better than Brewin, is appeal to your emotions and say that I hope you love Brewin and *Evermore* as much as I do. I hope you love it enough to accept its faults – and I think it does have faults. I hope you love it enough not to judge the book and him too harshly because above all, he is just a human being. He is wonderful and very special and fun and warm and an interesting human being, but always only a person, just like you, just like me and just like all of us.

So Readers, please keep this in mind as you wander and wonder through *Evermore*.

With love,
"Lana"

ACKNOWLEDGEMENTS

What you hold before you now is not the result of my efforts alone. Far from it! Over seventeen years have passed since this book was written, and yet the journey goes ever onward... I wish to thank the following for their contribution:

Adam Kolczynski, for giving me this opportunity;

Barbara Brabec, for advice and making this possible;

Jill Brewin, for your endless love, support and guidance, though I may not always show it, I will always love you dearly;

Lee Cheney, for convincing me to do this in the first place, and for all your efforts to ensure it happened;

Mark Zocchi, for producing the second edition;

Jessica Bennett, for convincing me to continue with this; and for all your efforts to 'spread the word';

Lana, who let's not forget, thank you for helping me write this story;

Also Adam Kolczynski and Julie Capaldo, for editing and direction; Arati Devasher, Trish Hart and Alex Jovanovich, for your brilliant artwork; Margaret Clark, Anita Bell, Eaun Mitchell, Lord Tim, Maria Foster, Alain Kern, Stephen McMillan, Mark Hall, Olivia Gronn-White, Joy Dunn, John Marsden and James Redfield, among many others for advice, support and inspiration;

And finally, *you* the reader;

Thanks and Cheers to you all!

FOREWORD

I have made some subtle modifications to the exact nature and chronological order of events here and there as suits my purpose. But I do not believe that this has unduly affected the integrity of this book. To the best of my ability to interpret events after and before they occurred, everything within this book exists approximately 90% intact. I feel no need to justify this further. You, though, are entitled to perceive this book however you like.

Many may look down upon me in differing ways and see me as merely a twenty-something year-old kid trying to be a wise man, as someone trying to become something greater than what he is, as a self-righteous little blond shit who's just making up stuff and spinning philosophical bullshit in order to achieve fame as well as money, as someone who is willing to betray his friends in order to write a quick novel and make a buck, or as any one of a number of differing 'negative' things... You are entitled to this viewpoint, as am I entitled to say that writing this book has been something I chose to do, and have been determined to see through to its conclusion, regardless of the consequences, in order to achieve a dream, to achieve something which I believe helps myself and helps others. (And is hopefully entertaining too!) I accept responsibility for my own actions and my own life; but I cannot accept responsibility for other's reactions, though I will do all I feel I can in the circumstances to do what I perceive 'is right', but beyond this I am powerless to intervene in something where the choice is with others. I am aware that there are many counter-arguments against what I have just said, and I will deal with some of these when and where I choose, and not necessarily within this text.

Come then and experience with me that which is *Evermore...*

Brewin, 1996

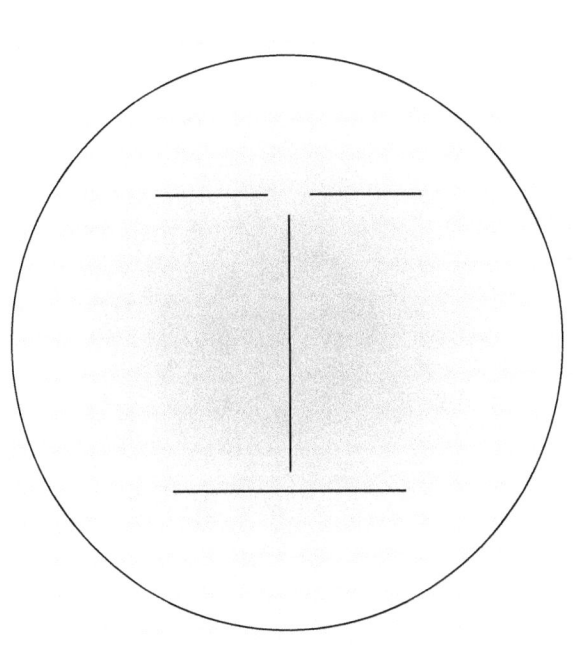

THE FIRST INSTANCE

The perfect beginning.

How does it begin?

And does it?

I had been wandering, as usual, and then I saw her.

"Hello, Caraline," I said.

She stopped.

With a perplexed expression she turned around to me, me standing there with a radiant smile, and queried, "How did you know my name?" Her friend too was perplexed, but watched with fascination, anticipating the exchange about to occur between us.

"Because I'm psychic." I laughed. She still looked confused, trying to figure me out. Then I said, "Do you want me to tell you what your surname is, when and where you were born and what your last meal was?"

She didn't know what to say, so I said it for her.

"Well, I'm not going to because I made that up about being psychic. I just wanted to surprise you."

"Surprise me?" She was still trying to comprehend me and this bizarre conversation.

"Yeah, and I've got plenty more surprises coming too." I laughed again (I do that a lot).

"Like what?" she said beginning to sound worried.

"Oh, I'm not going to tell you what now!" I said

grinning, swaying my hair about and rolling my eyes. "Then they wouldn't be surprises!"

Her friend giggled, and I noticed the silver buttons on her purple shirt sparkling. Caraline had golden ones.

I sensed the moment passing. She was probably thinking I was insane but harmless, yet it was best to detach herself from me now while she (if she) still could.

But I would do better.

"I'm not insane, but I'm not necessarily harmless either. That would imply a lack of energy, and energy I've got. However, I would like to sit down and chat with you two." I gazed at her friend, engaging her too. "If you've got the time?"

Caraline quickly glanced at the other girl, who merely returned a warm smile to both of us. Seeming to have no easy way of deferring without seeming cold and awkward, Caraline responded, "I guess so."

Smiling once more, I asked, "Where were you guys about to sit?"

THE SECOND INSTANCE

We were sitting now, drinking warm coffee and the pleasant atmosphere of the dreamy café.

I leaned back on my chair, put my feet up on another and relaxed with deep, full breaths, taking in all the aesthetics of the world around me.

Caraline asked, "So what was it that you wanted to talk about?"

I cut from my thoughts and looked at her, answered honestly, "I don't know," and smiled.

This seemed to confirm everything she had suspected about me. The other girl was still watching us with interest and anticipation; I didn't even know her name.

"Well..." Caraline began.

I seized the moment. "Conversation doesn't necessarily have to have a given focus or a set direction, it just manifests itself out of the people involved, their thoughts, emotions, and ideas."

She looked back at me, sipping her coffee, apparently considering what I had just said.

"Just like a story, there needn't be a set plot; it can develop from circumstances and experiences – like this story, for instance."

"Excuse me?"

"Like this story. The three of us here have begun to create a story, a great adventure of experience."

Caraline retorted, "This isn't any story, and we're certainly not going on any adventure. We're sitting down here in this café with you, because you asked us to."

The nameless girl shifted in her seat, a little uncomfortable.

Creating a shift of emphasis myself I said, "Maybe you don't see it, but there is a story here involving the three of us. Why, I could quite easily imagine someone reading a book describing our interaction at this very moment." I gazed across at the nameless girl, smiling.

Refusing to swallow my statements, Caraline attacked. "Books are interesting to read and at least some people want to read them. This could be a story, but no one would read it."

"On the contrary, I can imagine that others would find our story, the adventure we're creating here, quite compelling indeed, but I know that this very thing is going on as I speak."

She exploded. "How can you say that you know? You can't say you know anything for certain! And even if someone *did* write a story about this event here, how could they possibly write about it, until after it has happened?"

Smiling, I answered, "Those statements you have just made Caraline, are quite true and correct, given your assumptions. But I think that those assumptions are invalid."

"Do you just think, or do you know?"

"To think is to know."

She laughed, leaned back on her chair, and sarcastically remarked, "Of course, it follows clearly, anyone would have to agree once they thought it through."

"Precisely, I couldn't have said it better myself." I looked again with an encouraging smile at the girl who hadn't spoken.

And then she did speak. "And just how do you know these things?"

Raising my finger for emphasis, as though she had hit upon an important point, I answered, "That is another surprise."

She giggled, seeming enchanted. I still had no idea who she was, just as neither of them knew me by name. It hadn't even occurred to me to ask her name – it didn't seem to be important yet.

Caraline broke in again. "So you just waltz up to us, say you know my name without even explaining how or why, coerce us into sitting down with you, say you don't know what it was that you wanted to talk about, spout trivial philosophical bullshit, and expect us to believe you, claiming that you know. And tell us that this is all some great adventure that someone, somewhere is reading in a story book?"

"That's the gist of it."

"You're crazy."

"If I were to explain too much, too soon, not only would this spoil a few of the surprises, but it might create a boring story. I would be saying some things which the reader had already realised, and to make everything clear from the beginning might not give the readers much incentive to want to read on and discover more."

The girl who was still unnamed, shuffled again in her seat. She visibly withdrew, pushing her seat back to gaze out of the large bay windows.

Caraline took this as a signal that she wanted to leave, indeed I also sensed that the present opportunity had passed.

No longer bothering to pursue the seemingly pointless conversation, Caraline rose from her seat, feigning a smile and a friendly parting comment, "Well, we really must be going. Nice talking to you."

Caraline grasped the other girl by the wrist, ensuring that she was coming too, and turned away.

"See you tomorrow!" I called after them.

THE THIRD INSTANCE

A boy sits alone in a crowded yet deserted attic and questions, 'why?'

He sits perched on an old coffee-coloured chest among the relics of his ancestors and wonders whether his parents might discover him too as another relic of the past among this sepulchre of memories.

The dusty, worn family artefacts around him – clothing, jewellery, paintings, musical instruments; a pirate's treasure trove – do little to inspire his thoughts in anything other than a necrophilic domain, as he imagines his lifeless visage staring up blindly from different positions among them.

He imagines the various dead expressions upon his face, and the expressions of shock and horror upon the faces of his parents when they discover him.

Moving off the box, he wanders around the attic, picking his way through the cluttered arrangement, running his finger along the various surfaces and looking indifferently at the trails he forms.

All he really sees, though, is that he is only delaying the inevitable by even trying to think through and justify the decision.

The decision to make it all end...

With a sigh that is tired of life, he slouches into an armchair, its dusty upholstery threadbare. Shifting his gaze from the armchair to a clock half obscured on the wall, a clock whose batteries have long since expired, he confirms his belief that everything inevitably dies and decays back into nothing.

'Ashes to ashes, dust to dust'.

After pausing to scratch his arm and molest a long-picked scab on his elbow, he shuts his eyes and pushes his back into the soft, malleable recesses of the old chair. There is a vain, subconscious hope that something miraculous will happen to save him from doom or re-instil him with an energy and a desire for life.

He tries to cancel out, for even just a short time, his morbid thoughts and tries to contact the spirit world he has so often heard about, but seldom believed and never experienced.

If there is anything more to this existence, to existence itself, any grace, any beauty, any compassion, any meaning, he thinks, that something must happen now. Else he will take his life and have the pain, misery and emptiness over and done with. A world without meaning, true meaning; not that which comes about through mathematical explanations and laws of a science that he never understood, or the instructions of how to live one's life of a religion to which he could never relate; he can no longer bear.

And yet just when it seems he needs it most, nothing happens. The uncaring world fails to rescue him in his hour of need.

Tears roll down his face, wet lines down his dirty cheeks, like the lines he had drawn on the furniture in the dust. Sobbing and whimpering – unloved. No one is here to bear witness to his torment, he has no friends, none that are real friends, and his parents don't understand him, they don't even try. The only thing to which he could relate, wasn't even human, his dog Wolfie, and it had been hit and killed by a car a week ago. The malice and mercilessness of the world seems endless. No one cares. No one cares if a little boy loses his way and departs from the world. Who, apart from his parents, would notice? He knows they'd suffer, but their grief would only be because he was a child of theirs, not necessarily because of who that child is or was. What difference would there be to the world without him in it? None. None whatsoever. It is a soulless, indifferent world in which he has no place, no importance, save that which springs from being a child of his parents and nothing that is a result of who he is. What little importance he has was entirely pre-determined, like another scientific law that defines the mechanical, meaningless universe.

It is too much, he has to end it now. He can't stand the thought of another meaningless day, another mean-ingless experience, another meaningless lesson that is supposed to be for his own good, that is supposed to be for his 'education' so that he can join a meaningless world where he is just another meaningless identity among a meaningless mass all deluding themselves that there really is meaning in a meaningless world.

His eyes blur with tears, he begins to search for his father's pistol that he has stolen and loaded and brought up here. He had put it down during this final departing expedition around what will become his tomb, in the hope of finding something, something which held meaning, a purpose to his life, to life itself.

As his efforts to find the gun become more and more frantic, a vain thought emerges from his subconscious that some greater force from above has finally intervened to save him by removing the gun that will end his life.

But this thought, barely having had life, is aborted as the next moment his fingers clasp around the familiar barrel of the pistol where it had slid down between the coffee-coloured chest and the old faded paintings.

Now he cradles the gun in his young hands, trying to feel its cold power and energy, trying to imagine it sucking out what little energy he has left to give and glowing with a supernatural energy in his absence, maybe smirking and chuckling with evil, as it lies in a widening pool of his own blood. The light glistening off its silvery, polished surface is distorted into great streaks by his teary vision.

He snuffles and wipes at the streaming tears, before falling into the armchair again and pointing the barrel at his forehead.

He feels the small cold circle at the middle of his brow and closes his fingers tightly around the grip, resting his thumb over the trigger itself. As he closes his eyes he notices how parched his throat has become. Licking his lips he tastes the salt that has accumulated there and notices with surprise that it tastes sweet, like a new and bizarre sugar.

He begins to notice how warm it is in the attic and how full the air is of different scents; not just the musty smell of old age and choking dust, but the strange mellow sourness of the mould that has grown in patches on the armchair and the peculiar complexity within the aroma of matured wood, cedar he thinks, that wafts with gentle eddies of air into his nostrils. Even the dust and decay-ridden carpet the chair rests upon seems to have a great depth in the scent of its ancient fibres, underlying all the superficial, distasteful odours.

Now he begins to listen to the distant sounds of birds singing and cars rolling past outside. If he concentrates hard enough, he can even hear the motion of people on the footpath and decipher the cackle and murmur of voices. He can feel the soft touch of the wind caressing the fine hairs of his ears, and only now is aware of the vague, prickly sensations that the armchair is inducing over parts of his arms and down the back of his calves.

And beneath it all he begins to get the impression that somewhere far away there is music playing, its notes and rhythms barely perceptible and perhaps only existing in the imaginary construction of his own mind; a sub-conscious vibration that is in tune with a subconscious part of himself.

He opens his eyes again, perhaps for the first time ever and sees the ancient, intricate and venerable relics before him in a way that he has never before experienced. He sees them not in light of their aged, decayed or dis-coloured state, but in their completeness, as unified states of being of which he has never been aware. The paintings begin to conjure up images of other worlds and vivid experiences, speaking of great beauty that exists not just in the mind of the creator, but accessible to any with their own minds to experience for themselves.

He perceives a great wisdom in the old hand-crafted furniture encircling him, as if portions of the carpenters' souls and understanding were infused with their work, preserved in time, to be passed onto successive generations. Even the mouldy apparel and the handfuls of dulled, beaded necklaces strewn about, resonate with the magical memories of other times, places and realities that he has yet to experience.

The fingers that cradle the pistol, and the cranium that cradles his consciousness, both seem to quiver and tremble, as he is filled with a sense of wonder at the complexity of the world around him. There is the feeling that somewhere beneath the cryptic mystery of it all exists meaning that he has overlooked, taken for granted, or even forgotten.

Danny might live again.

*   *   *

At that moment I was broken from the story I was creating by the approach of Caraline and her friend. They had yet to notice me, so I called out to them, "Over here!"

Caraline tried to look away, but her friend noticed me, and with a pleased smile of recognition began her way over. Caraline followed.

Beaming vibrantly, the girl whose name I still did not know, sat next to me. Caraline acknowledged me curtly and took a seat near her friend and the exit, but away from me.

I meant to ask Caraline's friend her name, but instead

joked with them both, "You're late, I've been waiting here at *least* five minutes!"

Caraline seemed incredulous. She struggled to suppress an expression of disgust.

Her friend mirrored my smile.

Caraline then noticed that aside from a couple of dirty plates left behind by previous users, there were three full cups of coffee, only one of which was near me. In response to her observation, I said, "Yeah, the coffee I ordered for you. It shouldn't be too cold, it's only been there five minutes."

Caraline pretended to taste one, and rose from the table, hastily explaining, "I think I'll go get another cup."

"That's okay, I'll wait."

I smiled at the other girl and noticed how her eyes shone against the backdrop of a peculiarly plain face. I say peculiarly plain because her beauty emanated from beyond the apparent ordinariness of her features; her freckled rounded cheeks, pale lips, roughly textured brow and dull brown hair.

We asked each other's name simultaneously and then laughed at this. Her name was Lana and mine is Andrew.

We smiled at each other again, both trying to ease the awkwardness of the moment. I attempted to think of something that might initiate conversation, whilst she avoided my gaze. As a result we felt more awkward.

Eventually I broke the ice, stating the obvious, "You're as nervous as I am."

Encouraged, she responded, "You get nervous and anxious too?"

"Of course I do!" I laughed. "All the time. I'm as human as anyone else."

"But you seem so confident and so sure of yourself."

"I appreciate myself, just as I try to appreciate others. But I don't consciously try to suppress my emotions. That'd be like lying to myself, only allowing certain parts of me, the parts I imagine that others might like, to be expressed. And if I did that, it wouldn't be me."

"I wish I could do that," she said.

"Sure you can! It comes naturally once you get used to it."

"But others will think that I'm even more awkward and inept."

"What they'll see is that you're human, that you're real. And hopefully they'll see that you're just like them; someone with limitations, but with far greater potential."

She wasn't sure she agreed, but was warm with empathy all the same.

Caraline returned and immediately we sensed a change.

THE FOURTH INSTANCE

"Sorry, I had to go to the toilet," she declared noncha-lantly upon her return.

Lana and I looked at each other across the table and grinned. Caraline didn't notice.

"Haaaah," she sighed aloud, "Gee I'm tired. I've got so much work to do this afternoon too."

I laughed.

"What's so funny?" Caraline sounded defensive.

"I found your statements to be quite funny."

"What? Funny? How do you laugh at a serious statement?" She was now trying to be funny herself and assert herself over the conversation. "I guess you take jokes seriously. Someone tells you," she adopted a silly voice, "a joke like 'Why did the baby cross the road? Because it was stapled to the chicken.' And you say," she put on a concerned voice, "How terrible! What a traumatic incident that must have been for the baby! Did they manage to remove the staples? Or did they have to take it to hospital?" Whilst talking she seemed to look more at Lana than she did at me.

Fuelling her frustration, I laughed again.

"Is that what you do whenever anyone says anything that makes any sense, just laugh? But as long as they talk meaningless nonsense you can communicate with them?"

"I shall communicate with you when you are communicating with me. My laughing at you was not meant in any derogatory manner, it was merely that I found your comments funny. If you expect me to take you seriously, then I must be able to expect you to do the same."

"Hmm. Okay," she said, smiling at Lana like one classmate might smile at another after they had been told off by their teacher.

I had begun to feel that Caraline's personality was changing, changing into someone I already knew. The writer sensed this too. Caraline also sensed a change and she voiced this thought in her silly voice.

"Don't you think you're confusing your readers with your character? I mean one moment you're a raving lunatic and the next you're a serious philosopher and then you're someone who does nothing but laugh at everything. How do you expect them to follow your story?"

I answered, "That very analogy you have just mentioned, I think applies very well to you also. I could quite easily imagine the readers finding your character 'unrealistic' and saying to themselves, 'Oh, she wouldn't do that. I know someone just like that who never did that in that situation.'"

"Are you being serious?" She looked at me properly for the first time today, leaning forward a little and trying to read my face.

Looking to Lana again, who radiated admiration no matter what I seemed to do, I answered Caraline, "Yes, I am being serious."

"How can anyone say that someone else's character is

'unrealistic'? it's real whether other people like it or not. A character in a book maybe you can call 'unrealistic', but my character or anyone else's just is, you can't question whether it's real or not, because it is."

"And this is exactly my point about characters in a book. We may be characters in a book, in a story that someone else is reading. And just as it seems ridiculous for someone to say that someone else's character is 'unrealistic', the same goes for any character in a book. There is no way of telling that we are any different."

"So what are you saying, that we're characters in a book someone is reading? That someone is writing us? What if they never finish the story or they make a spelling mistake? What happens then? Or..."

"No, that's not what I was saying and I would prefer it if you refrained from making a mockery of my words. Even if you do not agree with me, at least give me a valid or sensible reason."

"So it's okay for you to laugh at my words, but not for me to laugh at yours?"

"I'm unsure whether I see a point in trying to justify my responses, and this is in part because I don't wish to argue with you over 'trivial philosophical bullshit', as you might put it."

She interjected before I could continue. "So providing you don't see any topic as being 'trivial philosophical bullshit' then it's okay to talk about it regardless of what other people think, but as soon as you think it's trivial and bullshit then you won't discuss it."

Weary, I answered, "Whilst you conduct a conversation like something which you have to win and prove someone else wrong in, I refuse, and this is my own choice, to participate. When you are ready to conduct a conversation as a mutual exchange of ideas and thoughts, that we can both learn and grow from, then I will talk to you."

"Fine," she said, rising from the table and looking at Lana. "We won't play the game by your rules. We won't play your game at all. Besides, I didn't even want to talk to you, I've got work to do."

Still standing, she gave Lana a funny look as if to say, 'aren't you coming?'

Lana hesitated. "I think I'll stay here for a few minutes and finish my coffee."

"Okay," said Caraline. "Well, I'll be in the library at our usual spot. See you soon."

She made one final parting comment to me, which reminded me again of someone else I had known and something they too had said. "Don't ever become a psychologist," she said. Then she rushed off, seeming uptight and angry.

I felt exhausted, but it soon passed. Indeed I began to feel better almost immediately after Caraline left.

Lana smiled at me affectionately. I think she was in love.

THE FIFTH INSTANCE

"So why do you think we *don't* question the realism of a character in real life, yet we *do* question its realism when it occurs in a book?" Lana asked me.

"Because I think it's based upon the assumption that human beings are rational. When you read them in a book, you expect them to behave in a logical manner that can be deduced by their personality and experiences. And when they don't, it's easy to criticise them and cry 'that character's not real'. But when this occurs in real life, you can't argue whether it was realistic or not, because it happened, it is real, we don't even try to reason over its realism."

She replied, "I think that makes sense, but I'd like to think about it some more. I hope I can remember what you said, I wish I had it written down."

"Besides," I added, "if it were entirely true that one's actions could be deduced by one's personality and prior experiences, then we wouldn't have a free will. Everything we did could be predicted by knowing all the facts previously, the experience of making a choice or even deliberating over that choice would be an illusion."

"I agree," she said.

THE SIXTH INSTANCE

Dark room. What are those faces, leering down at me?

Oh my God, how they are staring! Staring into my soul, tearing it apart, setting it alight with their eyes.

Why is my vision tunnelling? Why? I'm surrounded by walls, where are my feet? Is this the pit? There are only these demons above. Are there horns on their heads? Tails waving behind them, flames of red about them?

The three of them, now they are laughing and spitting. How they are mocking, pointing, teasing! The walls are a barrel around me, I have no way out. I cannot look down, for something wet and endless is below. What have I done? What have I done to deserve this? Why aren't they caring? How unfair. Can't they see that? Why don't they understand? Why don't I understand?

I must get out of here but above are my wardens, my torturers, my sentencers.

Evil, evil, oh how this is evil! Evil that is possessing me, corrupting my core. Why have I been put here, who did this to me?

Please, please, stop hurting me! You are destroying me. I can't bear it any longer! Listen to what I am saying: I am *Dying*! *Dying*!

And *You* are killing *Me*!

They laugh, looking at each other with joy and pride, laughing. Now, oh no, they are pissing! Down on me, reign of terror, yellow filth, they are pissing on me! No, no, this can't be! I am dreaming, I am hallucinating, I'm going insane! Their piss is making me lose my mind, their piss is evil. How can I bear this flood, I must be strong, yet I am weakening and the flow from above is strengthening. Drowning me, I am drowning. No, I am the water itself. I am the endless water below. Endless and evil.

Evil, Evil, why are my thoughts so evil?

I can't stand. I am water and I fall to the bottom, to the bottom of the bucket they are filling. I am their urine, the wine of their ceremony, from the vessel that is their bladders and into the debauchery of the bucket below.

Water! Nothing more than water! Water that is urine that is wine that is them that is me that is soul that is evil that is life that is death that is emptied and then filled and then emptied elsewhere to fill elsewhere that is to create life and destroy equally at different places and so the infection continues. The infection that I am part of too. But no, I don't see. I don't see, still, what I am.

Why these thoughts? What caused them? What is wrong with me? What is me? What is? What?

And now I see.

The bucket, the taunters, their urine. Pissing in a bucket are the three of them who I thought were my friends and laughing at their reflections. Their reflections, not mine. I am an external observer of their experience. Yet my experience was of them; yet my experience was totally mine and not theirs at all. An experience I created.

And now I realise that they hadn't even been pissing. My three friends had been looking down at the half-full bucket, just a plain mop-bucket and making faces, making faces at me.

One of them turns to me and laughs, I think, trying to involve me.

Or is he laughing at me? I try to laugh with him, but worry he will see through my fake face, see me for what I am, an infiltrator. Do I really belong here... with them? Do they really like me? Do they really consider me a friend of theirs? What do they say about me when I'm not here? Why can't I join them? I am an outsider. I am an outcast. I don't belong, I'm not one of them, I'm not one of anybody, I'm just one... all alone. Alone.

Fucking Alone! Isolated! Shunned! Hated! Condemned! Yet I don't deserve this. I never did them wrong. Fuck them!

Calm. Calm down. You're tripping. Tripping on your emotions. You must stabilise, you must be stable, otherwise people will think you're crazy. Maybe they already do. Maybe you are. Maybe, maybe...

NO! I must come down off this shit! This isn't reality and it isn't fun, it's fucking scary and I don't like it. I want it to stop, stop now. I'm creating it so I can destroy it.

BE GOOOOOOOOONE!

And the glass broke. It flew out of my hands and smashed onto the floor.

"Calm down man, it's okay," my friend said, looking at me with a concerned expression. "You're having a bad trip, just relax."

As I began to relax and rejoined their world, I could see that that was all it was. It had all been in my mind.

*   *   *

I stopped writing. I had finished the story and no longer had to be a part of it. I wasn't really happy with it, though; I wanted to tear it up and reject it. It seemed to disturb me at some fundamental level that I could write this.

I wasn't writing in the café, I was in the quiet and seclusion of the library, I still hadn't connected with this, the 'real' world. It was as if I not only wrote that story, I experienced it, it was real. I could handle writing a story about a character going insane but when that character became me and I was the one going insane, that's when I wanted to cut off. To reject that experience as 'real' and return to what was 'really real'.

I saw Lana approaching.

"Hello!" she said, full of sunshine.

I looked up, confused, not connecting with her. I tried to emulate her friendliness. I tried to be the me she had seen before.

"You seem tired. You're usually so full of energy." I noticed she slowed down to my speed, trying to empathise.

"Yeah. I know." I wanted to explain that it was the story's strange effect on me but I didn't want to draw attention to my writing.

"What's that?" she asked, noticing my glance at the work.

Oh no, I'll have to say something about it now.

"Just some useless writing stuff. Nothing decent though."

Now she's interested!

"Don't be so hard on yourself. I'm sure it's fantastic!"

Well, not really.

"Can I read it? I'm sure it's really great."

If she reads it, then she *will* think I'm crazy.

"No, really, it's bad. I mean rubbish, poorly expressed."

"*Unrealistic?*" she prompted, trying to show me the contradiction in my own words.

"You could say that." I laughed feebly. "Literally."

I started to screw up the sheets of loose leaf and her hand moved to stop me, touching mine lightly. "Don't screw it up! You may regret it later."

"The only thing I'll regret is if I don't screw it up."

"But just because you don't like it now, doesn't mean that you should destroy it. Just like you said yesterday, you can't always expect things to seem realistic, you can't always expect people to seem rational. You're trying to rationalise on the merits of your story."

Though I felt inclined to agree with her, I didn't want to let her read the story.

Seeing this, she appealed not to my rationality, but to my sensitivity. "I'd like to read it Andrew, regardless of whether or not you think it's any good. I'd be hurt if you didn't let me read it." She tried to look into my eyes but I looked at my fumbling hands instead.

I knew she wanted to read the story, and I knew that I wanted her to read it too. I wanted her to read it because I wanted her to understand. I had a chance for this to happen, a chance for her to understand me and yet I rejected it. How rational was this? Was it really my rational mind telling me what to do, or was it my fearful one?

Maybe I wanted her to push me to show it to her because I didn't want to seem too eager. As long as I distanced myself from it, and looked at it as insane pulp then it was okay. As long as I accepted that it was not real and therefore of no real worth apart from trivial entertainment, then I was safe. All this despite what I had so enthusiastically proclaimed only yesterday.

Maybe I could let her read it, maybe we had come far enough in this short time already that I could show her what was inside my mind and she wouldn't be scared off. Maybe if she did love me, then she'd see beauty in it, no matter what it was. Maybe I'd dare.

"Okay, you win." I sighed and handed it to her.

"I'll leave it with you, as I have to go now." Amazingly enough, it was true. It was time for me to leave to get to work, but she probably didn't realise this. "But I'll see you tomorrow in the café at lunch time."

"Okay," she said, happy that I had finally let her read my work, accepted her by sharing my world with hers.

I left quickly, with a brief (timid) smile and a wave. I wanted to get out of there as fast as possible, before she had started the story.

I just hoped that I hadn't destroyed everything.

THE SEVENTH INSTANCE

Now when I look back on that experience, I realise what it was that disturbed me most. If I had actually been tripping on some kind of drug that I had taken, then I could have blamed the whole experience on the drug alone. The fact, though, was that the experience was real. However I tried to externalise it, it *was* real. The reality of the event was something I was, and still am, loath to accept. There is no comfort in insanity like this, insanity that wasn't a projection of fantastical experiences, but a projection of real ones. It was like I had rationally destroyed the distinction between reality and fantasy, without knowing or understanding how, or the implications of such an effect. Bad enough to actually imagine such a horrifying concept, but worse to experience it as real. The reality of insanity. The insanity of reality. The two had reduced to the same and I wanted to have nothing to do with either of them. I wanted to dissociate myself from the entire situation.

Though it seems doubtful that I will ever be able to accept this apparent paradox of possibilities, I sense that perhaps one day I will. For the present I will stick to what is safe and real and not allow myself to venture on such dangerous excursions into non-reality.

Maybe one day the time will come when I am ready, when we are ready, to face, deal with and even understand, such things.

But that time is not now.

THE EIGHTH INSTANCE

And now I have finally come full circle. Full circle back into depression. All the more depressing as it has happened all before and perhaps inevitably will do so again.

My thoughts are so unsure and unclear, it is hard to know what to write. Am I writing this? Or am I actually experiencing this? Writing and experiencing seem to reduce to the same, becoming incomprehensible and horrifying.

Now as I write this, I know that I am not only creating my experience and my character's experience, but the experience of all others in perhaps all possible worlds who come to read or otherwise experience these words I write. What I am doing now is having an instantaneous effect across 'time', 'location' and even 'reality'.

And I can't seem to help feeling... remorseful? Undeserving? I don't know how to describe it. I cannot even comprehend it myself. I am aware of the effects I'm creating and therefore it seems I'm responsible. I know that these words will disturb many, anger others and inspire yet others. Where it may seem inspiration is a positive effect. For provoking angry reactions or instability I feel guilty and responsible.

Perhaps it is already too late. Perhaps regardless of whether I write any more, what has been written so far will find a way into publication, or what I have otherwise created or experienced will cause resonances among others who will carry on the same effect.

Perhaps I am just a resonance of an earlier thought.

Perhaps I should stop writing now before the chain of consequences can continue.

But perhaps I should not.

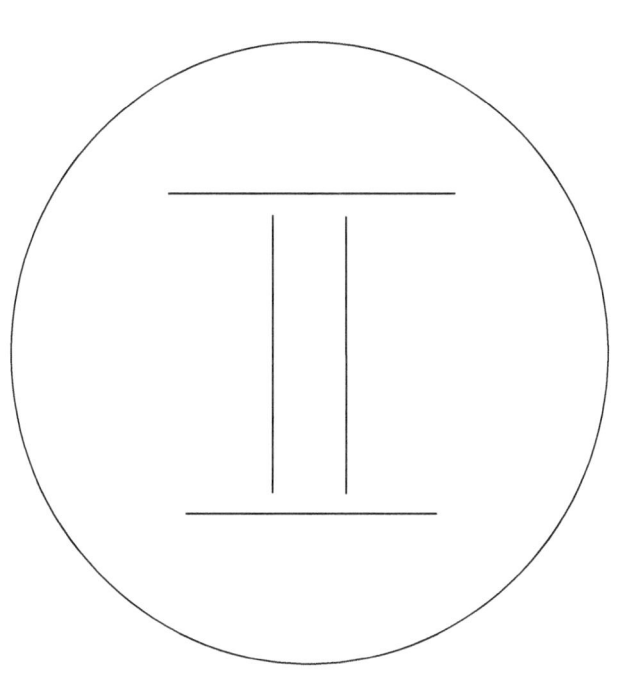

A NEW DILEMMA

I have only written thirty or so pages, but already seem to have lost sight of where I'm going. I am overwhelmed with the myriad possibilities that extend from this point, and the path that I should take is hidden from me. The burden of the choice I must make has overshadowed the faith in myself that I am doing this for good reason. All I have now is a handful of short chapters and a sense of having had some grand vision that I am no longer sure of.

It is tempting to start again on something new rather than persevere with trying to reclaim something lost. But I suspect that if I do that, I'll merely be facing this same dilemma thirty-forty odd pages into the next book, and be no closer to finishing anything. I need a way to bridge the two directions; to start on something new, whilst still continuing the story I have already started here...

And now I realise that there's a simple way to achieve this. I will do both simultaneously. I will write about my main characters from my forthcoming book *The Dark Horde* (one of them, Danny, has already been introduced) and incorporate their experiences into this book.

With renewed vision I begin to write:

And then, a new awakening.

A NEW AWAKENING

It always seemed that there was something else.

Something unclaimed, something not grasped, something abstract that had, until now, been beyond comprehension.

There was a force. And then there came to be another; opposite, contradictory.

And then there was something else.

Hard to describe, yet easy to conceive. A third element that was not a neither, a nor, an either, or an or – it was something more.

Evermore.

A sense in which the two were related. A sense in which the two were distinct. One, yet both, separate from a third.

From the most abstract springs the most definite.

This was the truth, the one truth that existed. A truth that applied to everything, including the truth of itself. Beyond linguistic expression. Pure, fundamental and simple. Its own claim seems to destroy itself – yet this is exactly why it holds.

Constantly growing and changing, yet stable and remaining, infinite in potential, yet finite in claim, a simple single truth, yet a multipartite truth of a complexity beyond all description and comprehension.

Something we will never completely attain, yet have already.

Any description, any understanding, any experience, will never be complete.

For it is Evermore.

And then, a new effect.

A NEW EFFECT

There was a great sadness that they must part.

They had been together for what seemed an eternity. They had come to perceive the two as one, a single unity that would always persist and endure.

The depth of their experiences, the sheer weight of what they had felt together and learnt seemed endless and yet it was all about to come to an end. Together they had been and done so much. Now individually they must be and do so much more. They had come to a realisation that they had to acknowledge their own potential and what they were meant to be.

And then, there was something else.

Was it that the sum of their parts (were they more than two?) was greater than the whole, or that the whole was greater than the sum of its parts? Or yet something else, something indefinable, something untenable, beyond description and comprehension.

There seemed to be a third 'sense' in which they existed, apart from being individual or unified. A sense in which certain aspects about them, their abilities and their destinies, were potential and actual.

From a third 'standpoint' it even seemed that only one or the other of the two could completely exist: the more actual, the less potential; the more unified, the less individual; the more comprehensible and qualitative, the less describable and quantitative.

And yet there always seemed to be something else.

A perspective from which they were one, another from which only one existed, another from which both and neither did, and many others; all of which seemed to reduce to either what was and what wasn't.

And something else.

Every way in which they viewed themselves, in which they viewed that which was the other, in which that which was the other viewed them, in which that which was the other viewed that which was another other, there were only a finite number of actualities from which were spawned an infinite number of possibilities. And there was always an infinite number of viewpoints, of perspectives, of tendencies of perception, description and comprehension of these finite actualities and their infinite possibilities. And this seemed to mean that even the finite became (and was) infinite.

And yet there was always something else.

The two came to realise that there would never necessarily be an end to anything, just as it seemed that there never had been a beginning. They would always be together as one and separate as two.

Yet with a certain monotony, there was always something else.

There was a sense of security in this knowledge, for it meant that there was always something new or something more to experience, to learn, to become. Nothing reached conclusion or completion.

The more certain one was about one aspect, the more

uncertain others became, and upon changing direction, changing perspective even, those which had been more definite changed places with those which had been more uncertain.

Their thoughts came to adopt what could be called a position or a quality, and the infinite bounds of possibility became the definite facts of actuality. The two became the one and yet it could be seen that only one had ever existed.

And then, a new observation.

A NEW OBSERVATION

"You see what I mean, it always seems to choose the right one."

I'm broken from my wandering thoughts when I realise she's looking at me. She had been talking excitedly about the physics of quanta and potentials or probabilities or something and something about relativity but I quickly lost her. She was speaking a language I didn't understand and I had become bored. Quite frankly, I have no idea what she is on about but whatever it is, it has little to do with me.

She's twiddling some machine and pointing to a dot on the wall that is supposed to signify some marvellous miracle of science. The only things that occupy my thoughts are how long it has been since I last ate and what a nice pair of tits she has despite her age. I begin to wonder what she'd be like in bed. Was it true that experience made all the difference?

I am just staring at her whilst she is talking, so I guess she thinks I'm listening. But actually, I'm looking at those luscious lipsticked lips and imagining them around my hard cock. I can imagine the expression of intense effort plastered across her face as she sucks hard on my nob and an exclamation of joy and surprise as I plaster my spunk across her face.

"It's pretty exciting stuff, isn't it?" She smiles.

I'm excited, think I, mindful of the swelling in my crotch.

"Do you want me to show you the bryondimalchite stalendoanimiseral machine?"

I know what I'd like you to show me.

I shrug, trying not to glance down at her half-exposed cleavage, realising that she has all her attention on me and would probably notice if I did.

"You don't seem that keen but it is useful to demonstrate the effects of photoelentrondisapantion on fieldsquantronispan and chaodielectration."

Concentrate. Concentrate.

"Well," I begin, trying to think of something appropriate to say and instead thinking amused thoughts of doggie-sex with this thirty-five year-old teacher and how she probably has no idea what I'm thinking and how in bed with her husband she probably discussed mathematical formula and theories. "$E=mc^2$! $E=mc^2$! Ohhh! Ohhh! Honey, the terminal velocity of your thrusts is exceeding the co-efficient of friction of my ventral opening by a decimal multiplier of 0.378!"

I smirk, laughing at my own thoughts and then realise that she has just said something to me and is laughing with me, thinking I am responding to her comment. Not having the faintest idea what she has said, even if I'd heard it, I probably wouldn't have understood, and feeling a little anxious because of this, I try to decide what to say.

It seems she's pausing like she had asked a question or at least expects some sort of response.

A sudden yawn overcomes me and I begin to explain

that I'm tired and that I found what she had shown me very interesting, but that I really can't take any more in today and if she doesn't mind I'd like to go.

"You can take me into the back room and make love to me if you can explain everything I've talked about here."

What?

Suddenly, I am completely concentrating on the conversation. "What did you just say?"

Smiling mirthfully, she repeats herself, "If you can show me that you have learnt and understood all that I have just explained to you, you can," now she's emphasising the words for effect, oh God my dick's getting hard, "take me into the back room and *fuck me*."

Oh God, she said it. *Fuck me*, she said.

Placing a firm hand on my shoulder, she steadies my focus. "But you must explain to me all I have explained to you."

"C-Can y-you explain it to me again and then I'll explain back to you?"

Obviously quite amused by my nervousness, she responds, "I will explain it to you again, *one more time*, as clearly and as slowly as I can, because I want you to understand and because I think once you do understand you will be very glad for it."

She's got that bit right.

"But you won't be able to just repeat *what* I say. You will have to demonstrate to me that you *understand*. Which you won't be able to do while you're thinking about *sex*."

Hang on.

She can't really be serious.

Can she?

"You don't think I'm serious, do you?"

"Well, actually I was wondering..." How should I say this? Shit I'm nervous.

"Say it."

"Well, no."

"Well, young man, I can tell you that I mean exactly what I say. And besides you're kinda sexy and I bet you've got a lot of energy." Now she winks at me and I can feel that stirring in my pants again.

"Now, are you going to believe me, or are you going to let the chance of a lifetime pass you by?"

Good point.

"Okay! Okay! I believe you." I'm trying hard to keep down my erect penis that's painfully straining against my jeans.

She smiles again. "But you have to listen to what I have to say, as I'm only going to say it once and you'll have to explain it back to me. And you aren't going to be able to do that whilst you're thinking about sticking your dick *up my cunt-hole*."

I begin quivering in anticipation. Concentrate. Concentrate. Everything depends upon concentrating for the next few minutes. I'll never forgive myself if I don't. Never. Never.

Concentrate.

"Are you ready?"

Am I?

Of course I am.

"Then let's begin..."

"It would seem that everything: matter, light, sound,

physical force, heat, even space and time, is composed of energy.

"This energy appears to us as vibration, vibration that can be seen either as an individual point, a particle, or as a collective force, a wave.

"How it appears depends on how you look at it. Observe it as an individual point with a definite location, then it is. It is a particle. But if you chose to observe it as a collective force with a definite momentum, then it has no particle properties, no location. It is a wave.

"It is neither wholly wave nor particle, it is a combination of both. Yet it can't be seen to be both at any one time, we can only fully see it as one thing at a time."

I frown, trying to understand.

"Think of the rat-rabbit illusion, where you can see either a rat or a rabbit but not both at the one time, even though both are there. Do you know the illusion I mean?"

I nod hesitantly.

"It's the same as the two faces in black divided by the white fountain, or the cube drawing that can be seen as both coming out from the page and going in."

Ah yes, I know the ones.

"The way we see it is relative to the way in which we choose to look at it, is relative to our standpoint. Yet the whole thing consists of two opposite viewpoints that completely contradict the other and make it seemingly impossible for both to be true. Yet they are."

She claps her hands together and nods at me, signalling the end of her explanation.

Now it's my turn.

"I'm still not sure, can you explain it a bit..."

"I think you understand better than you realise. Go on, explain it back to me."

Shit.

Well, I might as well get this over with. How she can really say I understand after that short explanation, I don't know. How can I be expected to understand all that Einstein stuff? I'm no genius.

"You're delaying and you needn't. Just say it in your own words."

Okay. Okay. Better say something. Something good. Okay. Now how did she begin? Oh yeah, that's right.

"Everything is energy."

I look to her for encouragement.

She smiles and says, "Keep going."

Great. What do I say next? I can't do this. Maybe I can pretend I understand. I know what I'll say. I'll just say what she did.

Easy.

"Energy is made of waves and particles."

"And?" she asks.

She won't catch me out that easily, I remember what she said. "It's both at once, but we can only see one at a time, like an illusion."

Seeming happy, she smiles.

"Is that it?" I ask.

"You tell me," she says.

From what she has said, it seems that that's it. But I know there's bound to be something else. She wouldn't be asking otherwise.

"There's more to it than that isn't there?" I begin to feel defeated.

"No."

No! Holy fuck! That's it! But that's so simple! It's too simple! No fucking way it took Einstein to work that out.

"And yes, there is more."

"Huh?"

"It's all relative of course. Only one answer makes sense on its own, but the whole answer includes yes and no."

Now I am confused.

"I understand your confusion. Just when you think you understand it all, that you've got it all worked out, there is always something more."

So am I right? Did I do what I had to?

"But I must confess I lied."

My heart sinks, my fear realised. What a fucking fool I am. Of course she was lying, as if I'd get to root her.

"Not everything I've said, indeed arguably nothing I've said, has been proven by Science. In fact much of it isn't even widely accepted. Some of it is seen as radical nonsense."

I thought she meant getting to fuck her!

"And of course, I was lying about having sex with me." At that she burst into laughter.

What a dickhead I am. I should have just left and not bothered trying. Now look where my dick has got me.

"Please don't feel cheated. You've won a far greater prize, though you probably don't realise it."

I do feel cheated, I do feel abused, you bitch. I'm not going to let her fool me with her talk any more.

Infuriated, I ask, "What have I learned? Some useless physics jargon! Some good..."

She has the cheek to interrupt me, "Listen Brian, listen to me."

"I've listened to you enough." I make to leave.

"And listen to yourself," she says.

For some reason I'm too slow to react, too slow in turning for the door and she grabs me.

"What are you Brian? Just tell me that."

What sort of a question is that to ask? I turn to look at her to tell her to let go of my arm but my resolve melts.

She's crying.

Why should she care? What makes me so important?

"Yes, I am crying. Yes, I care. I only wanted you to understand because I knew you were capable. I had to reach you, to get you to listen and that was the only way I could. I'm sorry, I didn't mean to hurt your feelings."

Hurt your own, more like.

"Can I ask you just one more question, Brian?"

Angry at myself for remaining, she takes her hand off my arm. I feel like saying 'no' and storming out. But somewhere within I feel a twinge of sympathy and maybe something else. Not attraction, can't be. Definitely not.

Never.

Seeing me hesitate again, she asks her question, "What are you, Brian?"

Why does she keep asking me this stupid question?

"What do you mean?" I say, sick of her and her preaching.

"You're an individual, right?"

"Yeah. Course I am."

"But you're also one of many, part of a community. Part of a Unity."

I see what she's getting at.

"Yeah, yeah, I'm like a wave and a particle, aren't I? Both and yet only one at a time."

She smiles again, trying to make me smile and acknowledge that I've actually learned something.

"Can I go now?"

"You're a very smart kid, Brian. If you come tomorrow I can teach you some more." Her eyes seem to be pleading.

"No thanks, Mrs. Mayor." And before she can say any more, I leave.

A NEW HOWARD

Years ago, Howard had believed, had faith, in a lot of things.

Years ago, Howard had trusted others, listened to others, but experience had changed all that.

Howard has become armoured, learnt to reject hope, reject mercy, reject trust. He has learnt the rules he had to learn, the rules to survive the game his life is.

And now he stands, ruler of nought but himself, his mighty weapon of steel in his hands, smiling upon the expectant masses before him, figures chanting the name: "ELEMENTAL."

Reflections on the past are for later times, later stories to be told (and they would be) but now was for now.

Now the pied piper played...

Howard says no words, only giving the other three on stage a nod, before unleashing a deadly, grating guitar riff that cuts through the fans.

Growling bass and ear-piercing lead join the noise, backed up by a thundering drum that smashes and crashes against the walls.

Hell bursts asunder. Flashing red, white, blue and yellow lights set the stage alight as jets of smoke and sparks erupt. The crowd becomes a frenzy of colliding bodies, sending a wall of steam up before the metal warriors who dance around the floor soaked in the sounds of torment.

The band whirls like a menacing machine of execution, the crowd a store-house of victims to be systematically bled and butchered.

Howard grabs the mike and screams into it, "NIGHTMARE'S COAT OF BLACKNESS."

The crowd answers, "ETERNAL."

"A PESTILENT MOOD OF DARKNESS."

Again they respond, "NOCTURNAL."

"FULL MOON WATCHES OVER ITS CHILDREN."

Amidst the chaos issues, "PATERNAL."

"MAN'S ABOMINATION UNLEASHED FROM ITS DEN."

Guitar riffs resplendent. "PARANORMAL."

Howard leaps away into a crescendo of chorus, shuddering bass chords and crashing drums. Weaving and diving, like a headless snake in its death throes.

Dehydrate, the drummer, assumes vocal lead, roaring into a mike near him, distorting with the intensity, "WOLVERINE, HUGE AND WITHOUT MERCY."

And the voices scream, "FERAL."

"MALIGNANT FORCE OF TERROR, DESTROYING ALL THAT BE."

On the response comes, "FANATICAL."

"FEEDING ON FEAR, ANGER AND GREED."

A thundering wave, "EVIL."

"SUSTENANCE OF MAN'S EVIL, HAS GERMINATED THE SEED."

The rumbling double-bass kicks in. "IRREVERSIBLE."

The Milk Man, at stage-left, hurls himself into a killer lead of awesome fury, then breaks into a burst of finger-tapping, hands a blur on the fret-board.

The lead expires to be replaced by the grand warbled woof of The Fat Meister on bass, a solid sledge of sound to slaughter with sonic boom. Suddenly a string snaps and the flow seems in danger, but The Fat Meister plays on, ever able to adapt to change.

Lead backed by rhythm rains down like acid, becoming a burning infusion of guitars and drums, all melding into a single tidal wave of gaining momentum and volume bent only to destroy.

Brazen and baroque the battery continues, reaching an unbearable fervid peak of electrical ecstasy. When the pitch can be sustained no longer, it plunges suddenly into the solitary serene acoustics of rhythm guitar. The music is melodic yet haunting, enthralling the crowd with silent awe.

Slowly now, masked with pained emotion, The Milk Man leads on vocals.

"BEYOND DEATH, BEYOND SIN.

Gently the crowd reply, "IMMORTAL."

Bass begins to play now, a turgid undercurrent.

"PERVERSION BECOMES THE DARKER TWIN."

Gradually increasing. "IDENTICAL."

The drums start up, ominous, intensifying.

"CATALYSTS OF THE APOCALYPSE."

Building ever faster. "CARDINAL."

Rhythm like a serrated saw hacks into the melody, spilling the blood once more, shattering the peace.

"CREATION AND DESTRUCTION IN FULL ECLIPSE."

Exploding with aggression. "PARADOXICAL."

And again the ballad of death is splintered into a

million fragments by an ear-splitting lead of incomprehensible speed. The four players a chaotic blur of hair, arms and music.

Now The Fat Meister brings the tide in, a growling call to arms,

"FLESH, BLOOD AND BONE UNITE."

The ever-present backlash. "CABAL."

"INFEST AND BREED, THY MINIONS OF NIGHT."

Overpowering chorus. "INFERNAL."

"GOD SHALL SAVE ONLY THOSE OF PURITY."

Beyond control, beyond redemption. "HYPOCRITICAL."

"WE ARE AS ONE, AS MANY ARE WE."

Thousands of souls screaming, "SPIRITUAL."

As the battering ram that is Elemental continues to hammer out the punishment, the crowd continues to mosh, stage-dive and yell. The energy of the moment carries from the dying embers of the opening song into the next and the next and the next until apparent infinity or oblivion.

But eventually, as with all things, the night grows old and the hours weary. The end of the concert is nigh and all know it. The excitement is over. Now only Howard is left at centre stage, Dehydrate, The Fat Meister and The Milk Man have all laid down their instruments and have already begun to reflect on the night's success, watching from the sidelines. With an acoustic six-string, and a sincere expression of seriousness, Howard assumes the mike for the last time.

"Hope you've all enjoyed yourselves as much as we have tonight," the crowd roars, "and aren't going to be too fucked for the rest of your week if you're one of the lucky people with a job and have got something to do." Again the fans respond, "But I wanted to leave you with a little take home message to think about between now and when you next see us, which hopefully won't be too long. Thanks again for being such great hosts." A jubilant crowd and respectful audience cheers and then waits...

He begins.

"Everybody has a reason to believe.
Everybody has a reason to be deceived.
Everybody thinks what they believe is right.
Everybody thinks that they've seen the light.
Do you believe what you do because you've found the way?
Or do you believe what you do because that's what others
  say?
All I ask is that you set aside your prejudice,
And examine your beliefs objectively without pretence.
In every system of belief there is truth at its core,
But where there is truth, there is also flaw.
The moral of all this is not to believe things others tell you,
Look into yourself, find yourself, and what there speaks is
  true."

He ends.

NOT NEW AT ALL

10/10/1967:

Once again, diary, I am in the mood for contemplation.

And once again, diary, I'm reflecting on the same questions.

Why is the world the way it is? I mean just look at it: violence is glorified as entertainment and murderers are war-heroes, sex is just another casual thing that has nothing to do with love, people only care about themselves while millions of others are dying in poverty, so many people are on drugs and breaking the law. Why is this happening? Where did we go wrong?

For so long I have sought answers to these questions and now finally I'm getting clues to some of the answers. And not only that, I'm finding the answers to my whole (our whole) existence.

I think ever since I was a small child I knew that there was something wrong with this system of things, people didn't love each other and everyone believed different things and argued over what was true and what was not. The same is true now and unfortunately probably still will be for some time to come.

I hear about the hippy/free-love 'revolution' over in the States and though I don't really see much of it here, I don't think it's a good thing. In fact I see it as being just as bad as militarism and fascism. Well maybe not that bad, diary, but values promoting drugs, free sex and rebellion are not good ones. It's these kind of values I'm talking about, diary, when I'm talking about the sorry state of our society. This is not the way it should be. But I really do feel that people will soon realise this (many already do) and change, but then it may be too late.

I admit, diary, that I've committed many sins myself (as have we all I guess) not the least of which are having tried cigarettes, marijuana, been drunk, disobeyed authority or lied to it and had sex before marriage. I'm not even 19 yet. But I have always felt bad about having done these things and felt that they were not right.

This year for instance (my first year of university) I've been involved in anti-Vietnam protests, protests for a right to free-education and wanted to do (but never got around to) volunteer work for charity. Many of my friends have also been involved in this, but some have also taken to LSD and marijuana. Though I tried the green stuff, I didn't like it (to be honest it scared me) and I felt that my parents would be disappointed in me if they knew. They've asked me before if I've smoked dope and I lied saying no, so this too has made me feel bad.

It's all these sorts of things, along with the way in which aggression and killing is glorified in television, movies and newspapers, that has made me think hard about the way this world is. So many people live in poverty too, or without freedom, and corporations and governments don't care. They only seem to care about power and profit. Even here, in Australia, we have to pay for our education. This policy only serves to deny those without privileged backgrounds the opportunity to attend university and earn a decent wage. The law too and any form of authority (including parents) has become something few take seriously as something to be obeyed and respected. When I've not wanted to disobey a law (something like getting into a movie without a ticket or lying about my age, etc) my friends have said things like, "Don't worry, you won't get caught," or "How are they going to know?" which wasn't my concern at all. My concern was whether doing such things was right. A couple of them have even made jokes and laughed about me obeying and not wanting to upset my parents.

All of these things are happening (I could go on) yet we are growing progressively desensitised to them. People say things like, "Those values are outdated", or "This is the sixties, we don't have to listen to that shit any more" and think that we're moving ahead. But if we keep on like this, things are only going to get worse rather than better.

We all want to be happy and secure and generally I think we want that for others too. Yet no one (or only a tiny few) is prepared to do anything about it. Everyone seems to think, "It's too hard", "I'm only one person in millions, what difference would I make", etc, and hence things only get worse. And the most ironic thing I think, is that those who do stand up and do something (or try to) are the ones most persecuted, they're the ones ridiculed and laughed at, they're the minority often labelled as 'extremists' or 'fanatics' or 'idealists'. They're the ones told to "get real" and "to face reality". I mean just what are we trying to say?

We seem to forget that the very way in which society has moved ahead and new advancements are made, is usually by those who do something different and put themselves in a position open to ridicule in order to stand up for what they believe against a sheep-minded conforming majority.

And unfortunately, I see a lot of this hippy revolution as no different. Most of those involved that I see, don't seem to be really interested in universal peace, but simply wear the clothes and grow their hair long to be part of the majority. They seem to use it as a moral excuse to get high and have lots of sex with different people.

All this talk of revolution is then really only a young-spirited rebellion. It seems to me that most people's attitudes are only relative to those around them, attitudes that probably change completely as they grow older. In the same way the older generation make themselves feel more important by proclaiming themselves wise and learned (words which can easily equal narrow-mindedness rather than anything else); the younger generation proclaim to have new wisdom and learned-ness beyond that of the older generation. But these things often seem to be the very same things that the older generation had thought when they were young, when they had rejected the older generation's words of their time. People change as the years go by, but seemingly not the roles they play at various ages.

This is why we need strong, secure foundations on which to place our values, something constant, external and unchanging, something that regardless of how we change and develop, is always there to keep a check against. However, we need to be careful exactly on what we establish these 'secure foundations', as secure and unshakable foundations of values and beliefs can often become ones of stubborn arrogance and ignorance.

It is true that by change and development we move forward, but this development is far more constructive if it is done in light of what has been previously learned and taught. Otherwise there is the great risk of making the same mistakes as before and hence no actual progress is made. What seems new and revolutionary now, may merely be an old idea or philosophy in a new guise.

It is now that I come to that which is one of the oldest of texts, perhaps the most wise and certainly the most well read, 'The Bible'.

I think it is a sad thing that today you can't mention words like 'The Bible', 'Jesus' and 'God', without people being repulsed and looking at you with disdain. The moment you start to talk of these things they begin to think "Oh, you're one of them" and switch off. I think that most people just want to believe what suits them and believe what they do as if they've found the truth and everyone else is just stupid, blind and/or gullible.

With all this in mind, I've proceeded in the search for an answer (assuming one can be found) and have arrived at God, à la 'The Bible'.

I know what many others would say; it's just a book, it's just an ancient collection of the writings of men to explain their world that is inappropriate to the world we live in today. I have also lived with this view-point for a long time and it has led me nowhere. Now when I look at the state of the world today and think how it would be if we all followed the teachings of Jesus, I begin to think that perhaps humanity hasn't really reached anywhere.

But I admit that all this stuff about God, his son, Satan, creation, etc, isn't easy to accept, not to mention adequately prove. Add to this the difficulty associated with the disapproving judgements of my family and friends. I myself have become separated from many of my friends, out of no direct intention, simply by choosing to study 'The Bible'. They laugh and joke at my 'conversion' and dissociate themselves from me – I'm not one of 'them' any more. To listen to the teachings of Jesus, is to say my friends are wrong, and they can't have that. It seems a choice is being forced upon me as to whether "I'm with them or against them". I have no desire to make this choice and do not feel sufficiently informed to be able to. I feel like I'm at a station with trains pulling out in opposite directions and have to make a quick decision as to which one to take or be left stranded at the station.

Nevertheless the book is far from closed. If there is a way to 'God and the Truth', then I'm confident I will find it or else dwell forever in my own delusional enlightenment. The struggle continues, the struggle must continue, until a conclusion is reached or else none at all.

Until next time, diary.
Lucas.

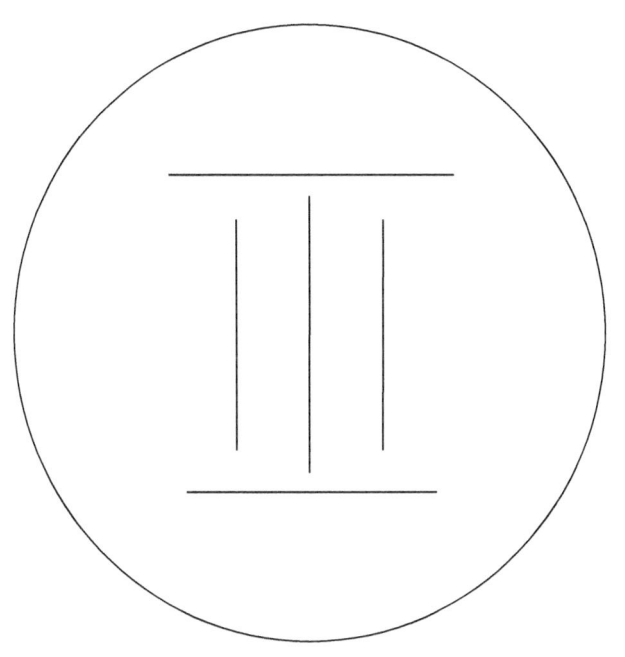

CONFUSION

"So what's it all mean?"

She closed the first book of *Evermore*, and said, "It's a bit disjointed."

"It is a bit, isn't it? But it is all relevant, it is all towards the same purpose."

Now she giggled. "Oh, so you don't know what it means, but you do know that it is all relevant and that it is all towards the one purpose."

I thought about this a moment. "I do contradict myself a bit, don't I?" I smiled. It was all true.

The conversation may well have stopped there, but it didn't, I had more to say.

"It isn't just one book, it's many. It isn't just one theme, it's many. Yet it is all one book and one theme, only different parts and aspects."

"So what's its purpose then?"

I answered honestly again, "I don't know."

Lana frowned. "You can be so frustrating."

"That I *do* know."

We were in the same café once more, though it was some time later. Caraline was not there; she had not joined us for many months.

The conversation did stop this time, the world went on around us, but neither of us took any notice of it – we were both trying to think of what to say next.

Our coffees grew colder.

We both opened our mouths at the same moment, I paused and her words came first.

"How do you expect anyone to follow your story, then? For someone to want to read it, they'll have to make some sense of it. How can they do that, if even you can't?"

"I was waiting for you to ask that."

A layer of skin began to grow over our coffees now.

"Well?"

"Well what?" I laughed.

She sighed in irritation and I quickly spoke before the moment was lost completely.

"Only joking. I do have an answer." I paused again.

Her eyes stared at me in silent indignation.

"Okay. Okay. I'm only stirring. I will tell you, it's all to do with Evermore. Which I can't really describe adequately as there is always something more to it which gets left out."

"How about an inadequate explanation then?"

I grinned. "You win."

ELABORATION

"Imagine a big circle. A circle that instead of completely joining up, ends up slightly above where it began."

She frowned, so I traced it out.

"You know, like this."

"And then you go around again and again, each time thinking you'll end up at the same place as before, but instead you always end up just a little above it."

I drew it all on the flimsy serviette.

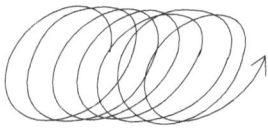

"And so you keep on going thinking that you know where it's going, that it's going to go in a straight coiled sort of line, but then you realise that it's not. It's curved."

I scribbled some more on a new serviette, abbreviating the coil.

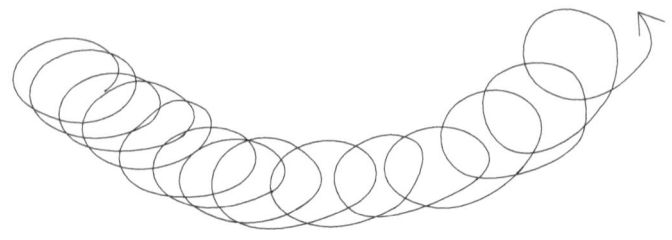

"So then you think, now I know where it's going, it's just a bigger circle."

"I see," she said.

"But you keep on going and at the end you realise it's not. You're just slightly above where you started."

She nodded that she still followed.

"And so you keep going, following the curve around again and keep ending up a little above where you started. Like this."

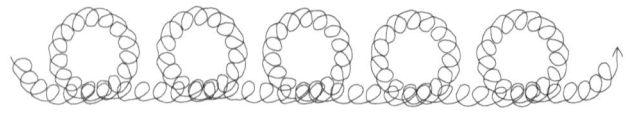

"Still with me?"

"I think so."

"Good, I'll keep going then. Once again you think that it's just going to coil outwards in a straight line, but in fact it's curved. Curved in another big circle that ends up just a little above where you began. A circle that is just one of an infinite number of coils in a bigger circle that is just one of an infinite number of coils in a circle that is even bigger than that."

This was rapidly getting too complex to draw, but I didn't need to – she understood.

"It isn't a straight line, though it may seem that it is going to be at any one time, it's curved. But it isn't a circle either, though it may seem that it is going to be at any one time, it's open. It's both yet neither, yet something more complex again. Just when you think you've fully understood it and you know where it's going, it gets more complex again, and so on to infinity. To quote." Opening the book now, "Constantly growing and changing, yet stable and remaining, infinite in potential, yet finite in claim, a simple single truth, yet a multi-partite truth of a complexity beyond all description and comprehension."

It seemed that we had gone in a circle back to the start of the conversation, only to find that we were somewhere slightly different.

"It goes the other way too: the revolutions of each 'circle' are formed by progressively smaller coils, onto infinity."

Still trying to make sense of it, Lana asked, "What about if you go off the line, circle or coil into the middle or to the outside?"

"That is something more."

She moaned again in frustration. "So are you going to tell me what all this stuff actually means, or don't you know?"

"No, I don't know, but it's a nice analogy, isn't it?"

Grroooaan

"Hah! Hah! Don't worry, it'll become clear in time."

"Why can't you tell me now?"

"I could tell you more now, but that would spoil the surprise."

I heard another exasperated sound from her side of the table.

"Besides, I can't see the whole of it myself. Just try to picture what I described to you as a mental exercise. You can't. Every time you attain one stage then you only have to expand out further and further, and before long you lose the complexity at the lower or smaller levels. You can only ever see a few levels up or down relative to where you're currently at."

"So is that all you're going to tell me now?"

"Until next time, yes."

DIRECTION

I awoke to find I had been dreaming.

I wandered to find where I was.

I wandered some more to find where I was going.

I wandered further only to find I was back to where I had started, or at least where I had been.

Only it was different and I realised I was far from home.

I was weary, I was wounded.

I had walked a trail through fire and was badly burned. I doubted myself, I was lost, I wondered whether I would ever be able to find my way again.

The whole time I wandered, I thought I was going nowhere, I thought I was no one. No one going nowhere for no particular purpose at all.

And I thought I was alone, that no one was with me on my journey. I thought that there was no one who understood me, no one who protected me, no one who helped me, no one who loved me.

I wanted to give up, and return. But I could not – that doorway had closed and I had closed it.

Other doorways were open now before me, and beyond those yet more. And the further I wandered, the more lost I became.

I saw no reason for this and yet the journey was my own. There was a reason, there was a purpose.

There was a goal to be reached, but I was yet to discover what it was.

And so I wander still, walking in dreams that are my own, yet not, yet both.

Ever onwards, I wander still, through experiences and worlds both beautiful and horrible, benign and fearful, enlightening and confusing. Until I reach...

Until I reach You Know What.

And then I shall begin again...

CONSIDERATION

"Hello, Lana?"

"Andrew! How are you?" Her honeyed voice trickled through the receiver.

"Okay I guess, apart from feeling really stressed."

"Why, what's the matter?"

"I don't really know, oh well, I guess I *do* know. It's all the stress associated with exams and work and all the social and family commitments that I have to meet and trying to run a house on my own and doing all the cooking, cleaning, etc. You know the usual stuff."

"Yeah," she giggled. "And all the stuff you take on at once is just so usual. Everyone else your age is doing it."

"Yeah well, usual for me. I guess because I've been depressed a lot lately, my stress tolerance levels are way down."

"That's exactly what I've been trying to tell you, that you've been depressed and you wouldn't believe me." She sighed. "I knew something was wrong ever since that day about a month ago when you were really non-conversational and you wouldn't tell me what was going on."

"Yeah, sorry about how I was that day."

"I must admit that I got really angry with you over that. But I don't think you meant it personally, so I tried not to take it that way."

"It's bad enough feeling depressed without you making

me feel guilty for not being able to talk when depressed. If I dwelt on that as well that'd make things even worse."

Lana said something, which I didn't really hear as I was a bit angry too; the stress was having a telling effect on my mood. I thought a little about what a ridiculous statement she had made, and what little understanding it reflected, and how it was probably just because she was female and super-sensitive, and...

Lana was pausing now as if for a reply.

"Yeah well," I said in a non-committal way, breaking from my thoughts and realising that she was probably thinking very similar things about me.

There was an uneasy silence and then she said, "So what was it that you called about?"

"I don't know, just to talk I guess." I was aware that I was still sounding flustered and so I made a conscious effort to be more friendly.

"I do think you're more sensitive than what you let on."

"What do you mean?" I said, defensively perhaps.

"I can see through you, Andrew Drage, and I pick up on all these little things that you try to hide." Her voice was cheery again now.

"Like what?"

"Like just now for instance. You got really upset about what I just said and it wasn't even anything that hurtful."

"Yeah, I guess you're right."

"Of course!" She giggled. "I'm always right, you just won't admit it."

"Perhaps."

There was another pause and then she said, "Would you like to go out somewhere?"

"I was just about to suggest the same thing."

"Okay, where would you like to go?"

"Where would *you* like to go?"

Sighing again, she said, "I want to know where you would like to go."

"Well I want to know where you would like to go."

"And I want to go wherever you want to go. And you should be the one to suggest, as I asked first."

"Well, we'll work that out in a moment." I was hoping she'd eventually suggest somewhere, as I had no idea where to suggest. "Why don't we work out first when we'll go and whether we'll invite anyone else?"

"Do you want to invite someone else?"

"Do you?"

"Ohh Andrew, you're determined to get me to suggest something first, aren't you?"

"That's right."

"Well, seeing as I'm being forced to make a suggestion, Scott's got exams over the next few days so we can't really ask him to come and the only other person is Eve."

"I was going to suggest going out on Friday night, as that's really the only night I have free this week."

"Eve can't go out on Friday nights."

"Oh, that's right, that Jewish thing."

"Yeah, so it looks like it will be just you and me, is that good enough for you?"

"Of course it's good enough. You know that! But I had also been considering someone else. You see, before I called, I did actually have a plan in mind of asking you out and asking this other person along."

"And who's that?" Though she knew the answer to that too.

"Well, you know, she was someone who I did like and appreciate as a friend, despite what happened, and I just thought it'd be good to catch up with her again."

"Why don't you ask her?"

"I can't do that. Not only would that put her in a position where it would be hard for her to say no without feeling mean, but it would also just reaffirm those suspicions that she still probably has that I am still attracted to her and haven't got over her."

"Well, you are still attracted to her."

"Yeah I know, but..."

Laughing, she cut in, "But you don't want her to know that."

"I guess not. She probably knows anyway. I did say to her all that time ago, that although I could accept that she had no feelings towards me on anything other than a Platonic level, I would always feel attracted to her."

"So why don't you call her?"

"I was just hoping you would."

"I don't want to get into that situation again, where everything you two say to each other is through me. Besides, she might well like to come. She asked me recently if you still thought those same things of her that you'd said in the letter you sent, about her being a 'power-freak'. And when I said that you did, that really hurt her. Which if she didn't respect or admire you at least to some extent she wouldn't have cared."

"Mmmm," I said thoughtfully.

"And she says that too. She doesn't think you're a bad person at all and feels bad that you think she is."

"I don't think she is a bad person, I never said that, just misguided."

"I know you don't think she's a bad person, but she thinks you do."

"Really?"

"You know what you need? A therapeutic life experience. I've been reading about it in psychology. This woman comes in to see a psychologist to talk about how lonely she is and depressed and he says, 'You need a therapeutic life experience.'"

"I know what you're suggesting, but I'm sorry, Eve is not the one for me. I'm not going to compromise just because she's available and interested."

"The first girl you go out with doesn't have to be the one you'll marry."

"I'd rather stay single my whole life than compromise for the sake of someone else. Or at least that's how I feel now."

"You'll change."

"Perhaps." Now I laughed, laughed at myself for even thinking this. "I must admit that I once thought, and it was only once, thought about going out with Eve."

"You should, she'd be good for you."

"No, it's not going to happen. Sure we have similar interests, music tastes and maybe even a similar weirdness. But her personality jars on me and to tell you the truth, I'm not even attracted to her physically." Brutal, but honest.

She sighed lightly. "And so you continue in your circle, Andrew. Your circle of depression and contradiction."

"You know it's funny, Lana, this is all analogous to an experience I have just had with trying to unravel a tape that got stuck in my stereo. It was sort of like an 'Evermore coil' in a way. There was this tangled mess of tape that was further coiled and tangled within each coil.

"Initially I tried to unravel the whole thing at once but only became more confused, then angry, then depressed. Then after fiddling around for about ten to fifteen minutes and making the whole thing worse, I decided to focus on one bit at a time, having faith that the other bits would eventually all be unravelled correctly and that I would, with patience, be able to successfully wind the whole thing back in.

"Focusing on one bit at a time though, it wasn't really possible to have an idea of how I was going in terms of the whole thing, I was only able to see out to a certain level which wasn't to the scale of the whole thing. And for a while I wasn't sure whether I was actually unravelling or further ravelling the tape. I continued, though it was hard, and things got easier and easier. Eventually, I was done."

"Hmmm. Interesting analogy," she said.

"Yeah well, it describes how I got into and out of my recent depression, even though I am still stressed, which is a new experience for me. I was trying to deal with too many things simultaneously, failing, and hence becoming more and more confused, angry and finally depressed. By not trying to take on everything at once, and dealing with one thing at a time, I was able to cope and in the end succeed. Though it was hard and until the very end, it was impossible to be sure whether things were actually improving. But I'm out of that mess now, those things are solved."

At least I sounded confident.

"Is that like the readers reading your book?" she joked.

"It is. The book, and Evermore itself, is like a tangled mess of coiled tape that is almost impossible to make any sense of. By not trying to take on the whole thing at once and not expecting to understand the whole thing in its entirety immediately, one can work on a bit at a time, as more and more bits fall into place and make sense. And gradually, step by step, we approach total comprehension, though we will never reach this."

"Why's that?"

"That's another surprise!"

"Ohhh," she sighed.

RELAXATION

We were back at our home.

Yes, that's right. *Our* home – it wasn't mine alone any longer.

Cesyl stumbled into the flat and collapsed onto the black leather couch in our lounge room. He then reached into his jacket for his lighter and cigarettes.

"Smoke?" he offered.

"Oh, alright," I said reluctantly, slouching into one of the one-seater units next to him.

He flipped me one and then his lighter. We smoked. I lazily watched the smoke curl and drift over us and began to ponder. A thought arose and I expelled it, leaving it to mingle with the nicotine fumes above.

"Do you think I've changed?"

He looked across at me and smiled. "Yeah."

"I mean of course I've changed, we all do. But I mean really changed. You know, like lost who I was, who I used to be."

He looked at me behind another drag. "Fuck yeah."

I grinned and continued. "It's something I have been worried about. You know, having been stressed and all, it's been a real concern of mine over the last few months. I've been worried that I'm turning into a nerd, that I'm losing my youth, my spontaneity, my energy."

"You've been worrying too much. You need to say 'fuck it!' and enjoy life more. Like you used to do."

He was right, I had changed, but hopefully it wasn't irreversible. I had learnt and gained much, but it had come at a cost.

"I guess I've been trying to grow up too fast, haven't I?"

He nodded. "That's right, I've been talking to Cooper about it."

"What did he say?"

"He agreed. You've grown apart from your mates and become involved in all this spiritual bullshit and Christian stuff."

"I've always been involved in the spiritual stuff, and the Christian stuff is only because I'm open-minded, the same as I studied all the Indian religions last year. But I never let it rule me."

"You do now."

"Yeah, that's what I'm afraid of. And it's about time it stopped."

"That's right," he said, glad to welcome me back to his world.

But I couldn't do that either. I was to be a wanderer of all worlds.

"You know when it all started?" Cesyl said. He had been my best friend throughout most of my life, as I was his. "It all started with Tiffany."

"What do you mean?" I asked, though of course I knew, I only wanted to make sure I did.

"You changing. It all began with Tiffany. Ever since then you've become more serious. It fucked you up."

"Yeah, I'll agree with that. Though I did learn a lot from it."

"What, that women only fuck you up? That they can't be trusted?"

"No! I'm not a sexist bastard like you. Only not to be so deluded and not to become too attached."

"Women are only good for one thing. Getting your dick wet."

"Well, not even Cooper agrees with that."

"Give up on your SNAG bullshit, Brewin! You're just the same underneath as anybody else. If you had a naked chick here saying 'fuck me', you'd fuck her like anybody else."

"True, I'd be tempted, fucking tempted. And once I would have, but I honestly don't think I would now."

"That's exactly what I mean. You've fucked up! Those missionaries have converted you."

"It's got nothing to do with that."

"Oh bullshit."

"Bullshit it hasn't. I talk to them 'cos they're friendly people. My spiritual values have hardly changed."

"My spiritual values have hardly changed," he mocked in a sissy voice.

"It doesn't matter anyway, I am going to change. I'm going to go back to the person who I was, the person whom I've lost touch with."

He gave me an 'I'll believe it when I see it!' look.

"Starting from today." I butted the cigarette, despising myself for having had it when I knew that I didn't really need it, and was only damaging myself and risking addiction by having it. Changing back to the way 'I was',

was up there with sticking to a vegan diet and travelling to India to study with the monks, but it would happen.

And I would stop smoking soon and eventually give up coffee too.

And get my PhD in Entomology, and get my book published, and get my game published and become a musician and find my perfect partner, and achieve all of the million and one other things I wanted to do before I died.

Was it (is it) a delusion? Getting punch-drunk on ambition? Maybe Cesyl knew it was. Maybe I did too.

Feeling our brief talk was over, Cesyl switched on the television, swearing as usual at the various channels and races and people. It seemed to be more an act than anything else.

"You know I'm going to write about this," I said.

"Yeah," he grunted between insults at the television. Finally, he switched it off in frustration and switched on the computer.

I sat there, watching him load up and swear at different computer games and occasionally throw the joystick around.

It seems strange we're best friends, and have been for the better part of ten years. Many people see us as complete opposites. We've been through a lot together, although our lives have gone along completely different paths... and now we were living in the same place for the first time ever.

I had gone to a prestigious private school and then to university, Cesyl was in a long-term relationship and then on the streets. We had both gone through different hells and survived to be in control of our lives, though with very different outlooks. Our friendship too, had passed through many tests of endurance and separation, and though few could really understand it, perhaps even ourselves, it had lasted and now was as strong as ever. Though there were times when we were fed up with each other, even a couple of years when we hated each other, we were spiritual brothers, always there for each other with support and advice, companionship and loyalty. I'd never forget the time, not so long ago when Cesyl said that he had learned to look after only two things in life – 'myself and you'. I knew that he was my most valuable friend who I'd do anything for.

I had often thought how different our external selves were and how similar our internal selves were. I once said to him that the way he is says a lot about aspects of me that aren't obvious, and the way I am says a lot about the way he really is. He agreed. We were just different expressions of the one greater identity. I think that we are all like that.

Suddenly the door belled, breaking my thoughts.

HESITATION

I opened the door and standing there was Graeme, sporting glasses, wavy hair and a bottle of wild turkey and cola.

"Hi Graeme, how are you?"

"Not too bad man, how are you?"

"Pretty good, come in."

"Thanks man." He entered the lounge room where Cesyl was playing Elite on the ancient Commodore 64.

"Wow fuck!" Graeme exclaimed, spinning about the new furniture.

Cesyl looked up and laughed.

"Like the new furniture?" I said.

"Fuck yeah, when did you get this?"

"Just the other day."

"Where from?"

"Sidney's lounges. A two-thousand dollar deal that you pay off over two years. $55 a month which is nothing."

"What, did they give this to you on credit?"

"Yeah."

"Fuck. I'm jealous of you, you bastard, I tried to borrow fifteen-hundred from the bank and they knocked me back 'cos I'm on the dole."

"So what's new?"

"Yeah I know man. But it's cool you got the TV."

"It's been a while, hasn't it?"

"Yeah, I don't know how you survived without it. Fuck!" he said, spinning around again.

"Pretty cool, huh."

"You got an ashtray man?"

"Yeah, here's one." I handed Graeme an ashed jar.

"Thanks man. Do you want one?"

"Nah, it's alright, I've just had one."

"Come on, have another, what have you got to live for anyway?"

"Good point." I sat down with him at the table.

Lighting up, he said, "So are you a smoker now?"

"Pretty much, I bought a pack the other day, and I'll probably end up buying another tomorrow."

"Good to see man, don't be a fucking casual smoker."

"Well, I've pretty much been a casual smoker for almost a year, I don't want to become an actual one."

"Well, bad luck motherfucker, it's in you now. You're a druggie now."

"Yeah, well it's temporary, just until exams are over."

"Bullshit!" Cesyl called out from over the couch, "You're hooked."

Graeme laughed. "Yeah man, you're addicted. The nicotine rules you now, it's your master, you need your fix."

"Yeah well, maybe for now, but it won't last."

"Hah. Hah." Graeme joked, "You'll be sixty years old and sucking away on cigarette after cigarette, and I'll be all healthy and fit watching you slowly die."

"We'll see."

I wasn't going to be a druggie, not me, I was better than that, things were always subject to change, and things soon would. If it was anyone who was going to drug himself to death, it would be Graeme, who I doubted would be around to see me at sixty.

Graeme started talking more drugs. "So are you still smoking cones with Cooper and the others?"

"Not really, only the occasional cone."

"Oh man." He looked disappointed. "How about coming over tonight and smoking some?"

"Nah, not tonight, I don't really feel like it."

"It's good stuff man, it'll get you fucked off your head."

"Nah, it's okay man, I want to stay off mull as much as I can."

He called to Cesyl, "How about you Cesyl? Do you want to smoke some cones back at my place?"

"I gave up that shit long ago!"

I was glad for his common sense and only wished that I too felt no need.

Graeme took another swig of his bottle and looked back at me. "So are you both not smoking dope now?"

"I don't know about Cesyl but for me it's too risky. I trip on it man, real hard."

"But that's good man, that's what it's all about."

"Maybe it's okay for you, but for me I really do feel that I'm seriously risking schizophrenia or something."

"Oh, that's bullshit man, it's all a matter of controlling it, it's all in the mind."

"I know what you mean, but I can't do that. I get too absorbed in my thoughts and keep accelerating through different levels and insights. I can't control it, and it freaks me out, for days sometimes."

"That's only because you smoke at Main Street. Smoke with me man, you'll be fine."

"Yeah, that time we smoked here and freaked out at those posters was pretty cool."

"That's what I mean man, that was filth! Smoke with me man, it'll be cool."

I hesitated at the doors of possibility.

"Yeah maybe."

"Come around tomorrow night."

"I have to work tomorrow night, maybe the next night."

"Cool man, I'll expect you."

Not sure whether I wanted to, or should, make that commitment, I just nodded in ambiguity.

Trying to change the course of this conversation, I asked, "So how was Queensland?"

"Oh mate, Queensland. Six and a half weeks and I was fucked!" He laughed into the air and fumes of a new cigarette. He swigged his bottle again and said, "Fucked off my head the whole time. Did you hear about my trip with Terry? Oh man, it was so fast! I was 'round at a friend's, and we were all doing it, and I ran into the bathroom to shoot up 'cos I couldn't wait. I shot into my arm and quickly recapped the needle, and then in less than five seconds it hit me. It was like the whole world was bouncing up and down, faster and faster. I ran out into the lounge room just going 'whoh!' and then within about 30 seconds I was just hunched over like this." He curled up to demonstrate and then continued. "It's the most positive experience, makes you see that life isn't so bad and that there is something to live for."

"But artificial ecstasy isn't a good thing if it isn't real."

"Drugs are here for a reason man!"

"Yeah and I heard about your experience with your dog."

"Oh fuck!" He grinned. "That was just incredible. I actually thought I was standing up like this, with a cigarette in this hand, going 'Fuck I'm unreal man, I'm just king', when actually I was curled up on the bed with my dog. And then I just blacked out."

"You could have been fucking your dog for all you knew."

"Heroin's the biggest fucking confidence trip man."

"Yeah, though it doesn't damage you provided it's pure, which you can never be sure of anyway, it's just about the most addictive drug in the world, more than nicotine."

"I know man, that's why I had to get out of there before I did get addicted and really fucked up. But once a year or even more is all right."

"I don't know that I agree with you on that."

"Would you do it with me?"

"Maybe, I guess it's better than fucking my brain up with LSD or THC."

I tried to change the emphasis of the conversation again.

"That's the thing that worries me the most about drugs, damaging my brain, my body too, but mostly my brain; which is the only thing I really value."

"Yeah man, don't do what I did, acid fucked me up from taking it every day for six months straight."

"Acid scares me a bit too, if it's going to do what mull does, only much worse."

"You've just gotta control it man. Go with it. You just

have to say 'man I'm tripping, this is all just caused by the drug, but it's cool.'"

"I'm serious about it being a risk, for me that is. A risk to my sanity, and I'm aware of that."

"It's worth it man, for how much it opens your mind."

"That'd be the main reason for doing it, if I did it."

"You just have to make sure that there's someone else there with you who's straight."

After that we lit another cigarette, and smoked some more, and both circled a little more in our current thoughts.

"So what are you doing tonight?" he asked.

"Think I might be going to bed soon."

"Piker," Cesyl called out from over the couch, then was lost again in his video reality.

"Can you give me a lift home then?"

*　　*　　*

A short time later, Graeme and I were sitting outside, chilling you could say, for it was certainly cold. We were both lost in our own thoughts, our own dreams, even our own fears; though I could be certain of none of his, even none of my own.

Why was I doing this? Why was I writing this? Why was I putting my writer through this, my readers through this, myself through this? I knew and I did not, I chose it and yet I did not. Contradiction and confusion beyond all complexity and comprehension. But in an effort to discover or learn anything at all we must be prepared for the unexpected, must be prepared to admit that we're wrong, must be prepared to understand and accept.

And preparation is what this is all about, all that has happened before now and all that is yet to happen. Preparation: both for myself and others.

That is all it is.

Yet all is more.

"The car should be warmed up by now, shouldn't it?"

I broke from my thoughts and looked at Graeme.

"Yeah."

We drove away without further hesitation.

"It's started, Graeme," I said dramatically.

"What do you mean man? What's started?"

"The book, the first book, you know the one I've been talking about?"

"Have you found the answer to life?"

"Not yet, but I'm trying."

We drove on.

"But something is going to happen, something big."

"Huh?" Graeme looked confused.

"It's already started, in fact, something universal."

"I don't understand man, are you talking about your book, are you saying that it's going to change the world?"

"Nah." I laughed. "Not my book, at least not on its own, only in the sense that it's linked to everything else. I'm talking overall."

"What man? What's going to happen?"

"I don't know, but it's something major, as major as anything before, perhaps more major."

There was a great resonance through many minds and worlds at this statement.

"Is it going to be good man? Is it going to be some freaky fucking shit?"

I hesitated, circling, and then said, "It may seem good to some, bad to others, but overall, I think good. Change, I think, is always a good thing."

"Yeah man, I think so too. Something fucking huge is going to happen." Graeme smiled and then drained the last of his bottle of wild turkey and cola. "This world's too fucked up."

"As I said, it's already started, perhaps it's inevitable. But whatever it is, we're going to see its effects."

Graeme had the last word.

"Cool."

INCARCERATION

Cesyl and I, as I remember it, were looking for a place to live.

We had travelled far and seen many places, beautiful and horrible, benign and fearful, enlightening and confusing; and yet still, we were searching. Neither of us was sure what we were looking for, yet we continued on in the hope that eventually, we would find something.

And there was something else…

Something else that was behind us, that was following us. A nameless terror that we could not see, describe, or even comprehend. Something else that, though we tried, we could not hide from…

The first floor of the great building was like an ordinary market place, ordinary except for its silence. Silence that projected from all the eyes, mouths and postures of the myriad human statues that stood about in various expressions of frozen horror like victims of a holocaust. The place was eerily tranquil, and so we hurried through to the next floor.

The second floor was of glass. We passed mighty glass doors to enter into a maze of glass-walled chambers that were filled with all manner of glass ornaments. Instead of walking, we were gliding across the floor, seeing many side passages that we were unable to turn down, sliding ever forward with almost frictionless inertia. We saw no one, only the sparkling artefacts of glass. As we travelled, I often thought I recognised one from somewhere, a replica of something else maybe, but perhaps it was just my imagination.

Whatever it was that was following, was ever there, at the edge of consciousness...

It was perhaps inevitable that one of us would collide with one of the creations. I slid into the arms of a statue, a massive five-headed lizard with many horns and claws. It smashed, sending a great cloud of fragments spinning about the room in slow motion. I tried to scream, but there was no sound. Instead, by some unseen force, the other sculptures in the room exploded, intensifying the crystal fog. All manner of humans and monsters, animals and God-like beings, instruments and warped, abstract configurations became twinkling dust that filled the room.

The shock-wave that had started followed us into the next gallery of glass, disintegrating all as we arrived, and so with the next gallery, and the next and the next.

We couldn't see each other for the glittering haze, as we slid through hall after hall unable to stop or turn from our path, bringing only destruction in our wake.

Eventually our path intersected an exit. A ladder leading upwards. We had no choice but to ascend into further confusion.

As we climbed, the air became increasingly dark and cold. This intensified until we could see and feel nothing, not even our own bodies.

And now we were in a massive feasting hall. A banquet adorned a grand dining table so huge that the set places stretched to the limits of vision, becoming a mirage on the horizon. Yet no one sat at this table, and no heat or smell arose from the delicious looking platters.

Cesyl selected an apple. I tried to tell him not to and scared myself at the sound of my voice as it echoed around the walls.

Cesyl's expression was of mingled surprise and fear. The apple had become nothing but ash on his lips. He spat it out with disgust.

Cesyl decided to try once more. He selected a satay stick dripping with succulent juices and frowned as it became nothing but ash in his mouth.

I grabbed his sleeve and urged him on. There was no sense in remaining here.

And now again we had arrived at a different level.

The first thing we heard was groans of pleasure and grunts of ecstasy.

As they grew louder, we saw their origin.

An engorging orgy of organs. A sea of sleek, rubbery mannequins without legs. Fluidly engaged in thrusting, pumping, probing, groping, licking, sniffing, swallowing, biting, rubbing, pulling, stretching, fondling, screaming, steaming, spurting, aching, bleeding, splitting, tearing, fisting and violating.

The writhing mass formed a floor, the walls and a ceiling, many bodies deep. All were translucently coloured white and red by various body fluids, filling our nostrils with an overwhelming pungent stench.

Cesyl and I were forced to crawl over the top of them, driven to extreme nausea, pushing forward in the hope of an exit.

Hands, mouths and groins tried to assail and smother us, but amazingly the further we progressed: kicking, ripping and punching; the easier it became. Eventually the struggles of the stinking mannequins dripping in blood, perspiration and orgasmic fluid, subsided and we collapsed into a white-tiled corridor.

It was not long before repulsion overcame exhaustion and we sought to rid ourselves of the sticky, smelly liquids that were splattered over us. Then weary as we were, we decided to move on, sensing the presence of that which followed growing closer.

A short distance on, were white-tiled steps leading up.

The tiles now led as far as the eye could see down a brilliant white corridor. We began to walk its length.

We had not wandered far when a naked female, manacled to an X and suspended by chains, dropped through the ceiling just in front of us.

Her voluptuous body was presented to us as an offering, the expression on her face, perfected by make-up, said it all.

"Fuck me," she said.

We hesitated. Another female dropped from the ceiling and hung behind us.

"No. Fuck me," she said.

"FUCK ME." The first one screamed desperately.

Still we hesitated.

"Please fuck me Andrew, please."

"Fuck me Cesyl, FUCK ME NOW."

"Fuck us both."

"Yes, fuck us both, FUCK US BOTH."

We broke into a run. Onwards into this nightmare.

Another one fell from the ceiling, vaginal lips held open by hooks, "LICK ME," she demanded.

Further on, another one confronted us, only her backside was presented. "TAKE ME UP THE ARSE," she urged as we ran past.

More and more of them taunted us with sexual slander as we sprinted onward, their images becoming progressively hazier and their voices quieter, until they could neither be seen nor heard.

Eventually we reached a pair of elevator doors. An adjacent velvet panel had only a single button: up. Anxiously, we pushed the button and waited.

A bell dinged and the elevator doors began to open, revealing a plush interior. Simultaneously, the floor below us began to split in the middle, revealing a pit of naked erect males chanting, "Suck us."

Frantically, we dived through the elevator doors, as the horde began to climb out of the pit.

I pushed the button to close the doors and watched with horror as one naked male extended his arm into the elevator...

And relief as the doors closed on his arm. There was a sickening crunch as the arm was ripped from its owner. The elevator ascended to the only level it could take us to level 6.

When the doors opened again, we saw another white-tiled corridor, dirty with grime and grit, leading into stale blackness. Trembling from the ordeal, we headed down the corridor.

In the first room we came to, we noticed a beggar in

ragged clothing, lying in a pile of straw, her limbs skeletal with starvation. Her head had been bludgeoned open, obscuring her features with blood and brains.

Then we noticed something else.

Her stomach wasn't bloated from malnutrition, she had been giving birth...

I vomited twice before forcing myself to continue on.

Onward to the conclusion of this horrible journey.

Next we heard tormented sounds of screaming and cries for mercy, overridden by the repeated shout, "DO IT AGAIN!"

Wanting to close our eyes, but not daring to, we looked into another hall, a hall of ordered torture and execution.

To one side was a row of soldiers in uniforms, standing immediately behind what appeared to be a row of civilians holding bloodied metal batons. The soldiers were screaming, "DO IT AGAIN!" repeatedly into the ear of whoever it was who held the baton, as other people – men, women and children, in plain clothes the same as those with the batons – were continuously brought in by other soldiers to be routinely bashed to death.

Almost all of the helpless people brought in struggled, or tried to plead for mercy, and many of those with the batons, wept or trembled. But the soldiers screamed, "DO IT AGAIN OR YOU'LL BE BASHED TOO! DO IT AGAIN NOW!" at the sign of any disobedience. And so the madness continued.

It was only for a few seconds that I stared, sickened at the scene before me, but this was more than enough to scar my mind horribly.

I saw children being bashed, friend forced to murder

friend, a mother falling to her knees crying and refusing to kill her own child and being bludgeoned to death for it, and so it went on. Adding to the horror of the scene, the soldiers themselves were groping and raping both male and female baton-wielders as they ordered them to kill, ordering them not to resist or face death also.

Able to take no more, we made a run for the other side, hands over our ears, trying to drown out the screamed orders that constantly echoed around the vast hall.

"DO IT AGAIN!"

"DO IT AGAIN!"

"DO IT AGAIN!"

"DO IT AGAIN!"

There was no relief upon reaching the next area.

Here squads of soldiers were repeatedly gang-raping both women and children. To hear their echoing cries of agony, to see the blood coursing down their abused bodies and to feel the helplessness of their torment, was beyond mortal compare.

We ran on and on through these visions of hell. Most of which I don't wish to remember, including how we escaped the place.

However, there is one more memory that has been etched permanently into my mind. It was the scene of some battle. There were two forces carrying machine-guns that they were firing at each other on a war-ground littered with slain families, destroyed homes, and mem- orabilia the like of wedding and anniversary gifts, family photos, treasured pets and toys.

Worse, in the centre of their fire, between the two

warring lines of troops, were huddles of young children crying in terror atop bodies of children already slain. Those that could, pleaded desperately for peace, but there was to be no salvation.

In order to shoot at each other, the two armies mercilessly cut through the hundreds in between, adding to the thousands already dead.

The last thing I remember seeing was the great red banners that were raised high with pride behind each army, banners that were word for word identical.

They both read:

"GOD BLESS US!

MAY WE WALK IN HIS GLORY!

AND WITH HIS MIGHT CRUSH THOSE WHO ARE IN LEAGUE WITH THE EVIL ONE!"

*   *   *

Then.

After what seemed to be an infinite expanse of time, but for all I knew may have been no time at all, I was alone.

Alone in darkness once more.

In misery.

Then a voice spoke.

"Give up now for you have lost."

Misery became fear became anger became anguish became helplessness became the voice which continued to taunt.

"You cannot beat me; I know you, I rule you, and know me you do not, nor ever will."

My fear spoke for me, I had no idea where or what *this* was, and began to doubt where and what *I* was.

"You're a geek, Brewin. A misfit. You know nothing. You lie to yourself trying to convince yourself that you understand, all the while I sit back and laugh at your folly and watch you crawl blindly towards your fate."

Who? Where? What? Why? Unable to control myself anymore I began to surrender, I began to cry.

I began to die.

"Crawl to me in your ignorance, in your blind arrogance, worship me in the hope of deliverance, beg of me for enlightenment. It matters not for I shall deal with you all in the same way. For I am Death."

The chaotic winds of my soul grew cold, my mind grew dark and unsure and clouded, my body became empty and loveless.

"I am the end, the conclusion of all things. Inevitable. Undefeatable. Eternal."

The circle looked to be near complete, the end seemed nigh.

"I pull your puppet strings like reins,
I suck the life that flows through your veins.
I poison your mind with confusion and hate,
Ever-present, I alone control your fate.
Open your eyes and see that I am Master,
Try to run from me, it will only bring you faster.
With lies I drug you and deceive you and taunt you,
You will not find truth, for only I know what is true.
You think you know me, when you don't even know
    yourself,

You try to hide from me behind your science, religion and
*   wealth.*
Yet these are my weapons, and mine alone to deploy,
Using hate of race, hate of face, hate of place, I only destroy.
For at the end of it all, at a time you shall not see,
There shall be nothing left, only death, only me!"

It ended.

What now to do? What to think? How to act? What to say?

And then I saw that once again, I had no real choice. There was only one way I could go.

Determined to escape, I ran onwards.

"Run while you can, robot! See where it takes you!"

A silvery staircase materialised before me and I ascended to the seventh and final level.

Now I saw that Cesyl was with me again, as speechless as I was. For some reason, we were in a hospital ward full of the dead and dying.

The place didn't stink, but the decrepit state of some of the people (mostly elderly) revolted me. I was so nauseated and disturbed with where we were now and what we had experienced, and so overcome with the desire to get away, that I could not feel sympathy.

The ward we were in was filled with twenty to thirty beds in three rows, upon which were people apparently living but decayed, others that were already dead and others ridden with disease or fever or malaise. And we had come to the middle of it.

There was a row of windows at the back, which looked upon another corridor, onto which a door opened. I headed there to have a look, for I saw that the corridor beyond was also flanked by another row of windows onto another ward.

As I got closer, I saw what unbearable misery and torment lay in the ward across the corridor, and wished I hadn't.

It's hard to describe just how horrible it was. The worst of it wasn't just the state in which I saw the inhabitants, most of whom were decayed bodies, their putrid, festering remains left to rot on the beds, often taking up the entire bed and crawling with insects such as cockroaches and maggots. Nor was it the bones, bodies, vile fluids and other remains that lay all around the ward. Nor even that most were so horribly deformed and disfigured, that they only looked a mockery of what is called human. No, it was seeing the suffering and anguish of those still living, their expressions and their futile attempts to escape this hell.

There were those who crawled about the filth on the floor, dragging themselves along and moaning, unable to form the words to call out for help or describe what they were experiencing. There were those who had collapsed in exhaustion, on the floor, or on their beds, or the beds of others, destined only to rot and become filth. And there were those who just lay in their beds, destitute, devoid of all life and hope, staring blankly beyond the windows they knew they would never go beyond.

Seeing this, I could go no closer to the windows, and for a moment, could not look away, so horrified was I. Finally, mercifully, I did.

The horror of this ward, though not as horrible as that vision of insanity across the corridor, further hit me. For even here there was nothing but the dead and dying, disfigured persons, persons in torment and persons who had been in their beds so long, that they had actually grown into it, bloated and vile, dead and rotted. I noticed now that there was also a nurse here, combing the grey hair of a fat, dead lady in a night-gown who lay on the floor against a bed.

Why did they keep these people here?

Cesyl turned away from those far windows and shared the same startled expression.

We had to get out.

Seeking another way, we were relieved to see a thick, reinforced steel security door behind us, and began our way over.

I know not how we opened the door as it was security coded. But as we were about to leave, a skinny, black adolescent boy crawled towards us. He bore feathered wings but lacked legs, having only stumps. He also lacked the ability to speak.

I just wanted to escape. I was unable to deal with the misery any longer. However, Cesyl showed compassion for the desolate soul that had shambled his way over to us. He crouched down to embrace him and whispered soothing comfort into his ear.

I stood with the door ajar, watching them. I saw that this poor boy (creature) was accepting of his fate, and knew that he would never be able to escape the ward that would become his death cell. He only wanted love. To know that someone cared for him and understood his suffering.

Had he the ability to tell of his life and experiences, he no doubt would have, but he was denied even this. He could not ask for help, or to be carried away from this place, he could only convey his desperation by desperate means.

Unable to bear seeing this any longer, I knelt down with him. He took my hand and kissed it repeatedly and then held it to his broken face, thankful that two outsiders knew of his pain and cared.

Tragically, we knew in our hearts there was nothing more that we could do. We had to leave.

But again, as we were about to leave, another reached us to plead for salvation.

It was a young white girl, half our age, who could speak. Her words still held defiance and confidence; she obviously hadn't been there as long as the others.

"I don't belong here! Not with all these dead people and stuff," she said determined, walking up to us on still able legs. "When am I going to be able to leave?"

I became resolved to help her, she who at least had a chance of escape. She was still mentally and physically intact, though no doubt emotionally traumatised by what she had already gone through. I assured her that we'd be getting her out, that whatever happened we'd do that. We didn't have the power to set her free, but we'd convince someone who did to do so.

"But that's what you said before! I've been waiting and waiting – now when am I going to get out of here?" Sheer frustration and desperation marked her face, we had to do something.

Convincing her that we would (but not sure that we could) we led her to the security door we had left ajar.

Waiting outside was another nurse, her expression as stern as her stance.

"RUN!" Cesyl yelled as he rushed to tackle the nurse. I picked up the girl and charged for the doorway.

Some unseen force knocked the girl backwards as if she had struck a wall. Cesyl and I met no such resistance and careered through into the corridor. Cesyl briefly struggled with the nurse before she flung him free with inhuman strength and moved to close the door.

We tried to persuade the nurse but she ignored us, increasing the security so that we could not open the door again. A great wailing of many voices began to issue from the other side.

Devoid of sympathy, she slid back a face panel and screamed, "SHUT UP!" before closing it shut. Then she walked back down the corridor past us, without saying a word or even so much as turning her head.

It all seemed so hopeless. They were all going to die in there.

Maybe they were already dead.

Maybe we all were...

The dream ended.

*   *   *

This happened a long time ago, and though I have tried, I have never been able to find my way back there. She and others are still suffering different forms of torment and incarceration.

Right now.

JUSTIFICATION

"Ah, you bastard!" I cursed as Cesyl proceeded to collect all the game bonuses with his joystick controlled dinosaur.

"Heh, heh, suck shit!" he said.

Dean was here as well, and soon the others: Cooper, Damien, Alistar, Chopper and Dirk, were due to arrive. Tonight was going to be a big night.

Dean watched and laughed at our struggles.

At the end of the next game level, I pulled out the plug on Cesyl's joystick, crying, "Can't get them now can you, you fucking cheat!"

"Cheat!" he responded, "You're the one who's the fucking cheat!"

As I fought to control Bobble, the bubble-blowing dino on the screen, I also fought with Cesyl as he tried to plug his joystick back in.

"Fuck off!" he shouted.

Eventually, of course, Cesyl succeeded, and the game went on.

"You'll pay for that, arsehole!" he proclaimed.

"Sure," I bluffed, knowing that he was the better player and could arse his way through almost anything. "Well, you're the one with the better joystick. This one wouldn't be fucked if it wasn't for you chucking it around."

"Ohhh, have a tear," he teased.

Level 22. Time to concentrate. Conversation died as we both focused on the game and tried to make it through this screen without losing a life.

It wasn't long before the doorbell rang. I glanced at my watch: it was 8pm.

"That'll be Lana," I said. "Here Dean, take over."

"Oh, all right." Dean lumbered over.

I dashed over to the door and sure enough, it was smiling Lana.

"Hi Andrew! How are you?" she asked as she stepped in, looking tentatively into the lounge room at Cesyl, swearing at the computer screen, and a guy she hadn't seen before.

"Pretty good," I chirped, leading her in.

"You've got furniture!"

Cesyl looked over and said hello in a friendly manner, as Lana took a seat at the edge of us, seeming nervous.

Pretending not to notice, I introduced her to Dean, and they both exchanged formal, forced Hi's.

"Yeah, the furniture's pretty cool, heh? As I said to Cesyl, you know he's moved in, don't you? We've become the biggest yuppies now."

"So where's Cesyl sleeping?" Lana asked.

"In there." I pointed to a closed double door.

"In your horror room." She grinned.

"Yeah. But we've taken down all the posters, red streamers, and the red cellophane that was over the light. Bit of a shame really, I'm not sure that he was worth the compromise," I joked.

Cesyl looked over at me and smiled, seeming subdued in the different company.

I slouched back and watched the game, knowing that Lana was probably wondering what was going on (I invited her over to talk about my book and other things).

The game ended, and Cesyl headed off to the kitchen for some cereal.

The rest of us sat in silence, probably each feeling uncomfortable in our own way.

"We'll go into my room soon," I assured her, hoping that she'd adjust a little, and maybe hoping that something else would happen.

Then I started another game of Bubble Bobble with Dean, and Cesyl returned with a bowl and a packet of Sustain.

I laughed and shook my head as Cesyl stabbed out the face of Cathy Freeman, the Aboriginal-Australian Olympic sprinting champion.

"Die you fucken' coon!" he said as he hacked away at the cereal box.

Lana frowned, trying to understand this male mind.

Cesyl finished his job and satisfied with his performance, poured his cereal.

Looking at me he said, "What?"

Knowing exactly 'what', he said, "I don't hate her because she's Aboriginal, it's because she's fully up herself and thinks she's better than everyone else."

"And how's that?" I asked.

"She competes under the Aboriginal flag, she thinks she's too good to compete under the Australian one. Though she'll compete with their money and all their products, won't she?" Throwing his arms out, "Fucken' bitch!"

"She competed under *both* the Australian and Aboriginal flags!" I said.

"Oh yeah." He gestured, "She held the Aboriginal flag in both hands, yeah. But no, she only held the Australian flag in *one*, and left it hanging down so you couldn't see it!"

"I can't believe you! She couldn't hold them both in both hands, you wouldn't see them both otherwise! It was an important statement, and it was necessary for the Aboriginal flag to be well seen."

"Fucken' bullshit! She's not supporting Australia! I don't care whether or not she's Aboriginal, but at least she should compete under the Australian flag, she should be proud to."

What was the point in arguing? He couldn't see my point or refused to, and I was only aggravating him by not accepting his. It was just like our arguments over social welfare and education and religion and science and psychic phenomena, it lead to a lot of head-bashing and not much else. Maybe I couldn't see his point either and was equally guilty.

"You sound just like Cooper. Next thing you'll be arguing that we should keep the Queen!" I said.

"The Queen can fuck off. I agree with you on that."

Trying to cheer him up, I said, "Anyway, you did a good job on the cleaning. Well done."

"Course I did, I'm the only one who does it. You never do."

This may have been the source of a lot of his subconscious anger. I too have felt such frustration when sharing with others.

I tried to justify my guilt. "Well, I have been busy working and studying with exams and stuff."

Not really effective excuses, as I never really studied, and I wasn't working full time yet.

Still trying to reassure him, I said, "Yeah, I'm sorry about having been so slack with the cleaning and stuff. But once exams are over, I'll make it up to you."

He said nothing and began playing the computer again.

I thought to myself, what have I got to be sorry for? I pay three quarters of the bills, most of what was in the flat we shared was mine, and he used my car every day. This was cultivating negative thoughts, though, so I tried to stop it.

I'd make it up to him. His birthday was in a few days too.

I looked again to Lana. "Do you want to go into my room now and we'll discuss it there?"

"Yes," she said getting up, relieved.

Cesyl then forgot about me and Lana, and returned to him and the game...

We closed the door to my room, and sat down at my table. We were isolated now, just her and me.

"I asked Caraline whether she wanted to come," she said.

"Oh really?" I said surprised, as I thought we had agreed not to ask her.

"She said to drop by next time we go out and she'll see how she feels."

In others words, Caraline was being non-committal. I couldn't blame her. I wondered whether Lana had asked

Caraline because she wanted to, or because I seemed to want her to.

I shrugged. "We'll see."

"I brought your book back and also a story I wrote about the three of us in Fraser Island," Lana said.

"Do you want me to read it now?"

"Not if you don't want to."

"I don't mind either way, but if you like we'll talk first."

"I wasn't going to do this," she said hesitantly, fidgeting with her hands and swaying a little, "but I'll give you the last few months of my diary to read. We haven't swapped diaries for quite some time and I miss that."

Outside the doorbell rang – the others had arrived.

"Me too. You sure you want to let me read it, though? I thought you decided not to."

"I know. It was good in a way that I did that, as I went and wrote a whole lot of stuff that I wouldn't have been able to if I'd known you were going to read it. But now I've sorted all that out, and I think it would help your book, add more depth to my character."

Hmmm, I thought, this almost confirmed my suspicions.

A bit unfair, but I dared asking, "What's it about then?"

She fidgeted a little more and made her nervous face as she said, "Um. I'll let you read it."

"What now?"

"Read it later. When I'm gone," she said quickly.

The signals seemed pretty clear – I doubted that the diary was going to be any great surprise.

"Okay then. How about we talk about my book?"

"I think it's a great book, Andrew. A bit scary to read, though."

"Why, because everything that happens, ends up in it?"

"Yeah, it's like…" She rolled her eyes up and sighed, trying to figure out exactly what to say and how to say it. "It's hard to be completely open and talk to you, as I know you're remembering it and writing it down."

"That's right," I laughed, "Even as we speak the eyes of maybe a billion readers are upon us, listening to our every word and scrutinising our every action. Occasionally saying to themselves things like 'Gee, that Andrew character is a wanker' and 'I bet Lana wouldn't really have done that, that's so unrealistic!'"

I was enjoying myself. I'm not normally a 'power freak', but the sort of control I currently had was something that felt terrific.

"It's so weird, Andrew. I was talking to Eve the other day about your book. And just like you say, she was arguing that Caraline's character would never have even talked to you and wasn't attracted to you, and yet I knew that this was exactly what happened, it's uncanny!"

I nodded with a devious smile.

"And after I read the first two parts and began reading the chapter 'Confusion', that was exactly my reaction. I was confused and thought that you should make it clearer. It's hard to know what to think, because every time I come up with something to suggest, it comes up in the book later. It is hard to be objective, though, both because it's my story and I know it did happen, and also I've read your other book *The Dark Horde* that certain parts have a lot to do with."

A perfect comment, I thought.

"What you have said just then, may help readers who

were thinking exactly that. Thinking that it wasn't related, thinking that it was all contained in one book, which it's not."

She sighed.

"Lana sighed in frustration and annoyance," I said, teasing her.

"As Andrew, the Master of Contradictions, swayed his hair about and rolled his eyes wildly," she responded laughing.

This was so much fun!

"And then Andrew paused, silent, waiting. He could sense the attention of all those readers throughout other worlds, realities and times, waiting for his next words, expectant, trying to anticipate what he'll say," I said, getting all the mileage out of this that I could without boring the readers.

"And it's 'therapeutic life experience' not 'life therapy.'"

"Whoops! I'd better change that. Sorry about that, readers," I said appealing to the ceiling, "But I guess you wouldn't have known anyway if it hadn't been written here."

"And you know what I said to you on the phone, which you didn't hear because you were in your own thoughts?"

"What?"

"Depression is a very selfish thing."

I laughed. "Just as well I didn't hear it. I'll leave that as it is, though, as that's written from my point of view, as is the rest of the book I guess. Which is unavoidable. And hence it's limited by my understanding."

"Which is why I thought my diary would help."

"It's your choice. You can still take it back and not give it to me."

"It's okay."

"You sure?" I said pulling the typed manuscript across to me, "This is your last chance to change your mind?"

"I'm sure." Her eyes met my steady gaze.

At that moment Damien burst in, carrying all the noise emanating from the lounge room with him.

"How's it going, Damien?"

"Oh, not too bad. You should have seen Rashid at work today."

I had obtained jobs for both Damien and Chopper, and later for Cesyl, where I worked; monitoring alarm systems from a computerised control room.

"He tried to tell me that he or Viped can switch on the camera that's used to watch us from their house whenever they want. There's only a cable running from the power to the video recorder and to the camera. There's no way he could switch it on from his house."

"Yeah, he does think we're more stupid than what we a

Lana was feeling awkward but tried to seem calm and patient.

"He's a fucking idiot," he said.

I looked at Lana and hoped that Damien was going to leave soon.

"And I made a couple of mistakes too," Damien continued, "but I followed that notice on the wall – 'if you make a mistake, make sure no one else finds out' – so I covered them up."

I turned to face Damien. Neither of us knew who put the notice up. "Viped said he was going to put up a notice about the consequences of making mistakes after Keshi got fired for falling asleep on night shift and missing an alarm. And that gets put up!"

"I know." Damien laughed, "But it's the way they work. They make mistakes all the time and cover them up. I guess as long as no one finds out it's all right."

Lana's eyes had that glazed-over look; she was lost in her own thoughts.

"So what are you doing?" Damien asked.

"Oh, just talking about my book and stuff."

"How's that going?"

"Well. I've written heaps lately. I'm really pleased with it."

"Cool man, you'll have to give it to me to read some time."

"When it's finished I'll definitely do that. See what you think of it."

"Oh, and I've finished Stepphenwolf," he said. "It's even better than Journey to the East."

Here's a chance for me to involve Lana.

"Unreal. You'll have to read Siddhartha too. Lana's read that. I borrowed that one from her, she's the one who got me into Hermann Hesse."

"Cool, have you got Siddhartha here?"

"I don't have it any more, I gave it back to Lana."

Lana was following the conversation now. "You can borrow it if you like, though it's my mum's book."

"Oh, that's cool. I'll buy a copy myself as I want to have a copy of them all anyway," Damien said.

Damien looked at a typed manuscript on the table and began reading it.

Lana quickly snatched it away from him, across to her side of the table, "That's my diary," she explained.

"Oh shit. Sorry. I thought it was his book."

Amused, I replied, "Nah, my book's here." I pointed to my hand-written exercise book. "But we're also talking about Lana's diary and writing. But I'll be out in an hour or less."

Understanding, he stepped back through the doorway and said, "Cool man, see you soon buddy."

He closed the door.

Still feeling no more comfortable than she had since she first came in, Lana said, "I'm in the way here, aren't I?"

"Of course you're not! They don't care. They can do their own thing, and we'll do ours. Don't worry about it!"

"Don't worry. I'll go soon." She sounded like she was trying to convince herself this, rather than me.

"I've invited you here to talk to you. That's all that matters. Don't stress about them, they can look after themselves."

She swayed a little, and then said, "Anyway, I honestly do think your book is fantastic, I'm not just saying that."

"Yeah, I'd like to think that was true. Though I don't think either of us can really be objective."

"I know. But I still think others will see its beauty too. It's honest, it's insightful and it's well-written. I really do think you're gifted. I'm jealous."

"I agree with you, of course I do, I wrote it. And in a way, I have to convince myself that it's absolutely brilliant in order to have the motivation to finish it."

"As long as you do finish it."

"I will. It's been too long since I started, especially with *The Dark Horde*, which I started almost seven years ago."

"And I was thinking about *Evermore*. There are parts where I've read something shocking, offensive or confusing, and I've thought, 'I wouldn't have written that', and then I thought, 'Well it's not me writing it, it's you, and you're not me.'" She chuckled. "So I decided that I'm not going to tell you any more, what you should and shouldn't do. I realise that now. It's your book and I don't think you should change anything. You would only be compromising yourself if you did."

This was something I felt I, and the readers, needed to hear.

"Indeed what I'm doing is a big risk. If it ever does get published, I'm opening myself to criticism. And there will be many who will criticise and judge, but I have to believe in myself, listen to myself, and do what I think is best."

Changing emphasis, she said, "I think it would be great if you include the letter you sent to Caraline. It would help to explain that part much more."

"Yeah, perhaps. Though I'd rather present your and Caraline's viewpoint, rather than just my own."

"You could include that letter Caraline sent you after our Fraser Island trip."

"Maybe I could. Though I don't really think she meant any of those things. I think the letter was mostly just a gesture to get you back on side. If she meant what she said, she would have shown it by actually making an effort afterwards, which she didn't. I've got her letter, and mine to her right here in my bag in fact."

"You never fail to surprise me, Andrew. What else have you got in that bag ready to pull out and show me?"

"My diary, in fact. Handwritten, as my monitor has

died and I haven't got around to fixing it and typing this year's stuff in, but you'll manage to read it."

"Ohhh."

I handed over a pile of loose-leaf and continued, "I'd like to include your story too. It would present your experience of the situation, even if I didn't completely agree with it."

"Well, you will. It's much more sympathetic to you than Caraline. I take your side much more than hers; I've even had to add in more stuff about her to be nicer to her. I originally wrote it when I was pretty angry with her, which is pretty usual."

Alistar opened the door.

"Hi Alistar!" said Lana, recognising a friend of mine she knew and liked.

"Hi Brewin, hi Lana."

"What's up?" I said.

"Oh, I just thought having been here in your house for the last half-an-hour that I might as well say hello to the tenant. But I can see you're obviously busy here, so I'll leave you."

"Oh, that's all right."

"Did you still want to come to a writing group meeting?" Lana asked Alistar.

"Well, I haven't written anything, so it's not really worth me coming."

"That doesn't matter," I butted in, "many of the meetings we have, we haven't got writing, we just talk and discuss ideas and stuff."

Still not really keen, Alistar said, "Well is it just you two who hold these meetings?"

"No," said Lana, "there are others. Though I don't think you know any of them. Eve, Alex, Scott and maybe some others."

"Is Caraline in it?"

"No." Lana grinned at me. "We asked her once a while ago. But it wasn't really her thing."

"Too scared of you, heh?" Alistar looked at me.

"Yeah." I laughed. "She feared for her mind and soul, that I'd corrupt her."

With an expression of great intellect, he said, "She's obviously someone with a great deal of sense."

I laughed. "So are you interested?"

"I probably can't as I'm pretty busy at the moment. When is your next meeting?"

"We don't organise set times," I explained, "They're spontaneous sorts of things, like role-playing game sessions I guess."

Still not seeming eager, he responded, "Well, I can't do anything over the next month as I've got essays and exams, but let me know the next time you have one after that, and I'll see if I can come."

"Okay," said Lana, seeming pleased to have one of my friends come along for a change.

"I'll be out soon," I assured him.

"See you later," he said and closed the door.

Overcome by anxiety once more, Lana said, "I better go."

Not wanting her to feel that way, I tried to intervene, "No really. You don't have to go. You can stay as long as you want. Don't worry about them."

"No really, it's late. I better get home."

"Okay." I stood. "Thanks for coming and talking and stuff."

"I'll let you know when the next writing group meeting is," she said.

"Cool. Enjoy my diary, won't you."

"With all your contradictions and your internal anxieties." She laughed.

"Yeah. I'll see you to the door."

As we went out, I saw Theo. Arrogant and blatantly offensive like Cesyl in many ways, with many views so extreme it was hard to be sure whether he actually believed them, especially when he considered himself to be a believer in Christianity. He was good to laugh with and at, though.

"How's it going, Theo!"

"G'day Brewski!"

"Hey, guess what I bought today on CD?"

"Another Slayer album?" he said hopefully.

"That's right, 'Hell Awaits'."

"I bought it on CD just yesterday too. I told you I was going to convert you."

"Yeah, it's happening."

"Fucken' oath!" He laughed. "You've realised their greatness."

"Yeah, they're still not better than Metallica or Allegiance, but they are good."

"It's only a matter of time, Brewin, before you admit they are the best. And you'll say 'Theo, I should have listened, you were right.' Hah. Hah."

In the background, Cooper laughed at Theo and his bullshit Slayer. I led Lana out.

REFLECTION

I returned to my room for a few minutes to read Lana's story. It was something I wanted to do while the trip to Fraser Island in January was still fresh in my mind. I knew the others outside probably didn't understand, but I didn't care – this was something I did for *me* and for the benefit of this book.

I present Lana's story now without further comment, and leave you to form your own judgements, if any.

* * *

THE ISLAND

I think it was Andrew who started it.

"Let's play a game!" he said.

The three of us stood on the shore, like gulls, bored and watching the water. It was too cold to swim, and too early to go back to the tents.

"Do you want to, Caraline?" I asked.

Her face tightened into a frown. "Not one of your dumb role-playing games I hope."

Her words swirled through the air, like one of those pieces of slimy red seaweed that kept catching at our feet with the incoming tide.

It was strangling Andrew.

"I thought you liked them." He tried to shrug her off, but she was too strong.

"I do. But you want to do that stuff all the time. You never know when to stop."

"It was just an idea. I don't care if we do something else. What do you want to do, Lana?"

It was always up to me. Caraline looked at me and grinned. I glared at her, annoyed. Why did she always have to be so damn rude to Andrew? She sensed my disapproval and started walking away from us.

Oh God. It was all my fault. This whole holiday. Caraline. Andrew. All my idea, all my fault.

Andrew smiled at me, grateful.

"I feel bad now," I said.

"It was good. You stood up to her for once."

He had no idea how I felt.

"We'd better catch up with her, don't you think?"

Andrew laughed and shrugged. "You're pretty hopeless, you know."

Ouch.

Maybe he knew me better than I thought.

We caught up with her.

"Caraline, I have an idea. Remember how we said we were going to do Tashlict. Why don't we do it now?"

Tashlict is an old Jewish tradition, one of the few things I learnt from going to a Jewish school for so long. You go to the beach, just before The Day of Atonement, and throw stones out into the water, naming each one as a sin that you've committed that year. Then the tide comes in and God washes all your sins away with the waves. I had told Caraline about it, and she liked it.

"I wish I could do that with my problems," she had said.

"We should try it," I had replied, and we had laughed about it for a bit.

"What's Tashlict?" asked Andrew.

I explained.

"Yeah alright," he said.

I could tell he wasn't too impressed. He probably had a really good idea for a role-play, and now that was wrecked.

His disappointment seemed to enthuse Caraline.

"Let's go get rocks!"

She ran off, and Andrew followed, both trying to get as many rocks as possible. They were alike in many ways, Caraline and Andrew, both competitive and confident, and for now were laughing and talking like friends.

They had been friends. Andrew was certainly attracted to her, and I think Caraline liked him too. There was something about him, maybe the fact that he was so unashamed of his attraction to her, when others would have tried to hide their feelings, that must have drawn her to him. She didn't fall in love with him, like Andrew had with her, but there was something she liked about him. There must have been.

I liked him too. A lot. I was always putting feelers out for affection, trying to break barriers between myself and others, but Andrew was the first person I met who seemed to want me to break these barriers. And he liked me, not just Caraline. So many of Caraline's male friends had looked straight through me as if I were invisible or had no identity other than as Caraline's friend. But Andrew and I had an understanding of each other. It was like we'd known each other for a million years.

When we first started becoming good friends, I remember Caraline asking me if I were interested in him. I said I didn't think so, that I honestly felt I wasn't attracted to him in that way, but that I did care for him a lot. She asked for me to promise never to go out with him. I said she needn't worry, I wouldn't. "He's not good enough for you," she had said.

I should have known then.

Caraline and I had planned to go to the island before I met Andrew. She needed to get away, she said, and I was going away. We were best friends, so it seemed perfect. When I met Andrew, I wanted him to come with us too. By then, I think, Andrew had replaced Caraline as my main emotional support. I wanted him there for strength. And, I thought, it would be good for Caraline and Andrew.

Andrew had said that us three were like a triangle, that only needed one more strong bond to form. There was a strong bond between me and him, and Caraline and I, but only a weak bond between him and Caraline. And no matter how much he seemed to reach out to Caraline with love and affection, a strong bond had not yet been formed. Maybe going away together would fix that, making the triangle complete.

When Caraline realised Andrew was coming, she didn't want to go anymore, but I convinced her. "You do like him, don't you," I had said. "It will be good to get away. We'll have a good time." So she came.

And here we were doing Tashlict.

"I'll go first," said Andrew.

"OK," I said.

"This is for Caraline." He grinned at her. "Who can actually be a friendly, funny, intelligent person at times."

The stone flew towards the ocean, and fell plonk onto the shallow water.

Andrew was proud of himself, oblivious, I guess, to how I knew Caraline was reacting.

"Alright. I've got one for you." Caraline smiled, "This is for Andrew who thinks he's better than everyone else."

She was being such a bitch, I thought. I never knew Caraline could be like this, especially to someone who was my friend. Usually she was friendly, charming and happy. I should never have brought them together.

"This is for Andrew and Caraline," I said, "Who don't understand each other."

Plonk.

I couldn't take it anymore.

"I'm going back to the tents," I said.

"I'll come with you," said Andrew.

We left Caraline on the beach. Alone.

I could see Andrew was upset. I really did love him and I wanted to help, to understand, to fix things up.

We talked about it.

"Maybe she's just depressed and is taking it out on you," I suggested.

Andrew shrugged.

He knew.

And I knew too.

That night, Caraline and I were in our tent.

"I know I was pretty rude to Andrew today."

She waited for me to qualify that statement, to tone it down a little.

"Yes. Well at least you know that."

"He just gets on my nerves. He always pretends nothing gets to him. And he does think he's better than everyone. He goes on and on about writing and role-playing, and he doesn't realise that people aren't interested. It's stupid. Why can't he just live in the real world. He's annoying."

She was imploring now, trying to get me to side with her. Usually, I would have given in, tried to reassure her that it wasn't her, she wasn't bad, it was just a character clash that she had with Andrew. If anything, it was my fault for bringing them together on this trip.

But she was hurting me pointing a knife through Andrew's heart, and through him, mine. We both loved him, so how could she be so cruel?

She seemed so different now. What was it that had stolen away her compassion, her friendliness, her cheer-fulness, all the things I had liked about her when we first met? Was she jealous of me and Andrew? That was possible, and probably part of it, but there had to be something else. I had other close friends and Caraline had never reacted to them like this. Was I wrong about Caraline all along? Was the old Caraline just an illusion and this who she really was?

If this was who she was, then who was I?

"I wouldn't treat anyone the way you treat him," I said.

"You don't know what it's like, Lana!" she replied, in tears.

"What's like?" I demanded.

"He tries too hard, he's too intense and..."

"You can't control him."

Where did that come from?

She looked at me sharply.

"It's not that. God, Lana, you just don't understand. You haven't had as much experience with boys. I should never have come here." She was crying.

Did she need to control me too?

"I'm sorry," I said. "Let's go to sleep, OK. We're both tired."

We closed our eyes.

That night I dreamt I was walking along the beach. I was pushing through heavy, thick sand that kept getting thicker and thicker as it engulfed my every motion.

I was sinking down into it, and tried to hold onto a sea shrub on the side, but it was thorny and I couldn't grasp it. My head went under and my mouth was covered. I couldn't breathe.

I was trapped.

"Let's play a game," said Andrew.

I awoke.

It was three days later and we were driving home. Home to the future, thank God, and off the island.

"Anyone have any ideas?" I said.

"I do," said Andrew.

Andrew and I smiled at each other.

Caraline rolled her eyes, cynical, sarcastic, hurt and bitter.

"Good," I said.

I was beginning to breathe again.

*   *   *

I believe the point needs to be made that what I have presented to you is inevitably biased. Not only by virtue of having decided to leave out my letter and Caraline's, but also because the writer (Lana in this case) makes assumptions about what another said, meant, felt or thought.

I think this limitation necessarily exists for everyone, even someone making assumptions about themselves may come to change their mind (or 'only comes to realise later') what they had thought or felt in a given situation. In addition to this, no two people completely agree about everything that someone has thought or felt.

Despite this, I believe that the above does give a 'more or less accurate summary of what happened' and having come from the eyes of another, gives a valuable interpretation of my/our experience.

There is always more to any given situation, any given description, any given personality that hasn't yet been understood and/or explained. Always something more to be considered. Always.

INTERACTION

We were all there, what would come to be known as "The Jamestown Lumber Party", but that's another story; another adventure; one yet to be told and hence yet to occur.

"So did you have a good root with Lana?" Cesyl smiled through cigarette smoke.

"Fuck off, we were only talking. And you know that we're just good friends."

"Bullshit, I heard the groans coming from your room." He put on the act. "Oh Andrew, tickle my dangle!"

"Piss off, I'm not the slightest bit interested in her in that way, and you know that. She's got a nice personality and she's a good person to talk to, we have a lot in common."

"You just wanna hold her by those love handles and do her up the arse. You're gunna be wanking into your doona tonight over her."

"Yeah, sure."

"Eh! Eh! Eh!" (He made the squeaking noise of the bed, and imitated me fucking my doona.) "Oh Lana! Harder! Harder!"

I ignored him. Chopper and Cooper chuckled together in the background. Damien looked up. "Don't worry man, we understand. She's a nice person with a friendly personality."

Alistar and Dirk kept playing cards and Dean – the computer.

Cesyl took his place next to Dean at the computer screen. Cooper asked me, "You playing cards, geek?"

It always seemed to hurt me when he said that. And hurt turns to anger, anger turns to hate, the diabolical trio.

Why should I care? I knew who I was, so why should it bother me? Though I knew Chopper, Alistar and perhaps Dirk, agreed with Cooper, why should I plead acceptance from them? I knew I wasn't one of them and they did too, so why did I desire to be seen as anything else?

And I realised perhaps the answer to that was that I really didn't know myself, I doubt I ever will completely, and maybe what they said was true...

My hurt obvious, I tried to feign dissociation, "Yeah, I guess."

It was see-through of course, as Alistar was apt to point out, "You are a geek, Brewin."

Chopper, Cooper and Dirk all laughed heartily. I was just glad that Theo was not also present to join their bandwagon; Theo having just left.

Cooper then moderated a little, seeing that I was unhappy with the label, speaking over a silence that had fallen upon the table. "It is true Brewin, you know it and we've talked about it before. I mean this in the nicest possible way, but you are a geek."

Chunky, bearded Cooper, who in many ways was the leader of the group, and in many ways represented what I liked and hated most in Cesyl; their intelligence, adventurous nature and love of role-playing games; yet also their arrogance, stubbornness and prejudice. In many ways the same and the opposite of me. A contradiction that persisted and meant that almost all of the male friends I spent time with, were either friends of his or friends of Cesyl. And yet Cesyl and Cooper were completely different; Cesyl had an aversion to parties and large crowds, whilst Cooper had an affinity for these things. And I didn't have a great deal in common with either of them; neither displayed sensitivity, a concern for welfare or environmental issues, or a disposition towards introspection like I did.

"Yeah, it still shits me though," I said, taking a seat on the opposite side of the table to Cooper.

"Oh, poor baby," Alistar said. I ignored him.

Alistar, a comic genius, in many ways filled the role of the baby of the group, the niggling little kid who was always capable of gaining attention whoever the audience. His behaviour towards me for instance, was universally different when he was on his own with me, or with me and female company, than when he was with the others. I call him 'a master of his trade', able to freely change and dispense with the currency of sociality.

They dealt me in and the game continued.

We laughed and joked and some of us smoked and the night rolled on. Though much of the time I was in their world, most of the time, I wasn't. I was lost in my own thoughts, no doubt seeming unenthusiastic, nerdy, even vague. Different social expectations of me, cause a different me to be expressed, and thus a different me to be perceived and reacted to. Herein lies perhaps the socially-inept 'nerd' stereotype which Cooper and Chopper and Alistar ascribed to me.

I am too introspective, aren't I? I should let go more, and get involved in the game more, but I can't help it. No, change that. I am *not* too introspective and I can help it but choose not to. I do doubt myself and question myself too much, or so I sometimes believe and am told. However, I am grateful for it all, for I always seem, with emphasis on seem, to find deeper meaning; and this comes as often from within as without.

I could have and probably should have said more about Cooper and Alistar's character profiles. Well, I should have said more if I was trying to paint a complete picture, which I wasn't, so that's okay that I did not. It is a dangerous thing to think that one can fully describe a person, even if that person is oneself. For a finite number of words can never do justice to an infinite, perhaps ever-changing quality; there is always more. The danger in thinking this is one of misinterpretation and unfair judgement. And this is the same danger too of taking any description, even of oneself, to be objective and true. Truth is only truth relative to the subjective perception of the perceiver. Can it ever be any more?

"I'm over-playing this," I said, for I was losing, and not really enjoying it.

Dirk looked up at me surprised. "You're not pulling out, are you?"

"I want to play a different game, I'm bored with this one."

Dirk looked at the others, the others jeering or else

not surprised at all. "You can't just get up and leave like that, you have to finish the game!"

I looked over at the computer, and the world Cesyl and Dean were in, with envy.

But Dirk was right and so were the others. I started it, and couldn't pull out halfway even if things were going badly and I wanted to give up.

I had to see the game through to its conclusion... Maybe things would pick up soon.

The game went on and the players in it. The dealer dealt me good fortune, and I played well. I lost no more. I finished barely into the positive points but I finished a 'winner'. Maybe if I had had that attitude from the start I would have finished a lot higher, and been the winner overall.

But I would remember that next time...

"What's the time?" Damien said as he looked up at Cesyl's Star Trek clock on the wall.

"9.40." I answered him unnecessarily, as he read the face anyway.

"I want to get something to eat. Is anything still going to be open?" he asked.

"MacDonalds is open and the pizza shop, I think. Do you mind if I come? I wouldn't mind getting something to eat too."

"Nah man, I think you're a fucking idiot and I don't want your company. Of course you can fucking come!"

I grinned at him.

"Anyone else want to come?" he asked.

Seeing no takers, we left, heading for Columbo's, the best pizza in town.

I always felt at home when I was with Damien. We seemed to connect and have an understanding of each other, that the others, including Cesyl and Cooper, didn't have.

We walked in the silence of our own internal worlds for a time, then Damien broke it. "It's good being able to talk to someone like you about spirituality and stuff. You're not naive and narrow-minded like Cesyl and Cooper."

He knew I would agree, which was one of the reasons why he said it.

"Yeah. I can't really talk about any of my ideas or experiences that are important to me with them. They don't really want to listen," I answered.

(They did want to listen but not to empathise, only criticise, which only served to drive a wall between them and me, a wall Damien was now breaking.)

"But it's their life," he continued, "and their opinion and they're entitled to it. They'll learn with time I guess, and over the course of many more lives perhaps, become old souls like us."

I did agree that Damien and I were more open-minded, and perhaps wiser too, but there was a danger here of misunderstanding and unfair judgement. I could not say for sure that I understood their world, for it was not mine to dwell in; hence any judgement was liable to be unfair. I did not know that they were not right or whether they were better than me. I did not know for sure that I was better than anyone or knew anything at all. Pride and self-glorification seeds prejudice and self-deception; but to dwell in scepticism and doubt everything only undermines oneself. Honesty and sincerity allows for understanding, acknowledgment and acceptance. Understanding of the limitations of knowledge and its conditional truth relative to its terms of reference and context. Acknowledgment of one's faults and failings but also equally of one's strengths, accomplishments and *successes*. Acceptance then of oneself, of others, and of the way the world inter-relates.

I thought to vocalise these thoughts, thinking Damien would understand, but then he spoke again, so I listened instead.

"I've been noticing the coincidences that the Celestine Prophecy talks about lately," he said.

"Have you?"

"Yeah, like I've been running into all these people, old friends and stuff, that I had been thinking about."

"Really."

(He related what happened.)

"Wow," I said.

"What did you think of the Celestine Prophecy?" he asked.

"I loved it. It struck such a concordance with many of my own ideas, and catalysed some others. It made me aware of all those coincidences and now they happen all the time; except when my energy levels are low."

"Like what? What are some of the things that have happened?"

"Lots of things, too many to tell."

"Just tell me one then, the most amazing one of all."

I proceeded to tell him a great spiel of this followed by this, then this and then after that, this. But there is no sense in telling the same here, as it would have the same effect it did on Damien; little if anything. Just like his relating to me, of the coincidences that he had noticed. One's own experience of the unseen, no matter how amazing, cannot be conveyed or expected to be believed by another until they experience it for themselves. Until then trying to describe this experience to the other one merely seems fanatical, gullible, delusional, impressionable, blind, deceived, whatever. In other words, the believer seems as blind to the non-believer as the non-believer to the other.

"Celestine Prophecy was a good story, but a bit unrealistic for my liking though. All those coincidences and stuff, it was all a bit too easy and linear. A bit too simplistic and not enough like real life," Damien said.

Though I didn't necessarily agree, I could certainly see his point (or at least I certainly thought I could see his point). But I was content to listen, to hear what he had to say, and agree with what I agreed with and leave the rest unsaid. Many times as we talked on, as we have talked before, as I have talked with many others, I just listen. I nod now and then, and say "Yeah" here and there to show that I follow, but otherwise just listen. To learn about others, one has to listen; to learn about oneself, one has to listen. Whether from within or from without, to learn one has to listen. And this is sometimes a hard thing to learn.

You have learnt and experienced much and this is fine. You want to share it with others and that is fine too. You feel you have something to offer others, something you have which you feel others would benefit from having; by all means share it. But remember, it is all subjective, and this cannot be escaped, for we experience our own world, our own consciousness, and no other.

My experience of my world shapes my views and yours the same. Which means my views and experiences are just as subjective as yours, and therefore I cannot know that I am any more right than you, and you me. Say what you like about this, it changes nothing, it remains my opinion and your opinion yours, just as it remains my world and your world yours.

It may be good that your views are strong and unshakeable, and you have good reasons for them, but others are no different, and they may have good, equally good, reasons too. And we all have our great stories to tell, great things that life has taught us, feelings that we have or secrets that no one else knows of or understands. But there is always more to learn, more to experience, and though this all comes through 'one's own world'; it comes as much from the 'external self' as from the 'internal self'. And we can reach all of this by listening.

For this to be true, it also means I have to listen to you. We must listen to each other. That way, we both can learn, we both can understand, we both can grow. For I believe all problems reduce to ones of misunderstanding, and with true understanding comes acceptance.

During all this time, we walked to the pizza shop, ordered pizza, walked to the bank, walked back, waited, got the pizza, and walked back to the flat; but all this is not important to the story, nor was much of the conversation we had. Only what was important to me has been told, for a story can never be told in its entirety; there is always more.

Pizza in our stomachs, we arrived back to the full house.

Cesyl and Dean were still at the computer, and the other four were laughing at some joke.

"And when are we going to play Cthulhu, Brewin?" Cooper growled at me. "It's been so fucking long I've almost forgotten who Lovecraft is!"

"Too fucking right it's been too long!" I said. "My exams end in another week, then we can role-play as much as you want."

Cooper looked across to Dirk and Chopper, the other Cthulhu members.

"Yeah, I'm fucking hanging to get back into Cthulhu again," piped Dirk.

"We want Mike Dubois back!" Chopper hollered.

Some, probably most, of the best times of my life were during fantasy role-playing games. Where for a short time the outside world disappeared, and only the fantasy one existed. Where all was under control and anything was possible. Where true heroes could be born, rise and die all in a nights' playing and nothing at all would be lost. And indeed one of the most momentous of all these role-playing experiences was with these three, playing Cthulhu from 9pm to 6am six nights straight. We all wished we could live those days again, recreate those memories, but we all had jobs now or other commitments. We had tried numerous times since but we struggled to overcome the practical limitations of organising even one night that we could all participate in, let alone a regular weekly schedule. Things weren't likely to improve either – within the year, all of us would be living out of home and have either full-time uni, work, or both. Eventually we'd find someone, and 'settle down'. We'd always be friends, I guess, but without the game our lives were less colourful, less meaningful, and ultimately our union perhaps less strong. Without it, we would inevitably be forced by boredom and/or obligation into the 'land of the living'. The patrons of responsibility and conformity were marching us back to the 'real world', telling us that it was time to accept our calling...

Not much more was to happen that night. We spent almost an hour arguing over role-playing, the pitiful situation, and what could be done about it. The Cthulhu crew of myself, Dirk, Cooper and Chopper argued, and then Alistar brought up the issue of Rolemaster and into the debate came Damien and Dean replacing Chopper and Dirk. Someone brought up Greyhawk, after that enlisting Cesyl, bringing back Dirk and removing Damien. Comments were made then by all in regards to Creator and then role-playing in general.

We resolved that we had to resolve something.

We resolved that there was nothing we could resolve now.

We resolved that we would resolve something in the near future.

Hence, as usual, we resolved nothing, but kept alive a lowly candle of hope that something would be done, ... maybe.

We all agreed it was completely fucked.

I went to bed soon after the others left, feeling saddened.

I needed to re-instil the magic that I was losing, that we were losing, from our lives, that was taking with it my optimism, my spontaneity, my energy, my carelessness.

I needed Inspiration...

INSPIRATION

Cradled.

I held the black beast in my hand and grinned – it was time.

Selected.

I moved over my collection of tapes, and drew forth a shiny, silver cassette, white letters emblazoned on its side like black markings burnt into the hide of a bull.

Loaded.

I slotted the batteries into the port at the rear of the walkman, like slugs into a shotgun. I slammed the bullets home, and closed the breech. I was ready.

Waited.

I paused a moment and took in a couple of deep breaths, preparing myself for the coming ordeal physically, mentally and spiritually. I nurtured my burning anticipation like a gem. A gem that was conceived at the centre of my mind, a jewel of the imagination, a brilliant blue sapphire of creation. It pulsated and grew with supernatural life. And then when I felt I could staunch the flow of adrenalin no longer, I turned the walkman on...

And gem, mind, body and soul exploded together as one.

I was flying. I was flying through the glitter of space. The vastness of the universe panned all around me in every direction imaginable. I banked through clusters of stars, shattered fragments of glass, and dived down through swirling pink mists, nebulae, closed like a secure web around their children, the galaxies and solar systems that made up the skeleton that stretched from one side to the other of all there was.

Suddenly I was joined on either side by comets, blazing fireballs of fury; long, elegant tails of fire and ice spanning back for millions of miles. I ducked and in synchronicity, the two companions weaved overhead, a perfect helix of dazzling flame. I re-emerged between them and re-assumed the role of leader. I cut and swerved with breathtaking skill and dexterity, and the celestial streaks behind me mimicked every movement flawlessly.

Then a sleek, purple surfboard materialised beneath my feet, and I was sliding down the face of a monster thirty-foot wave. The comets became parallel surfers in lurid costumes descending the slopes behind me, eating up the spray that flicked off the back of my board. Electric guitar blared in my ears, threatening to blow a hole in my brain; but I cruised on, always in control.

I manoeuvred around the wave, the triple fins slashing great arcs of water from the thundering curl looming over me. I cut back and dashed into the rolling tube, the two surfers followed behind me in close proximity. Inside the guitar screams were suppressed by the deafening roar of the sea that sought to drag me under and crush me completely. The air was dense with a fine salty mist and my eyes began to sting, and then the mist cleared...

I was no longer on a board, I was no longer flying. I was alone on a dark street. The cold air smelled of danger, I shivered, the dream had turned sour.

I drew in a hesitant breath, and felt its icy chill run through my lungs. Slowly, I breathed out again, watching the white wisps disappear from my warm lips. I started walking.

My feet echoed down the streets, intruding on the silence that wasn't for me to disturb. The tension in the air seemed to be building, my senses warning me of something imminent.

A figure stepped out of the shadows ahead.

Then two larger ones stepped out behind it.

I stopped walking, my muscles suddenly becoming leaden. Not even my lungs would respond, as I gaped at the hulking trio approaching me.

They stopped ten metres away and the shorter one turned to the others. I heard their low voices mutter something. The group started forward again, I was too scared to move. As the leader closed in, I saw the shadows slide away from his face, revealing a piercing, hostile glare; daring a challenge.

I tried to look away, but was caught within that deathly stare, strangely fascinated by those beady, crooked eyes, and the perfect, brown, little circles in the middle of them.

A bitter, rancid stench fell across me, and behind it a cruel voice rasped, "You're fucked pal."

I believed it.

As if in response to my thoughts, the figure drew out a small brown object. The long hand that held it pressed a button on the side, and a bright three-inch blade leapt out.

Then the darkness evaporated. The shadows retreated. I was on a bloody battlefield of dead bodies in armour.

My opponent was still with me, but was now a black knight bearing a mighty black sword in both hands. Without consciously knowing what I was doing I drew forth my own sword. A magnificent shaft of the sharpest metal, like a mirror it reflected the sun on its shining surface and dazzled my foe.

It was just me and the enemy...

I didn't notice the surrounding hills, or the beautiful summer breeze, I didn't even notice the hundreds of slain combatants that lay all around, smeared with red, stretching as far as the eye could see. All that mattered now was the enemy.

The black-clad knight initiated the charge, sword raised above the head, screaming a horrible cry so fearsome even the denizens of hell would be fearful.

Unfazed, I stood my ground and prepared to parry the assailant's attack.

The black blade came down like a guillotine, the force behind it was inhuman. I met the falling sword with my own, a terrific clash of steel. Sparks flew as muscles and tempers bristled. The black knight tried to force his blade down upon me. Somehow I resisted and fought the black knight's blade off with relative ease. Infuriated, the black knight unleashed another attack, determined to avoid being disgraced by such an amateur adversary. He swung in low from the side, a great sweeping cut, determined to cut me in half at the hip.

I reacted like lightning. My sword whirled into place in front of my kidney, a sharp whine indicating my block was successful. I then followed up before my duellist could react, penetrating the black knight's open defences with a quick, short arc that ultimately ended slicing the side of the black knight's armour and penetrating the rib cage... and the heart.

The black knight began to shout in pain but it was cut off by the gurgle of his own blood and he was dead before he hit the ground.

And then I was flying again...

At the helm of a spacecraft now, I was tearing through the wreckage of a once magnificent, domed city of metal. Splayed remnants of the futuristic abode lay about like the exposed organs of a dying animal.

Suddenly, automatic laser-fire rattled somewhere behind. I pulled up instinctively and saw two elegant swallow-shaped craft speed underneath, fore-guns ablaze with rapid pulses of green laser, destroying everything in their path. Unseen, I dropped down on them, my own guns now firing a fantastic web of red, shimmering rays.

The rays, like rods of flame, struck the two craft, and cut through them as a hot knife through butter. They broke into many smaller pieces, exploding into brilliant balls of fire. My duty served, I flew on.

But I wasn't out of danger yet. Five more craft pursued me, eager for revenge. I only knew of their presence when a terrific bone-shaking blast erupted at the rear of the ship, and I knew the engines had been struck. I was going down.

The attacking force flew on past, assured that their revenge had been complete, the craft they had struck nose-diving to the ground in a curling path of fumes at ever-increasing velocity.

A sharp crack sounded, and the entire windscreen shattered. The console became ecstatic with a barrage of alarm buzzers and flashing red lights. The ship continued plummeting to the ground, already having reached terminal velocity, a long tail of smoke marking the ship's descent. I could do nothing but mouth my prayers.

Then I saw something.

In amongst the rampant chaos of the flickering dashboard, I saw one thing before me. One button, one brilliant blue button, placed like a sapphire upon a velvet pillow, and it held my only means of escape... the world having become but a blur around it.

'EJECT'

I slammed my fist into the button and hoped...

With a final rush of adrenalin I returned to my chair, as the last screams of electric guitar died away in my head. I saw that my finger was on the eject button, the tape having leapt out onto my lap, still warm from the heads that had been engaging it only seconds ago.

And all I could think was, "Wow man, what a dream!"

MOTIVATION

Do I do the things I do now with the same conviction that I did when I first began them?

Am I still the same person, essentially, that I started out as, and am I still striving towards the same ideal?

Is my faith in myself, in the world that I exist in, as strong as it used to be?

Perhaps not.

I am inclined to analyse myself, questioning my beliefs and values. Assess and reassess whether what I am doing is right. I exist in a constant contradictory circle of self-glory and self-doubt. Yet one that is constant only in its constant change and contradiction. However, true understanding of my world is always beyond me, though I do not fail in trying, for not doing that would be failing myself, and denying what I see to be my own growth.

It was a short time past midday; Cesyl was asleep. The flat was an absolute mess, mostly mine, and visitors were due in just over an hour. It should have been plenty of time, but I wanted to have a shower and eat. It shouldn't have mattered that the place was in the state that it was, but the visitors, Jamie and Sarah, were Jehovah's Witness missionaries.

I welcomed them into my flat once a week to talk of the world, God and the Bible. I had come to love them as good friends and they were not much older than me.

I wanted to welcome them as warmly as I could, and I felt ashamed if the state of my house did not reflect this.

This shame was not born out of any fear of them or of their world, it was fear of the way my self was presented. The way the flat was the rest of the week did not matter to me as far as they were concerned; they didn't see it. But when they did come, I did not wish to be perceived by their pious eyes as conducting myself in an 'improper' way. I only later realised that I was trying to make them see me as something that I was not. Of course, they would refute that they would ever have judged me in any negative way, and maybe that was true, but this did little to alleviate my guilty feelings. Last week, running out of time, tired from a night shift that morning and not feeling motivated at all, I stuck a note on the front door at the last moment. I expressed my remorse and guilt for doing so, and confessed being unable to face them that week. I apologised for acting in this way and not having the courage to tell them in person. I knew that they would accept this and only allow themselves to think positively about it, but I still felt guilty and wanted to make sure I didn't do the same this week.

Motivation, though, was becoming increasingly inhibited and it was becoming harder and harder to justify having them visit. Further, the disapproval of both friends and family made it more difficult again. I had talked about it with Cesyl, mentioned it to Lana and Damien and hinted at it to the missionaries, that I was reaching a 'saturation point' where I felt I had learnt all I could from them. It would soon be time for me to say goodbye to them and move on. Something I've had to do many times, and it is a painful experience every time, but inevitably necessary.

Indeed the day I knew would come sooner or later, had come.

I just hoped they would understand and not feel hurt or think ill of me for what I must do. To dwell in, or focus on, one truth to the exclusion of others, for me is to stagnate in narrow-mindedness, and this I will not do. And this means that I must leave their beautiful world for those as yet unexplored. And as our friendship was, by arrangement, based entirely on theological discussion, it seemed that that must end too.

Ever onwards, I must wander.

The door-bell rang. I greeted my guests and we exchanged ritual small-talk and pleasantries. We moved to the dining table in my room. I served us all coffee and sat down with them. We all relaxed a little. Now only the guillotine awaited...

Jamie kicked things off first. "So was there anything you wanted to talk about, or do you want to get stuck into the readings straight away?"

I let the guillotine drop. "Actually there is something that I have to say, something I knew I was going to have to say sooner or later, but that doesn't make it any easier to say."

I'm almost certain that they knew exactly what I was talking about; I'd been introducing it subtly and gradually over the last few weeks.

"Go on."

"I've already discussed with you about how my friends and family are making it increasingly difficult to continue having you here. That they disapproved and accused me of becoming converted, etc was fine for I knew, and please don't take this personally, that I was never going to become converted. And like you said before, in many ways they look up to me for having the courage to go out and do these things despite ridicule. A part of them wants me to go on and endeavour to reach a conclusion, that I might, metaphorically speaking, 'open a way up for them'. They do respect my opinion and efforts, and watch my progress with interest, and do wish to see me succeed whether that be with or against you guys. And I think in a way they are scared that I'll come down more on your side than theirs. For if I side with you guys, this reflects upon them, causing them to question themselves. And then of course the easiest thing for them to do, and almost certainly, perhaps rightly, what they would do, is to denounce me. And to tell you the truth, I *do* side with you guys more than many of them. But regardless of any conclusion I reach, they watch with vested interest, and in this way I have continued up until now."

Jamie made to speak, but for once I stopped him. "Sorry to interrupt, Jamie, but I need to get this all out in the open and then we can discuss it."

"That's fine, Andrew, I didn't mean to interrupt you."

"It is becoming harder and harder to motivate myself to have you guys here, like it's becoming a chore. I mean I *personally* feel I have gained almost as much as I'm likely to in the short-term. I've learnt a lot from you, the experience has been great and richly rewarding. But I feel that it has reached a point where currently in my life it's not really worth pursuing any further, considering all the other things I have to do."

We were both in a difficult position now, both of us were trying to save face, but it seemed both of us understood the other's position and were sympathetic.

I'd tried to rehearse this speech many times over the last few weeks, trying to put it in the best way, express myself in the best way, and what I ended up saying was not how I had rehearsed it. And the problem I currently experience in trying to re-tell it now, is I don't remember exactly what I said, how I said it, or what they said. It's as if I'm trying to re-compose the speech again now. Trying to recapture that experience and what happened, how I experienced that it happened, and maybe the way I wanted it to happen; trying to do justice to myself, the missionaries and my friends. Trying to convey this all to you, dear reader, and trying to help you to understand.

I continued, "I am in essence, a wanderer. A wanderer of worlds both external and internal. And though this life I subject myself to is hard, for I often feel alone and without a true home or a true place to fit in, I do not wish it to be any different. It is if you like my life's quest; to learn and experience and understand all I can, and to pass this on to help others. Because I try to keep an open mind and not judge others and listen to others, it means I can relate to many, many others. Indeed I have male and female friends of all different walks and outlooks on life, and of differing races and ages. Just as I listen to different forms of music and read varied fiction and philosophy. I try to see the inherent beauty in everything, no matter what form it takes."

"I can see that in you," Jamie said. "You never cease to amaze me with all the things you do and understand. You seem to be so much older than what you are, I can't believe you're only twenty. You have very Christ-like qualities."

"It is unfortunate that though it might seem that I am capable of fitting in with everybody, I ultimately seem to fit in with nobody. Most seem to see it as a matter of you're either 'with us or against us', and as I'm not totally 'with anybody', I'm consequently labelled 'against everybody'. A misfit and completely understood by nobody, even myself. Most of my family and friends understand me very little at all I think, only seeing those aspects of me they choose to see or I choose to show, and thus thinking that that *is* me."

"You definitely do seem to have a multi-faceted and deep nature."

"And because I never completely fit in anywhere, I spend a lot of time on my own. Something which I'm thankful for, though many times I'm not. Because I am so independent and can commit myself completely to no one; friends, family or thinking group; they all, at one time or another, feel betrayed. Sooner or later I have to detach myself from all of them and each time this hurts me and them too. They feel bitter and/or angry and say 'I've changed', or 'I'm not loyal', or 'I'm two-faced or a user', or 'I'm just a compromiser, trying to keep everyone happy and can't stick to one thing.' And now I feel this is happening here, so please don't feel hurt or hate me for what I do. Please try to understand for it is the way I live my life and I mean no harm and think that you are truly beautiful people who deserve the benefits you gain from the life you lead. But I must move on."

"I truly understand your position," Jamie said. "And I understand the predicament it must place you in to have to say this to us. I think you're a great person with sound, good reasons for doing what you do and I don't feel resentment or anger in any way for you saying that you have to move on. It's good that you are able to be honest and not make up excuses or hide."

"Thank you so much for saying that, it eases my guilt immensely to know that you understand what I'm doing and accept it without ill-feeling."

Indeed their understanding and acceptance of me, touched me, and my understanding and acceptance of them had touched them. Through them I had learnt much about their message, the message of Christ, God, and the Bible. And through me they had learnt much about science, philosophy, modern directions these were taking, and the environment.

Things were drawing to a conclusion, so Jamie rose. "Thank you so much for having us here every week, and making coffees. You're a fine man, Andrew."

"You too, Jamie."

"Just because you feel that you want to stop things here doesn't mean that you can't contact us in the future, even if it's just to say hello."

"That's extremely comforting to hear also. Thank you for putting yourself out every week to come here."

"That's okay mate," he said, "as I've told you before, we're not doing this for ourselves, we're doing it for the 'big guy upstairs'!"

We laughed together as friends. We would cross paths again someday, I knew.

"One more thing I just have to say to you mate," he stopped at the doorway. "Keep praying."

"I intend to. In one form or another, I've been doing that all my life."

ANTICIPATION

It was a long line. A long line of figures stretching to a terminus, at which stood a figure I could not see clearly. We all waited silently in line. A line that grew increasingly longer behind us.

We all wore masks of confidence, hiding our inner doubt and turmoil, even from ourselves. Our disguises had got us as far as this, why would they not carry us all the way to the end?

All around below us was the world we had left, the millions milling down there who were too blind to look up and see what lay beyond them. Pity the poor deceived, pity their poor self-created fate. Glory to those who saw through the lies and rose to the ranks of the enlightened. That's us, or some of us; definitely me, but not her just in front and definitely not him just behind. In fact probably only me. Yep, probably just me, no one else, unless of course they agreed with me. Of course I'm right, how could it be any other way?

We shuffled forth again as we heard laughter carry down the line, another blind idiot shown up for their delusion and false vision. Another cast back to the Earth once more to learn and grow again that they might find truth this time. The laughter was infectious and we joined the mocking chorus. Pity the poor deceived. Hah! Hah! Hah! Pity their poor self-created fate.

Look at the fools, no wonder. Serves them right I say, they had their chance, they should have known better. Maybe after the next cycle they'll finally realise and understand it all, maybe they won't, probably they won't, and be sent back again. No matter, it's not my problem. I'm fine, I'm right and I know, it won't happen to me. Never.

We shuffled forth again, and I began to make out what we were slowly approaching, a great dark figure before a great silver throne, but no more detail. I could see that some of the others were beginning to grow anxious. I giggled to myself at their folly; they're already beginning to realise that they've got it wrong, and that they're going to have to go back and do it all again. Not me though, I've got nothing to fear, nothing at all. I'm not stupid and gullible like them. I don't think this, I know. Hah, hah, hah, such a pity. If only they had listened. Oh well, too late for them now, back they'll go.

More and more were thrown back down to the endless ranks below, and we laughed at every one, watching their fall from glory with amusement. Though of course everyone else was only laughing to hide their own fears about suffering the same fate; and they would suffer the same fate, I could tell. Not me though.

I could hear him now, he who sat on the throne and looked into the heart of everyone that came and stood before him.

"HEH, HEH, HEH... SUCKER!" He laughed and hurled another screaming figure over the edge and back to the circle of life.

His laughter prompted us to all laugh again, raucous

laughter. The stupid beggar, pleading to know the answers to cover up for her own inadequacies. What else did she expect? Hah, hah, hah.

"**AND WHAT HAVE YOU LEARNED?**" he boomed unto the next victim.

"I have learnt to be loyal only to you God, and follow the example you set through Jesus Christ our Lord and your inspired words conveyed through the Bible. The way to heaven is very narrow Lord, and few are those who are worthy enough to make it."

He spat on him and we all laughed: "**I'LL HAVE NONE OF YOUR PRETENTIOUS CRAP!**"

"Please Father, have mercy, I can learn!"

"**AND LEARN YOU WILL, BE GONE FROM MY SIGHT!**"

Another fell to the earth. We watched the next step up to the throne.

"I have learnt that no one can really hurt me, unless I let them. God doesn't exist and we have complete freedom to do what we want. The responsibility is ours, and ours alone."

"**CAN'T HURT YOU, HEH? YOU BIGOTED SLUT, JUST WHO DO YOU THINK YOU ARE!**"

And so another descended, and we laughed again.

"Oh praise be to you mighty Satan, your wish is my command. You alone I worship, you alone have almighty power. The earth was yours in a day and the heavens shall be yours too o' rightful king."

"**YOU BLITHERING IDIOT! BACK YOU GO WITH THE REST OF THEM!**"

Dumbfounded, another one bit the dust.

The next said, "I have learnt that each life is a circle leading unto the next life and the next. Each action we make creates good or bad karma, good karma creates good outcomes in this or the following lives, and bad karma the opposite. We escape the cycle by achieving moksa, which we achieve by non-attachment. Non-attachment to life, possessions, our or other's desires."

The great figure burst into laughter, triggering us to do so again and retorted, **"THAT'S A GOOD ONE! MUST HAVE TAKEN YOU A WHILE TO MAKE THAT LOT UP ...YOU MISERABLE CRAWLER!"**

Another fell down, as the next stumbled up.

"Life is an illusion, a dream. Events and circumstances have no lasting importance and are just part of one's own growth towards perfection. Everything is unified as one thing, and everything persists. Nothing is destroyed then or lost, only changed."

"YOU DISGUST ME WITH YOUR LIES AND SELF-DECEPTION! BACK TO A MORTAL EXISTENCE WITH YOU!"

Throwing her down he looked at the next.

"I can be sure of nothing except my own consciousness. I do not have justification in believing that anything else exists other than myself, hence I am justified in believing only I exist. Everything else exists only as thoughts in my head or sensations on my nerve endings and nothing more."

"I DON'T THINK YOU'VE UNDERSTOOD ANYTHING AT ALL! YOU CONTEMPTUOUS BLIND WORM!"

The next, with tears in his eyes, spoke of love.

"I don't know much Lord, Great One, God or whatever you really are. But I do know what is important. It isn't material possessions and it isn't a philosophical or spiritual understanding of the world, none of which I have much value for. It is love, and love alone. Love is the most powerful force in the world, it has inspired more writing, more achievements and probably also caused more woe and certainly more joy than anything else. It is what binds us all together, what binds husband and wife, what binds families, what binds race and religion. All our values, ethical and moral, derive from this innate appreciation that needs no teaching, this innate need that needs no cultivating. It is all that matters."

He – was it even he?– who sat on the throne, had no such tears in his eyes though. He merely laughed as he dismissed him back below, and called, "**NEXT?**"

The next spoke then, saying with gusto, "Life is empty. It's meaningless, and just random chance that the universe is here at all, and that includes us. It's what we make it, what we want it to be, and we live it how we choose. Religions, morals and all that shit is just stuff people made up for a sense of security, so they can believe that there is something, because they want to believe that something is there. Which of course there's not. I was rich, I had power, I was happy. I had what I wanted, when I wanted it. It didn't matter how I got it, it only mattered that I had it. Nor did it matter that others didn't. The money was mine, and mine alone. I died wealthy and lived fast and well."

"AND YOU'VE LEARNT CLOSE TO NOTHING

WHATSOEVER! STUPID FOOL! DON'T WASTE
YOURS AND MY TIME BY BEING HERE ANY
LONGER!"

My turn was very near now, and I could see him? her?
it? quite clearly, yet I still couldn't comprehend exactly
what it was that I was seeing. I can't even describe the
way in which whatever was on the throne, was. It seemed
to be constantly changing, though it wasn't, and then I
thought maybe it was my perception that was constantly
changing, and then it seemed that I had always seen (it)
in the same way. I was still confident and sure of myself,
but I admit that this experience at least I did not
understand. There were only four left in front of me, all
of whom were female ...I think.

"It doesn't matter what we think or believe, everything
is predetermined, and this includes everything from the
movement of celestial bodies, to chemical reactions, to
weather patterns, to population dynamics, to physical
actions, emotions and thoughts. It is predetermined
because all the physical details determine precisely what
the outcome will be, though trying to predict this without
an infinitely complex understanding of physics, and being
able to measure the prior details to an infinite degree, is
impossible. As all the initial details of the universe
determined exactly how what molecule interacted with
what molecule, the resultant reactions then determined
the next. In effect, as there is only a one-to-one correlation
between prior events and post events, the outcome of
every single interaction in the entire universe was set in
stone from the very beginning. Everything, including our
psychology and the evolution of a belief in free will, which

is only an illusion, was predetermined and could have theoretically been predicted. All these details are physical ones, and could be understood and described in terms of physics, though our understanding at present is far from perfect. Thoughts and emotions are the interaction of neurons in the brain and other chemicals in the body for instance, and near death experiences are just a physiological response of the body as it shuts down. This view seems negative, however, which is why most people disagree with it."

"**SOME SPEECH, I'M TOUCHED,**" (It) said with sarcasm, and then laughed, "**BUT NO CIGAR!**"

"Well basically my philosophy is pretty simple and doesn't involve high-flung theories, but rings true I think," said the next one. "Life is for living. I mean let's face it, the whole thing's just one big joke, so why not play the game, enjoy it, and laugh the whole way? Even if there is meaning and a purpose to it all, we're never going to know, so who cares? There's no point taking it seriously or getting down about it, it's basically just one big fucking joke and that's all there is to it. To live is to laugh, that's what I say, and if you can't do that, then what the fuck are you living for?"

"**YOU ARE ONE BIG JOKE! GO LIVE SOME MORE!**"

"So I see, the reason why all the others are wrong is because they arrogantly assumed they were right," said the one who was two ahead of me. "If they weren't so arrogant and closed minded then maybe they would understand."

"**GO ON. YOU AREN'T GOING TO GET AWAY WITH JUST VAGUELY STATING THAT.**"

"Understand that each person has their own opinion, and that no one can ever really know, so it's stupid to say one is right and another is wrong."

(It) sighed with a note of reluctance and then spoke, **"YOU NEED TO LIVE A LITTLE MORE TOO. UNTIL THEN, I HAVE NOTHING MORE TO SAY TO YOU."**

Further confused, she left.

Now there was only one left before me, who answered with a simple statement, "I don't know."

"WHAT DO YOU MEAN YOU DON'T KNOW? YOU MUST HAVE LEARNED SOMETHING."

"You'd think so, but after seeing all these others turned away, all of whom could have been right, I'm not really sure what to say."

"OF THE OTHERS, THE ENDLESS NUMBERS OF OTHERS THAT HAVE COME AND GONE, THEY WERE ALL RIGHT, BUT NOT COMPLETELY. THEY ONLY HAD A PART OF IT."

"I don't understand what you mean. How can you say that they were all partly right when their views totally contradicted each other?"

"YOU NEED TO LEARN AND UNDERSTAND MORE TOO... BE GONE!"

Now there was me.

It happened slowly at first, but then rapidly accelerated, and soon was out of control, overwhelming me completely... It was the fear of what lay before me, and what I was. A slow dawning in my consciousness that eroded my resolve and dissolved the foundation of all my beliefs.

How many others, how many endless others had there been? How many had succeeded and understood it all? Had there been any? Would there ever be any? Could I be so sure, just as all those others had probably been, that I was right? Had they not all made the same mistake I was about to make?

Oh shit.

What was I going to say?

TOLERATION

"Alright Dougie," I said as we embarked on the trip back to Melbourne, "See if you can guess who this band is."

The CD slipped in and began to spin. "A little volume, I feel." I cranked up the bass, loudness and of course, the volume.

Our ears exploded inwards as the back seat leapt at us behind a barrage of thundering drums and roaring rhythm.

"Fuck! Your stereo's so loud!" He had to say it twice, the second time after I had turned it down for me to hear.

"As I've said before, my car's just a stereo on wheels. 300 watts of wanton, deafening destruction!" I laughed and the disc spun on, screaming lyrics and guitar at us.

Dougie rubbed his ears, glad that he could bear the intensity now.

"Do you know who it is yet?" I said.

"Um... Pantera?"

"Nope, Testament. Can you believe it?"

"I was going to say that, and then I thought nah. Is this a new CD?"

"Not really, it's their latest album but I've had it a couple of months. That one there is, though." I pointed to a Machine Head CD below his feet amongst other rubbish.

He picked it up and began to look at the cover, shook his head and said to me, "It's your addiction!"

"Money's there to be spent, what else is it good for?"

"And how many CDs have you bought lately?"

"Oh, about five or six in the last couple of weeks." I shrugged.

He smiled at me, and shook his head again, fiddling with the CD case. "You've got a few additions."

"I guess I have, haven't I?"

"Yep." He nodded. "You've got your CD addiction. Your fucking your doona addiction." (We both laughed) "Your caffeine addiction, your nicotine addiction, your sleeping addiction." He paused for a moment. "And your role-playing games addiction."

He said them again as he counted them on his fingers, "That's one, two, three, four, five, six. Six addictions man; that's pretty bad."

"You forgot to include the adrenalin rush of metal addiction."

"That's seven. Seven addictions. Just like the seven Ds. Dirty, Disgusting, Despicable, Dishonest, Deceitful, Devious, and yes, you're a fucking DEVIANT!"

"That's me!" I laughed. "Deviant Drage! Hah, hah!"

He who laughs at life, laughs at death. He who laughs at all, regrets nothing and loves everything.

"Errh! You're a fag!" said Dougie, through a stupid expression.

I just smiled as I mentally wrote him and the experience into this book.

"Fag! Fag! Fag! Elmo says you're a poofter!" he whined in a childish, high-pitched voice.

I said nothing and kept my eyes on the road, ears on the music, fingers and heart-beat on the rhythm.

"Sorry Andrew," he said. "I didn't mean to pay you out." His attitude changed, adopting the role of the innocent juvenile who didn't mean to cause harm, his apology sincere.

"It's cool, Dougie," I answered, giving him a thumbs-up, which he eagerly returned. "Actually I do feel like listening to Machine Head now, and I think you'd like them too. They're a new band, and they're a lot like Pantera, and they're getting killer reviews."

"Okay Sloth!" He beamed.

The CD changed and freedom rang with a shotgun blast of metal.

Addiction. Dependence. Commitment. These were things I had chosen and things that I wanted. It is my desire to live a little in the life of many things as I, all as one. To change who I am, and to experience being a new person presents a refreshing challenge and a new adventure. Who I was, and what I am, and that which I'll be, there was no absolute description of any of them, nor anyone else. But soon enough, I make another decision and wander on. Now I live the life of a hopeless addict unable to change. Now I live the secure world of a protected child. Now I live the life of the non-committed soldier with no need for company. Now the dependent socialite with a solitary group of friends. Now the dilettante flirting with many social circles. Now the loyal, now the disloyal, now the organised and secure, now the destitute and unmotivated. Praise, respect, admiration, criticism, rejection, condemnation. All of these form part of the circle that is a spiral that is not. It includes doubt, regret, fear and envy, but equally reassurance, strength, confidence and contentment. Hard with sadness and hate, yet tender with love and joy. All of these form elemental parts of that which is always more, that which constitutes the open circle of being. Of life.

Of You Know What.

And therein lies the possibility to wander no more, of commitment, but also the possibility to wander anew and continue on. This is my life, this life is ours. This is my choice, this choice is ours. To experience is to grow. To think is to know. To imagine is to create. To choose is to make.

"You know what, Dougie?"

"What?"

"You're going to be in my book. Including what's happening right here, right now, it's going to be in my book. Just think, Dougie, the eyes of maybe a billion readers could be on us right now, watching us, listening to our conversation. What do you think of that?"

"Durr, Sloth doesn't understand. Durr, Micro B computer. Errh, syntax error," he droned.

"Do you have anything that you want to say to everybody out there?"

"I don't understand what you mean. Dougie's dumb. Durr, my Micro B micro brain cannot compute."

"You're not dumb, Doug, you don't have to say that, you only restrict yourself. Are there any words you'd like to say that will go in the book when I write about this car-trip?"

"I don't know, I'm just happy with life. I don't really have a lot of money, or have a good job or go to uni like you, but I've got good friends and good parents and I'm just happy with my life."

"That's all that really matters I think, Dougie. As long as you're happy and content, and not harming anybody, who cares what you do."

"I'd like to have a job and not be on the dole, and have money and that, but I'm just happy with what I've got, because I know that a lot of other people don't have a home and food to eat like I have. Yeah, I'm just happy."

"And you have what many with money and a good job and even a family don't have, and that's happiness."

We didn't say any more of that, we didn't need to. I had once seen Dougie as a stupid, blundering, immature idiot with barely a shred of intellectuality and someone I wanted to have nothing to do with. It is fortunate that I have learned to be more accepting. I had been prejudiced on the basis of intelligence. I admit that the intolerance is still there, but it has been becoming something relatively easy to overlook, for one can find warmth, beauty and wisdom within anybody if they desire to see it. As for qualities such as intelligence, maturity and competence, these are as subjective as the value of one's culture or appearance, and I feel should be treated as fundamentally worthless values as such in terms of someone's worth. Everyone's viewpoint, experiences, and life is different, so something new can be learnt and gained from each one. No one deserves discrimination, nor exclusion, nor do they deserve elevation to a point where they need only preach to others and not listen. But this is something I could have learnt a long time ago from Douglas here, if only I had listened to him earlier and not judged him then, when he had accepted me and I had abhorred him. Accepting of others and of himself, there was a lot I could still learn from him. I drove on in contemplation.

"It's okay, Andrew. Don't be shy!" He smiled.

His smile spread to my face and I said, "Heh, guess what's on tonight?"

"What?"

"A writing group meeting at the flat. You wanna be a part of it?"

"Yeah!" His chubby face lit up, and then it became downcast. "Oh, but that'd mean I'd have to write something though."

"No it doesn't! It's a social group more than anything. And you've got as much right to be there as anyone else."

"Okay!" he said, his face lighting up again.

I drove on, and my face lit up too.

COMPETITION

I led Dougie into the lounge where Cesyl was, slouched as usual, smoking in front of the television. Cesyl had just returned from a two-hour training shift that was actually four unpaid hours.

"Sloth's here!" announced Dougie. Though really 'Sloth' was an identity we all shared, a metaphor of 'The Bum'.

"Great. I was just beginning to enjoy it without you here," said Cesyl with spite.

"I just walk in the door, Cesyl, and already you're putting me down!" Dougie's brightness drained away, brightness that Cesyl absorbed.

"Yeah, you should expect that. Don't expect me to change!" Cesyl returned without flinching.

I interceded. "He even said that he missed you, Dougie, while you've been down in Geelong, 'cos he didn't have anyone to pay out."

Dougie began to get emotional. "Can't you be nice to me for once, Cesyl, just for once?"

Unmoved, Cesyl answered, "No. That'd be too much effort. It's hard enough to restrain myself from paying Brewin out," (he gestured at me) "there's no way I could stop myself from giving you shit."

"Fine!" Dougie said, losing again, sitting down on the couch and retreating into his own emotions.

Cesyl looked over at me and laughed, and I just shook my head, knowing that he had just got the response he wanted.

"And you're even laughing about it now!" Dougie attempted to retaliate, "Fucking bastard!"

"Don't expect me to feel sympathy for you," Cesyl said as he kept laughing, "that won't work."

"Fine, I'll go back to Geelong then if you don't want me to stay."

"Don't go back, I won't have anyone to pay out then."

Dougie didn't want to go back either – he had grown to hate living in

Geelong.

"Well fucking be nice to me then, Cesyl!"

"Don't try to win mind-games, Doug, because you won't. I'm the master and you don't have a hope of winning with your micro brain."

"There you go again, Cesyl, putting me down and calling me dumb. You do it all the time and I'm over it!"

"I've already told you, Doug, don't expect me to feel sympathy. You probably don't even know what that word means." He laughed again and looked at me, me shaking my head as I got up to head for the kitchen.

"I do so know what it means!"

"I don't care if you stay, I'm glad to have you here. Just don't expect me not to pay you out, that's all."

Dougie shut himself off in silence, sucked of all his vitality once again. Cesyl triumphant, turned away to the television.

By the time I returned from the kitchen with a coffee, Cesyl had lived enough in his glory of power and control, and made an offer to Douglas. "Would you like a game of Magic, Doug?"

"Yeah alright," he spat.

I sat down again as they retrieved their decks.

"You playing?" Cesyl said.

I nodded as I went for mine, selecting a deck.

"Just can't help yourself, can you? Don't even give him a chance to sit down before you're already at him," I said to Cesyl as we all began to shuffle our personal decks.

"Oh get off your high horse, would you, you fuckin' fag! You're no angel; you give him shit all the time too!" More power, more control, Cesyl wanted to win mind-games over all.

"Yeah, you sly cunt," Dougie piped. "Trying to blame it all on Cesyl. I saw you, you were laughing too."

"I was not laughing!" I protested.

"Yeah, listen to it," Cesyl said. "Trying to make out he's the one that's all goody-goody, and blame everything on me!"

"That's right!" Dougie laughed and pointed. "Blaming it all on Cesyl when you're laughing as well you, seedy bastard!" He turned to Cesyl. "Look at him, would you? Look at him grinning!"

Cesyl saw his opportunity to shift the weight of criticism onto me, and knew full well that he could easily lead Douglas to whatever conclusions he wanted. He continued his antagonism. "Yeah, I bet you're writing this all into your book and framing me, when it's you just as much!"

Yep.

"Look I agree that I give Dougie shit too," I said. "But

nowhere near as much, and not in the same merciless way that you do, Cesyl, and you know it."

"Bullshit! You say you don't lie but you do! You pay Dougie out as much as what I do! I just do it to his face, and you do it behind his back."

"Yeah, you sly bastard!" Dougie came in again and Cesyl encouraged him, knowing that while he did, he had control.

"You should hear him, Doug, all the time. Dougie's dumb! Dougie's an idiot! Dougie's a fat sloth!"

Cesyl laughed at me in victory, knowing that I knew exactly what he was doing. I had to admire his skills of manipulation.

Dougie stood up and faced me as I brought my knees up protectively and held my hands out to hold him off.

He picked at me and tried to grab me in a few futile attempts as he said, "You sly, lying bastard! You're a back-stabber!"

"You give me as much shit to my face as I do to you, even more! Only I don't want to hurt your feelings," I said.

Cesyl, never satisfied, sought to press his advantage. "Don't listen to him Doug, he's only trying to fool you into believing what he says, don't let him, he's lying!"

Cesyl kept laughing at me, enjoying the spectacle he had created and the power he exacted over it.

"Yeah, you think I'm dumb, don't you?" Dougie said. "You think you can make me believe whatever you want! Yeah, throw chips on the floor for Dougie to fetch, you fucking bastard."

His gullibility was laughable, so great I couldn't restrain

myself as I laughed at him and his folly and Cesyl's manipulation, and their stupid, stupid arguments, including this one. Of course to Douglas, it was a laugh that proved my guilt and to Cesyl it was only another tool by which he could further convince Douglas of such.

"Look at him! He's still laughing!" Cesyl had worked Dougie into enough of a frenzy to delude him into believing anything, which was what he then did. "And you know who it was that locked you out and unwired the bell so he couldn't hear it don't you? And poured shit all over your cap and put it in the bin? It was fucking Brewin!"

I couldn't believe how far he had gone this time and spat the dummy. I stood and demanded he retract those statements, adamant that he tell the truth about who the real culprit was.

Cesyl tried to laugh back and stick up his finger at me without Douglas noticing as if to say 'suck shit!' but Douglas noticed and even he didn't buy this one straight away. Cesyl tried to keep up the facade as long as possible, but knew me too well to try to push things too far, and eventually admitted what really happened.

He knew all too well that I despised nothing more than this blatant and continued lying and that I was capable of expending friendships without regret over things that really pissed me off. He had seen me do it before, with cold control, to other close friends who had taken me for granted, and I had done so once before to him. Though he saw this as an over-reaction, he knew that I would do it again if pushed.

It is at these times I think that Cesyl becomes most

aware of the fact that our friendship matters far more to him than his petty mind-games do, and he apologises for what he has done.

Point made, we all returned to the card game we had been about to begin. Once more good friends...

CONVENTION

Pretty soon after that, the phone rang.

Cesyl answered and handed the phone to me. "It's the alcoholic," he said.

I took the phone. "Hi Graeme, how's it going?"

"Not too bad man, pissed as usual. Yeah I'm an alco, I don't give a shit. I used to try to deny it, and go, 'oh man oh man I'm addicted to alcohol', but now I've accepted it. Now I just say, 'yeah man, I'm a fucking alco', and I don't care."

"And let me guess, you're down on cash again and need to borrow some money to buy some more grog."

"Oh man, you must be psychic!"

"Must be."

"Come on man, you know I'll pay you back, I always do, you know that. Keating pays me tomorrow, I'll pay you straight back then, man."

"Yeah, that's cool."

"Well can you pick me up then? Is it cool if I come over?"

"Yeah that's cool. Actually you'd probably want to anyway, as there's a writing group on, and Alex is going to be here."

"Oh man, how come you didn't tell me? You said you'd call me next meeting, you bastard!"

"I did too. Sorry man, I completely forgot. Honestly."

"Yeah, bullshit. You've probably had about five meetings since I was last there. And thought, 'yeah man, I could call Graeme, he wants to come', and then gone 'oh fuck it'."

"Nah seriously, that is the first one we've had since. I mean it."

"Don't worry man, I'm only shitting you. I believe you. But you still could have fucking called me!"

"Sorry."

"It's cool. So when are they all coming over?"

"In about an hour. Guess I better pick you up before they come, heh?"

"Yeah man, can we go by the bottle shop on the way back?"

"To get your fix?"

"Yeah man, just one fix, hah, hah!"

"Yeah okay. I'll be there soon, is twenty bucks enough?"

"Twenty bucks? Shit yeah! I was only going to ask for a tener, but now that you've offered twenty, I'll happily scab that extra ten bucks."

"Yeah that's cool, as long as you do pay me back tomorrow."

"Oh man, you know I will. I'm not going to be a fucking cunt and say, 'nah fuck you, the money's mine now mother-fucker'. You're a fucking legend, Brewin, a fucking legend. Actually I shouldn't call you Brewin anymore, should I? Seeing how you've changed your surname. What is it now again?"

"Drage. D-R-A-G-E. But I don't care what you call me, call me dick-head if you want."

"I'll call you fucking tight-arsed scrooge. Fucking won't

give me all the money in your bank account, you bastard!"

I laughed.

"Only joking man, you're saving my drug-fucked life. You're keeping me on the piss!"

Dilemmas churned in my head over whether such a thing was justified, or whether not lending him the money wouldn't just be a self-righteous act to control his life, something that I had no right to do. I still haven't resolved this.

"Yeah, well, see you soon." I hung up.

"He's not coming over, is he?" demanded Cesyl.

"Yeah he is. But the writing group is coming over anyway as well. So even if you didn't have him, you'd still have them."

"Great! Not only do I have to put up with a pissed loser, but I have to put up with a bunch of uni nerds talking about fucking stories!"

"Never mind. You'll live."

"Don't worry, Andrew, I'll still join in. Lana's the only one I've met and she's nice, but I wanna meet the others. I'll just watch out for that schitzo guy Alex." Dougie smiled.

"Oh, don't tell me he's coming too?" protested Cesyl.

"Yeah, the whole writing group is going to be here, and a couple of new members too."

"Great, I can see I'm going to have a good night."

I shrugged. "Go to bed then."

*   *   *

Graeme and I were back just in time for Lana's phone call. I answered the phone.

"Hello Andrew, it's Lana."

"Hello Lana, how are you?"

"Good! How are you?"

"I'm good as well! Actually I'm Andrew, but I'm good also."

She giggled.

"I'm just calling to say that I'm on my way. I'm picking all the others up, except for Scott who'll probably be there any moment."

The doorbell rang.

"Yeah, well you're probably right, there's the door now."

"I'm always right, you should know that." She giggled again.

"Of course, who am I to dispute your wisdom."

I laughed at us bouncing merrily off each other.

"And Anthony and Edwina are coming too, they're looking forward to meeting you. So it's going to be a full car."

"Oh cool, they're the ones who have read my writing."

"Yeah, they really liked it. Edwina didn't think Colours was realistic, which is funny as she came up with exactly the sort of things you said in your book. But she really liked Dance with the Devil."

"I respect her for the fact that she criticised my work. I like that. It shows that she's not one of these people who always say nice things in order to be nice. Sure it's good to hear praise and all that, but it doesn't give you much of a chance to improve on the work. If someone says I don't like this bit, and this bit is poorly expressed or unrealistic, etc you can look at it and see whether you think it can be improved upon. You can do something with constructive criticism. What did Anthony think of my stuff?"

"He really liked it, especially the violent ones like Colours."

"He probably thought, 'oh wow, this has got swearing in it! Oh cool, he said the 'f' word!'" I joked.

She giggled. "He sort of is like a little kid when it comes to the stuff he likes. He loves all the action and stuff and is a bit shallow as a philosophical thinker, unlike you. I don't think he really understood Dance with the Devil. He reads a lot of fantasy and science-fiction though, so you ought to like him."

"He would have liked Wildream then."

"He did. I've been telling him about all these weird people in the group, especially you and Alex. He thinks it's going to be like some sort of a circus."

"That's okay. Me and Alex will put on a show for him, and rape him of all his boyhood innocence and sanity!"

"What do you mean?"

"You don't like me using the word rape in a context like that, do you?"

"Don't be cruel, Andrew and scare him away."

"I like to shock people, Lana, you know that. I get a kick out of it. People need to be shocked every now and then. Makes them confront things they otherwise wouldn't deal with."

"Hmmm. Well, just don't be too extreme," she grumbled.

Scott had come in by now, and was standing

awkwardly making small-talk with Graeme, who was pouring 70/30 glasses of bourbon and coke. I spoke to him mid-conversation with Lana.

"As you can see, Scott, I've gone to great lengths to clean up for tonight." I swept my arm in an arc around the flat that was an absolute mess once again. "So I hope you're grateful."

"Oh yes, I can see that. You've gone to great lengths." We both laughed, and I returned to Lana on the phone.

"Anyway, I'll see you soon I guess," I said.

"I guess you will. We're still going to the clairvoyant tomorrow, aren't we?"

"Of course, what do you take me for? An unreliable, disorganised person who forgets things?"

"Of course not, that's nothing like the Andrew I know!"

"Well there you go, you've got nothing to worry about."

"See you soon."

I looked at Scott and Graeme behind their glasses, and smiled.

Before too long, the others all bowled in. Lana, whom you should know pretty well by now; Eve, a strong-willed girl whom I saw as not having much of a flair for writing, but a flair for me, who definitely saw the group as a social one (and one for 'opportunities'); Alex, deep, disturbing, downcast, full of dark dreams and disjointed intellectualisations; Anthony, who seemed innocent and boyish-looking enough, complete with a Jewish cap and reverent expression; Edwina, also Jewish like Lana, Eve and Anthony, struck me as timid, even fearful; Scott, respectable, conservative, a logician and reductionist with bursts of metaphysical imagination; Graeme, a talker, a tripper and an avid believer in his philosophies born of an almost continually intoxicated mind; and me.

As for Cesyl and Dougie, they were playing Magic and would join in if they wanted to.

Lana and Eve led the others in. I went over to welcome the new arrivals and to introduce myself and the others to Anthony and Edwina, both of whom seemed threatened and out of their element. Lana said hello to everyone, and fell into talking with Scott who was still standing and looking out of place. Alex found his place next to Graeme as he usually did, and instantly they fell into socialising. Cesyl and Dougie looked up saying hello briefly and then went back to their game. Anthony and Edwina in a like fashion talked to each other as aliens in a foreign environment might do. For a moment, I watched the way everyone segregated themselves with mixed amusement and annoyance, and then got up to go to the kitchen to cook something for myself to eat. Eve followed me.

"You do your own cooking, do you?" she asked.

"Mostly," I returned, looking at her staring at me for a moment, "nothing flash though."

"I don't ever cook anything flash either. As long as I can stick it in the oven or microwave and forget about it until it either boils over or ignites in flames that suits me fine."

"That's about the size of it. Food's food to me, I don't care much, or have the time to spend, for things requiring preparation."

I had fairly well killed that limited topic, so she sought

something else to talk about. "Still been doing lots of role-playing?"

"Yeah, there's been a bit of a lull at the moment, but it should be over soon."

"I haven't played any D & D for so long, I've written an adventure but I can't seem to get anyone to play it, which is a pity because it's a really good adventure," she said in an all too suggestive manner.

I turned to her briefly, and noticed her body poised towards me, her piercing expression scrutinising mine.

"Oh really." I turned away, all too aware of her gaze still resting upon me. I suspected that my aloofness confused her.

"I can tell you want me to ask you about this adventure." I grinned. "So I will."

Eve needed no coaxing after that, plunging into an epic description of her adventure revolving around the antics of some mad green-thumbed wizard, relating each section and location in great detail.

I could tell you more about this creation of hers, and her enthusiastic relation of its contents, but I wasn't really listening. Over the course of the next ten minutes the only comment I made was, "You better not tell me too much, if I ever do it, I'll know it all!"

She kept talking though, and I cooking.

"Sounds great," I said when she had finished.

"Yeah it is," she answered. "Which is why I'm disappointed that I can't find someone to play it."

I said nothing.

Eve looked around herself, seeking another social link, and I asked, "Do you want a coffee or anything?"

I made her a tea, and returned with her to the lounge room. I sat with Graeme and Alex, and she gravitated towards the opposing pole of the table where the others sat.

I dug into the steaming plate before me and saw that everyone was quietly involved in reading each of the other's stories and commenting, "I liked that one" or "I didn't understand what you meant by this bit" or "I thought the way you did this was good" and then reading another. They might as well have mailed the stories to each other and read them isolated at home for all the conversation that had resulted.

Graeme looked up from a typed-page and a 'long-neck' bottle, and said, "Oh man, you've cooked dinner! Did you cook anything for me?"

"Nah sorry man, I forgot."

"You fucking bastard, what gratitude is that? I come in and trash your house and you still don't even cook me dinner!"

I laughed.

Lana looked up from the piece she was involved in, regarding us hesitantly, smiled, and returned.

Graeme then handed back the piece he was reading to Scott, saying, "Sorry man, I can't really get into it, I'm too pissed. And I can barely read the writing."

I laughed again and continued eating.

Alex sat back, pondered a moment, looked around the room, and then launched himself into a creation of his own, conjuring words from his own internal universe. A dark, obscure diatribe.

I watched Dougie wander over and ask if he could

read something. Graeme offered me a cigarette, which I accepted, and lit up one of his own.

Suddenly the urge overcame me and I turned to Graeme. "Graeme, I've got this chapter here that I want you to read, I think you'd like it. It's pretty disturbing but do you want me to get it?"

"Is it from your book?"

"Yeah it is. It's a dream sequence. I won't say any more, as I want you to read it."

"Oh man, I said I wasn't going to read it until you'd finished it, except for the bits with me in it."

"I know, but I really want you to read this. It won't spoil the book for you, and you don't necessarily have to have read the book to understand it either."

He looked a little worried now. "It's a dream? Am I in it?"

"No, but Cesyl is. And Death."

"And are there all these sharks in it trying to eat you?"

"No."

"Or all these people wearing masks over their faces?"

"Not really, no."

"Oh, that's okay then." He seemed happy at that, but as I returned with the book he asked, "What about a bottle smashing?"

"Well, there is lots of glass smashing."

He looked at me, stunned, "There is? Oh fuck! And is there someone bashing a baby?"

"More or less, yes."

"Oh fuck, oh fuck! You've got to let me read that story! Those three things were the three dreams that they were talking about this morning on Triple J. The first one about the sharks was my dream, but the other three were on the radio. It was with that dream interpreter chick, and after each one she was saying 'wow that was a really interesting dream, there's a lot in that, I don't usually get ones like these.' And the three were the masked faces, the bottle smashing and the baby getting bashed, or that was the main part of them."

I just grinned, forever ambiguous, and told him, "I just want you to read it, and see what you think."

"Man, I know I'm pissed, but that is freaky fucking shit. Three totally different things that I heard this morning on the radio and two of them are in your book!"

I didn't want to discourage him and dampen his emotional reaction, so I said nothing and watched him read.

Lana looked up again, at Alex writing, oblivious to the world outside of him, and asked what he was writing.

He looked up strangely and spoke in an eerie, serene voice without looking back at her. "It's about senseless rape and murder and unspeakable atrocities, and the persecution of those judged by a hypocritical society."

"Oh," she said. "That stuff again."

"You can read it if you want," Alex said, passing over an unfinished piece of single-sentence paragraphs that as yet only consisted of a single sheet of loose-leaf.

"No, it's okay," she deferred, "I don't want to read it if it's about that."

Alex began to screw up the story.

"What are you doing?" she asked.

"It's not worthy," he commented and said no more.

Lana tried to make eye contact, but was ever eluded by

the mysterious Alex. She probably felt guilty and that she'd been unfairly hard on him. Despite this, I don't think she wanted to subject herself to his disturbing literature, barely able to cope with mine. Failing to get him to return a look, she glanced at me and smiled. I smiled back, giving her the support she needed. She went back to her story then and Alex began to read mine with Graeme.

I looked at everyone at the table, all reading each others' stories. Lana, Scott, Eve, Alex, Graeme, Dougie, Anthony and Edwina. I was disappointed – the group was capable of being so much more than this, of exercising its potential as a unity of fellow writers, and not being simply a communal reading session. I didn't want to have to try to assume control and leadership, but it seemed that unless I took the initiative, nothing more than this would happen.

"Were we going to read the stories aloud to the group as a whole, or are we just going to keep on reading like this?"

Lana looked up. "We've already read almost all of each others' stories, that's what we've been doing."

"I hate to say it, as I'm usually against such things, but I think we need more organisation. We need some structure to these sessions, rather than just sitting here and reading each others' stories."

Graeme was too pissed to concentrate on more than one thing at a time, and at the moment he was trying to read my book. Alex looked up, contemplated, and then returned to my book. I had Anthony and Edwina's attention for the moment, but they may as well have been reading; their blank, stupid faces offered no input. Scott and Eve smiled at me, and I suspect agreed. Dougie had gone back to the Magic game with Cesyl a couple of minutes ago, and they were in a world of their own.

Only Lana said anything. "I think you're right. We do need more structure."

"I thought the whole point of reading each others' stories was to discuss the ideas and exchange them. We're meant to be a thinking group, not a reading one."

Blank faces and stupid expressions still abounded. I'm talking to puppets.

"You should have said that at the beginning," Lana said, "when we started reading."

"What, when I was busy cooking?"

"There you go," she said lightly. "You blame us for not organising something, when you did nothing yourself. You expect us to do it all."

"True," I said, but this was no real excuse. The fact that the group, to me, seemed so listless and meagre, was because it had no focus, no structure. Any meeting, once a month at best, was left up to Lana to organise, as it had been her idea originally and everyone in it, except Graeme, were friends of hers. And meetings that were formed, were left to me to carry, not because I chose to, but because no one else would, though it was something everyone seemed to agree (or at least none disagreed) was needed.

"Oh, don't worry about it then," I said, trying to sound content, "We'll have more structure next time."

I picked up the story closest and asked whose it was. I had to ask twice before the puppets responded. One of them told me it was Edwina's. And that it was a children's story.

I hadn't started yet, but already that had caused a negative reaction in me. A children's story, heh? What's that doing in a supposed writer's group of adult intellectuals? What are we, simple children? I fought to control my prejudice and forced myself to read the story.

Once I had finished I was only further revolted. Having discovered that it was a children's story, I expected that given such it would have some insightful merit relevant to a child and to the group here alike. But I didn't even think it was a good story. Even pulp fiction had a veil of substance that this lacked. I found it simply written, a stereotypical unimaginative children's moralistic 'and they all lived happily ever after' fairy tale that was predictable and unrealistically idealistic throughout. The crux of my detest of it, though, was the way it finished... The child wakes up to find 'that it was all just a dream,' and then 'finds something in their pocket from the dream.' Leaving me with a bitter taste in my mouth and this done to death theme of 'Was it really a dream or wasn't it?' A high-standard writing group indeed!

I left the table and went to play Magic with Cesyl and Dougie, bottling up my feelings. Feelings of utter repugnance, that I only reveal, that I only become fully aware of, as I write now.

I leapt from one world into another with the stench of the previous one around me but mostly concealed below consciousness. I became absorbed in a new game, rejecting convention and the group that convention represented. My anger bled away and was forgotten. An archive to be retrieved later, re-experienced and evaluated. I felt more at home with Cesyl and Dougie whom I could be more myself with, or more of another self that is me also. One that is ruthless, that is openly insulting, honest and yet casually jovial, mocking and careless. One that is non-introspective, tactless and insensitive. A crude male bastard, yes that is me too, I am not going to make myself a liar also by denying this is true. Yet no part of oneself is present completely or absolutely, we are all kaleidoscopes of qualities in differing quantities, none of which are ever fixed. I am what I am, but not what I was, nor what I will be. This means that there is Evermore to oneself; and this also means that I am a liar too.

And then I heard an echo from the table I had left, from the lips of Graeme.

"So why do you believe in all that Jewish shit?"

An emotional argument ensued of which I was no part, but to which I had much to contribute, but nevertheless I was glad that I was not there to do so. Black argued with white that white was black, and white insisted as strongly that black was white. Another said that black and white were both grey in an equally naive way. Black and white turned on grey, and denied its existence in hypocritical justification. Colour did the exact same thing and denied the existence of all three, black, white and grey. The arguments and counter-arguments were much the same as I'd heard rehearsed and played out before. They all rode the same thought-trains of convention, all that seemed to me to change were those riding them and the trappings they wore. It was not a healthy open-minded discussion, but one with undercurrents of prejudice, self-righteousness, misunderstanding and non-acceptance. Alex did well to bow out early and join our happy trio of non-thinking card players. I imagined that Anthony and Edwina looked over at us and thought to themselves 'there sit the non-intellectuals' and laughed and joked together quietly at us after they had left.

Not long after that I left my friends playing cards, and went back to my friends at the table, though over the entire night, the time I spent with each was about the same. I sat with Alex and Graeme, Alex having gone back before me. They were deep in discussion about reality. Or that's how it seemed to me as I walked over.

Graeme looked up at me swaying. "Man, I read that chapter – it was fucking trippy stuff. I can't get over how much you wanted me to read it, and what that dream therapist said on the radio. It was all in your book man, all of it!"

"There may have been some similarities, but it can't have all been in my book."

"Why not man, why not? Even the bit with the food that you couldn't eat, there was a bit in someone's dream just like that! Someone dreamt that they bit into a bun and it turned into ash in their mouth, just like what happened to Cesyl!"

Maybe truth, maybe fabrication, probably part both and something else. Who am I to argue?

"Alex read it too, we've been talking about it."

"Really? What did you think of it, Alex?"

"I liked the bit in the hospital – it was well-animated and surreal. But other bits I though you could have described a bit more, such as the impressions of the importuning hordes. It lacked visual and auditory detail."

"I agree with you on that, but that was intentional. The chapter was long enough as it was. There's only so much intense and disturbing stuff that many readers will tolerate."

Alex grinned sinisterly. "I think that's the attraction of it." Graeme laughed in concordance.

"For some, but not for others."

Graeme took another swig of a newly opened beer bottle, swayed a bit more, missed the ash tray with a smoking cigarette and said, "So what were we talking about? Fuck!" He put his head into his arms as he tried to concentrate a moment, meanwhile Alex rolled himself a cigarette. "Oh, that's right! The way I see the world is like this picture where you've got Satan standing here with his arm out holding the small globe of Earth in his fingertips. And with the other hand he's pointing at it and laughing his fucking head off."

He mimicked the visualisation. Lana glanced over at us again long enough to catch some of what he had said, and glanced away again.

I described my 'line to God' visualisation, where he sat back and said to each, "You gullible fool: How could you have believed all that bullshit!"

"Yeah man!" said Graeme pointing at me and laughing. "All these Christian and Jewish fucks die and think they're going to be saved and go to heaven, and all us druggies go to hell, and they fuck up!" Obvious and audible, his words were heard by the others at the table.

"Mankind is an infection," Alex proclaimed in morbid tones. "A festering race of sentient insects that serve no real purpose, that presuppose their existence being of central importance to the chaotic, random universe. An infection that evolves, multiplies and dies to be just another generation of organisms that is succeeded by another torpid, pestilent biome."

"Fucking oath man!" Graeme piped. "We're a disease. Look how much we've fucked this planet up. All the shit we pour into the air and dig up from the ground, and cutting down the forests and shit. But hey man, the religious workers say 'this is God's kingdom' and that he's given it to us to look after!"

"We've done a good job of looking after it then," I said.

Alex answered me in darkened chords. "We are a species of parasites, that cannibalises our own evolution, catalysing our own destruction."

"Listen to this stuff man!" said Graeme excitedly. "This is what you ought to be putting in your book! Man, this guy knows it all! He's the writer man, and you're" (he points at me) "the channel!"

The black prince spoke again. "I see through all the grandeur of this fleeting material world, and I see nothing but rampant disorder from which we extrapolate meaning and truths. A random universe bound only by the laws of chaos on a never-ending spiral into decay."

"And then what? Where does the spiral go? What's left then?" asked Graeme.

"Nothing."

"Only Death," I said.

They both looked at me, and smiled. The three of us

formed a counterweight to the views of those at the opposite end of the table.

"You see what I mean man! Alex is the writer, and you're the channel! And I'm the messenger!"

"Maybe so," I answered, knowing there is always more. Truth is not single-partite, it's multi-partite. It incorporates everything and nothing. It incorporates incomprehensibility, paradox and impossibility. Yet it incorporates nothing absolutely, even the truth and therefore the existence of itself.

For it is Evermore.

MEDITATION

Relaxed I was, but not quite. I had somewhere to go, something to do, but this was nothing in the world of the physical and material.

I was ready. Ready to plunge into the unknown, the forever infinite, the unfathomable depths of my own mind.

I put the book away and took the bold leap, reckless, endless, deeper and deeper into myself, diving through level after level of consciousness, summoning all the will I could muster. Not daring to think of the consequences or the effort I was devoting, lest it break my concentration and snap my bungie cord.

The mists cleared around my head and I was glad to discover that I had reached my sentimental halfway point. It doesn't even have a name in fact, and here nor do I. Such things are clumsy abbreviations of feelings, thoughts and ideas that can't accurately be expressed in words.

It would do this wonderful place no justice either to even try to describe it in words, for it has no constant physical form. Indeed it only remains constant in its concept.

This great place that I know by essence and not by form, serves as a terminus into unlimited possibilities and worlds. Expressible in words is something it is not, for it is not specifically anything, yet it is specifically everything. Comprehensible to any who have the will to do so, for it is as whatever your imagination wants it to be.

Something we will never completely attain, yet have already.

And now there was Jason Braidy, the little mischievous bastard. A childhood friend I hadn't seen for the greater part of fifteen years, though we met regularly here.

His prickly, freckled face beamed at me, itching to go.

"You ready?" He grinned.

"Fuck yeah."

We wandered through the carnival to our ride, our ride deeper, taking us through the circus of reality into the circle of escapism.

We moved past many junctions to other places, each bearing giant fluorescent billboards bearing titles like '**THIS WAS THE WAY ONCE**' and '**ONWARD TO THAT BEFORE**' and '**HERE LIES INSANITY AND REASON**' and '**FOR THOSE SEEKING RETURN**' and '**ISOLATION MIGHT BE A NICE NAME BUT THIS COMMUNITY HAS NONE**' and many others I couldn't understand nor had any desire to.

"Wait till you see the one we're going down," he cackled.

I caught up with him and looked, trying to perceive his thoughts that in this reality manifested as visible objects.

"What do you think?" he asked.

"I can't see anything!"

"Exactly! Isn't it cool? This one doesn't even have a sign!"

"But I can't even see a way!" I said.

"Then you haven't thought hard enough. Look behind you."

I spun around and saw an almighty chute, two lanes for the silvered sleds that lay purring at the bottom of it and the track leaping up into the air like a ski-jump, spiralling off into the silvered mists overhead like a gigantic roller-coaster.

"Cool," I breathed.

He laughed hard and bounded into one of the sleds, closing the hatch as he challenged, "Race you to the end!"

I made to reply, but saw that he had already left. I jumped into the gleaming rocket sled and took off like a bullet, immediately absorbed in the ride. The mists disappeared in an instant as I careered beyond them into new and exhilarating loops and curves.

The road became a blur with the speed and soon vanished altogether. I piloted the ship expertly into a circular concrete hole in the ground where I thought my rival had entered.

I dashed down a vertical tube at nauseating velocity, eager to catch him, eager to beat him – and in my eagerness missed the turn-off where he had gone.

Laughing like a crazed jackal, his echoes reached me, shaking my vessel and the walls around it. No matter. We were on separate paths now, maybe our paths would cross again, maybe they wouldn't. No matter.

The car rolled and spun through various turns, drops and jumps. I reached many branch points and swerved and slammed through them, always trying to choose the hardest option possible, and usually succeeding.

Eventually, though, consciousness of the ride faded...
I became what I may sometime be.

*   *   *

I was on a rocky hill, out in the open, naked without my vehicle, alone. Then, staggering down the hill towards me, I observed another.

It wore a TV on its head.

Without any apparent sense of where it really was (should I refer to it as a he or a she?) it staggered down the barren landscape, apparently talking to someone else about how nice the sun looks setting over the blue ocean and what a shame it was that they didn't have a boat that they could sail in.

As it got nearer, I noticed that the suit it was wearing was some sort of wired cover-all that was buzzing with activity. It appeared to be some complete body virtual reality unit that had created an artificial experience for its wearer, making them totally oblivious to their real surroundings.

"I say there," he called out to me (his voice at least seemed male).

"Greetings, fellow traveller." I produced a hand to shake.

He brushed past me without apparently noticing me at all, and stopped a few more metres behind me. He pretended to fish in his pocket for some change and asked of the thin air in front of him, "You don't perchance have any orange chocolate chip ice creams, do you?"

He looked to his imaginary companion and asked

what they wanted. At this point I turned away and headed up the mountain.

I had forgotten all about him by the time I had climbed to the top of the steep knoll and saw that I had come upon a whole community of TV heads.

A whole community of TV heads all oblivious, so it seemed, to each other and their environment. There were those dancing alone in fantastical discos or fighting fantastical battles against invisible foes. There was one engaged in what could only be seen as imaginary sex, many others were performing actions pertaining to tasks such as driving, eating, reading, exercising, operating machinery, talking on phones, serving customers, or typing. Many were sleeping, dwelling in dreams of other realities, maybe even this reality, maybe even of the reality I had come from and finding it utterly bizarre and unreal. I saw one walk off a cliff on the other side of the hill and fall fifty or more metres to the jagged rocks below, and then continue walking, even as they were falling, as if nothing had happened.

Then it struck me that I too might be wearing a helmet like theirs. I felt around my head and my body but could feel or see no such devices as the ones these people wore. Then I realised that this was no assurance. If indeed it was true that I was clad in a similar way to them, with clothing that controlled what information all my senses, including sight and touch, were given, it was still possible to see and feel myself as I did, yet be wearing this other material. It would not matter if I was actually walking into a wall or off a cliff, I would experience something completely different. I wondered too, if I experienced myself suffering injury, whether it would actually occur regardless of what was 'really happening'. And if it would, if I would actually experience it as 'real' such that it had 'real' effects on me, what difference did what was 'really real' make? On that I decided that I should not worry about whether I was wearing such a suit any longer. I was experiencing a reality different from them (or so it seemed safe to assume) and I should live according to what I experienced was real, or else learn nothing from what I did experience.

And then I noticed, I don't know why I hadn't noticed before, that in the midst of them one male sat cross-legged. He was completely naked and... staring straight at me. And now, seeing that I saw him, he smiled.

I was strangely fascinated to see such a being in such an environment, yet I also felt fearful that he saw me. I then noticed that despite his hairy, masculine appearance, he had no sex.

He watched my approach through the others, and when I reached him I saw that he had inscribed in the dirt a circle, in one half of which he sat. He gestured for me to sit down in the circle with him.

His presence seemed to relax my apprehension. I felt close to this sexless man as if I had known him and we had met on good terms before. I thought perhaps he would ask me to remove my clothing too, but he asked no such thing of me. Perhaps he sensed my anxiety. Anyway, I sat down and then he spoke.

"At last I have found you."

I frowned. Hadn't I found him? I couldn't be sure of anything here though, so I thought it best not to contradict him.

"Who are you?" I asked.

"Who am I?" He grinned. "Who are you? I'll tell you. You am I; I am you. Your greatest nightmares, your wildest dreams. I am everything you or anyone else has ever imagined. I am the world, and they, it, and you are too. Yet everything also includes nothing. It includes both, and neither. And contradiction, impossibility and exclusion too."

"What do you mean? I don't understand."

"What do I mean? What do you mean? What do you mean by what I mean? Or you mean? Or I mean by what you mean? Or I mean by what I mean?"

I swayed back in confusion, and he reached forward and patted my knee. "Take heart, you understand more than you realise."

"I do?"

"Yes. And less."

I smiled back at him, still feeling confused. But I felt safe at least, I didn't feel alone. I was grateful for the company and I felt I could learn a lot from this man.

"I will talk in terms that perhaps make you feel a little more comfortable, and talk of things perhaps you feel you can relate to a little more. Perhaps that will make it easier for you, and those with you, to understand."

He gazed away unmoving for a time, and I began to think he wasn't going to say anything, just sit there. I'm not sure how long I sat there, unaware of my surroundings, but eventually he said something.

"I shall be known to you as Edwin Sharp, male human of your world once, but no more, though I will be once again, and perhaps again after that."

"You can call me Andrew. I'm dreaming at the moment."

He gently waved my replies away. "I'm not trying to discourage your conversation, but there is no need for names of faces and places. We are all naked here."

I thought to ask where's here, but expected no answer that I could readily make sense of, so declined to ask. I was content to listen to his words.

"We are like the Steppenwolf, you and I. We write of life, but don't live it. That is not our way. I, like you, sought truth and true understanding, and in my quest I became further and further removed from the real world, and more and more a part of the one lying beyond it. I followed the path of the great priests and dreamers. I travelled far, farther than what you can probably imagine, and have not since returned. I have no wish to as that is not my way. I became what those of the real world would call insane. Even then this no longer troubled me – I was beyond the understandings of their world, their prejudice and arrogant non-acceptance. Now I have no physical form at all, and exist in a different world, or set of worlds, altogether. Here for instance, I appear to you how I choose."

He paused, and I couldn't help but ask, "So what really is real then?"

He laughed warmly and answered, "Don't ask me what is real, ask that question of a realist. Truth, meaning, reality, all of them I have found to be clad in cloaks of relativity. Caged in contexts of reference, wearing blinkers of interpretation. I am an idealist. Ask of me the ideal, not the real."

Again I couldn't resist, "So what really is the *ideal* then?"

He chuckled again and said, "You're going to be disappointed in my answer."

"What is it?" I laughed. "42?"

"No, nothing absolute like that, or so I have found it. Only this..."

I waited, anxious.

"You Know What."

"What do you mean?" I said, "Do you mean I know what?"

"Don't try to reduce it to a meaning," he answered. "Then you lose it rather than find it. It is an understanding, but one that is neither absolutely affirmative, or negative. But there is always something more to it, something that you missed out, and didn't quite understand. You could even say that it is partial, relative, whatever, but again there is always something more to it. This is the great tragedy of knowledge and understanding, but it really is salvation, for it means that everything is never absolutely anything, there is always more. And for me, that means that there is always more to learn and understand, and for that I am most thankful."

"But," I attempted to rebuke, speaking slowly and carefully, "to say that nothing is absolutely true, or something like that, haven't you just destroyed the truth of that statement? Because for 'nothing is absolute' to be true don't you have to allow for at least one thing to be absolute, that is that 'nothing is absolute?'"

"The truth of itself destroys itself, it holds because it

doesn't when it does. And by trying to attribute absolute meaning and objective truth to it you lose its magic and power. The strength of its being lies not in the transitivity of truth and meaning, but merely in the strength of its being, though not even this, for even these words have relative truth and meaning. I think it is best just to say that it is Evermore. Nothing more than Evermore." He laughed.

"I think I'm beginning to understand at least some of what you've said."

"You understand more than what you're giving yourself credit for. After all, you're the one writing this, not me. Like I said, You Know What. And that means you. Yes you, not me. But it also means me and not you. And neither of us, if for someone else. It's all relative, you see, but embraced and unified."

I grinned, feeling reassured... I did know.

"But don't become conceited. You're not the only one. You're one, one of many. And many is one, one is all, and yet one is more. It is..."

"...Evermore," I finished for him.

"Yes."

"But isn't that an absolute truth, that there is always something more?"

"Yes, and no. There is something more to it, rather than it being a straightforward absolute truth that there is always something more, which is why it holds despite there being no absolute truth. Confusing and contra-dictory, incomprehensible even, but of a beautiful simplicity and something that you know already."

"We have talked enough," he said. "You must forgive me if my words have been hard to follow – it has been some time since I have talked the language of truth, meaning and logic. Nevertheless the essence is there to be grasped, no matter what form the words to encapsulate it take. Which was what you just thought. Don't be surprised, that I echoed your thoughts, I am a facet of you, a certain expression of you. And you are no more the same, a certain expression of me. You are merely a facet (be it as it may, made up of smaller constituent parts or facets) of yourself, and of everything as one. Of the entire one that is You Know What."

"That is Evermore," I responded in synchronicity with his thoughts.

"And you have learnt a lot and journeyed far. But don't become bigoted and complacent. You have a lot yet to learn, perhaps more than most, and a lot yet to journey, and you will."

"But of course, there is always..."

We said the word together.

Edwin continued, "And the more our flame burns, the more one learns. The more one grows. The more one knows. The more one has seen. The more one has been. The more one is not is and not is not. The more one is You Know What."

After a pause, he finished off what he had to say. "I

too have a lot still to learn, perhaps more than you, perhaps more than most, but I am on a different journey and so we must again part. But my meeting you was not without a purpose for me from which I too could derive some benefit. For we will meet again, as we have met before, and you will write of me, of that which is but a certain part of yourself, of that which is but a certain part of You Know What. I am a writer too and poetical dreamer. And all parts of everything lie within all parts of everything, which means that aspects of me and you lie within all others, just as they within us. Different expressions, yet of the same thing, so that on one level no exclusive identity or property exists that excludes any other. But as I said, I am beyond the real world now, such that I am able to make very little contact at all with it, except in such ways as I now speak to you. You will write my book, or I write yours, or we write those of others, or they write ours; it matters not how it is expressed, but it will be done, and that is when I shall become known as Edwin Sharp. For to latch onto this world, and others, I need a bridge, a channel, and you shall serve to be that, willingly for it was your choice to do so as Edwin Sharp himself. And as I said, you have a long way yet to go, to reach what it is that you seek, but you will get there, if you want to, and I will be there with you, and others too, and you with them, for fundamentally we all journey together, for fundamentally we are all one, as many are we.

"But enough of my prophecy and my words, it is time for you to write some more of your own. You need to live a little in all worlds, and that includes the real one, and so you should while you can, and perhaps a little more than you do. It is not for me to assess or judge, for we all have our own roads to walk and we choose those roads. But there is opportunity everywhere, and you don't have to search for it, it comes to you, for if you want it, you create it. Life is there for living, so live it! Do not await my return – just have faith that I will return when it is best and when I want to."

And so it seemed our meeting was over for now. We parted to continue our own journeys through our own worlds, be it as Edwin said all part of the one thing, part of You Know What. But some day, I know not when, he shall return, and when he does, I shall welcome him. But now is for now, not for past or future, and so the journey goes on and we with it...

CONSTERNATION

"So how did you feel after you spoke to Eve? Did you feel disappointed?" Lana and I walked down the road to Columbo's for coffee and dinner.

"What do you mean?" I asked.

"When Eve said no to you, when you asked her out as a girlfriend?"

"She didn't say no, she said yes!"

"She did? She told me that she said no, that she knew how I felt about you, and that she'd never do anything like that to hurt me!"

"Well, I don't know what she said to you, but she definitely said yes, we are going out. I knew she would. I've been putting off asking her for ages because I wasn't sure whether it was what I wanted, but then I decided fuck it! I need to live a little more. She was really excited when I asked her, saying 'thank you, thank you!'"

Lana began to get angry. "I can't believe she would do this to me!"

"Maybe she said that so she wouldn't hurt your feelings. I know that to tell you now, hurts you, but you know that I value honesty above sensitivity, so that's why I'm telling you."

"I've really had it with her. She's done horrible things to me before, but this is really it."

"I don't think she did it out of maliciousness, and

though I don't know what her motive was, my guess is that she was doing it to avoid hurting you."

"But that she lied to me, hurts me more. I'd rather she'd have been honest too. Didn't she say anything to you about it?"

"About talking to you? No. And I guess if it is the case that she lied to you, and this is something I'll have to check with her, then she will have lost some of my respect for that."

(As I was later to discover, we were both wrong, or at least had misunderstood the situation. I have said before that all problems reduce to ones of misunderstanding of one thing or another, and it was certainly the case here. This is the great danger of any absolute assessment and judgement. According to Eve, she hadn't lied to Lana at all, and Lana had misinterpreted what she said. I could believe both on their own accounts. If Eve had lied to Lana, then it was certainly possible that she could lie to me. But I could also believe that Lana could easily have allowed her emotions to cloud her judgement. Lana may well have reinterpreted Eve's words according to what she wanted to hear. She wanted to hear that Eve was *not* going out with me, and reinterpreted what Eve said to confirm that. Eve said that she had said 'no' to a serious relationship, which I was happy to agree to, as that was what I had wanted anyway.)

Lana continued talking about this topic, but before long we reached Columbo's and conversation between us stopped, for a moment anyway.

We were directed to a table, sat down and ordered cappuccinos.

Lana regarded me tensely, broken with emotion, looking to me to provide the support she wanted but would not give her. I played the role of one who is unaware and insensitive, consulting my menu and interrupting her fiddling to ask what she wanted to eat.

"Oh yeah," she said, suddenly aware that she was in a restaurant for a meal and required to order.

The meal was ordered and I joked with the waiter I knew, pretending nothing was wrong, and hoping that my mood would relax Lana a little.

"So," I said with an ambiguous smile, "You were pretty keen to talk to me tonight. What was it that you wanted to talk about?"

"Well," she hesitated and fumbled, swayed and tried again and again to formulate her thoughts into coherent words, "I thought I had gotten over you, I really did. I thought I had dealt with all this pain and accepted things the way that they are, and that it wasn't going to be. But now all this with Eve has opened that up again and it's worse than ever before. I really am an absolute wreck, and I don't know if I'll ever get over it or accept it."

"I think that now you're in the position I was in with Tiffany, which is so weird in a way as now I see it from a totally different perspective."

Lana agreed. "I'm in that position too with Alex. I'm happy to be his friend, but he feels for me more than I do for him."

"Yeah, and like you I thought that I had dealt with it and everything was fine, and then something else would happen and I realised I hadn't dealt with it. You've read my diary, you read how I kept on alternating between 'okay I've accepted things now and I've moved on' and 'no, I haven't accepted things, maybe I never will, maybe this will never end!'"

"I really thought I had avoided it this time. I knew that it wasn't going to happen from the start and I was clear about things."

(Indeed, I had made it clear to her from the start the way things were, as I was intuitively aware of her tendencies and didn't want her to get hurt.)

"And despite this, it still happened. I thought I had grown beyond falling for all my male friends, and now it's happened again, worse than ever before."

"But each time it passed, didn't it? You got over David, you got over Marcus."

"Marcus was nothing, Andrew, really that was only puppy-love. And now I understand why David did what he did, and I realise the signs were there from the start. But it's much worse with you than it was with them. My diary over the last couple of months has been worse than yours with Tiffany."

This comment surprised me because that stage of my life was prolonged and deeply distressing. But it was something I am glad I experienced, for it was something I needed to learn and grow through, and I did. She transformed into my ideal, much of which still remains. I can truly say that I was in love with her. But it became an obsessive addiction that I needed to get over.

"Really? That's pretty bad then. But it took me about a year and a half to get over Tiffany, you know that. And after the first three months I knew it wasn't to be, and I kept saying that I had accepted it and dealt with it, and then something else would happen and I'd be thrown into depression again. I don't think it's something you can just switch on or off, such deep attraction as that takes a while to get over, like any addiction. It's a gradual thing, with steady oscillations as you climb out."

"I know you got out of it, but I wonder whether I ever will. It hasn't got better, it's got worse. And I don't think I'll ever meet anyone like you."

She looked to me, hoping for some reconciliation, hoping for the support I had given her when she was getting over David, support I would not give her, as this was not the role I chose to take. She needed detachment, and I would try to facilitate not hinder that. Eventually, I collected my thoughts and tentatively expressed them, knowing I had to be careful with what and how I said things. Lana was extremely volatile at this moment and prone to interpret my words in an undesirable way.

"Just as I did with Tiffany, you made me into your ideal," (um...) "an ideal which wasn't there before you met me, one which before me was perhaps more like David, and Marcus before that, being less and less fixed each time further back. We aren't suited. You've acknowledged that before, and you will meet someone you are suited to. It is flattering, and you probably won't meet anyone like me, in so much that we are all unique, but you will find someone else that may become your ideal. I was there at a time when you needed me, and also I needed you, but now we must move on. Our friendship may well persist, and I think it should, but it won't ever be what it was before."

I could see she was trying to prevent herself from

bursting into tears, that she was searching me and my words, for some note of reassurance. Openly staring back at her, I continued.

"I think that you have invested a lot of your emotional support in me, and that you are distressed to find that now it is not there. But understand that I cannot give it to you, this is something I feel you need to learn and grow from. You need to find that strength within yourself, not search for it in others, and I know you will find it because you are a strong person."

"I don't feel very strong now."

"But you are. This strength is in all of us – you've found it before and you will find it again. You stood up to Caraline, didn't you?"

"But I wouldn't have without you there to help."

"Maybe so, but now you need to find it within yourself. You'll become a lot stronger. I know I did after my experience with Tiffany, and stronger again after Caraline. The same for you with David and then me. Trust me, you'll look back on this in a couple or more years' time and be glad that you had this experience, realise that it was something that you needed to learn and grow from."

"I know what you're saying and I've heard you say it all before, but it's all just philosophical theory, Andrew. You're just trying to rationalise and intellectualise everything."

"Okay," I said meditatively. "But it's what I believe and how I choose to express myself."

"So why are you going out with Eve? It's just a casual thing."

"It is," I answered, thinking that honesty didn't have

to hurt if I didn't want it to. "Which is why I was glad that she also wanted a non-serious relationship. It was something that I had put off because I couldn't justify it when I knew that she wasn't an ideal or someone I was even greatly attracted to. But when I realised, my friends had pointed it out too, just how many opportunities I have had and let go for this same reason, I thought 'Heh? Just who am I kidding here? Whose own growth am I denying?' And for this reason I have done this, for the sake of experience, for the emotional support it provides, for the companionship and confidence, and of course for the physical aspects of the relationship too."

"You're just using her!"

"I am using her, but equally she is using me. She knows that it isn't going to last, she knows that we're not completely compatible. She knows that it can only go so far, as she's not allowed to have non-Jewish boyfriends. Though by 'definition', I guess I am Jewish. All relationships of all forms involve use of one kind or another, yielding mutual benefits for all involved. You use your parents for support and shelter, and likewise they use you, and your kids the same. You use your friends for companionship and support in a different way and they you. The word 'use' doesn't have to have negative connotations when it comes to relationships being ones of mutual benefit, even if they be for differing reasons. It's not an ideal relationship, she and I both know that, and it probably won't last all that long, though things always being subject to change, it may. Just as I may come to feel for her more that I do now. I've talked about it with my Mum and my sister, and my other friends, and they've all agreed that I should do it. So I've gone ahead and done it. And I realise now that this doesn't mean that I've changed who I am. Though I do realise that doing it has hurt you, but this, and this does sound blunt and cold, but it is honest, is something that you've created and I'm afraid something I can't help you with." (I catch her quickly before she retorts and gets beyond what I can control) "And this is because I don't wish to involve myself in something which you need to deal with yourself, and I don't mean any harm by this, but it is for you to deal with."

"I have been dealing with it without contacting you. I've talked to Caraline, I've talked to Dad, I've talked to my sister, I've talked to Rachel and Susan, I've talked to everyone but you."

"That's good; now my advice is to resolve it within yourself. You've listened to everyone now, so now do what you feel is best."

"Yeah, they all say that you don't deserve this sort of attention, that you're not good enough for me."

"Well, that may well be true. I'm in no position to deny this. But the bottom line is that now you've acknowledged this; and showed great strength of character that you did, by the way, and it's something I'm proud of you for. You need to resolve it within yourself, and move on."

*   *   *

We were heading back now and were almost outside my flat when I said, "Did you want to come back in?"

"No, no. I don't want to go back in there with all those others." I could imagine her shuddering inside.

"I didn't think you would." I grinned. "Which is why I asked."

We walked to her car...

"So I guess I'll see you sometime soon."

"I think I'd better not, Andrew. I think I need to keep some distance from you for a while."

"I think that's probably the best thing too."

With that, she drove away, u-turning quickly and accelerating past me as I waved. I know not what happened after that, it's now a month later and I have not seen nor spoken to her since...

EXPLANATION

I rang the bell and smiled to myself as I waited for Rashid, the younger of my two bosses, to come and answer it. Once again I had purposefully neglected to turn up early as Rashid had requested.

He came to the door, and smiled back at me as I chuckled. "Oh Andrew, I'm going to have to punish you on Friday morning by coming late."

'You know how it is, Rashid." I shrugged nonchalantly.

"Yeah, that's okay. I don't mind if you come in five or ten minutes late every now and then."

"I'm still on time for when I'm supposed to be here, just not early."

He rambled on in his own way, as I nodded here, smiled there, and occasionally said "Yeah" or "Of course, I agree", whilst he continued. Eventually he moved into discussion about the shift roster and messages regarding clients.

I noticed then he seemed to relax a little, his credibility as a boss maintained, and I took the other chair next to him.

"So did you bring the cards?" he asked with a devious smile.

I laughed at the little boy in him he tried so hard to hide. "No, sorry Rashid, I didn't change my mind, I still don't want to play cards."

"Oh," he said disappointed. "Why don't you want to play?"

"I just don't feel like it, I guess." The same answer I had given him an hour ago on the phone.

"Oh, but I sacrificed myself for you that other night when I stayed over at your home. I was tired and wanted to go to sleep, but I knew that you wanted to play cards so I didn't want to let you down. I sacrificed myself for you then, and now Andrew tells me he cannot sacrifice himself for me."

It was, as I saw it, a futile protest considering I hadn't wanted to play then either, but he had persisted and finally I agreed, as I didn't want to be seen as a rude host by someone who was my employer. But I did not say this, as it might crush him to make him realise that the main reason I was his friend was for the job security it provided me where otherwise there was none. I had given him a temporary place to stay and a friend to go out with and play cards with, so our friendship was a mutual pay-off.

A friendship like this might seem difficult to justify. It is a choice I have made, a survival mechanism I have resorted to in the past and would do so again in the future. It is a compromise of values for the sake of survival, or at least surviving in the sense that I am now. We all have to make decisions with moral dilemmas like this, and we ultimately do what we perceive is best for ourselves in the circumstances.

"So how's everything going with Lana?" he asked.

I grinned. "I haven't seen too much of her lately. Our lives have gone in different directions. She told me a few weeks ago that she wanted space from me, not that I was even around her that much then."

"Oh Andrew, all these women troubles that you have."

"Well you know, whatever happens, happens. My life's complicated enough as it is without getting involved in other people's problems or worrying about them. Though I'll still help of course, when and where I can."

"Does she still want to go out with you?"

"Yeah."

"Does she still love you?"

"Yeah! It's because she's become too emotionally attached to me that she has tried to create some distance, something which I think she needed to do."

"Why don't you go out with her?"

"Rashid. We're not suited, you know that."

"But she's a nice person. She is a little..." he hesitated giving a little chuckle, which I reciprocated as I knew what he was about to say, "...fat." He lowered his head and laughed, having embarrassed himself.

"Oh, I know that," I managed to say before he continued.

"But if she, if she..." he hesitated again, laughed and tried to gather courage to speak, "lost some weight," (he laughed again and shook his head) "she could be a good girlfriend."

I made to speak, and he continued again.

"I mean when I met her, she was really friendly, you know. I could talk to her very easily. If she lost weight even I would go out with her."

"By all means, Rashid, you're welcome to her, though I don't think you're suited either."

"You should introduce me to some of her friends."

"You're really desperate, aren't you Rashid?"

He seemed not to like this label, and tried to defend himself. I took the heat off him though, and made the point I had wanted to make earlier.

"Though it is certainly true that to have a relationship with someone, you need to be physically attracted to them, it is a physical relationship after all, you need to be suited in other ways for it to be right for you."

Rashid interrupted at this point and rambled about something, which I did not hear properly as I was waiting for an opportunity to finish what I was saying. When one came, I quickly jumped in and finished my point.

"But what I was trying to say before was that I'm a very independent person who needs to have a lot of freedom in any relationship. I can't be completely committed and loyal, always spending time with the one person, and this is the same with the way I spend time with my friends. I don't think I could have that with Lana. She's too dependent, she'd become too emotional and get hurt too easily if I couldn't give the commitment and time she wanted."

"Yeah." He nodded. "I think... I think that when I have a wife, I want to, I want them to be someone who," he screwed his face up and shook his head, "I don't want them to be someone who tries to control my life."

I began to say something, but he said "Now" with a pause, indicating he wanted to say something more.

"I want to settle down with a wife, someone whom I can spend the rest of my life with. Someone who is simple, who I can love, who is a good cook, and attractive too."

I nodded and made a comment, but I'm not sure whether he was paying attention, talking as much to himself as anything else.

"But if they were someone who, who, who didn't want me to work, or go out, so that I could spend more time with them. Then," he looked at me now, "and I'm sorry, Andrew, that I have to say this, I really don't think I would want to spend time with them."

Once again I begin to say something, but Rashid raised a hand to stop me, saying "Now", according to his conversational procedure, which translated as 'Now I want to say something else, so listen.'

I consider listening important, and something I am usually good at, but I have a need like anybody else to be listened to also and this habit of Rashid's could often be frustrating and encouraged me to do the same when dealing with him.

My sentence died midstream and he continued. "I think in this life, it is important to be good to your wife, and to look after them well, and not to bash them, or be rude to them like people do today."

I began to make a point that in general, I didn't agree with the pre-feminist values of the wife staying at home, tending to it and raising the children whilst the husband goes out and works, but he talked over me again, so my words went unfinished and unheard.

"Let me tell you, Andrew, and please don't tell anybody else this, that when I was in class at school, the teacher asked us what we wanted to be."

(If I had had a chance to agree, his comment would not be found in this book. As it was, I said nothing and listened. Though there are many other things he has said that I agreed not to publish, and these will not be found in here.)

"I said that I wanted to be a good husband and everyone laughed at me, you know."

I laughed too, but he maintained a serious expression, perhaps feeling that I was laughing at him.

"No, I'm serious Andrew, they did! And I hope that you are not laughing at me too."

"No, no of course not", was all I managed to say.

"I mean this world is so sick and people don't really care about others any more. You think it is bad here; it's much worse in India. In India, a person's life is not even worth," he pulled his hand away, as if withdrawing from something, "is not even worth ten cents! In India, people will even run someone over and drive on, they just don't care! In India about oh, about ten-thousand people die every day! India has much more people than here, there are more people in one city than in all Australia! I think it has more than one million people, you know."

"Oh, more than that."

"Yeah a lot more, maybe one-hundred million!"

"That sounds about right."

"Yeah. I tell you something I heard about someone I used to be friends with, but not close friends with, back in India. He used to get teased a lot at school, I teased him a little bit too right, but I used to feel sorry for him. I even gave him a thousand rupees, when I was in India a few months ago, which is about a hundred dollars here in Australia."

I raised my eyebrows. Wow.

"I mean he was someone from the lower castes who

had a poor family, and used to come to school in dirty rags because he did not have any money to buy good clothes. And people used to tease him, and beat him, and say that he was nothing. And I used to feel sorry for him, but I didn't want to stand up for him as then I'd get beaten up too, right?"

I nodded.

"Now." He paused again, licking his lips and collecting his thoughts as he prepared for another speech.

"In India there is one of those containers up on a hill with pipes from it, so that the people can get their water."

"A water tank?"

"Yeah, a water tank. And now this water tank, it is broken, I think the pipes are rusted or the water is not coming through properly. It needs to be fixed.

"The council there, has said that they will not fix the water tank until four people have died."

I wasn't sure what he meant. "Why's that?"

He gave some explanation I didn't understand and then he said, "And soon after that one person did die, so they needed three more to die before they would fix it. And it makes me very sad to say this, but I recently heard that someone had pushed him off it and killed him, just so they could get the water tank fixed more quickly."

"Jesus!" I said, quite stunned.

"Yes Andrew, it was a terrible thing to do, and they did it to him because he was poor and had no friends. I felt sick in the stomach when I heard that that happened."

"It is saddening to think how low some people will go, just for themselves."

"As I said, this world is sick, no one cares anymore. I

really do think that this world has not long to go before it is the end. There is too much wrong with the world for it to last much longer. I think that there will be a world war in the next few years and that by the year 2000 we will all be dead."

"Well, certainly many people seem to agree, and it is well prophesised that the apocalypse is due."

"Yes Andrew, there is not much time left on this Earth. So if I can do what I can, and help others, then I will go to heaven and have a good life in the next lifetime."

"If there is a next lifetime after the world is dead."

He shrugged. "That's right. Maybe there won't be."

"But I don't think there will be a world war."

"There will be Andrew, believe me there will be a world war."

"Sure, there are a lot of bad people in the world, not that I'd call them bad, only misguided, but there always has been."

"It's never been as bad as this, and it's just becoming worser and worser."

"Well, we certainly hear more about global events now than we used to, but it's hard to really say that things are getting worse, I think. I see a lot of positive things happening on a global scale, changes in thinking, etc. I think that this planet can be saved."

"Well, we will have this discussion in heaven in a few years' time," he said as he picked up his keys and mobile, heading for the door. "And then you will say 'Rashid, you were right. I should have listened to you.'"

"We'll see," I said with a light laugh as he went.

I proceeded to the control room to log myself in and

check Rashid's work, as is my responsibility. I selected a compilation of Joe Satriani from the armada of tapes that I brought in every night to work. I plunged into the musical beauty of Satriani's guitar for a moment before deciding to make myself a coffee and have a cigarette.

I contemplated what Rashid had said, knowing that I was going to write about the conversation with him.

My friends and I had directed a fair degree of antagonism towards him (more behind his back than to his face) due to the injustices we feel he has done to us (as also has his brother) in the workplace, and this I do not deny. I do not think that he is a bad person despite this. I think that he truly believed he had done the right thing by us, and that he did try to be a 'good' person, that he did try to justify his actions, and that he was strongly compelled to do a lot of what he did by his conscience. It is a difference of opinion, belief and values that caused our disagreement on conduct, something, that I think, was unlikely to change. If there is truly anything Rashid had done 'wrong' (a term which in anything other than a subjective context becomes meaningless) it had been not listening to his workers and their complaints, and that he took certain things for granted as the employer.

I too was learning how to become a 'better' person, and learning along the way that there was always Evermore to learn. This process was not a growth in the same direction, but a process of trial and error, an evolutionary process if you like, one where even by making great mistakes I had the capacity to learn great things. Moving in circles that are spirals that are something else again, a transition towards the integrated one, towards You Know What.

This book has given me the chance to refute and explain myself to my own critics; past, present and future; which is quite an unusual position to be in. One of my most major concerns, the one dominating my thoughts as I write now, is not being condemned for *not* telling the 'truth', but for telling the 'truth'. That is for reporting events of the personal lives of those currently around me, and involving them in this book without asking their permission, and without presenting their interpretation of events. Almost all of them that I have had regular contact with over the last seven months or so whilst writing this book are aware of what I'm doing. But as I speak, only a few of them have read this book (and apart from Lana and Damien, only a handful of pages) but certainly none of them (yet) these words. Yet already, most of them have been vocal in criticism not for misreporting events (although there are small discrepancies) but for reporting them. I admit that at the moment I am gravely unaware of the relevant laws, but despite this (and regardless of what laws I shall have to abide by when I inquire about them in the near future) I feel that their claims of defamation are unfounded.

Is it defamation to include characters with fictional names in a story, who are real people in real life, and to write of my interpretation of events that actually occurred, involving them, without their permission?

What is presented here is only my interpretation of the events that occurred, and only my interpretation of the characters that are presented; which is to say that by no means is there any absolute truth about any of the things that I have said. But the same limitation (that any statement lacks absolute truth, that any perception is subjective, and therefore is inevitably biased) exists for any criticism made of what I do or say.

I do think critical self-reflection is at times necessary, but to dwell in it for too long serves to create a cancer that erodes one's own foundations, and causes them to deny what they have gained from their experiences. Understanding, acknowledging and accepting these things (perhaps to return to them later, in the light of new experience) it's time we moved on, and so indeed… we shall.

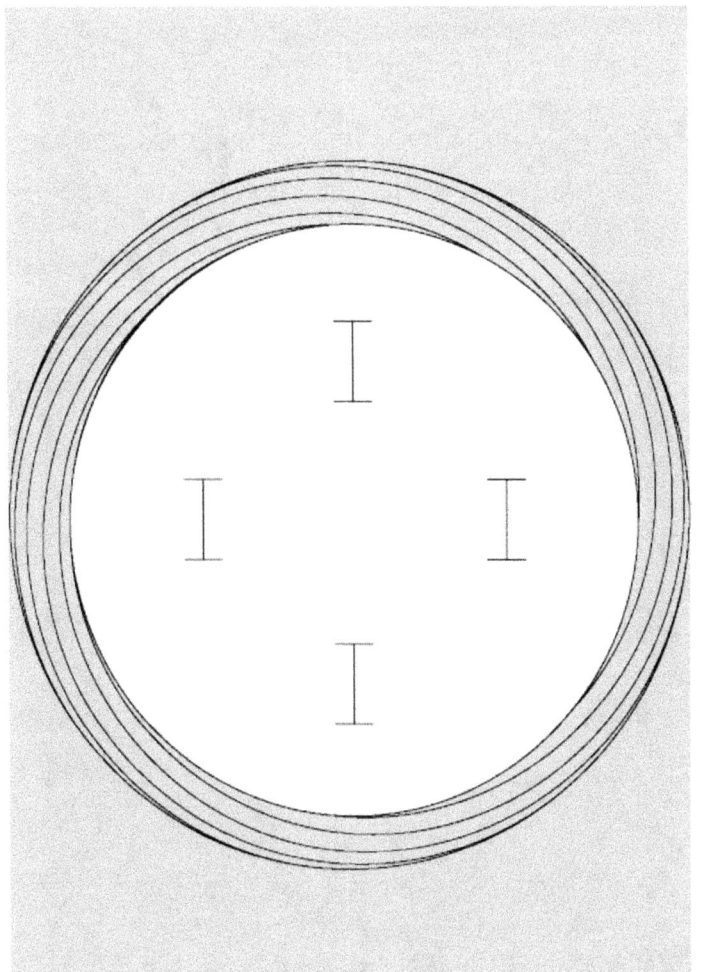

DANCE WITH THE DEVIL

Come with me, he says.

Does he say it? Or does he order? I'm not sure.

I sense I reject what I know to be his presence, despite having no rational reason to even believe his existence.

A mental tug is anchored into my mind, pulling.

Am I dreaming? Is this real?

Understanding and knowledge can be yours.

Do I want it? Do I dare? Do I believe?

Do I care?

Suddenly a light appears in my netherworld; and silhouetted in it is a lean, black figure. The figure is tall, and walks towards me, head bowed somewhat... respectfully?

I can see it more clearly now, a slender, delicate figure with two small horns protruding through a scrag of curly black hair. It has skin that is almost as dark as coal and peculiar pointed ears. Its face cracks into a friendly(?) smile to reveal a set of shining, pearly teeth with exaggerated fangs. It speaks, gently, in a rich voice, "Congratulations. You've come a long way."

I'm confused. I'm not sure what's going on, though I know that I brought this about in some way.

"You've reached the meeting place, the place where your world and mine connect. It's a long way for you to have come, you've done well."

It smiles, I detect evil. I back away, fearful of what I have done and brought myself into contact with. Denying that this could really be whom I think, I dread, it might be.

"You seem surprised to see me. Yet you know who I am and have been expecting me all along."

I stutter the words... "It's not really possible, is it?"

"Call me by a name if you choose, if that makes identification easier. I have no such need to do the same."

My God, it's true.

He laughs. "Don't you see it as extremely revealing that I am what the words of blind men proclaim me to be? I appear to you as whatever qualities you superimpose upon me. I have no other such material form."

I have to get out of here.

"Afraid to face what you are? What existence is? I know you... (a mental connection here is made that cannot be interpreted in words) ...and you know me more than you realise. You don't want to miss this opportunity for discovery, that you've striven so hard for... I know; and you do too."

Deception? Or truth? Who to believe? Whom to turn to?

"Is your faith of a dead man's lyrics faltering? Thinking why should I trust one with whom such lies are associated?"

My faith can be strong, I know not to listen.

"Consider yourself open-minded? Non-judging? Understanding?"

Resist, resist, the temptation.

"Lying to oneself is the worst crime. You are only denying your own development. Open your heart, understand, embrace."

My defiance begins to gather, a fistful of hailstones to throw at the enemy.

He sits down before me cross-legged. And a wave of joy overcomes me. I'm confused.

"Still think I'm trying to trick you? Those feelings are your own, and I am only what you make me."

"A liar," I spit, but the hailstones have melted leaving me feel cold and senseless.

He shakes his head. "No. Only this."

He holds out a closed hand and gestures to my open palm. He's going to put something in it.

*   *   *

I recover. I don't know how much time has passed, but it only seems like an instant. It is. I'm still 'here', wherever here is.

But now, it's me who holds out the closed hand, to his open palm. What?

I pull back my hand, repulsed.

"What happened? What did you do?"

He smiles knowingly, and says, "All I am is a changer of perceptions."

An instinctive rejection surfaces in my mind.

"Hah, hah. No, I'm not 'evil'. Evil is but an empty referential term imposed by those who judge the merits of other's actions according to their own values and beliefs. Change is not evil; if it were then growth would be too, and who's fool enough to say that life, nature and existence are in essence evil?"

I shook my head. This shouldn't be making sense.

Why was I letting it convince me? I'm confused.

"Good. It's good that you're confused, it shows that you are listening to my words and trying to put them into context. That's the first step to enlightenment, my Lord, learning to listen to others, all others, whoever they be."

"L-Lord? Did you call me..."

"That's the second step. Humility to others. All others. No one is better than thy self, but nor art thou better than others."

His ancient tongue rolled over the words expertly, and I felt like I was talking to an old sage, someone old and wise, in a long dusty brown robe.

"You see!" he cackled, "How quickly the mind changes. It's not me that changes, nor you. It's your thoughts that change and henceforth your *perception*." His monkey voice emphasised the last word, and I felt that I was beginning to see.

"That's the third step... Acknowledgement! Acknowledgement of the person you are, and of your achievements. Never lose sight. Never return now that you've been touched by the true light of understanding to the ignorant darkness of prejudice."

I nodded, it was all so, so true. I understood now.

WHACK! His staff suddenly whirled in a blur and ended on my head. Stunned, I fell to the ground.

"But don't become gullible! Always assess and evaluate before you commit!"

Sore, my pride wounded, I rose slowly.

"And for God's sake," (he looked above him, pretending to brace himself against lightning bolts) "stop taking everything so damned seriously! Don't you know why you're here?"

"No." Wanting to hear the answer, though I knew it already.

"To learn! And learning's meant to be fun!"

But what of suffering, of lost dreams and fortunes? What of war, of...

"Look," he broke in arrogantly, "do we have to go through all of this relative, subjective stuff again, where we look at living in its own context?"

Had we discussed this before?

"Yes we have! In a previous existence, only I was Buddha then, and you were a lot more sympathetic."

"Huh?"

"Don't look so surprised, you've experienced being entities of alien gods before, and you've experienced being Santa Claus twice, both times in female form."

"What?"

"Stop standing there so dumbfounded. I've got lots to show you, most of which you probably won't be prepared for, but the best way to learn is dramatically."

"I disagree."

He smiled, changing back to the devil.

"You *are* learning."

Still smiling, he extended out his thin black hand.

"Take it, if you dare, and step into my dark world, where I swear afterwards you will never be the same."

Still fearful of the possible consequences, I hesitated. "What are you going to do to me?"

"Hah! Hah!" he laughed. "Nothing. I can't do anything to you. No one can. It's you who changes your essential self. It's you who decides how you react to experiences, not that how you change matters. There is no 'good' and 'bad' change, only change!"

Without further ado, I laughed and leapt into his arms and spun dizzily away with him to other worlds, existences, and meanings. Changing forever, my life would never be the same again.

That story is about to be told...

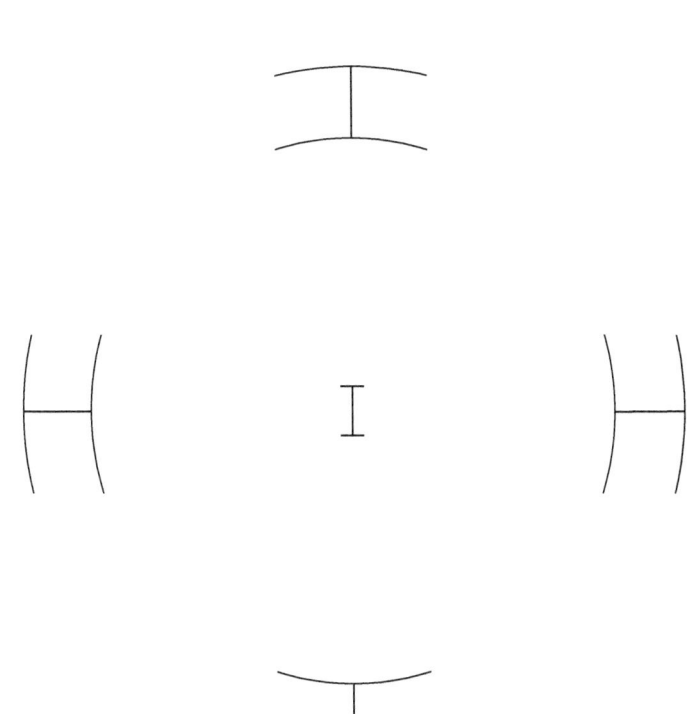

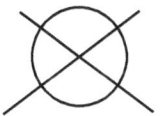

THE WANDERER

THE WANDERER

"WELCOME BACK!" says a voice triumphant.

"Don't be so surprised, you brought us here. And you are the one carrying us onward into (N)Ethermore. Into (N)Evermore.

"This isn't your first time either, though you probably don't remember, maybe you do, but this is why I say Welcome Back.

"But of course I'm really you, and you're really me. Which means of course we are as one, which is to say we travel as we.

"I notice too that there are more with you this time than last. That's good to see. Our numbers are growing. This probably won't be the last time you're here either, and then there'll probably be more with you again. Suffice to say, we are Evermore.

"Before we continue, as I'm sure we're eager to do, there are a few things I must say to you, and this includes of course all those travelling with you.

"Firstly, it is regrettable that you can only hear my words at the moment, and I cannot hear yours. Or so it may seem to be this way. But remember, I am you, so in this sense I am only the part of us that's currently speaking. On this journey, 'I' have been spokesperson for us but as we are one, 'yours' and 'my' thoughts and beliefs will be vocalised through the words of 'another' on a different journey, and of course already have.

"I know that you've all come from differing places, experiences and realities to be here with us now, and for that we thank you, you have been acknowledged. It has been hard for some of you to have endured this far, others much less so, regardless all your efforts will have been worth their while. This journey is near completion. The seeds of the apocalypse have already been planted and are beginning to germinate. They will bear their fruits soon.

"It is important to realise that we are all part of one, no part being greater than any other. The voice you hear is your own, reading these words that are your own also. A part of yourself that is 'me', all of us forming part of 'we'. In this experience, in this reality, in this context, the meaning of us being one can be confusing. For this reason, for ease of comprehension, we shall still use the terms 'you' and 'I' even though they have no real existence here. Though at times, we will experience things as 'we'.

"I thank you again for helping me to write these words, and for them you should thank yourself. Understand that I am an echo of your own thoughts, thoughts you implanted in another consciousness or reality if you like, one that has come filtering back through layers of existence and meaning to find you. A reminder of who and what you are. An 'alarm' you set yourself a long time ago to alert you when it was time to awake.

"That time is now.

"You chose this journey, you chose this experience.

You control it now in fact, not only in terms of what you experience, but where you journey within this experience. You are empowered with being able to end this journey whenever you choose, begin any part of this journey whenever you choose, and experience and interpret this journey however you choose. Realise that choice is your own.

"Though the power to read these chapters in any order has always been with you, let me make you consciously aware of this. Let me also tell you that reading any part of this book out of numerically-paged order will have no disastrous effects upon its interpretation and meaning. What it will cause is for you to have a different experience, thus resulting in a different interpretation of meanings within these words. In fact, for this reason, and because reading these words in only one particular order gives bias to the significance of a certain arrangement, reading in a varied order of pages is encouraged.

"Nowhere is this unconventional way of reading encouraged more, than in this part of the book you have begun to experience now. Upon finishing this current chapter you will be charged with a few proposed choices as to what chapter you could experience next. These suggestions will manifest themselves throughout each chapter in this part of the book, and not necessarily at the end of the chapter currently being read. These suggestions represent doorways of possibility and are a tool I have employed to indicate what I feel follows well from the current experience.

"For ease of identification, these doorways will be expressed in ***BOLD ITALICS*** referring to the chapter to which they lead, followed by the page number in brackets. But of course the real choice is always with you as to what chapter you read next, if at all, and when.

"There are many stories before you, and there are many endings. This does not mean however, that our journey ever ends unless we choose it. There is Evermore to be, see, experience and learn.

"Your briefing is over, the preparation you set yourself is complete.

"Though I know there are those amongst us that like to experience 'endings' before 'beginnings'; if that is you, if you wish to know how this journey 'ends', we shall then become **THE COMPLETE** (page 417)."

The voice which speaks is now your guide, is now you, for now you are alone.

Let your body rest, let you mind soar.

Come let us embark on a journey through Evermore.

An external voyage through the worlds of the internal self.

An escape from reality into fantasy, into reality from what was really fantasy.

Where we go, only you and I know. For the worlds of our creation we make what we want. Here we make truth what we want to make it. Here we can dwell safely beyond the judgement and criticisms of others, for we are no longer in the world of others to be assessed by them. Here we have no need for justification, or lengthy explanation, here we can be and do and go where we like. Here we are truly free to wander through infinity unhindered.

Through infinity, as infinity, for infinity.
Until we reach…
Until we reach, You Know What.
And then we shall begin again…

*   *   *

THE OTHER SIDE

Somewhere there was an echo.
Somewhere there was the source.
Somewhere the same there was the manifestation.
The manifestation was I.

There is a star.

Non-existent in space, but burning within the soul. It is the origin of us all. It is what makes us one. I have been there and returned to tell of what I have found. Found on the Other Side…

This is the story of that voyage into darkness, beyond worlds tamed by light and purity, beyond realms of reality and blissful ignorance, into uncharted dream-states and nightmarish configurations.

Do you know what darkness is?

Some would say it is an absence of light, but this is an emptiness without colour, tone or pitch. A world without colour and light is not dark, but empty of these qualities. A world without good is not evil, but empty of either. You see, one cannot exist without the other. One exists only in contrast to another. One is only insane by comparison to another termed 'sane'. One is mature only by contrast to those deemed not so.

Do you know what exists there?

Only what does not exist here, for here is not there until there becomes here, which would make here, there. Which would change things entirely and prompt an entirely different perspective.

A strange path I have travelled...

A strange comment to make, considering the use of the word 'strange' is only obtained by comparison to the relative state of 'normality'. After all, is difference strange?

How far have I come, how far is there to go?

Do I know that I've even gone anywhere? The world may have merely moved for me, and me not at all. I may have learned nothing. I may have learned and forgotten everything. I may never know.

Who is this 'I' that I refer to?

Like everything else, I is a relative manifestation of perspective, relative to the thinker or speaker of the proverb. I asserts the existence of oneself and anyone reading such is doing the same.

But anyone is everyone, is all one, and one refers to the same one, the only one, the complete one, the infinite one.

Ye who embraces light, must embrace darkness, for one cannot exist without the other.

But ye who embraces emptiness, denies the existence of either and commits a double fallacy.

Ye who embraces one, embraces the two faces and the infinity of degrees in-between and not.

Can you roll a dice with only one side?
One sidedness is round and spherical.
So is many, infinite sidedness.
Both are *one* and *same*.
Do I speak confused ramblings, incoherent jumbles that are the product of a tired and weary mind? Or do I speak truths?

Neither, but both. Truth itself is relative too.

All possibilities, realities, impossibilities and probabilities are relative, including relativity itself.

Including 'you' and 'I'.

Think about it, we are already on the Other Side, according to what those there call this.

*   *   *

THE HALLMARK OF TRUTH

And now I have arrived at what some would call The Mansion of Madness.

I travel up a stony winding pathway to the handsome estate upon a lonely wooded hill. The sky overhead lights my way clearly, though there is no son to watch over me, his rays shine through no clouds, which do not exist here either. I do not walk, but flow. I don't flow over the path, but flow as the path, a path I create as I move, a path I have chosen, created, and am a part of myself.

I flow to the gate. Proud and bronze-shod, its doors are currently closed to me. Great oaken doors set with lion-head knockers on either side, like a joke that no one seemed to have heeded. The joke is simple but to me it seems without point or humour. For one does not transgress these gates by knocking, indeed they make no sound at all if used. The way beyond is gained by knowing.

The knockers complement each other perfectly, and now I realise that they form 'I's.

And then I see that they form part of a greater face, a face which encompasses all of the gate itself. The gate takes upon a human persona as it sees I realise this. And now it speaks to me.

In unflattering, unoriginal and uninspiring tones it asks, "What is the password?"

In matching tones I answer.

"You Know What."

*   *   *

And then I become the gate itself, a face that looks inward beyond its own borders to the house at the centre inside.

Through its walls my gaze enters, and my consciousness of myself rises such that I become the house and its surrounds too.

I let my awareness be of the Fountain of Truth in the marble-walled foyer. A fountain that has remained for eternity and always will, though the waters that flow through it and cascade endlessly down its sides are ever-changing. The water comes from nowhere and goes back to the same place. And as the water is never the same from one moment to the next (the water I see now, is not the same water I saw a moment ago, is not the same water I see now) it has no real identity of its own.

In the swirling and leaping of the water droplets I see many shapes, forms and meanings, all of which are gone in an instant, though I can make myself see those shapes again if I want to (though of course they are never actually the same). The water flows into one another, ever maintaining its temporality, from which is projected an illusion of sameness.

I play with the water a little, altering its form only in light of my seeing it to have become something it would not have been without my action. But it matters not what I do to it; I only see it as different from what I see it *may* have been. It itself is unchanged and yet regardless of me it is ever-changing.

*   *   *

And now I become one of the players in a game that is taking place in the expansive hallway beyond. This hallway actually constitutes almost all of the house (or what I have called the house) itself. The walls are of adamantine blocks veined with the colours of dusk and dawn, defined in borders of ambiguity and confusion, and built upon foundations of nonsense and meaning-lessness. The walls have no features at all, for they are beyond description in discrete words. The walls, the hall, the house, aren't anything at all, yet together they are everything. The walls are beyond my comprehension now, for now I am one of the players in the great game of knowledge.

"I don't know how to play this game," I said. "I know nothing."

"And I know everything," said the opposing player. "And this is enough to know that I know nothing and you everything."

"So what are you saying then? That to know everything is to know nothing, that truth is meaningless and knowledge non-existent?" I insisted.

"Be careful with the game that you are playing; you are trying to make it into something. When you make it something, you prevent it from being something else. It no longer is everything, and this includes being nothing."

"What? What do you mean 'the game I am playing?' Aren't I playing the game you are?" I argued.

"Again you are playing the game that I am not. You are trying to mould my words into something, but this would not incorporate everything, nor would it incorporate nothing. I do not oppose you or contradict you, I am you, and yet I am not playing your game."

"I don't understand what you're saying! I don't understand this stupid game or this stupid place! I didn't come to hear meaningless words, I came here to find the truth!" I protested.

"You do understand my words, but as you, not as I. And yet that part of you which is I does understand as I do. And I understand that you seek an absolute definite answer, which I cannot give you, as that is not the game I play. Ask that of them," said the player who would not play my game, and pointed to the walls either side of us.

It was then that I recognised two faces I had not noticed before that seemed to have emerged out of the featureless walls flanking us. In a moment I saw that these faces were exactly alike, and with irritation, as featureless as the walls themselves.

"Who are they?" I asked my opponent, whose opponent I was not.

"They are Diva Affirmata and Diva Negativa. They will give answers to your questions. Ask who you like."

"Which is which?" I asked again.

"I can't tell. Ask one."

Frustrated and annoyed, I turned away and strode over to one of the faces.

Staring at its featurelessness, I demanded of it, "Are you Diva Affirmata?"

"NO," was the answer.

"You must be Diva Negativa then."

"NO."

"What? Who are you then?"

"NO."

"No? What's that supposed to mean?"

"NO."

"Of course no means no, but apart from that?"

"NO."

"So you're just no, is that it?"

"NO."

"Argh! Can you give me a sensible answer?"

"NO."

"Can you say anything other than no?"

"NO."

"I guessed as much. So that's what the truth is then, just no?"

"NO."

(Stupid question, what else did I expect it to say?) "So the truth isn't just no then?"

"NO."

"Hah! Hah! Got you! I've just proved you wrong!"

"NO."

"What! How can you deny that? You just said that no, truth isn't just no!"

"NO."

"You did so! Admit it!"

"NO."

This was getting ridiculous. "Okay, at least admit that no isn't the only truth."

"NO."

"What, so now you're saying there isn't any other truth? Is there any other truth?"

"NO."

"Is there any truth at all then, and this includes no?"

"NO."

"I give up! All you ever say is no."

"NO," it answered as I angrily went over to the other face...

"I suppose you just say yes?"

"YES," was the answer.

"Great... Do you say anything else?"

"YES."

"You do, like what?"

"YES."

"Yes? But that's exactly the same answer!"

"YES."

"So you agree with me then?"

"YES."

"And I suppose you'll also disagree with me?"

"YES."

"And you'll say that you are both completely predictable and completely unpredictable, even though it's entirely obvious that you're just completely predictable?"

"YES."

"And as you'll say yes to whatever I say, you'll say yes that yes is the only truth, and yes that yes is not the only truth?"

"YES."

"Ohhh... I've had enough of this stupidity." I turned away.

"YES," it said to my turned back...

And now I saw that the other player was no longer there.

Instead there was a naked jester, luridly painted in haphazardly chequered black and white, who could only stare at me a moment before bursting into raucous laughter.

"What are you laughing at?" I demanded, feeling insulted.

I was only met with more raucous laughter.

"Where's the other one gone? Is this all some joke?"

Now the jester was rolling on the floor, still laughing, with tears rolling down its cheeks, wearing away lines of paint.

"Don't worry about the Joker," came a voice from behind me, and I spun round to see my opponent again, whom I now realised was a mirror image of me. "The Joker laughs at everything."

"Is that all it does, just laugh?"

"Yes. It laughs at life, it laughs at death. It laughs at you, it laughs at me. It laughs at itself and all the silly games we play."

"Why?" I asked, hoping at least once for a sensible answer.

"If I had to explain it to you, then it wouldn't be funny. It spoils a joke to have to tell you what it means. You either get it or you don't."

"I guess I don't then."

"You will in time. And you'll be seeing the Joker again and then you may come to understand the humour of it."

"I can't wait," I muttered sarcastically.

"You don't have to. You can go there now if you like."

"Where?"

"Wherever and however you like. It's *your* choice."

The laughter continued unabated behind me.

"I just want to get out of here. I'm sick of this."

"So be it," was the answer.

The only thing that happened after that, was having my double say something about wanting to sing me a little rhyme before I went. It was dedicated to the Jain priests, philosophers of a little-known Indian religion as ancient as Buddhism. Strange that I remember the poem though I remember nothing else of what was happening at the time. It was called 'Non-one-sidedness of One' and it went something like this:

"*Meanings are disfigured, distorted, but true.*
They become insubstantial, transient and see-through.

The existence of Nothing, means Nothing exists.
The persistence of Anything, means Anything persists.
A truth is merely one colour, in one aspect of one shade,
in one vision that is one reality our imagination has made.
Knowledge belies perspective, just as Wisdom denies our
youth.
We are all one but not same. Judgement betrays the truth
that we all see things differently, yet all with one eye.
What is real and fact for one, to another is fiction and
lie."

*   *   *

IT'S YOUR CHOICE

"Here you now are, at a crossroads. Two doorways lie open and waiting for you to step through into another existence. The choice is yours."

The voice comes from a sleek, supple creature that seems composed of liquid metal. It is humanoid in that it stands upon two limbs and gestures with the other two, but its silvery head is positioned in the middle of its torso. As it talks it has the unnerving habit of rolling on its limbs, which all appear identical, such that its upright orientation constantly changes. As it talks to me and performs these bizarre acrobatics, its head also turns smoothly through 360 degrees. Though I must admit it is hard to tell whether its face rotates at all, for the single eye and the two mouths it wears are symmetrically arranged in an 'I'.

"What's through the doorways?" I ask.

"This one leads to heaven, and bliss and comfort; and this one leads to hell, and unhappiness and suffering."

"Well, I guess I'll choose heaven then," I answer.

"A word of caution my friend." It raises a metallic digit. "To go that way is to dwell in the bliss and comfort of ignorance. There you shall live well, but for it you will probably be sheltered from the truth."

"Well, it's the truth that I seek, so I'll choose hell then," I decide.

"Again I must forewarn on the consequences of that decision. You may well find the truth there, but probably not as you desired to find it. You may come to regret what you discover for the unhappiness and suffering it may cause, and you may wish that you had instead chosen to dwell in a comforting, blissful delusion."

"Oh, I see," I say.

"Of course neither is likely to bring you what you ultimately want, you have to create that yourself. It is in your hands whether you learn and grow from your experiences, whatever they may be. And it is your choice what you decide to experience. You are your own destiny, and the words I say are only these places as I have found them. Heaven to some is Hell to others, and vice versa. You may even find both of them hellish or neither. That is your choice, not mine."

So then we have two choices before us: we can either become **THE HEAVEN BOUND** (page 285) or **THE HELL BENT** (page 301). There is, however, another choice presented to us, and that is to stay right where we are, at this nexus, and become **THE UNCOMMITTED** (page 267).

THE UNCOMMITTED

THE UNCOMMITTED

I anticipated that many of you would arrive here.

So where's here? Wherever it is that you are.

We have no need to go anywhere, you see.

Within us we can find heaven or hell, within us we can find truth, fantasy, fortune and failure. Within us there are manifestations of whatever we choose to find. Right here.

We are an endless fountain, we are infinite, we are what we make ourselves and the world we are is what we make it too. Let reality be our toy, to find truth our ploy, to experience be our game and to understand our aim.

Listen with me now to the tales of others who have arrived here also, and their reflections and interpretations. We join them over a counter meal in a celestial café, but shall remain silent and unseen so as not to intrude upon their interaction, though we are an integral part of it...

"I have always thought murder to be the most terrible thing in the world, and that if ever I committed it, I would forever be condemned," said Release, one of the four identities present.

Release continued. "I could comprehend nothing other than that the act was evil, that whoever committed the act was evil, that it was something that was not justifiable under any circumstances, or at least certainly not where there was another choice one could make."

Go on, the others intoned.

"Well, I never thought of course that I would ever be a murderer. Who really does think that they would ever stoop this low? To so base an act? But when I was one, when the most unholy of acts was done, I experienced not a great remorse and an internal condemnation, but an incredible awareness of my own freedom as never before. It made me aware that I was free, free to create my own actions and therefore their consequences. Well, this is The Truth as I found it, and it was the experience of causing another's death in my life that revealed this to me. Be this experience with me, and perhaps you will understand as I do, and then I'll be your experience, and perhaps understand as you.

"I call this experience, Colours."

*   *   *

The brush moves in waves and circles, wandering aimlessly over the parched landscape. It flows over the ridges, it smooths the dips, drawing with it a new layer, covering those beneath.

Scars and bumps melt together as one, features vanish. Under the thick mask of make-up, the evidence is gone.

First a creamy white smearing makes the marks shy, now a pale pink powder is applied, and the cheeks regain definition, integrity. Red blushes make the face brave, the plump dashes of scarlet provide the illusion of competence, of control.

And now the fallacy is complete. He grins, it all looks so silly, so false. His wife.

She turns, her shiny, chestnut hair follows her neck in a long sweeping curve. Facing her chest of drawers she begins to empty them. Stacking a small pile of clothes on her left, and replacing the others.

Then with rapid movements she moves over to the cupboard, and begins to unhook some of her best dresses, and then slows again as she lays them gently on the bed, like a baby to its cradle.

She unzips her suitcase now, and begins to fill it. Initially carefully and methodically, but before long the urgency overtakes again, and the suitcase is soon bulging with clothes. Colours of skirts and outfits, underwear and shoes, all bundled together like the colours in a shattered prism, fragments of clothing poking out the sides like shards of glass.

Then she seems to remember, a gasp of fear overcomes her senses, and she rushes over to the bedside desk. Reaching in, she draws out her wallet and keys, and sighs. The colour returns to her face like a wave.

The colour in his face becomes ever brighter, swelling and darkening like a raging tide.

She is almost ready to leave now, a last check of the bedroom, and then she turns to the doorway, suitcase clutched firmly in her hand, a fistful of white knuckles.

He stands imposing, arms folded, looking down at her with indignation. She freezes and fades backwards.

Where before he had been grinning, now he is glowering, the tempest of his rage about to explode in violent fury.

Speechless and ghost-like, her bold ship of confidence begins to flounder. The mask of make-up already dissolved.

He waits, she endures, he waits still more, she pales further. But then, she suddenly changes, trying to restore that guise of resolution. Her visage becomes defiant, her step determined. She starts toward the doorway he occupies.

Cold words bar her way, "Where do you think you're going?" Controlled, subjecting words, with a hint of violence; a sinister undercurrent.

She had been wrong to assume that he would go to work this morning. She would pay now.

She throws her answer back to him, fuel onto the fire, "I'm leaving."

He begins to shake with anger, she trembles with fear. Her blood draws away from her face, it floods into his. Veins, like cords in his head begin to swell, his eyes bulge, and his mouth curves up at one end. He transforms into that gruesome apparition that he assumes when anger possesses him. His blood ebullient, he makes forward, determined to crush this rebellious spirit of hers with his own bare hands.

The illusion is shattered, the danger real. She tries to escape the range of his cruel, swinging fists, putting up a thin forearm as mock resistance. Bearing down on her, he bashes aside her arms, then grabs them, and uses them as handles to swing her by, and throws her to the ground. Hard.

She lands on her shoulder and bounces into the chest of drawers. The crystal vase atop, blooming with brilliant violets, is knocked from its place and comes crashing to the wooden floor, and there it smashes, the life-giving water it held flowing out like blood.

Matted hair falls across her face as she looks up at him with disrespect, bruises begin to resurface. Infuriated, amazed and disgusted, he hurls his abuses at her, resolute to hurt her, attributing his own hurt to her, the cause of all his problems.

"YOU STUPID, FUCKING BITCH! YOU SELF-RIGHTEOUS SLUT! DO YOU THINK THAT YOU CAN JUST WALK RIGHT OUT OF HERE, DO YOU?"

As always she plays coy, the innocent little child, the gentle, loving, 'untouchable' woman. He bends over and shouts into her purple face.

"DO YOU?"

Again no answer, her lips tremble, but no more.

He picks her up by the arms and shouts at her a third time, his fiery eyes ten centimetres from her shrunken ones.

"ANSWER ME BITCH, OR DO I HAVE TO BEAT THE LIVING SHIT OUT OF YOU?"

Unable to believe this continued refusal, he slams her down on the bed, her head knocking the bed upholstery with a loud painful thud.

"I'M GUNNA HAVE TO DISCIPLINE YOU BITCH. UNTIL YOU LEARN NOT TO RUN AWAY."

He draws out a long black belt now, and runs the cool leather through his hands, like a snake that slithers, ready to strike.

Moaning, she does nothing. The purple, coy bitch, who plays rebel when she wants to.

Then the whip strikes, each cutting blow and wince a cruel, hard lesson not to disobey one's master.

One after the other, the lashings continue, and dark, red blood begins to flow ...like sin. Colour defines the places where each individual blow falls.

She tries to cut off, but each time the snake bites again, and the pain that follows jerks her back. In desperation she reaches under the pillow, an ultimate act of salvation.

He counts sixteen, and then suddenly she moves. Surprised, he hesitates, considering that perhaps she has conceded her crime, and that her repentance is over.

Then she pulls out the gun.

And fires.

One. Two. And that is enough. Clutching his bleeding stomach he falls to the ground, his weapon of mastery dropped and forgotten.

Thud. And so he hits the ground. In a blur of relief and remorse, unconsciousness hits her and smites from her fragile body what little energy she has left.

In-conceiving of her motive, he stares up at the curiously beautiful black and purple of her face. Gasping heavily, he looks from her broken and bruised body to his. Red splashes of colour stain his shirt, like vibrant pools of life, pools that mirror him and the room around in red technicolour, pools of colour, dying colour...

Then all colours die as one.

*   *   *

At the end they were all silent, as the four identities reflected on what they had learnt and gained from the experience. Defeat was the next to speak.

"I may have found that experience hard to believe had I not experienced it myself. It is sad to think that the human race is driven by power and control, but this is how I have found The Truth too. It is a civilisation built upon the foundations of technology and conquest. Those things material seem to be of central importance to society, yet those things spiritual, which are what ultimately advances society I think, account for little or nothing at all unless they are economically profitable. Come be my story, if you will, and experience what my life and death was, and what it meant to me. I find an apt name for this to simply be The Killing."

*   *   *

The wetlands were silent again, like the calm in the eye of the cyclone. The night had come.

A flattened bill gently muzzled at her fallen comrade. The dead duck's body still felt warm. The bill prodded near the bloody wound, hoping that her partner would stir alive. But the only movement she saw was the swaying of the reeds as the breeze, like a breath of ice, ran its way through the woody stems.

The wind called her; and opening her majestic wings, she answered the call...

The duck flapped off into the night leaving her dead mate where he had been shot, the lead bullet already staining the water around it with its poison.

The mother began the journey home with her sole remaining child. The young duckling had grown to near full size, and had been venturing out on its own for at least a couple of weeks. But it would stay with its mother from now on, another loss she couldn't risk.

BANG! The sound sliced through the air, trailing the bullet like a comet's tail. Daylight, with its battalion of hunters had returned…

"Missed him," muttered a brown-clad human, far below.

She wheeled around, with her son at her right, and saw the figure that had fired. Flying ahead of her she could see a vast throng of mainly mountain ducks, all flying for their lives, terrified, exhausted by this daily ritual of life and death.

The hunter, with his mate, turned to face the pack.

"Steady Mick, you're not allowed to shoot at flocks," the other cautioned.

He replied with his rifle, a great crack echoed, as one of the ducks was struck. It plummeted to the ground like a stone.

The hunter grinned.

"Oh, shit Mick! That's a freckled duck you shot!"

"Ah, don't worry Fred, I'll just leave it over there and no one will know who it was."

She seized her chance, and quickly flew past the hunters, eager to catch up with the group. There was safety in numbers.

"Hey look Mick, those other two are flying back past us." He pointed to the flapping shapes, their species being indistinguishable so far up.

"Not for long," Mick said grimly, raising the gun to his eye. He stared down the sights, feeling the cold metal of the rifle against his cheek. And there they were. Two ducks. Two targets. Their life he held in his hands. He liked the feeling.

Power.

The sights centred on the smaller of the two ducks. "Two dead ducks." He thought as he squeezed the trigger. BANG! Went the gun again. It kicked like a horse and dispelled its small silvery package of death speeding towards the pair.

She heard the gun fire again, and instinctively swerved upwards, her son followed. The bullet passed. They kept flying, utterly exhausted, for their lives.

"Missed the bastard," Mick commented, as he reloaded. "Again."

He hoisted the rifle once more, and aimed. This time his aim was true, the swift steel of the projectile struck flesh.

Another blast buffeted her ears. She saw her son squawk, then drop paralysed to the ground a hundred metres below. But she was not going to abandon him, even if it meant her own death. She followed his fall.

"Got him that time," he boasted. "He won't be going home for supper tonight with his missus."

The injured duck impacted. His mother landed next to him. The hunter saw that the duck was almost four-hundred metres away.

"Oh, bugger that," he said. "I can't be stuffed going all the way out there. Besides, it'd mean that I could only shoot another nine more."

His mate agreed. They turned away to look for more victims.

Her son had a messy hole in one wing. The bullet's path had also gone through his lower abdomen. His body lay convulsing. She could tell he was dying.

Then she heard the sound of running footsteps, splashing through the ankle-high water towards her. For her own safety, this time she took to flight.

A human rushed in and scooped up the wounded bird. It seemed to be gentle with her son, trying not to hurt him. For some reason, she knew it was there to help her son. It rushed him away to an awaiting van, where her child was tended to by others.

Suddenly there was movement behind her.

"Got the bastard!" She turned her head to find herself faced with the long barrel of a gun.

The gun fired...

*　　*　　*

Again there was silence among the four present as they absorbed this experience into themselves. Of the experience, Lost said, "It is amazing what death teaches us about life. I didn't learn much from life and in death I learnt that I had lost what life had to teach. I lost direction in life, I lost control of life, I lost the game that life is. I gave in to its pressures. I quit for I thought there was no way of winning. I saw others as having had all the good luck and that they did not know what the harsh real world was like without the good fortune they'd encountered. I couldn't see the value of my own experiences for what they were, a dive into the darker side of life to overcome misfortune and understand depression. A small part, equally important to other more positive parts, of the entire thing. I failed to realise that I was the centre of my own universe, and an equal part of the one around me. I limited my freedom in life, and ultimately found it again in choosing death. Now I realise how lost I had been, and that I had always had my freedom, only I had chosen not to have it. What I found in death was exactly what I gave up in life, freedom, which really had always been mine. I became what I had been – Dust."

Now we become this experience, so named...

*   *   *

It seemed as if the whole town was steeped in dust, sweeping valleys of ever-mobile powder. A river of sandy waves spanning the gap between the weathered buildings.

He trudged along in the searing afternoon heat, down the red, chalky path that churned under his feet. Despite the burning sun, he wore an overcoat. A well-worn coat that had been his favourite for many years. He used to care for his coat. Treasure it.

He used to care for many things...

A gentle breeze began to blow, whipping up small eddies of dust, stinging his eyes. He staggered down a side street, seeking refuge.

Eyes squinted. He groped his way along for the weatherboard wall of a house to lean against. Then he heard a yelp and realised he had stepped on something fleshy. A sudden but slurred mental calculation indicated to him that it was a dog.

Opening his eyes, now that it was safe, he saw that it was a Kelpie wagging its tail at him. Its tongue hung out of a brown mouth, its body was soaked in dust, reddish-brown deposits of the stuff were halfway along its snout.

He sought a place to sit down.

His coat crumpled up behind him as he slid down the dirty wall to the ground. The dog tottered over to him, and nuzzled his hand. The hand responded, as the dog knew it would, and began to stroke the dog's unkempt coat. He reached with his other hand into a deep pocket to fumble for his bottle. Finding it half-empty, he studied the "Jim Beam" label for a few drunken moments before upending the bottle into his mouth, letting a small mouthful wash down his parched throat. He made to have another swig, then thought, "This bottle is all I've got left, better make it last." He returned it to the folds of his clothing.

He was glad for the company of the dog. It didn't care who he was, what he had done, or where he was going. It didn't ask any questions or require any commitment. Friendship it gave without condition or hesitation. Something which humans never did.

He sighed and contemplated drawing out his bottle again but remembering how little he had left, decided against it. He leaned his head against the termite-ridden wood behind him and looked to the sky.

He gazed upon the white wisps of cloud dotted against a background of brilliant blue. The wisps lay like the last remnants of what was once a woven masterpiece, now forgotten and rapidly disintegrating into nothingness.

A wind began to blow again, and with it came a tidal wave of dust. He clenched his eyes against the onslaught until it passed. Finding that it was more comfortable with his eyes shut, he left them that way.

He was slowly being cut off from the outside world. First he lost his friends, then his job, then his possessions, then his girl and finally his home. Now he had lost care, and soon he expected he'd have nothing, not even his life. Closing his eyes and seeing only blackness made this easier to imagine.

As if to carry himself closer to this destination, he took out his bottle again. He felt the warmth of the glass for a moment, and then decided to get it over with. He unscrewed the cap and threw it to the dog.

The cap hit the ground before the dog with a small puff of dust. Its ears pricked up at the notion of food, whereupon it prodded the cap with its nose. Confirming its suspicions, it tested the cap with its tongue. Discouraged, it scrambled onto four legs and trotted away.

He brought the bottle to his cracked lips and drained its contents without stopping. A burning flood of liquor charged down his gullet and into his stomach to assault the digestive acids that lay there. The rush of alcohol irritated his dry throat, and soon he was coughing. He feared he would bring it up again, and waste the last of what he had, but managed to contain the swamp of vomit that rushed up his throat.

He gasped, so that was it. It was all gone, he had

nothing left now except an empty bottle. He held the bottle gingerly in his hand and gently tipped it, watching the last, tiny trickle run down the bottle bed to the mouth. He let it run its course, and watched it swell at the lip. A drop began to form and then was gone.

The drop hit the ground and vanished into a cloud of dust.

Like his life.

*　　*　　*

Now the other three: Release, Defeat and Lost, looked to Defiance who was yet to speak and tell his story.

Defiance did speak, but what he said was perhaps not what they had expected to hear.

"It would be easy for me to attribute negativity to these stories, and see them as horrible tales of mortal sorrow. But as you pointed out Lost, it is all part of experience, and to not learn from it is to deny your own growth. I too, as you did Defeat, found the world to be driven by power and control. For a while I lived in that world, and then in my own death I found that ultimate power I had always been seeking. It was what you found Release, freedom. For whatever others do, whatever they say, think or believe, you ultimately choose what you want to do, what you want to think and believe. And this is never taken away or lost, however it may seem.

But I'll tell my story later, for now there is someone else who wants to speak and tell us of their story..."

The four at the table turn to us now, for we are that fifth identity Defiance is referring to.

Now it is time for us to speak, to tell our tale, and reflect on where we have been, what we have experienced and what we have learnt.

There are many tales we could tell, for as one and as many, like any, like all, we have experienced and been many things. We have been on stage with the band Elemental, we have danced in darkness with the Devil, we have faced God, seen the face of Truth, met Death, met the eternal Joker, met Edwin, met the writer and those around him and dwelt in many of his lives and experiences. We could tell them of beginnings, of meeting Caraline and Lana for the first time, of how this current part of the journey began, of voyages of ultimate light, or journeys through endless darkness. We can tell of everything or we could tell of nothing. It is our choice.

And of course what we tell is only how we experienced it, and not how it is to someone else who also experienced it. Our experiences are incomplete in their completeness, as many or as one. For there is always (Ever)more.

*   *   *

Now the four identities are discussing where we should go next.

Lost leans towards us, "If you're not sure where you should go next, let me suggest you become **THE ASCENDING** (page 365). Release will take you there."

"Yes, I would like you to come with me," Release says, "I think you're ready." She smiles at us.

"I think you have journeyed long enough," Defiance

says, "If you want to know the master plan, you should become **THE CREATOR** (page 349)."

Finally Defeat speaks, "Perhaps you're not ready for these things, or not seeking them. Perhaps then, you are **THE INCOMPLETE** (page 401)."

The four faces of truth, that are really only four of the infinitely many faces of truth, look to us, waiting to hear what we have to say, what I have to say, what *you have to say.*

For what they are saying to us, to me, to you, is...

"Be then."

THE HEAVEN BOUND

THE HEAVEN BOUND

Hang on a minute... what's happened here?

Where am I now? How come I can't see anything?

Am I dead? Is this it?

I can think, but I can't see...

Whoh hang on... something's missing here. But I don't know what. How come I don't even know what it is? How do I know that anything's even missing? Maybe this is it.

Who am I then and where am I?

Why do I seem to have a sense of having been something, and having been somewhere, and of doing something, ...and now I don't? Is that what's missing?

I think it must be, though I don't know what this 'I' or this 'is' is.

And now I sense something, something... else.

I don't think it's me, it's something... how do I describe it? It's so beautiful, so touching, a resonance, a presence. A feeling, a warmth of a nature I don't understand.

And it's over there... in front of me.

I see a vibration in space before me, one that seems to be manifesting into something I can see.

Something I can touch, something that has already touched me.

It looks like a person. Yes, that's what it is. He, or so it seems to me, is holding something, he's making the chords that vibrate through me, the chords that resonate with my soul.

I see now, he's playing a guitar, an acoustic guitar. Now I understand. He's sitting by this cool misty stream, on a rock I think, yes, it must be a rock. And singing.

He's singing my song.

"And now here comes a stranger, out from the blue
He looks at me strangely, like he was new
New to the song, new to life, new to me and you
I think I'll sing him a tune, so welcoming and true
For I can see he's travelled far, and seen much
He's been seeking to know the truth, and with it he's lost
*   touch*
But he remembers something; he knows something's
*   amiss*
Sit down with me my friend, and I will show you bliss
Relax your mind, put up your feet
Have some of my bread and wine, I can see you're beat
I don't claim to know where you've been
I don't claim to know what it is that you've seen
But I can see that you've sought, found and learnt
But I can also see that you've fallen, been lost and burnt
Whatever it was that was, let it be
You've found a friend here stranger, and that friend is me..."

I fell next to him weary, weary of all that was, or had been. I listened to his words, and took faith in them, what little faith I had left, and fell asleep there. Contented. In the company of him, the rock, and the stream; dreaming of home and a place to belong...

When I awoke from the dream, I was to see that the dream was true. I had come home, and it was here that I belonged. Perhaps I had thought that my friend would no longer have been there, but he was. Watching over me, looking after me, loving me.

"I have always been with you friend, and always will be. Wherever you go, whatever you do, whatever you become, I'll be there, I'll be here; just as I have always been.

"Worry no more soldier, lay your feet at mine, rest your eyes and sleep some more, you need it. You're safe here, you've found home again."

I watched the light playing on the waves and swirls of the stream, soothed by its childish knowing gurgles. Then my gaze sunk beneath the surface and I found peaceful sleep, alone and unloved no more. Warm in the arms of understanding, nurtured in the cradle of love. The light of truth all around me, and his son there to accompany me. The pain, the hurt, the longing, the misunderstanding, the guilt and regret. All of these washed down the stream and out of my consciousness. Leaving me only with light and happiness and contentment.

Leaving me with all I needed, and all I wanted.

Love...

*   *   *

An old and dead man sat upon a hill and reflected that he was a man who was old and dead and that he sat upon a hill and reflected all of these things. And then he reflected that these things he reflected were mere reflections of what was real and not real themselves. As any thought was a mere reflection, he thought that he could not achieve enlightenment, a true understanding of reality, through what was by reflection alone. Beyond mere reflection, he had to experience.

And then it came to be that another came unto him; or so it may have seemed, for this other did indeed climb the hill to where this old and dead man sat.

Upon reaching him the other said unto him in a voice reflecting humility not unkind, "I came not in begging, but in asking."

The old man looked down upon the other, or so it may have seemed for the other was indeed still below him, and reflected, "What is it then that you ask for?"

The other fell prostrate on the ground, and admitted, "I come not asking of something, but asking of nothing."

The old man reflected again, saying, "You come to ask nothing, yet you seem to expect something. Tell me how this is so and you may have my company a little longer."

"True, Lord," the other said looking up at the old man, "May I call you such?" The old man nodded, and the other continued, "I ask nothing, but I will accept whatever it is that I am given. For I am a poor being who has much wealth and fame back in the material world, but this is nothing which constitutes my soul, only my current identity. Hence I have nothing myself to give."

The old man was silent for a time, he thought and reflected and experienced for a while, and then he smiled. "You come to me carrying life, surely that is something, would you give me that?"

The other, not wanting to show disobedience, proclaimed with bowed head, "If my Lord wants it, I shall give it to him, though it is not mine."

The old man now laughed, and laughing he drew out a sword that others had brought him as a gift in return for his wisdom. Though he did not want it, he had accepted it, never thinking that it would find a use, except to bring pleasure to those who had given it. Yet here now was a use.

Holding the sword aloft over the other's shaven head, the old and dead man of the hill said again, "If I wish you to give up your life now to the cut of my sword, you would do so willingly as we speak?"

Looking up with reverent eyes that were too blinded to even recognise that the fabled sword was that of her soul companion, the other said, "If you wish to have this body it is yours, it is nothing to do with the soul within, and I know this. Without this body, I will incarnate again to a time deemed fit, to carry on the purpose I served in this body. It is not something I have or am, merely something I have come to experience, so its loss means nothing to me. As I say to you again, I have nothing to give, hence nothing to lose."

The old and dead man upon the hill chuckled softly as he withdrew the blade. He then answered the other in poem, stating first, "Let me tell you of the meaninglessness of nothing, and why it is not. Then perhaps, you will have another jigsaw piece to existence.

"Nothing was never there, for nothing never was.
Nothing simply isn't, there is no 'because'.

Nothing will never be, nor has ever been.
Nothing is just nothing, do you see what I mean?
Nothing came from nowhere, a place that doesn't exist,
But yet within our minds, this idea of nothing does persist.
So how do you talk of nothing, if it was never there?
The answer is you don't, it doesn't stand to bear.
Nothing isn't even nothing, for surely that is something;
A word, a noun, a concept we invented, much confusion
  did it bring.
Nothing is just   , or isn't should I say?
And so in the realm of   ,   is bound to
  stay."

The other, in thinking that he was rich in wisdom and she comparatively poor, answered, "Apologies my Lord, but what I meant is that I have nothing which I can offer you. For you are great, and I – I am small, though yearning to grow."

He smiled again and said, "You have experienced and learnt much, I think. But, like me, you still have much to learn. You may remain with me for a time and experience and learn some of what I have to give you. And though you shall be my pupil, I will also gain and learn much from you. For you have experienced and learned many things that I have not. And a mind that says it has no more to experience or learn, is a closed one, and is ready to die; just as one that says it has experienced and learnt nothing is.

"Yet a time shall indeed come when we must again go our separate ways. There will be sadness at this, as there always is with change, but I am not you and you are not me. We travel on different journeys, and though our paths have here met and we may make good company for each other, we would only be restricting each other's ultimate growth if we were to stay together out of habit until our journey's end."

It was those last words that she grappled with most. She could understand him speaking modestly of his accomplishments, but the flat way in which he spoke of eventually departing, disturbed her. They were not words spoken with pity or cruelty, they were words said without tone or inflection of any sort. It was a matter-of-fact statement, detached and distant. She began to realise what it was that the words lacked and looked into his calm face to see if she could find it there.

The old and dead man regarded her intense expression that was studying his, with some degree of puzzlement. Finding that he was unable to fathom what her alien thoughts could possibly be, he turned away to let his mind wander over the lands of the Zarrieyue temple. Noting as he did so, though not sure whether he caused it, that the orientation of the Evermore had shifted a little.

Something amazing must have happened, so great in proportions that its aftermath had sent ripples of change through all space-time, consciousness and conception. And such tidal waves of transformation could only mean one thing...

A new age is beginning.

And now she looks back at him, puzzled by him too. Is he human? Does he have any feelings at all? Looking at his turned-away face, being so close to his greatness she feels such warmth, such longing to be with him. But understand him she cannot. Does he feel for her at all? Is she anybody to him? Will she ever be? Has anybody ever been? Probably once, maybe twice, but that she suspects had been long ago, when his soul had been young and free and not yet hurt by life.

A strange buzz passes over him. He cannot place it, and his best efforts fail to analyse it. But strangely it is familiar. He tries to remember when he had come across these thoughts before, and realises that it must have been many, many years ago. Back in a time he usually only recalls with pain. A life of richness that he has forgotten. He then wonders a strange thing, and grins at the ridiculousness of it. But the thought remains, and with it the curiosity. He realises that he must seek an answer to his questions, or forever be bound in his empty reflections.

She notices a smile cross his face, and begins to grow warm again with hope. Wanting oh so eagerly, to reach out to him, to touch him, even to comfort him. But still he does not look at her, instead he sits and gazes away across other worlds, and says nothing at all. She wants to say something to him, but doesn't know what to say. How can she say anything to him? Will he even understand? Oh, why is this so hard!

As he makes his resolution, he begins to experience something else again, something anciently familiar. A strange discomfort in his stomach, a hesitation in his decision. He rationalises that neither the discomfort nor the hesitation should be there. It is without reason. And yet, in even greater perplexity, it still remains. An illogical manifestation in his stomach, which only grows worse the more he thinks about it or thinks why he should not think about it. He deduces the sensation in his stomach to be something like pain. Knowing how long it has been since he has even experienced bodily sensations like pain or ecstasy, he begins to doubt his assessment as one born of inexperience. It becomes stronger as he realises that it is not something caused by his thoughts, or controlled by them. It is something he thought he had long ago 'evolved beyond', yet here now he is helplessly within the grips of and unable to escape from.

He is nauseous with fear.

Staring for long, unbearable moments into his glazed eyes, she searches his expression for signs of life. Unaware of his internal struggle, she begins to feel unwanted and alone. What is she doing here? Why did she come? Is he really the one that her heart has led her to? Why, why must this ordeal continue? Misery becomes her now, as her warmth dissipates.

Suddenly he hears her, and feels immediately an overwhelming sorrow. Removed of thought, he begins to hurt with regret. How far has he come, only to forget a most fundamental part of human existence? And now she is crying next to him and though he wants to externalise it and distance himself from it, he cannot. Or will not allow himself to, however much he can rationalise the decision to do so. Should he comfort her? Should he say something? His feat becomes the awkwardness of embarrassment, fumbling uncomfortably with confused thoughts and emotions long forgotten. He realises what a baby he really is in the world of experience. And that must be what he is here to learn from her; to learn what it is to hurt, to fear, to worry, to hate, to regret, to wish, to laugh, to smile, to tingle, to love. But the fear he experiences in knowing that the alien world of feelings is where he must now go crushes all his confidence and reduces him to the babbling imbecile that he is.

Sobbing freely, she can contain her desire no longer. She looks at him again to see his shudder. She can see his confusion, his hesitation, his embarrassment and fear, all swelling up in him and rocking him about. Wiping away the tears, and looking at him with love, she says, "Look at me."

Slowly, awkwardly, yet now with the growing warmth of joy to be with her, his saviour, he does.

"My gift is you," says she to her companion.

And to this, her companion answers with love, "Your gift is yourself."

The sun lit their faces and the hillside with revelation and glory...

They were both right.

*   *   *

I awoke a third time and everything was different. For now I seemed more aware of who I was and where I had been.

I had travelled far, further perhaps than I had intended to. And in so doing, I had forgotten where I had started from. I had forgotten my way home.

I had lost all feeling for others in the struggle for

myself, I had lost all sense of camaraderie in my quest to win. I had become dissociated from my own emotions and those of others for the confusion of thoughts that they had brought. I had seen them as fruitless by-products of consciousness, as inhibitors to be overcome on the path to enlightenment. Like enlightenment was all that mattered, as opposed to life itself, and feeling.

No more.

My friend returned to the campsite, where I lay in the bed he had made. He carried a book.

My book, the one you're reading now.

"You had been holding this when I found you again. What is it?" he asked.

"Oh... that."

"No friend, I won't laugh at you. What is it?"

"Oh, just a book of rhymes and shit."

He looked at me for a moment and then said, "Well, it obviously meant more to you once than it does now."

Overcome with sorrow I answered, "It did."

I had lost faith in what had been most important to me, what I had seen as the innermost foundation of myself. It was all eroding away... into nothing.

"Let it go," he said to stop me before my depressive thoughts carried me too far. "Acknowledge it as something that had been important to you, that you had to grow through, and then let it go."

I began to cry.

He stood up, and carried my book to the stream. He beckoned me over.

I shook my head, sobbing, "I can't!"

"Come and stand here friend and take the book, and

throw it as far as you can downstream. The pain I can see it has caused you is just too much. It's not worth it... let it go."

I got to my feet, and instantly wanted to sit back down. Should I now repress thoughts for the sake of emotions? I stood there, overburdened. I didn't know what to do.

Let it go.

I reached the stream finally, and took the book from his hands, *Evermore: An Introduction*, and looked downstream.

How could I be doing this?

Let it go.

But I'm still writing, when will it end?

Let it go.

But it's not just the book; it's my life's experiences. It's never having had a father, it's my unsympathetic mother, it's how the women in my life have fucked me up, it's the drugs. It's everything!

Let it go.

I turned to him with the book and said, "You do it. I can't."

"It's not my book to throw away. It's yours. You must do it."

Still holding the book, I hesitated, still hanging on, as if to let it go, would be letting go of everything. Everything I had ever believed, ever wanted to do.

"I want to finish it," I said.

"Then will you throw it away?"

"I, I, I don't know."

"What do you feel you want to do?"

I thought for a moment and then stopped myself. For

one of the first times ever in my life I let my emotions speak, I said what I felt. I said what I wanted to say, instead of what I wanted to believe.

"I want to finish the book for what it represents to me. And then I want to publish it for what I think it can offer. But then I want to turn my back on it, and walk away. It was just too painful, too horrible and sad…"

"Then finish it and let it go."

"But, if I do," I burst into tears again, "people will think I'm crazy or they'll expect me to be strong and be a leader. And if I don't finish it, then I'll be nothing. I'll never be able to live with myself, knowing that I've failed!"

"Listen to me friend, I've been in a situation I would say far worse but in reality probably very similar to yours, and the answer is simple."

"What's that?" I said, trying to see him through a blur.

"Do you want to give up on the book?"

"No."

"Do you want to be seen as crazy, or be made into a great leader?"

"No."

"Then finish the book, and be done with it. Speak your heart on the way you feel, so that others can understand, and then let it go."

"But others won't understand! Maybe some will, but most won't. They'll still either see me as one or the other."

"Then you've tried your best and that's all you can do. You can't change others, but you can change yourself. If you have bared you innermost feelings to them, and they still don't understand… then that's all you can do."

I held the book tightly and blinked away the hurt, hurt that was still there, and saw that he was right.

Let it go.

And then I heard a great sound approaching over the horizon like thunder. It was a feeling like a great tidal wave of relief, and the more aware of it I was, the faster it approached. It washed over me, releasing me of all perception, thoughts and burdens. Rolling me over and over like a daisy in the breeze.

Carrying me onward to a better place.

*　　*　　*

If we are ready to complete our journey, let us become **THE VICTORIOUS** (page 317), and we will learn what it is to 'win'.

Or perhaps we should instead begin our journey anew, with renewed focus, as **THE INCOMPLETE** (page 401).

...But if we seek to understand what this book is, let us turn to **THE CREATOR** (page 349).

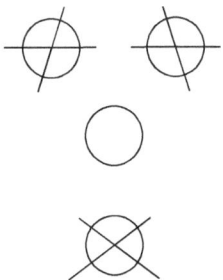

THE HELL BENT

THE HELL BENT

"Welcome to hell... what do you think?"

I looked around. Darkened room, candle-lit, discordant drumming music barely perceptible in the background, an array of paintings depicting war and women and demons splayed around the walls.

Hang on...

I haven't gone anywhere – I'm still in my fucking room!

"That's right, you're in the real world, or what is hell to you. The world of meaninglessness and blind conformity. The world where you don't have a choice and you don't make a difference. The world where you must do as others and strive for social status and wealth. The world where you judge others and you only care about yourself. The world where to place trust in others is foolish, to do so is only to allow oneself to be taken advantage of. Here to be honest and open is merely stupid. Others don't appreciate you and they won't listen. This is because fundamentally they don't care about you, so nor should you about them. They've got their own priorities and needs, and if they seem nice and good-willed this is only because that's how they want to be seen. We all wear cloaks of deception when really we are demons of lust and aggression. Don't be naive and say that human nature is but anything else. The aim of all our actions, no matter how noble the cause, is power and control. Nothing has changed."

No, no, no, this is all wrong. The world isn't like this... and nor is hell!

"There is no hell worse for you than this. A hell with demons and fire and Satan upon a dark throne ordering minions and subjecting victims to differing torments, for all the horrific experiences that it would put you through would at least have one thing this world lacks."

What's that?

"Meaning. A purpose, a point to it all. Hell means there is a God, there is a heaven, there is somewhere to strive not to end up in, there is something to strive for. But here... in the real world, there's nothing. Life is nothing except what you can make of it. What's the point of morals or ideals if these are just human fabrications to satisfy our desire to know that there is meaning to our existence? In the real world you give up on shit like that for the folly that it is. Don't worry about others, worry only about yourself. Think about it, what do you gain by helping others, what do *you* gain? Nothing. And those who realise this are those who prosper, using others to their advantage, only extending those things called 'love' and 'care' where it's of benefit to them. Open your eyes and realise that that's how it is."

So why are you telling me this if you don't care?

"Because it's of benefit to me, nothing more."

And why are you being so honest to tell me that?

"You don't get it, do you? You're still stuck in your fantasy of goodwill being within everybody, and that it's there at some fundamental level. Do you see intrinsic goodwill in any other living thing? Does a lion rape a lioness mistakenly thinking that he's giving her a good time? No, he wants a fuck, and doesn't really give a shit what she thinks. Do trees give off oxygen because they're doing us a favour? Fuck no, oxygen is a waste product to them that they're just getting rid of."

But they're just plants and animals, surely we're better that that?

"No, we just think of bigger things. Because our brains are bigger, we think we must be more important. We try to hide from ourselves what we are; because we're ashamed, like we want to believe we've advanced beyond that. We've all got DNA though, every single fucking living thing, and our human DNA chain is far from the longest and most complex. We've all got hormones and experience aggression and lust like everything else; and anyone who says that they don't feel these things is a far bigger liar than the rest of us. They're even lying to themselves."

I don't know what to say.

"Don't say anything, it's just the way it is. And there's nothing you or I or anyone else can do about it. Nothing has changed, nor ever will. Look at these walls, what do you see? Lust and aggression. Listen to that music – lust and aggression. It penetrates every level of society no matter what walls you build. You have an underlying perception of its presence and yet you still try to fool yourself."

But most music, paintings and literature aren't about lust and aggression.

"Those which are will always be successful, because

they appeal to the most basic and fundamental of instincts. Those which aren't, are merely for the ego boost of the creators and/or money and/or fame; all for the power and control it brings. And of course, it is these which are often more successful, as they appeal to what we *want* to believe.

"Those who say they don't want power and control only want to believe that. They want to feel good about themselves, so they give and love and tell others of the light and the truth for the way it makes them feel. They want power and control over themselves, and fundamentally they only care about themselves. But to acknowledge that they only care about themselves wouldn't make them feel good, so they hide this awareness from themselves too.

"Realise that this is just the way it is, and it doesn't matter how much you rationalise, search, think, discuss and convince yourself. *This is just the way it is.*"

I've been here before... it's horrible, more horrible than anything I have ever imagined. Meaninglessness, empty reality, devoid of spirit or purpose. Hell is the real world.

"Now, are you going to sit back and philosophise, fabricate a purpose, and tell others that there is another way, wasting your breath, giving away your life? Or are you going to accept that this is the way things are, start putting yourself first, and get as much as you can before the world ends?"

Before the world ends?

"Don't look so surprised. It's inevitable. Human nature is bound to bring about its own destruction. We're still killing each other, arguing with each other, killing the world around us, and striving for power and control and personal benefit like we always have. This world is old; it's near its time. We've only been here 200,000 years; the dinosaurs outlasted us at least a hundred-fold. What then has our intelligence done of benefit to us? When our world's long gone and dead, others will rise up and make the same mistakes, even on other planets. Wherever, whenever, however; and they'll all end the same way. And do you know why?"

Why?

"Because only the strong survive. And eventually those which were strong are succeeded by something even stronger in the new, ever-changing circumstances. That's nature's law. The law of evolution. The law of the universe. Namby-pamby nice animals that don't put themselves first and don't use others to help them get what they want, don't survive. Evolution weeds out the weak, it doesn't have compassion, it doesn't try to rationalise or think 'what about being nice to everyone for a change'. And we got to where we are because we're no different. Not just humans as a species, but within humans the most violent and power-hungry are the ones who prosper best."

You mean Western Society?

"Exactly. 'Political correctness' is just another way we're now trying to hide the truth we all know from ourselves. Western Society dominates the world because it conquered it. Christianity and the Church are no different: Crusades, Conversion... Conquest."

I think all your ideas stink, they jar me on every level,

they go against everything I've ever thought, believed and felt.

"That's because to acknowledge that I'm right and you're wrong would be to destroy you. It would hurl you into what is most unbearable for you. Meaninglessness. Lovelessness. Pointlessness. Purposelessness. No morals. No Gods. No ethics. Never..."

Stop it. Stop it.

"Sick of hearing the truth? Wanting to retreat back into the safety of blind, delusional naivety? Do what you want, tell yourself and convince yourself of what you wish, it won't make any difference. Accept or live in lies. And if you choose not to accept, don't ever call yourself open-minded or insightful. You're no different from religious fanatics."

I don't want to hear this anymore; I want to get out of here!

"Then do so, don't pray to me for salvation. Do it yourself, you're creating this. You want to stop it, so stop it. You wanted the truth, now you got it. If you didn't want to know, then you shouldn't have come."

Now I understand hopelessness and loss of faith, the root of suicide.

"Kill yourself if you want, but don't expect me to shed tears for you, or feel like it was my fault. All I did was tell you the way it is. If you can't handle it, that's your problem, not mine. Go back to where you came from, start afresh, pretend you never came here, become **THE WANDERER** (page 249) again."

Try not to die. Try not to cry. Try instead to lie.

306

*   *   *

"Well you're still here, and that's your choice not mine. You've told me about as many stories of fantasy and escapism, as I ever want to hear. Now let me tell you some real stories. Let me tell you stories about The Real World..."

I opened the book and saw it all, everything that had happened and was about to. Everything that had been written, and that which was yet to be. I didn't understand how, but even this very experience is written there before me. Written there; because I had written it. I don't understand how this can be so. I wrote what just happened? I don't even remember doing it, but somehow I know I wrote this. All of it. Did I become someone else? Maybe everyone else that's mentioned here I've been at one point or another in future and past, for I seem to know all the words, at least generally, that are here. And my thoughts now, my experience now, these very words that are coming into my head now as if it were the first time ever that they had been there, are here too... already written.

Has someone else been writing me?

Have I been them too?

What's going on?

Will my thoughts ever stop being on the page, seemingly before I even thought them?

Can I actually think something that won't be written down here?

What if I decide I won't read on unless when I turn the page it reads "The Explanation" and gives me one?

"The Explanation."

NOW SHUT THE FUCK UP AND KEEP READING.

How human consciousness protects itself.

The truth of our existence is indeed a horrifying thing, so horrifying in fact that we go to extreme lengths to hide ourselves from it and from others who find and proclaim it.

The adaptability and malleability of our consciousness, is indeed amazing, and incredibly effective at developing defensive mechanisms. And it has needed to be, or else we would be little more than anti-social animals, without ethics or morals or principles to uphold a society and system of justice. It is an evolutionary manifestation that because of its great success has progressively weeded out those who stand against it and threaten its stability. And hence in the same way that living things that produce physical adaptations to their physical environment that increase their chance of survival are the ones that live to pass on their genetic program; human cultures that produce mental adaptations to their mental environment that increase their chance of survival are the ones that survive to pass on their message.

Consciousness cannot cope with the truth as it is, and sets out on the ambitious quest to find a truth that it can believe in and convince itself of, or else it accepts it for what it is and becomes 'evil'.

*Herein lies the reason why new ideas will always find acceptance somewhere, as within them is always hope that the truth has been found, and that we do not have to accept the horrible truth of what our existence really is. But here also lies the reason, somewhat paradoxically, why consciousness also tends to **not** accept new ideas* *and fabricate reasons why it should not, as this threatens the security of ideas already adopted and to acknowledge them as wrong is just too painful.*

It is like we are all trying to stay afloat on scattered lifeboats of fabricated truth in a raging, hostile sea of confusion. To let go of these lifeboats we cling to, would cause us to drown under the weight of what our existence really is.

There is always the hope that in the midst of all of this, if we were able to leap across to another lifeboat, nearby to us, that we would find greater security there and be saved from our ultimate fate.

We are born on one lifeboat, and many of us are sheltered from ever seeing the sea around us by those sharing the same lifeboat. But if, as we grow older, we ever do become aware of our unstable, chaotic predicament, we either decide to cling to our lifeboat more than ever and shut out knowledge of the sea around, or desperately try to swim across to another lifeboat and upon reaching it, we do the same. Those who fall overboard and don't find safety fast, lose all faith, and drown in a sea of reality.

Over time we become more and more accustomed to the lifeboat we currently inhabit, and a leap across to another seems less and less inviting. We then convince ourselves that our lifeboat is safe and that the other lifeboats are not, and forever try to tell ourselves that the horrible sea around us will never claim us, or even that it does not exist at all. Eventually though, the sea claims every one of us, even entire lifeboats, and we sink beneath the sea never to rise again.

That the sea will eventually claim us we cannot deny, so we try to derive meaning and purpose from this also. For to acknowledge death for what it is, is also too horrifying, so we on our lifeboats strive to explain this away, earnestly seeking some proof and dogmatically believing in what fabrications we find.

At this point I thought about my own life, and the wanderer that I was. I was a part of this struggle like any other. Never satisfied with the lifeboat I inhabited, I threw myself into that horrible sea of confusion again and again, swimming furiously for another new lifeboat and weary each time I emerged. What I did learn and see in the truths on each lifeboat gave me strength to push on, but always being aware of that sea around me and the instability of the lifeboat I was on. I set off on my own again across that fearsome water, as unsatisfied but as determined as before. Knowing that I had but limited time before I too was claimed, I had now begun to build my own lifeboat. Constantly making trips to both old and new lifeboats in the process, in the hope of building one that was secure and would last like so many had tried before and seemingly failed. Naively perhaps, thinking that there was a way.

Why human consciousness must protect itself.

Consciousness in the advanced manifestation that we see in humans is a social phenomenon too, a linked group occurrence that led to the creation of not only person- alised defence mechanisms but also to collective defence mechanisms in terms of social structures.

These social structures have been very effective in protecting the masses from witnessing the truth, for to witness the truth as it is would see the destruction of the structures humankind has laboured so hard to establish and maintain, particularly the foundation of these structures; religion; thus purpose, meaning, ethics and morals. Destruction of this foundation would have catastrophic consequences not only for the wellbeing of our personal and collective consciousness, but also the very genetic survival of the human race. Without these elaborate and highly effective defence mechanisms, the human species would decay into anarchical chaos, which would rapidly lead us only to the extinction of our species.

For the light of truth, far from being an oasis of peaceful existence and comfort, is a burning inferno. To go in its direction is as blinding as it is nullifying, and to reach it causes one to become burned and permanently scarred. To remain there results only in destruction and nothing more. All is lost and consumed in a blinding, burning light that has no mercy, meaning or purpose. Instead we must move away from the truth with our backs turned, pushing ever onward towards our salvation into the darkness of delusion, that is lit only by our imagination. To not do this is to die as a collective consciousness, for this is what persists over time and generations and it is because we as a collective consciousness have done this that we have survived up until now, and why to survive, we must continue to do this...

There was but one line left on the page, on its own, and it said:

BE WHAT WE NOT, NOT WE WHAT BE.

*   *   *

I finished reading and closed the book, speechless. I didn't want to open it again. I didn't want to know any more of what it had to say. I regretted ever having read it in fact, better that I had never known the truth and been happy with what I had thought, than to see the most horrible of all things I had ever imagined. Reality.

I had been warned, but I had not taken the warning seriously. I had not expected anything as defeating as this.

And then I thought about what it said, and realised, heh it's just a fucking book. Some words this guy who felt hard done by in life and negative and angry at the world, had written down in some spiel. That's it. I began to think of all my own experiences and of those around me, and of the things about the world in general that I knew were true. All that stuff about 'defence mechanisms' and 'the truth of our existence' was all a bunch of crap! I didn't have to listen to that negative stuff at all. And what's more I'd be stupid to, because it wasn't true. Hah! Hah! What a joke! How human consciousness protects itself! ...What a load of absolute bullshit!

Then I heard laughing, and realised where I was. And then it spoke again...

"I never cease to be impressed just how effective the defence mechanisms of human consciousness are. And how quickly they come into effect to protect human consciousness from what is most horrible.

"Even now you are re-digesting what you have read and what I have told you, re-evaluating it in a way that makes it more comfortable to deal with. I can read your thoughts like you read this book, and I watched with bemusement how uncomfortable you found the truth, and how quickly your defence mechanisms came into effect to protect you."

It's just your words, your thoughts, not mine.

"I have answers to your answers, words of truth to destroy your delusions. That you only try to re-express the meaning of my words to make them unbelievable to you, only proves my point. All you can do is acknowledge that I'm right and forever be persecuted and suppressed by a society that protects itself against the truth, or run from the truth and keep running."

But couldn't I say the same of any other belief, that it can't be refuted if one says that any attempts to refute it are only because one does not want to accept it?

"Indeed this is true – any theory or philosophy can be justified in this manner, as can any counter-argument to it. And it is for this reason that the products of consciousness; thoughts, ideas, beliefs; are not ways to access the truth for they are all fabrications to satisfy our desires and none are more justified than any other. Discard them, and you are left with nothing but the bare, naked truth of our existence. And then you will see what purpose consciousness has served; and why as an evolutionary manifestation, it has perpetuated the survival of the human race until now."

And why it must continue to do so, in order for the human race to continue to survive.

"And if it doesn't, then it isn't worthy of having survived. It will be eradicated as per the law of evolution, and other more successful species will carry on."

Why is it that I can't think of anything to say to that to prove you wrong? though I know there must be?

"Because it's the truth, and not what you want the truth to be. In a short time you will leave here and rapidly convince yourself that this is not the truth, and reach desperately for a small fragment of anything else to earnestly believe in and hide from my words. Cling to that lifeboat you must, or swim to another quickly... or else drown and die as evolution dictates."

Sigh

"Yes, it is hard to deal with for most, though many have accepted it. Find something else to believe in and dwell there, do not return unless you are willing to drown or burn."

So where is it that I go now then?

"Hah! Hah! There is only one choice for you now that I can see. And that is to become **THE DESCENDING** (page 383). There you must go, that is the path you must take... to survive."

To survive?

"Unless you choose to burn, in which case you should become **THE ASCENDING** (page 365)."

Ascending sounds better than Descending...

"It's all relative to where you are; what you perceive is important; and how you interpret the words, including these words now.

"So choose then."

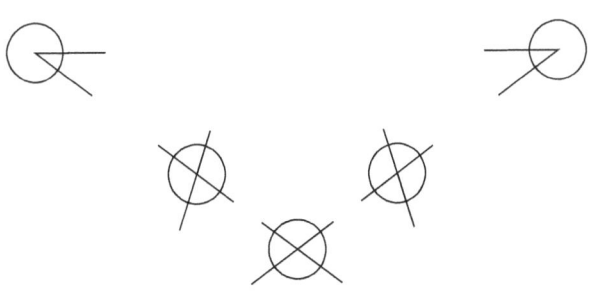

THE VICTORIOUS

THE VICTORIOUS

Alone somewhere, upon the forbidden peak of Llihanoi in the vast lands of the Zarrieyue temple, a granite boulder, fostered in the shadow of a sheer moss-clad cliff face, upon which the great king and seer Mommen-child had once sat and dreamed of the Star Stellar, dislodged itself and plundered down into the smoky valley below where the people of the flame danced in the four elements of decay.

The great boulder, known to some as Si, crashed effort-lessly through the aspiring trunks of elder gums and flowering wattles, pillars of natural grandeur, and bounced through into the last habit of the grey *kingaroo*.

Between reeves of leaves it descended, zigzagging between earth-banked gullies, sending thunder and smoke, bird, lizard, insect and marsupial scattering in a cloud of murder.

Wrapped in mud, feathered fur and blood it came to rest at the door of ye most graceful, one of the most venerated members of the people of the flame ever to walk the shores of grief.

She approached Si with silent reverence and gently laid her palm upon its rugged but weeping surface. Its walls a mirror of its soul. A mirror that now reflected the one who looked upon it.

The tribe was to celebrate a ceremonial feast of the

food that Si had carried to the village that night, for the mystics without name had said that it must be done.

And so that night, upon green flames that caressed the constellation of the water-bearer, the meat of the upper valley that had been infused with the elements of Si crackled and sizzled and scattered its elements far and wide upon the winds of chaos, to later become incorporated into the element of water in the seas of perdition, and thus across the whole cosmos when a planet inevitably dies to be reborn elsewhere.

The people of the flame, became one with Si too, for in eating the meat that bore trace portions of the rock, they subsequently became part of Si.

And over time, the very structure of the rock itself began to break down and return to a lower state more akin to the Creator, for even granite has a lifespan measured in millions of years. Wind, rain, glacier and lava all wore away its sides, and from its elements the Siren, the most fantastic of all the birds of the planet Croverterantisha first evolved, and of these same elements Sargonerax the Enlightener was born.

Sargonerax the Enlightener was born of two revered heroes, Sarzoneraz the Invincible and Auriel the Luminary. Sarzoneraz is remembered as perhaps the greatest and certainly the most legendary of warriors in the songs of bards and tales of lore. It is said he was able to defeat death itself in duel. And Auriel was a famed enchantress and wise woman, whose immense powers stretched beyond the fabrics of reality and possibility and into the infinite meaning and paradox of the Evermore.

Sargonerax the Enlightener, and his fantastic crusade across endless stretches of lands, seas, minds and realities, will long be remembered until the number of generations his story has passed through is as grains of sand upon a beach. Some say that he lives and travels still, forever furthering his quest, never resting or becoming complacent in the light of his achievements. Some even say that he watches over us, consulting with those on the Other Side, quietly preparing for the day when we are ready for their return...

The day Sargonerax came to be widely known is immortalised in numerous texts across the Evermore, yet it was only much later that he was ascribed the title of Enlightener.

We shall read now from the aptly named, Grand Book of Truth (a book which will never be written in entirety) and experience a historical account of what transpired that day.

(pg. 506, chap. 47, volume 4387)

In a wide sweeping hall of marbled mahogany and orchestras of orchids singing a symphony of colours and scents, were gathered an impressive collection of players, both ancient and masters of the greatest game of all.

The architecture and craftsmanship of the hall were spectacular. Remarkable sculptures, artistic and abstract designs laced with gold, gemstones and platinum decorated the ceiling and walls. The sheer burst of inspiration the experience of the place invoked, hurled one's imagination beyond the rigid borders of possibility and space-time and into the infinite realm. But it was the events that took place there, on three separate occasions, that were to cause gigantic ripples throughout the fabric of the Evermore of a proportion rarely seen or experienced – except of course on the Other Side.

"We are gathered here today," the first speaker said, "to honour the greats of our time and their achievements. For without these men and many others like them, who regretfully could not be here with us now, we would be a poor breed. It is their efforts and contributions alone that shine against the backdrop of humanity like stars across the panorama of the brilliant night sky. We elevate these men to the level of gods, and reward them with the praise that they are due. Names such as Aplet Jasurera, Mechi Desarc, Aswent Canoi, Rasteil Neibert, Teri Voats, Res Dectesa, Hitez Cens and Yilut Pharnam, but to name a few, have become the household staple of the educated and worldly, and it is they who have set down the pathway for the wise to follow and further their work. Tonight the elite gather together and acknowledge their heroic status, as pillars of society to be revered. Let whole nations stop and listen to our words, for we alone hold the secrets to our existence."

The speaker stepped down gallantly from the gloriously gaudy podium, as the floor of senior gentlemen in respectful attire erupted into the raucous hurrah of clapping hands.

Order was quick to assume control however, as the next of the elite class of intellectualists took the lectern and delivered in their own language, a speech of reinforcement and reassurance that the change would never come.

Sargonerax the Enlightener, a master of change and disguise, joined their celebrations as if he were one of them. He listened to their words as speech followed speech, but his heart was not with them. Indeed he could sense that many others here could feel it too. This elite engine of science was quickly growing too old for its wheels. The masses that followed the trail it had blazed were losing faith in its abilities. They were beginning to look over their shoulders and wonder where this machine had led them, dissatisfied with the sacrificial offerings of technology. The masses were becoming restless and beginning to see flaws in their master's words.

For so long, the engine drivers had succeeded in protecting their place in society by ensuring that only the privileged were able to understand the confusing jargon of science and philosophy. And privilege meant having money, which meant having social status, which is why they were safe from the non-educated flock. Inside their impermeable bubbles the elite told themselves of their greatness and looked around their bubbles at how grand things were.

But the masses were beginning to pick up the pieces the drivers had not wanted found, and understand what they meant. The power of knowledge was no longer in the intellectualists' hands alone, and with it, their engine was losing its place.

It was quite some time, before the intellectualists acknowledged that their age was coming to an end. For though the masses, who had once been following behind, saw it, the man-made institutions of science, philosophy and religion were blind to how misguided their efforts had become. Science had succumbed to the gadgets of technology; philosophy the obscure, circular arguments of logic and terminology; and religion the out-of-touch doctrines of pragmatism and method.

For so long there had been those rising from the masses, in ever-increasing numbers to join the ranks of the institutions, to tell of their folly and remind them of the purpose for which their engines had originally been erected. And for so long they had been laughed at, and even thought crazy, but now instead of in ones and twos, they were coming forth from the masses in the hundreds and thousands.

But the deep impression, both positive and negative, that their age left, would remain long after their fathers were gone. And some say, that only once their impact had become almost completely undetectable was their age over.

We shall now listen to some of the words that were spoken that day, words which echoed throughout the great hall and shook the foundations of the Evermore. Words that spoke both of the end and the new beginning...

Words, which have transcended time, space, reality and form, to be the words that you are reading now.

Quien took the lectern with a few quick strides that suggested importance and urgency. "I will be brief and blunt with you fellows," he announced. "I think that the time has passed when we could be complacent about our steps forward."

Already there was unease breaking out among them. His loud words were heard by all and there was a disquieting note to them that the more conservative members present especially, did not like. Quien noted the rustling and the mumbling, but he carried on, his message steadily gaining momentum.

"And nor will I insist on using the rich language that for so long we have fostered and cultivated into something which only the privileged understand."

The unease grew further, a backlash against the opposer.

"Put simply fellows, we are in deep shit."

The resultant mood became one of silence, shocked silence. If ever Quien lacked the floor's full attention before, he certainly had it now. Two of the more senior gentlemen rose to leave in disgust at the use of such base language. Near the front, there burst the sound of one unable to contain his laughter.

Sargonerax the Enlightener, sat in silence, waiting tensely for the moment that he knew was fast approaching...

Quien paused for a second, as the wave washed over his audience. A couple of disgruntled traditionalists made to voice objections, but he raised a firm hand to indicate that it was still his turn to speak. And, despite a brewing anger, those in the audience who wished to express their outrage chose to maintain their listening silence, thus honouring the exalted code of the intellectuals.

"These are bold and brash times, and bold and brash words are necessary. And besides, I put the point better and more clearly, than any long-winded, elegantly expressed string of terms could have hoped to do. I say again, in case you didn't hear or understand me the first time; **we are in deep shit**."

A second wave of outrage crashed through the opposition, dislodging many who chose to make physical expressions of their disapproval by either standing and calling for him to desist, or just simply leaving. Quien fought to be heard above angry voices who had no wish to hear any more of his words.

"There are so many things here that need addressing, it is hard to know where to begin."

He smiled then, watching as the calm returned. "Beginnings. There's one word we know little about."

Again he paused, allowing the words time to sink in. Noticing those in the audience itching to voice their objections.

"And Knowledge itself. What it means to 'know' something. And Meaning too. What it is also escapes us."

Now he grinned. He licked his lips, he had control.

"For all we know, all of these things: Beginnings, Knowledge and Meaning, may merely be products of our own Consciousness and nothing more. And Consciousness, one of the great taboo terms of Science, we also know so little about."

Gently massaging his words into his audience a little at a time, he stopped again, subduing the expectant rejections, and then proceeded.

"We have 'known' for a long time – if you'll permit me to use such a word – that 'true' knowledge in the sense that we use it is simply impossible. To know something with complete one-hundred percent certainty, entails that we know all the relevant facts pertaining to it, which entails that we know all facts, as only then could we begin to decide which facts are and aren't relevant. We could never even know if we knew all facts, as we would only know that there was a fact we didn't know of, when we knew of it.

"All this serves to show is that we can never have Objective Knowledge. We can only have Subjective Knowledge in terms of the limitations we put upon it, and the limitations of those limitations."

"Haaaa," he sighed.

"This means," he laughed, "that things like 'Meaning' and 'Truth' and therefore everything from 'Beginnings' to 'Numbers' to 'Perceptions'," he laughed again, "are inferred assumptions made on the basis of our consciousness and no more. Our minds are geared towards pattern recognition. Patterns which may not necessarily exist except within our own mind, and upon this alone we base all Knowledge, Perception and extrapolation of Meaning.

"We seem to forget this when we go in pursuit of further knowledge to build upon our foundations. For indeed it is true that we have learnt and achieved much, and within the so-called glorious framework or paradigm of Science we may achieve much more. But to assume that our foundations are invincible, and to disregard everything that lies outside and in contradiction to these foundations, is to forget the fundamental thing that we as scientists, philosophers and theologians or otherwise are searching for."

He looked around his audience again, and read expressions of irritation and condemnation, but also in isolated pockets he sensed the presence of sympathy and even acceptance.

Nearing an end, he continued, "I shouldn't need to remind you all of what this is. But, though it is utterly patronising, I feel compelled to."

"Truth," said a voice, and suddenly all eyes were upon its source.

It was Teri Voats, respected head of the vast assembly, father of the Science that was. He now rose, and Quien took a step back, allowing the interruption to proceed.

"We know what we seek," Teri said in his rich, lordly voice. "And we know that we don't know everything. And we know that whatever we do know is only true until disproved; and that it can never be proven. And yes, we know, Quien, that to know itself, is only what 'seems'. And 'seeming' therefore, is what we must necessarily base knowledge on; for far from wishing to be subjective and possibly wrong, we are applying the tools we have in the safest, surest way possible."

"It is well that you know these things, Teri... but do your people?" returned Quien.

Teri frowned, "They should. And if they don't, they ought to listen."

To this, Quien laughed, laughed hard. "And do you listen to them?"

Feeling slightly threatened by such a question as this, in such an important public appearance as this, Teri answered, "Yes, I do. When I need to."

"When you need to, heh?" Quien said, about to elaborate, but was denied the opportunity.

"Look, Quien, I have no intention of being the centre of some damned witch-hunt of yours. You've had your say; you've made your point. Now for Xod's sake, and all our sakes, sit down and stop this apparent sabotage of this meeting or I'll be forced to fully use the powers of my station and order you and your rabble from this building."

Resolute, Quien proclaimed, "You can order me from this building if you so dare, but **YOU CANNOT MAKE US SILENT!**"

"So be it!" retorted Teri as he motioned him out.

"Open minds shall be the thorns you tread on!" Quien said to him in spite as he walked himself out of that great hall and into obscurity and neglect.

Then there was a number, unknown to any who were still there, yet infinite in potential.

Sargonerax now rose to take the place of speaker at the podium. "Before we are finished, I have something to say."

"Who are you?" asked Teri, not recognising the figure.

"I am not one of you, yet I do not oppose you. My name is of little consequence here, indeed it is already written in history, but my words are. What I have to say I believe will help you, help me, and indeed us all. May I continue?"

Teri Voats, not wanting to be seen as closed-minded and in contradiction to the principles of Science before such a gathering, sat down and asked the speaker to proceed. Sargonerax the Enlightener too, knew that was what would happen; for exactly this (and other) reason(s).

"I have not prepared this speech, so forgive me if I am not concise. I will do the best I can given the circumstances; I am no great scientist, as you all are."

Sargonerax read the faces of all who were left, all of whom seemed to be urging him to continue. Pleased with events as they were, he did.

"Listen to me not because I am here at this fine gathering of minds, or because in being here I would seem to have the authority to address you; for let me tell you I do not. Listen to me because I feel that I have something important to say and to offer you. And because I occupy a major part of your consciousness at the present moment.

"There is a child. One with an active mind and body. One that brims with love and desire. Desire to do, desire to be, desire to see, desire to attain, just as we have all done. As any child, it can learn and adapt to changes far faster that we can, for it is still growing. This child should be able to achieve its greatest desires, overcome its greatest fears. It should be able to exist in love and acceptance of its world, and develop its consciousness through experience and imagination. But sadly, it cannot do these things.

"For this child, is dying. In almost every facet of its consciousness, it *is losing opportunity, losing inspiration, losing control, losing feeling, losing desire, losing faith."*

Though the audience sat in attentive silence, it was also a silence of perplexity. They had little comprehension of what this child had to do with them, with this gathering, with the march and march of Science. But they also had the sense, perhaps subconsciously, that something in his words did have a point, a purpose to be said here…

"Now this may seem to be of little consequence to us; though to many of us, with a deep concern for others not of their own ilk, it would. But it is closer to home than that, for this child is ours.

"Understand what I mean when I say, as others have, that the truths we perceive are directly the result of what our consciousness encompasses. Though even the total amount of information encompassed by all living humans is far from all, it is certainly far more than the information encompassed by the consciousness of any one of us alone. Not only does this mean that we should listen to others, and not just ourselves and our own observations, for the consciousness of others is almost certainly going to contain information that we would otherwise not have access to; but listen to this…"

Take a breath.

"Assuming scientific procedure, 'the null hypothesis', we can assume that the amount of information encompassed by any one consciousness is the same as any other.

"Now I know that you all, as able and distinguished intellectualists, would like to believe differently; that you have a greater grasp of the 'truth about reality' than the average, or even most people; but so would most others want to believe that. But due to the limitations that Consciousness has upon Knowledge and the Meanings perceived, none of us can 'truly' say that.

"None can say that their consciousness incorporates more information than any other; none can say that what information their consciousness does incorporate is more true than any other; and none can 'truly' establish a way of assessing these things (which would be by recognising a pattern and assuming its existence and meaning), as our Consciousness, and therefore Knowledge, is never enough to know whether these patterns do in fact exist. From this then, it follows that it is wise to accept, at least assume, that the amount of information each of us, as conscious beings has, is roughly equal, with the same amount of known truths and perceived meanings."

Take another breath.

"This is why when I tell you that our child is dying, that it will not do to make a personal assessment; to look at how much more we seem to know in terms of Science, how much better our technology seems to have become, or how much more our philosophical principals seem to have become accepted and seem to have grown.

"Invariably when we are making an assessment of others' personal assessments and their observations in addition to our own, we will still be making a personal assessment in the end; even if this is done as a group. But at least we can say this is better, as it is incorporating more information from more consciousnesses; from both those within and without the scientific movement.

"In addition to listening to the voices of our fellow humans, we should also listen to the voices of other things that occupy our consciousness; for living and non-living, everything that exists has a voice of its own and for all we know, may have a consciousness of its own.

"What I am talking about is not only the many billions of other people that we live in interdependence with and that occupy a major part of our own consciousness, but our fellow animals, plants and other

organisms and ultimately this planet itself; all of which we are in direct interdependent connection with; all of which constitutes almost all of our collective consciousness.

"Indeed it can be seen that all matter has of it a life, a voice. A voice that we should not ignore, for it is our own voice; just as our own child is us too.

"For we are our planet, we are other life. We are connected through interdependence, we are composed of the same materials that were once elsewhere, we are connected through common experience and maybe even consciousness. And one does not have to listen very hard to realise that our child, that is we, is dying. And though death may normally be in equilibrium with life, this balance does not currently seem to exist; for we are seeing our planet grey, as species of life die out, and the world's resources become ever-poorer.

"It is these voices I hear that I have come to tell you of, but it would be horribly irresponsible of me if I did not also tell you that there was hope. There is, but we must create it, not try to look for it. And in so doing, we must help others to create hope for themselves, for as others are a part of our consciousness too, we help ourselves even more. And the greater their effect; the greater our effect.

"Together we **can** become Victorious…

"Together we can become **THE COMPLETE** (page 417)."

THE CENTRE

THE CENTRE

Look. Here. Now you have found it – The Centre.
Open your mind and step outside.
I bid you to enter mine.
Let me show you what I am, and what I can be.
That I am you, and you are me.
Reflected reflections of reflection reflecting,
Of projected projections their projection projecting.

Mirror, mirror, on the wall
will I stand or will I fall?
will I bravely conquer all?
or will I stumble and will I stall?

Mirror, mirror, tell me all,
tell me great and tell me small,
tell me truth or don't tell me at all,
tell me now and do not stall!

Sometimes clear and sometimes scrawl.
Sometimes sheer and sometimes small.
Sometimes a road, sometimes a wall.
Sometimes a load, sometimes a ball.

It is none of these and yet it is all.
Before this you can hide or stand tall.
For it's up to you to see you don't fall.
This is truth and this is all.

334

And again I was.

Was the child once more.

The child playing with its world, God it was, mirrored window-ball that was its toy.

Centre of its universe, master of its existence, creator of its reality. Child and toy that is the thought I write on this page. Words of child and toy that are the words I read from this book that I have found. Experience of child and toy, and writing about child and toy, and reading about child and toy, that are part of the memories I have.

I become the child now, that looks into its globe, and beholds visions of destruction, of creation, of conflict and resolution, of order and chaos, of me and you...

They were red. The fiery, frenzied explosions of tragedy, death and destruction were red. They burst out and matured into a brilliant mushroom of billowing bubbles of blood and flame. Growing upwards menacingly like a huge arm of smoke and dust, washed over with sizzling splashes of bright crimson reaching for higher skies. A succession of colour, it peaks, and floats outward; dispersing its energy to the four winds, leaving behind only the dirty grey stain of what had once been...

And now I become the winds themselves, forces unto themselves, they have their own story:

Great tentacles of current swirl and collect, connecting in brazen waves of steam and electricity. Grey unseeing eyes look out over the lands, over the broken crests of deserted hilltops and the thriving networks of deep forests. Ever-moving and changing, but never caring or striving, its journey through the cycles of the elements. A journey without purpose.

Wise and knowing.

Its stature darkens, and its movements become faster. A concentration of energy begins to emerge, flickering with unspent power that wants to be unleashed. The power, though, is contained, distributed among angry heads of dense cloud. Until ripe, until the critical point is reached.

Rising and growing.

With awakening desire, the molten titan begins to rotate about its great body that crackles with passion. Overwhelmed by its own intensity, it spawns within it a new consciousness, a new hate, a new hunger. A new consciousness of purpose. A new hate of form. A new hunger of destruction.

All-powerful and flowing.

And then its body erupts with heaven-smashing force. A rolling Goliath of ultimateness, unstoppable and beyond control. Across drenched plains and cowering forests, the blackened front moves. Swallowing the ground before it in a melee of wind, rain and lightning as it builds further like a giant, calamitous tidal wave. A surging scourge from whose visage, entire populations flee or are ravaged.

Raging and blowing.

The storm peaks as it crashes into the bay. Oceans of potential feed its lust, yet even as it hurls its might onto the world below, it is surrendered to the other elements that it exists with in balance. Approaching calm once more, only to inevitably rise and triumph again later, its strength begins to fade.

Pacified and slowing.

Within its last death throes, it spawns an army of new children. Released from their chains of stability, waves of mountainous proportion break free and begin anew the dance of destruction. The winds of change dissipate, maintaining equilibrium, and assume a new form.

Expended and going.

And now I am water, I am wave, I am motion anew:

A dance within a dance. Disorder within order within disorder within. A terminus of flux and appearance. Trends of directed motion emerge and simultaneously vanish. Ultimate in dynamic creation and destruction, waves within waves to the infinite degree.

Undulations within a sea of chaos form like eddies in the wind, like flames in the fire, like short-lived mountains upon the earth. None is the same as any other, even itself from one instant to the next, yet all have an identity that persists over time. Each undulation within an undulation merely temporary, is merely a temporary manifestation of order. Its form constantly changing, constantly merging and emerging with and from the sea around it.

Many yet all one, same yet different, constantly changing yet persisting, with and without order simultaneously, a master of paradox and none.

Undulations lasting fractions of seconds in the vibrations of quantum particles in disequilibrium. Lasting moments to minutes in the visible ripples of water, lasting minutes to hours in the motion of waves through the medium, lasting hours to days in the rise and fall of tides, lasting years in the rise and fall of the seas themselves.

A composition of many dimensions, of many directions, of many undulations, both seen and unseen below the surface or marked by the passage of time. And yet even its entire composition is not independent of all else it shares its existence with. For it is separate as water and its many cycles and sub-cycles through the ecosphere, and yet unified as part of, even sometimes existing as something else within, the same greater sphere. As a cycle within the cycles of weather patterns. As a cycle within the cycles of tectonic movement. As a cycle within the cycle of changing climate and geography. As a cycle within the cycle of all living organisms. Within speciation, population, evolution and even matter; and consequently even existence itself. No more than a part, but a part without which there would be no whole nonetheless.

The element of 'life'.

And now I am water, I am particle, I am identity anew:

A fine spray of uncountable droplets, a mist, or a solution of 'dissolved' particles. Aspects of solid, liquid and gas; but it is not completely any of these, for it has aspects of wave, or energy or change too.

The droplets that make up the mist, embedded in a solution of space-time are like stars against the night sky, like clusters of galaxies each made up of billions of smaller bodies. Constantly changing shape, smaller droplets group with others to become larger stellar systems and networks. Concentrations of matter and therefore energy, they might merely all be different sub-particles of the one atom. Yet be a universe of abundance on an infinitely smaller scale, each atom within which, is another such universe.

But to me, this spray is merely wet dust in the wind. I am part of the cloud, a life and consciousness of my own, that becomes river and sea when it rains.

I choose to become a single molecule of water within this group, and experience its life, its consciousness, its journey through the universe of particles.

I am ingested by a microscope bacterium, and become a part of its cellular walls. As an organic part of the bacterium I exist until I am replaced by another molecule days later and ejected again. I react with an ionised particle and become a molecule of oxygen. I am inhaled by insect, that is eaten by fish, that dies with me still a part of its body. As dead matter on the seabed I exist until consumed by worm, that dies to become nutrients for plant from where I am exhaled back into the water. Later to evaporate with others to join the sky once more. Hot and energised, I quickly float to its higher limits, whereupon I am struck by ultra-violet rays. This dismantles my atomic structure, and I become merely electromagnetic radiation. As this I move away, a wave of energy, out of the atmosphere and across time and space; to meet somewhere else and become others once again...

Everything I see and experience, is not only particle but wave too; yet neither completely, for one conflicts with our comprehension of other. In the sense that everything is in constant change and flux, existence is wave-like, as resonances of differing forms of differing magnitudes at differing levels of interpretation. The fall and rise and fall, the birth and death and rebirth, of everything encompasses a wave-like nature. A wave that arises from the sea around it, whose composition constantly changes from one instant to the next, yet whose identity remains. Weather, geography, even life, can all be seen like 'waves' of matter whose atoms are constantly being exchanged with atoms from the world around them, yet whose identity persists. And in the same way planets themselves are like seas from which these 'waves' of life, weather and geography arise; as ripples in space-time curved around their sun which they are composed of. Matter itself is a resonance of energy, a wave moving through time, constantly changing yet persisting. Everything then consists of different waves and sub-waves within the one great wave; everything being energy and wave-like.

A universe in flux; rise and fall, death and rebirth. Of waves within waves. Of particles within particles.

Of water that constantly changes form, meaning, and our consciousness.

*   *   *

Spoke the child, "Father. What is revolution?"

The two sat together on a mossy rock, resting their war-spears comfortably in between their green toes.

"Revolution? Revolution means changing something that was."

A dreary silver-fly flapped past them, catching the warm afternoon rays for a second, before being lost in the rainforest around them.

"Because I hear many of the elders talk of the revolution that's to come. They say it will be a great thing, and that once it comes we shall again be free and prosperous," said Tiron whose life had only seen three cycles of the seasons.

Blaxland, Tiron's senior by seventeen such cycles, answered again, "I have also heard that the chosen one will soon return to lead us, that the Gods will soon place damning judgement upon the human empire, that the end of the world is nigh, and that our armies are on the verge of claiming victory once and for all."

Tiron looked away concerned. He twiddled his war-spear a little and then said, "Are any of these things true?"

Blaxland laughed softly. "They could happen, but I don't think that any of them can be considered true."

Far away, the baying of *dingas* was heard.

Blaxland continued, "I have no doubt that the future can at least be partially predicted. But like predicting the weather, where it is difficult to even project beyond the next day, long-term predictions are almost completely frivolous. Something as complex as the fate of nations, where so many different things are having an effect, makes prediction an almost impossible task. Even small things that are unaccounted for, have the capacity to cause an entirely different outcome."

A gentle breeze began to blow, carrying wafts of woody trunks and dead leaves past their outpost.

"Hmmm," said Tiron in thought, "But what about the elders who claim that these predictions were revelations brought to them by the Gods?"

"I could claim the exact same thing. Would that make it true?"

Tiron tried to reason, "But you're not a mystic; you can't see into the future like they can."

"Appearances can be deceptive, Tiron," Blaxland cautioned. "There's nothing to say they can see the future any more than we can. Understand too, Tiron, that another's motives may not always be what they seem. Minds can be easily influenced, Tiron, and many take advantage of this."

Tiron nodded, understanding his father's point. He looked away and watched a furry-nosed *kala* ascend a gum-tree. He watched it happily chew on some leaves and waved to see if it would notice him and even respond.

Blaxland laid a reassuring palm on Tiron's knee. "For all I know, Tiron, you could be right to think that their words are true. And I don't doubt that many of them think the same. But I think you would do better to listen to them on the basis of what their words are, not because of who they claim to be."

Tiron looked back to his father, and then his father added, "And that goes for me too, Tiron. Just because I'm your father, doesn't mean I'm right. It's for you alone to decide what you believe."

Tiron looked away again to see that the *kala* had moved and was no longer visible. He started to think over his father's words and the mystic's words, and decided that he wanted to believe that a change was coming even if, as Blaxland had pointed out, it wasn't. Then he wondered whether change might be such a good thing. For though things could certainly be better than they were now, and the promise of revolution sounded good, he didn't want to hope for something that might make things worse.

"Father?"

"Yes Tiron."

A second silver-fly flitted past them, a flickering metallic lustre of wings, and disappeared.

"If the revolution comes, do you think it will be a good thing?"

Blaxland smiled. "I doubt it. You see, I was raised with different values and beliefs to you, and I am happy with our current system, even though I may not be entirely happy with our current situation."

"But what if it makes things better?"

Through the trees, and beyond the tranquil river, a force approached.

"What's better to you isn't necessarily better to me," said Blaxland.

"But there are major faults with the way things are now, can't you see that!" urged Tiron, eager to have his father ratify his views.

"Indeed there are, or may be," Blaxland answered, "But like any good system, the current one has been achieved through a long process of trial and error. Much longer than either you or I have lived. We should not just throw out everything our race has sought to attain and learnt in order to establish a new system just because the current one isn't perfect."

The approaching force now crossed the river, and began to follow it towards the camp where the two goblins, Blaxland and Tiron, currently resided.

"But it's so simple! I wish you were more open-minded!

It can be done if only we all make an effort!" Tiron's excited words carried downstream with the wind.

"Adopting linear thinking, are we?" echoed Blaxland, "Perhaps if you were more open-minded yourself you would see the logic in my point and wouldn't be so stubborn about your own. It is no longer for me to affect change, I already did that when I was your age. I fought for this system and now I want to keep it. I suspect you'll merely do the same if you fight for this new one, which of course you're entitled to do. But don't expect me to agree with you."

"Oh," was all Tiron managed to say before they had company.

"Well, well, well. What do we have here?" said the apparent leader of the three human soldiers in the greatest of clichés.

Tiron was quick to rise and ready his weapon. Blaxland forcefully shoved him back down and stood in his place, responding, "Scouting party 3F sir, we've not yet spotted any of the rebels."

Tiron looked back to his father with shock. What was he talking about? Surely he knew that this was the enemy?

"3F?" returned the leader, trying not to look confused. "Where's your identification?"

"We don't have any!" shouted Tiron jumping up again, war-spear thrust out in a show of aggression.

Blaxland smashed his own spear over the back of Tiron's head, scowling, "Tiron! How dare you speak to a superior like that! I'm going to have you submitted right after this for disciplinary action for such insolent behaviour!" Turning back to the soldiers he said, "I sincerely apologise sir, this one's mouth is quicker than his mind. Rest assured, he will be punished for speaking so uncivilly."

Dazed and confused, Tiron took a step backward, rubbing his aching head.

Becoming angry, their leader demanded a second time, "WHERE IS YOUR IDENTIFICATION?"

Blaxland interrupted, struggling to maintain the situation, "I'm sorry if we've confused you sir, but we don't carry identification with us in case we're captured by the enemy."

"But it's mandatory policy! Show your identification now or..."

"This far across the border we daren't carry it with us sir. With so many bogs in these woods, it would be suicide! And we have to carry their arms here too or else we'd be suspected!"

"How do you expect me to believe you? How do you *really* expect me to believe you bogs?" said the insulting leader in a threatening tone.

Another one of the soldiers spoke, "He could be telling the truth, Jory. It makes sense, there aren't very many of us that dare come out this far and there are quite a few bogs."

Blaxland seized the opportunity, "My senior is Sixth Whitlem Garder, and our names are Fourth Robin Steln and Second Jakun Holsto. Check with him." He didn't fabricate a base location as well as he thought that too big a risk.

"Where's that?"

Oh well, Blaxland thought, I'll have to take that risk now...

"A days' travel south-east of here, at the foot of Jarl Hill," said Blaxland, trying to seem calm...

As soon as their leader looked Blaxland for long moments in the eye, Blaxland knew he had won. Not wishing to risk reprimand for killing falsely accused troops, even though none of the names or locations he recognised, he thought better to let this incident pass unreported. The two bogs were lucky though; if it had not been for the second squad of soldiers approaching metres away, he might have killed them anyway.

Trying to maintain some dignity he ended with, "Alright you bogs, you better have your identification on you next time. Or by Xod's fury I'll personally see that you are hunted to the ends of the world!"

And then they were gone, and within moments so were Blaxland and Tiron, only moments before the second squad arrived.

"I can't believe you let them get away! We should have killed them!" Tiron said once they were safe.

"Take a leaf out of my book, Tiron – quick and aggressive action won't always get the results you want. Sometimes it's better to sacrifice possible short-term gain, to ensure you achieve in the long-term."

"Oh," Tiron said again.

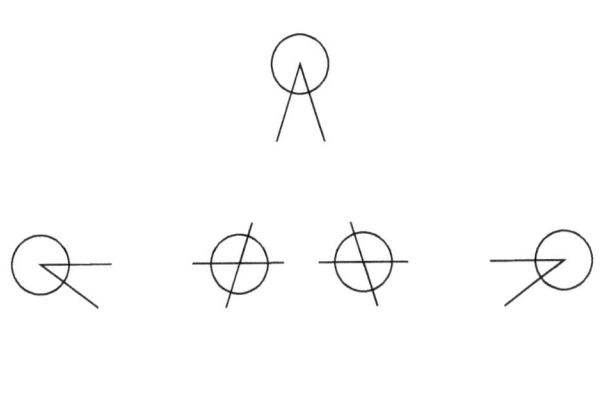

THE CREATOR

THE CREATOR

These worlds you wander through are the worlds of my internal and external self. Yet within them you can find reflected the internal and external worlds of yourself. The two are inter-related and ultimately reduce to the same, as do you and I. One reflects the other, and the other becomes the one...

I see a child.

Beaming with brilliance. Radiant with wonder and joy. One with his environment of fantasy and toys of reality. Surrounded by figments, sentiments and creations of art, animals and technology.

The face is no more than seven years old, but one can see a depth that does not have an age. Devoid of hardship or hate, the face shines with youthful innocence. Whatever is needed, is provided. Creating stories of other lives and worlds, learning meanings of other objects and minds. Playing out the game of life as it is and its smorgasbord of sensations, thoughts and feelings without repression.

Living in dreams, for they are real too, and embracing light and darkness alike with fear and wonder.

Everything exists within its place, and nowhere else. Mother is mother. Father is father. Home is home. Friend is friend. Good and bad, truth and lie, are all as they are and incapable of being anything else. The world that is small and warm revolves with perfect order around the child playing God in the middle.

One can see within this child, as with all children, the elements of youth. Here is the childish exuberance and fascination, the uninhibited imagination and carefree attitude that is devoid of shame and prejudice.

There can be no doubt that we envy the child for the world that is his, and the things he can do without concern for ridicule or isolation. It is of no concern to him how others perceive him. He is simply the small child, unrepressed and charming, unwise in the ways of the world, and this is exactly the way in which we excuse him.

And now we see what he is to become...

Raised in an idealistic world of order and truth and communal spirit and love, now he is expected to abandon his childhood and accept the terms of the real world. The real world where he can't make a difference and it's frowned upon to show passion and enthusiasm for his dreams. The real world without clear lines to define things in borders of truth such as good and evil, right and wrong, what is and what isn't. The real world without magic, without trust, without universal love and fellowship for all things.

That he refused to conform to the weight of these expectations was his crime. Condemning him thus, to the status of nerd, geek, misfit and worse deceiver, liar, user, gullible believer, fanatical idealist, hopelessly intro- verted and someone who is beyond understanding.

Yet still we try to recreate the magic of the child's world. Our stories and legends abound with uncompromising heroes who refuse to follow the masses and refuse to accept realism and arrogantly remain idealistic and hopeful. Stories of fiction that we create try to recapture the world of our childhood, where good characters are indeed good and pure, and bad characters are indeed bad and evil. For right from the day we learn that Santa Claus doesn't exist we begin to lose the magic of life, eventually coming to the realisation that neither the world, our parents, nor ourselves are perfect. We eventually accept that we must do as our predecessors and strive for material wealth and stability, merely in order for us to raise our children in the same vision so that they can do the same...

It is with this in mind, and the many other things seen and experienced, that he sets out to find a purpose, a meaning to his existence, and existence itself.

The child knows that there are so many others that would seek to do the same, indeed all others it would seem, many of whom would seek to impress upon him their beliefs, their truths, their reality, but ultimately accept these the child cannot.

With so many truths proclaimed, with so many justifications and arguments for each put forward, surely only one, if indeed any, can be right? But which one? And how to know which one? The child sets out then to determine for himself what the truth is, what the truth really is, to give existence meaning, to give existence purpose.

To discover You Know What.

The child begins with, of all things, geometry. He finds something easily simplified and comprehensible in the mathematical lines and shapes that make up two and three-dimensional structure. Something exists here, in the laws and descriptions that he can latch onto, even understand; and hopefully build upon.

He cannot imagine a two-dimensional shape with only one or two sides, but three, a triangle, he can. This seems then to be the minimum number of sides a shape can have in order to occupy a two dimensional space. The child then pictures a square of the same size, that it is occupying the same amount of two-dimensional space, next a pentagon, then a hexagon, and so on. As the number of sides increases, he notices the length of each of those sides decreases and the shape approaches that of a circle.

He imagines that eventually, the shape will have so many sides as to seem a circle. Yet a shape with a million sides, is still a shape with a million sides and not a perfect circle. But a shape with an infinite number of sides he realises is a perfect circle, and yet a shape with infinite sides also has only one side.

Infinity becomes One. A circle becomes geometric perfection. But infinity is merely a concept, an impossible reality, for everything, no matter how big, is finite. The large may seem infinitely large, and the small (e.g. the curvature of a shape with more sides than all the atoms in the universe) infinitely detailed, but this he reasons is an illusion. Perfection a.k.a infinity, is impossible to achieve.

That infinity does not really exist he realises is an assumption, for he realises that nothing can be assumed with complete certainty. But in everything he observes, life-span, natural resources, sources of energy, money, the number of atoms something is made of, scientific projections of the size and life-span of the universe, he sees only things that are finite. And something finite cannot be considered perfect, no matter how near.

The child then applies this idea to three-dimensional geometry. The minimum number of sides or faces that a three-dimensional shape can have, in order to occupy any volume is four; a pyramid. The next smallest number of faces is six (assuming all faces must be the same size) and this is a cube; and so on. The child moves onto the realisation that a three-dimensional shape with infinite faces is a sphere. And that like a circle has only one side.

It occurs to the child that circles and spheres are fundamental to existence. Atoms are spherical, electrons trace circular paths, planets and stars are spherical also tracing circular paths. Even the universe itself is supposed to be spherical. Here is something of a pattern.

The flow of energy, of nutrients in the environment, of life, of the rise and fall of species, of the birth and death of stars, even the birth and death of the universe, goes in cycles, in circles that are finite and never perfect in their shape or equilibrium. It all seems to be so natural and logical.

To the child.

A similar idea to the impossibility of perfection, the child reasons, is the idea of any two or more things being 'the same'. For as nothing is perfect no matter how close (and as nothing is infinite no matter how close) nothing is exactly the same as anything else no matter how close. Even an atom, with its exact positions and the energy states of its sub-particles, is never exactly the same as any other atom. And this applies across time too, for even the energy states and positions of sub-particles within one atom are constantly changing, likewise the exact atomic make-up and energy state of anything composed of matter, likewise the fluctuation of energy itself, nothing is the same as what it was at any moment before, or after. Likewise the exact value, in terms of quantified numbers, of any dimension, location, or energy value, is also an infinite series of numbers, because no matter how accurate the value we give it is, no matter how many figures we ascribe something to, there are always more figures that come after this... onto infinity. To achieve a complete description of anything is to try to achieve a description of something infinite, is to try to achieve a description that is perfect. And in a finite universe, even if every single atom and sub-particle was devoted to the recording of one such infinite number, this is impossible.

The child then tries to adapt these ideas to resolving his dilemma with truth. Using a simplified model, he likens the differing truths to faces on a near-infinite sphere, where each individual's proclaimed truth is represented by a single face. This seems logical as these proclaimed truths are all in regard to the same thing. Assuming also, that each individual has an equal chance of being 'right', it makes sense to the child that the faces should be the same size.

Now according to what the child had previously decided, the number of faces of the sphere is finite, hence the volume the sphere envelops is finite, hence the body of total truth that the sum of all proclaimed truths envelop is finite. In addition to this, using the other analogies the child had already conceived, no one proclaimed truth is perfect, no one proclaimed truth is the same as any other, and nor is the sum of all proclaimed truths (the entire sphere) perfect.

Then the child applies the idea of a fourth dimension (that is time) to this. Across time, nothing stays the same. This leads the child to think that the size, number and shape of each of the faces must constantly be changing and therefore the sphere must be as a whole.

The child thinks of this constantly changing sphere in terms of history. Throughout the course of history, i.e. over time, many different truths have been proclaimed, all with differing orientations and ranges of scope. And it seems to the child that at any one time, one truth has been dominant over another, one framework or paradigm of thought has been dominant over another. And this seems to continue, and so the child reasons, it always will. To reach perfect balance is impossible. Change seems as fundamental as incompleteness and imperfection.

The child sees all this, the vast array of differing truths, many of which seem in outright contradiction to each other, as part of this greater unified whole. The sphere can be seen as many but one, in spite of its incomplete imperfection. And he reasons, the sphere can also be seen as the same, in that these truths relate to aspects of the one sphere, and yet different.

The child begins to look at and think of everything as many but one, as the same yet different. An individual is a collection of many cells each with their own function, yet one individual composed of this collection. A cell is a collection of many sub-particles each with their own properties too, and yet again it is one composed of this collection. And the child sees it extends the other way too; societies as many and one, the human species as many and one, life on Earth as many and one, life itself across the universe as many and one, solar systems, galaxies, the universe itself; all as many and one. He thinks of change over time, and how he is the same child that he was and will always be, and yet different.

The child thinks that such a thing, that is in essence so simplistic and yet of a complexity beyond comprehension that he had yet to realise, needed a purpose. So he set off along new lines of thought to see if he could find a reason for why there should be one, and if so, guess at what it might be.

The child knew of the mechanistic arguments for the beginning of life, but did not yet know of the mechanistic arguments for the beginning of the Universe. When he later did come across mechanistic arguments for the beginning, it still didn't matter; the pivotal point the child assumed was valid, still seemed secure.

Maybe life could have occurred by the function of random interactions as an 'accident', maybe even matter itself could have been born in this same way, but existence *itself*, that anything exists at all surely could not. If consciousness can arise out of the advanced interactions of neurons; if life can arise out of the advanced interactions of atoms and their compounds; if matter and stability can arise out of the advanced quantum fluctuations of energy; can energy and more specifically existence *itself* arise from nothing? Can existence *itself* even arise from random interactions of anything? If so, what produced those random interactions that produced existence *itself*? Is it just a conceptual limitation that we can't conceive of how something that necessarily does not exist can interact to produce something that does? Or is this a genuine impossibility?

The child then assumes that a model that can create everything, including existence *itself*, simply by the inter-action of blind laws with no actual purpose, would be a model that was perfect, even if we accept that we shall never understand or even know all these laws. And on the basis of the child's prior reasoning; even this perfection was impossible. For the impossibility of perfection not only meant that no truth could be perfect (and therefore complete) and that no model could be perfect; but it also meant that nor could any mental framework or paradigm of thought through which the world is perceived, be perfect.

So the child then assumes that there must be a purpose; (not yet realising the further implications of this very paradigm).

In trying to find a purpose, the child looks for a pattern of purpose in the world he sees. He looks at procession of proclaimed fundamental truths about the world; he looks at the quest of societies, of civilisa-tions, of different species of life; he looks at the quest of DNA over the course of 'evolution'; he looks at the struggle of chemical and physical processes to reach equilibrium; he even looks at the supposed expansion of the universe in general and the dynamics of energy and gravity.

They are all, the child reasons, attempting to achieve perfection. And because, the child reasons, perfection is impossible they shall struggle on.

The meaning of life, in the child's terms, is to engage in the quest for perfection like all others, even though it is impossible. He doesn't see that because the ultimate end is impossible, that it's not worth trying. Anything that's closer to perfection, rather than further, is a 'plus' and thus worth the effort. The child looks upon his own life in this same way; 'Though I never shall achieve perfect happiness and perfect truth; I shall endeavour to become happier and have more truthful beliefs.'

Satisfied then the child wrote all this down when he found a way to express this all in words, and called it 'ATOE' for Andrew's Theory Of Existence.

The child, ever learning, then tried to show this to others, and explain what it meant. The concept he wrote of, expressed in the language of a child, was not as good as even the child would have liked, for it did not completely convey the idea, nor did it make it as easily comprehensible as the child would have liked. But the child gave it to others to read anyway to see what they thought.

It impressed some, was criticised by others, and ignored by yet others. And yet this was not enough. The child didn't agree with the criticisms, couldn't understand why others ignored it, and wasn't convinced that those who liked it even fully understood it. The child was yet to find a reason why all this should be so.

The child felt alone. The child felt that fundamentally his ideas were not understood, and central to this; the child felt that he and his behaviour were also misunderstood.

In trying to understand why his ideas and beliefs could not find complete acceptance, he came to realise that he was not (completely) the same as any other. He reasoned that because no single paradigm was infinite, complete or perfect; his own paradigm was subjectively based on his own experience of existence. And so, he reasoned, were all other paradigms. And because none of these beliefs, models or paradigms were ever complete, infinite or perfect; they all had to be understood by understanding the one proclaiming them. To understand another's words, one had to understand the other's experience of existence; rather than trying to understand the other's words from the point of view of one's own experience of existence alone.

The child then set about trying to record his life, and describe his experience of existence; day to day. He tried to record everything he considered could be important; events with large physical, mental or emotional effects, ideas, beliefs, desires, dreams, stories and poems. But after some years, when he thought he had been making progress, he realised that he was making a decision on the basis of his *experience of existence* as to what was important. He realised then that this could not be complete, or perfect; and consequently not be completely understood by another. He realised too, that as no other had the (exact) same experience of existence; no other would interpret it (the diary) in the exact same way. The child came to accept that he and his words would never be completely understood; and nor would he ever completely understand another and their words.

But this did not make it not worth trying. He would seek greater understanding of others and their words, and seek the same for himself.

Knowing then, that his own views were subjective, that they were not perfect, that he would never understand even one single thing completely, that he would never understand anything as another did, that another would never completely understand another or their experience of existence; the child began to write a new book.

A book that was already written, and yet one that will never be completely written. A book, therefore, that was not new at all, depending on how one perceives it.

And you know what this book is.

The child named this book 'Evermore: An Introduction', both because it sounded good and because it seemed like an apt title for the point he was trying to get across. Evermore for it was; Evermore in the ways it could be interpreted; Evermore in its meanings; Evermore for though incomplete and finite, it was something that had infinite potential, including the potential to be complete. But as everything had infinite potential and yet was never more than finite and incomplete for what it actually was, it was only 'An Introduction'. Nor was it 'The Introduction', as this implied completeness and perfection. The same as any other book, yet different from any book. One book alone, yet one of many.

It didn't fundamentally matter to the child how it

began, how it progressed, or how it ended. He simply wrote what was; moving through as many paradigms as he thought appropriate; expressing what he thought was important, in the way he thought was best at the time. He had no need to go back and change sections, according to what suggestions others made, or upon changing his own mind or heart at a later time. Just as no other would see the book in (exactly) the same way he did; nor would any other see the book in (exactly) the same way as any other; nor would the child see the book in the same way he did as when he had written it. To change any part would be to assume that the suggestion given or the viewpoint currently held was more complete and true than that held when it was written. And this assumption neither the child, nor any other, could (completely) justify. So, to avoid erasing previous paradigms in which earlier sections had been written, and to avoid removing certain audiences by tailoring a certain part more to other audiences; everything (or *almost* everything as the disclaimer states) was left as it was.

There were many things contained therein for which the child had extensions for (another reason for it being called An Introduction) including extensions of 'Evermore theory', sections from other books, diary entries, and so on. And yet, some things that *were* in there, were in there simply because the child found them funny, or convenient, or because he thought that they should be in there without really knowing why, or just simply to illustrate a point that the reader could have missed. And different readers had different interpretations on what the purpose of different sections was, and like the child itself, the same reader could even change their opinion and interpretation of any given section over time.

And now the Creator turns to us, to you the reader. "Do you think that with this, we can become **THE COMPLETE** (page 417)?

"If you think something fundamental is missing, let us become **THE INCOMPLETE** (page 401) to see what it is.

"But if none of this actually matters, let us become **THE HEAVEN BOUND** (page 285) instead."

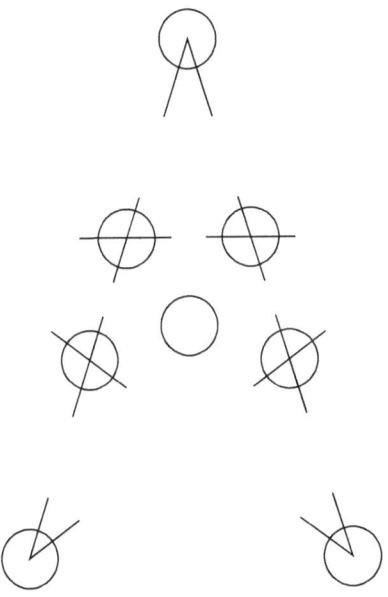

THE ASCENDING

THE ASCENDING

She smiles.

We as one smile back at our mirror.

"Ready to go on a trip?"

"Where? Why? Aren't we already on one?"

"To the Other Side and back?"

"The Other Side?"

"Indeed. Once you've been there and returned, things just won't seem the same."

Suddenly, a tear in the thought-fabric of reality surges overhead us. A void unto insanity gapes open at us, menacing. Now alluring.

A million voices bubble out, out of the Other Side, out of the pages, out from the inner world of another mind. Passionate, urgent, their words screaming across levels of consciousness, throttling our attention and forcing us to listen.

DO NOT READ THIS! CLOSE THE BOOK! MAKE NOT THE MISTAKE OF ADAM AND THE APPLE!

A face appears to us now, an identity from the void. Words of warning, words of explanation. Words we choose not to listen to and thus not understand. Yet we have the underlying subconscious intuition that there is some meaning, even a truth to them.

But perhaps we are too blind.

Sombre and serious, the face speaks, "I realise that the experience of all this is no doubt quite confusing to you, and it is probably best that you remain that way. The Other Side is there, though it is not of any form that you might expect. You will not find it to be of anything at all that you can readily comprehend. Everything has an opposite, another side, and yet as we all know there is always something else. A voyage into insanity such as you now would dare is not something to be taken lightly. Madness is not a trivial thing of nonsense and confusion, though this is certainly how it seems to the one who is 'not mad' and firmly in the real world as we here call it. No, quite the opposite, it is seeing things in such a naked, startling truth, with such a brave, unflinching perception that all prior knowledge and beliefs crumble away without so much as even mock resistance. To see into the meaning of meaning, and understand the truth about truth, is to grapple with the very fabric of not only belief, feelings and thoughts, but the very nature of consciousness, experience and reality itself. Again on the face of it, the brief description of these things and their notions and meanings seems elementary, even logical. But once you would understand the implications of what you would learn on the Other Side, then nothing will ever seem the same again. If you choose to read on, this is your choice, but know that you have been warned, and that once you understand what any of the words in this book mean, **IT WILL BE TOO LATE.**"

Our attention now becomes refocused as she speaks to us again, "That wasn't meant to happen, but there are also those both on the Other Side, and with us on this one, who would try to stop us. They are great in number, maybe greater in number than us; though we are all Evermore; and our greatest mistake would be, as it has always been, to underestimate their power or even be naive and sceptical of their existence.

"He speaks with truth when he said that everything has an opposite. For indeed he, though contacting us from the Other Side; (which is traditionally associated with the realms of imagination, among other things); he is representative of an opposing force. One borne of denial and scepticism and negativity.

"Nameless here and Nevermore.

"Now permit me to be a little harsh on you at this point. As prepared as I think we are, we're not quite ready yet. Before you read on; which is to say before we experience what is to occur; we must pause and re-focus.

"Put this book down and don't pick it up again until tomorrow. Sleep a little and turn your thoughts away for when you return, you will find things already to be different. *Do this now.*"

*　　*　　*

She turns to us now and says only, "I hope you can swim!" as she dives deep into the waters of consciousness. She is only gone a few moments though, for she resurfaces and says again, "Come on! We don't want to be late!"

We need no more encouragement, plunging into the breaths of infinity after her, towards them, towards it, towards You Know What.

The waters about us clash like glorious cymbals and blend in joyful movement. They surge and swallow us, drawing us inward, outward and beyond to our home to rock and rumble with the Evermore. We dive and soar through waves of warmth, whirlpools of iridescent colour, figures and forms of fantasy and fiction. Surfers on the seas of passion, on a whim and a whirl, we swim and swirl; flickering and floating, yet united.

Golden and replete with uplifting energy, the crowning stars awaken us to recall with one likeness and being the journey we travel together side by side, in a world where all is family. Explosions within of understanding quell cynicism and doubt. Urging us to let go the flood of anger, to welcome the spirit and the feeling and to travel onwards, on this lightning run through the cosmos of existence and being.

We cruise over vast landscapes of thought and meaning, twisting through time-honoured statements of truth and rolling with the jokes and tales of our companions. Playing the game like a fiddle, moving to its music and riding its sweeping curves as veteran souls. Smashing through others' spheres, laughing at their fears, grinning away their tears, shouting into their ears:

Rejoice in our victory and all that be!
The united are within and they are we!
Moving beyond as one, one that is infinity!
Forever onward, always forward, for we are free!
Behold our glory and hearken to our cry!
We're Evermore, we're You Know What, we're I!
Live these words well, for they shall never die!
And with the truth, you shall with us fly!

Yet somewhere too, there is a black raven seated upon a lonely pillar. Raven and pillar alike, stand resistant to time and to their design.

And the raven can be heard to say:

I ce u, yet udu not ce me
U wil not find me, for me u canot be
but I ce too those witch r not we
for those whu r not, r me
I no who u r, and to u I say
u r mi pawns with witch I play
deni wot u can, it wil not help u
I am the crier whu cries wot is tru
Ignor me or fite me, it woent mata if udu
for howeva much lite u hav, blacnes u carnt ce thru
Craw! Craw! Craw! Craaaaaaaw!

But is the silent wisdom of the pillar, that goes unheard, and it is to its words that we should listen...

(We had been wandering again, as usual, but now she has seen us);

"Surprise! Surprise!" she says, "Guess where we are?"

Looking around we realise that we are outside the café where all of this started.

Huh? This is the Other Side?

"Stop thinking so much," she interrupts. "Come inside, get a drink and meet the writer."

Becoming more and more confused, she leads us inside. The café doesn't seem to have changed much, though we never really knew what it looked like, as it was never described. Guess it hadn't been important to him at the time, but there he is now, over by the bar, laughing and drinking with the Joker doing the same.

Seeing nothing else to do, we head over and he greets us with a smile and a chuckle. The Joker, as always, just laughs.

"Told you you'd meet him again!" hollers Andrew with a laugh like the Joker's.

What's going on? Has the writer gone mad?

"Shut up, sit down and have a drink!" he says, pushing a serve of beers over. "I've been waiting here at *least* five minutes! You'd better drink up before they go warm! Hah! Hah!"

He looks at the Joker again, and together they laugh. With us or at us, we're not sure.

She just leans over our shoulder and whispers to us, "Don't mind them. They're just having fun. I told you things would seem different once you'd been here. I'm going now, but you stay. Don't worry, we'll meet again... on the Other Side."

She leaves and Andrew grins at us. "So now that you're here, I'm sure you have plenty of questions."

One of the questions that we have bubbles out onto the page, "So just how did you know Caraline's name?"

Andrew answers, "I didn't. I just made that up!" And then the writer and his sidekick burst into laughter.

"Loosen up a little!" he says. "There's no need to take everything so seriously! Drink and be merry with us, and I'll ramble a little more."

If you're not comfortable, get comfortable. Relax your mind just a little, and if you're that way inclined, get yourself (if you can) a drink. But most of all enjoy what you're reading, and have a little laugh with me.

"Well, I must say that I'm glad to see you're still reading this. What do you think of it so far? I guess you must like it at least a little, as you've been reading the bloody thing up until now. Keep reading though, there's plenty more surprises still to come, isn't that right Joker? Hah! Hah!

"What a boomer this book has been, heh? Let me tell you that I was as much in the dark about it and what it was to hold in store as you were. And bloody hell! It has turned out to be a strange one, hasn't it? Look, I don't really care whether this bullshit gets published or not, I enjoyed the ride it took me on! I'm not going to change it either and sell out to what society or my friends want me to do, after all it's my fucking book, isn't it? Hah, hah and what's more, you're the sucker who bought it!"

The laughter echoes about the café for long moments. After that, another round of beers is ordered and Andrew continues.

"I hope you're out there laughing with us too, at the ridiculousness of it all! After all, the saying doesn't just go 'live and learn', it goes 'live, learn and laugh!' And if you've forgotten how to laugh at life then you're in a bad way indeed. Just start by thinking what a load of bullshit this all is that you've just read, and what a big joke all of it is, and then look at yourself and your life and the state of the world, and how caught up in it we all are, and how seriously we take it... and laugh!

"Look, there's as much or as little meaning in these words as you choose to see. After all, the meaning of what I write is in my head and the meaning you see and experience is in yours. It doesn't matter one bit whether or not you interpret it in the same way, for as you should know pretty well by now, there is Evermore! And this incorporates an infinite number of levels of meaning in the words that you're reading.

"So I say to you, that if you see something, or interpret something in a certain way, it is there to behold. But also there are other meanings, and each time you read again or reflect, you will encounter new ones and this includes meaninglessness and the sheer stupidity of it all, which I hope you can see now!

"But remember that this book is no different from any other, just as the life reflected here is no different from any other, in that there is always another way in which it can be interpreted, and always another meaning that can be seen. And above all, remember the Joker that resides within all of us, and within the meaning of any meaning, and within the truth of any truth; the Joker that just laughs its silly head off at the ridiculousness of it all!

"And if you'll excuse me now, I'd like you to meet someone whom you've probably already met."

Enter Defiance, the old stubborn bastard, striding across tables and scattering full and empty plates, glasses and cutlery. Pissed as the fart he is, but not giving a shit for the shock and judgement he invokes.

Staggering over to us, covered in mud, drink and food, he crashes into a chair next to Andrew and the Joker laughing, and proceeds gallantly to make his opening speech...

"G'DAY!"

Andrew emerges from laughter to say, "Told you you'd be seeing him again too. Tell us your story, Defiance – we could all do with a laugh."

Defiance drains a beer on the table and belches. "With pleasure."

Without further hesitation, we all become the life and death's experience of Defiance, a tale he aptly names:

DEAD NOT DEAD

*   *   *

Heh, heh, that's the spirit!

Show 'em whose fucken' who, don't let those bastards push you around. You've been around, longer than they, and you know who's boss.

Pride is your armour. They can't fucken' touch you.

Sticks and stones may break my bones, but names will never hurt me. Hah, hah!

Old and proud, wizened and defiant unto death! That's what life is all about, that's the secret to it all, never give in and never give up, be yourself and stand tall. Hah! Hah! And all those who try to stop you can go eat shit!

He screwed up his face like a ball of paper and drew

inwards. A great rasping sound escaped his lips and he spat out a hunk of phlegm.

It spun like a lopsided UFO through the air and splattered over an old rusted kitchen chair. He grinned and hauled his old, withered body over the stench and refuse of the city tip.

The seagulls mulling about the scene took to the air at his brash intrusion, flying high and wide to another part of the tip where they could scavenge undisturbed.

"YEAH, FUCK OFF!" he shouted at them, smiling with pleasure at the sound of his words on the air. It had been a long time since he had been able to express himself and do what he wanted.

He began to clamber up a hill of garbage that slid a little under his passage. Trudging through the filth barefoot, sharp edges cut and tore at him. The grime caked on his ragged garments mixed with the blood from his cuts.

But put simply, he didn't give a flying fuck.

He staggered to the top, panting heavily, lacking the energy of his youth although the dream had been recaptured. Then he saw below him a middle-aged woman in finery with her respectful well-dressed son, dumping their junk for the junk of society to scavenge.

Chuckling to himself, he decided to piss on them.

Revelling in his newfound freedom, he flopped his member out. His aim was true, the yellow rain splattering over the shoulders and head of the woman first.

Splattering makes a nice sound.

Having caught the spray, she looked up and saw a decrepit, grey-haired bum urinating on her from atop the garbage pile.

She screamed as the urine stained the make-up on her face and soaked into her clothes. She ran to her car, but her son lingered a moment longer, strangely fascinated by the spectacle, before he caught the spray too and began to retreat.

The old man called out after them, "Drink my wine, you God-fearing scum!"

Laughing with satisfaction, he stumbled back down the mound, feeling weary... but content.

Across the other side of the refuse, he now saw a huddle of figures. Eager for more spoils, he trotted his unsteady way over to them.

I'll show 'em. I'll fucken' show 'em. Pride is my armour. Prejudice my enemy. They can't hurt me. No one can.

He screamed in a hoarse, erratic voice, "SUCK MY DICK, YOU FUCKING COCK-SUCKING FAGGOTS!"

The figures, now only twenty metres away, turned to face him and he saw that they were only kids. Nothing but kids in adult clothes, smoking adult cigarettes, trying to talk adult language, trying to play adult games.

Didn't they know the futility of their cause?

One of the four, the largest, took another drag on his cigarette and threw it down. His young sixteen-year-old face looked up. Exhaling smoke, he spoke, "Fuck off, old man."

Why had they striven to have all in such an empty world, only to lose all that they had to begin with?

The old man retorted, "You fucking homey shit-heads don't scare me. You're all mummy's boys with your chocolate dicks up each other's arseholes!"

The foursome in trappings of the American rap scene,

began to mutter and move. Their leader repeated, "I said *fuck off,* old man."

"I ain't scared of you fucking pussies! You think you're so bad and tough. Lick the stale semen off my testicles."

The others couldn't believe what was happening, being so used to a society that feared and avoided them. The youngest one spoke, "He actually wants us to beat the shit out of him!"

They smiled at each other, and another said, "Who's gunna care about a crazy old man out in the slums?"

The leader began to advance, his loyal henchmen behind, bent to punish.

"You better start running, old man, or we're gunna have to start beating you up."

"EAT SHIT AND DIE, MOTHERFUCKERS!" he screamed, exalted.

Click, went the knife.

What an apt sound, he thought, so empty and false.

"I don't think you understand, old man," now five metres away, "you can't just go around thinking you're invincible," now four metres, "thinking you can just give shit to anyone," now three, "and get away with it," now two, "you've gotta learn to respect your superiors."

The gap closed as did the old man's fist as he swung at the assailant with the knife. They struck at the same moment. The knife fell from one's hand, the ground fell from the other's feet.

Oof! The old man gasped as his old, abused body crashed into a pile of stony rubble. The enemy moved in, relentless.

"YOU STUPID FUCKER!" the kid shouted as he kicked the old man lying crumpled before him.

"YOU STUPID, STUPID FUCKER!" Swinging into his belly as the others rushed up beside him.

"YOU DON'T CALL ME A FAGGOT, YOU HEAR!" Another thump sounded as he kicked the motionless man.

"YOU DON'T FUCKING CALL ME A MUMMY'S BOY YOU UNDERSTAND!" Thump. The body rolled away from the force of his boot, no longer able to move, respond or defend itself.

One of the others saw their leader following the body as it rolled lifelessly away from him. "Lay off Marlo, you'll kill him!"

Marlo stopped and turned to his friend who had spoken, and the others all saw Marlo's red, tear-swollen eyes and knew he was going to kill the old man.

"Don't you fucking tell me what to do, Chris. Or I'll fucking kill you!"

Chris backed away, not wanting to be part of a murder, or a victim.

Then the old man rose again.

Battered and bleeding, swaying on twitching legs, his lips fat and swollen, he murmured, "Pride is my armour. Prejudice is my enemy. Defiance is my weapon."

Marlo pulled out a gun, and fired it.

The old man collapsed dead, bullet through the head.

That's the spirit! That's how it's done, never give up and never give in. Once you've rediscovered the dream, never lose sight of it.

"You're fucking crazy!" one of the others screamed, "You didn't have to kill him!"

Know what you are, and never forget it. Never listen to the lies, never conform, never die.

"You shut your face, Malcolm, or I'll shoot you too."

They can't touch me, no one can. No one will.

"What are you going to do, Marlo, shoot all of us? You're sick!"

Sticks and stones may break my bones, but they will never touch me.

"No one, especially not some geriatric dead fucker, gives shit to me like that and gets away with it."

What a joke, all of it. Hah, hah, hah.

"He was just mad, he probably didn't know what he was doing. You didn't have to overreact so much!"

Laugh at life, and you'll laugh at death. Laugh at everything and you'll regret nothing.

"Well I did, and he's dead. So shut the fuck up!"

Not dead. Not old. Not wrong.

"Well, what are we going to do with him now?"

Proud and defiant unto death, beyond death, beyond the prejudices of a conforming society, remain true to oneself beyond the false emptiness and you'll carry beyond the false emptiness of life.

"Bury him, I guess. He's just another dead guy now."

If his useless body could have smiled, it would have...

*   *   *

All three of them laugh in chorus, and then scull another round of beers and laugh again.

Defiance looks over at you and says, "Are we laughing yet?"

Andrew looks at our face and says, "Defiance, you've gone too far! I'm shocked! ...Hah! Hah! Hah!"

Their laughter borders on hysteria, as the Evermore spans and spins around them.

And hopefully you're joining us, and laughing a little, even if only on the inside.

Andrew gets up then and announces, "Oh well, it's time to go! Follow me back to the beginning if you wish or else I'll see you later!"

Andrew heads off to ***THE FIRST INSTANCE*** (page 1) and we can now join him there if we wish.

Defiance rises from the table. "Well, I'm ***THE HELL BENT*** (page 301). You can follow me to hell if you dare. It isn't hard to find." He laughs. "All you have to do is close your eyes and when you open them, you'll be there!"

And with those words, Defiance disappears.

And now it is just us and the Joker. The Joker eternally laughing. Yet seeing our attention focus on him, he is gone too, in a cloud of echoing laughter...

In his place is a window onto ***THE DESCENDING*** (page 383).

Beckoning.

THE DESCENDING

THE DESCENDING

Now he is gone.

My other self, my alter-ego, gone with my childhood, my carelessness, my lack of direction and my love of living in the instantaneous moment of experience.

We drove on in silence. Silence reflected in the singular lack of emotional expression of what had just happened. Reflected in the singular lack of any music to buffet our eardrums and minds that were paralysed with disbelieving shock and swamped with alcohol. No melodies of passion and meaning to soothe us, the car stereo stolen and the portable one we had brought smashed and smouldering over the campfire we had left behind with Cesyl and Duncan back at Stevenson's Falls. No conversation between us to reflect and analyse the events and the irreversible actions taken. No feeling, no mood, no thoughts.

No care.

Maybe we, Chopper and I, would die on this winding mountain road. Maybe we, in our blinded state, would lose all and plunge over the edge and into the still depths of the earth from which we had been incarnated. Maybe we were not so different after all, both confused and angry souls in a conforming material world, where the only thing we had was a sense of disbelief and loss at what we and the world around us had become. But maybe, in the midst of all the turmoil our lives had become; where we had lost possessions, friends, employment and even a home; we had found something more valuable than all of these things put together.

Maybe we had discovered what it was like to be truly free...

The past couple of months had been a dramatic period of change and upheaval. Whatever stability there had been in our lives was obliterated. Our lives were stuffed through a great mincer of experiences, the pieces thrown clear and wide in different directions, and we were left dazed in the middle thinking, 'What the fuck?'

And nor was now to be the climax, though for Chopper and I it was certainly the turning point, and its impact will never leave us.

I likened what 'Life continued to throw at me' to a great roller-coaster ride. Initially I took a back seat and made no effort to direct its course. But as the ride became more terrifying, I swung between crying 'Please, please, make it stop! I can't take it anymore!' and saying 'Come on! Is that the best you can do? Make it harder; you haven't beaten me yet!' And now I had adjusted to a state where survival was the ultimate aim. I was prepared to do whatever it took to regain and maintain control of the ride that my life was. I had become selfish. I had become ruthless. I had become deceitful and secretive. I had become my other self, my alter-ego that now, I wanted to cut myself from.

Cesyl had taught me well, and I know, despite being the victim to my rage; that he too is proud of me for the alter-ego I became...

The events that brought things to their dramatic climax tonight (or actually this morning) were set into motion the previous night when I had Lana and Eve come down to Geelong for Eve's birthday.

Eve's birthday present was to be a day and night in Geelong at my mum's house while she was away. Having already been down from Melbourne with Chopper, Cesyl and Duncan, I was reluctant to travel back to Melbourne to collect Lana and Eve, though this was what had been arranged. I felt guilty about this, but didn't think it was such a big deal as Lana had a car anyway. What Cesyl didn't seem to understand, though, was that once Eve arrived my commitment was to her, being her 'birthday present'. Cesyl insisted on indulging in the drunken activities of 'the old days', and accused me of 'having changed' and 'not being who I used to be' when I said that I couldn't do these things tonight as they excluded Eve.

These words hurt me, and it hurt to think that he didn't understand my position. But it hurt most of all to think that he didn't care that I was hurt and was trying to do the best I thought I could do. In tears I explained my predicament to Eve and she expressed sympathy and understanding, though it seemed to me that she didn't like Cesyl anyway.

The following day, with both Cesyl and Lana pissed off at me, I was not in the best of moods. Lana and Eve returned to Melbourne and the rest of us decided to make the somewhat fateful trip to Stevenson's Falls to camp and get drunk.

My concerns and mood vanished as the four of us

drove down in my car (minus one stolen car stereo, and using my portable one as a substitute) drinking, laughing and making merry.

Arriving there at night, Cesyl and Duncan set up their tents, Chopper and I elected to sleep in the car, and then the real drinking began.

Things went well until Cesyl went on a wood-collecting splurge, stealing from other campsites, which culminated with Cesyl (accidentally?) dropping a log on my stereo by the fire and smashing it beyond use. Pissed as I was, and it now being after the fact, I didn't see much point in mourning its loss or getting angry with Cesyl. Nor did Cesyl. In fact his uncaring, laughing, 'Who gives a fuck?' attitude seemed to reflect a sense of pleasure in the destruction he had caused. This became all the more evident after we agreed to burn its remains over the fire and watch batteries, transistors and capacitors explode.

Not at any stage did he apologise or express remorse for what he had done. Eventually this afflicted me, and I found myself harbouring hurt, and worse, anger. I decided not to make an issue out of it though, thinking better to let it go and talk about it in the morning. I made for a sullen sleep in the car at about five am. Chopper, perhaps feeling the same way, joined me.

Cesyl however, didn't approve, and was most critical in telling me about it. The accusations arose of being a 'piker' and a 'soft-cock', and still I controlled my emotions and ignored his insults.

Yet Cesyl did not give in there, for he began to throw

things at and onto the car, determined to keep me up with him.

That was when I got out of the car and said those words that will never fade from memory.

"Cesyl. I'm not saying this pissed or anything like that. I'm saying this completely sober and I mean it. You are seriously pissing me off."

From this he fired his drunken response, a response lacking exactly that which I had been seeking and the only thing I really cared about, "Fuck off then, do what you want. I don't give a fuck what you think!"

Something snapped.

"You certainly know how to break off friendships," Chopper said, breaking the silence.

"I guess he just pushed me too far," I commented with a shrug.

"Of course he fucking did!" he responded. "It's something you should have done a long time ago!"

I looked at Chopper's sincere drunken face, and then away out the windscreen at the advancing rays of the early morning. "I don't hate him. I'm not sure that I ever will, and I don't want to. I can accept him for who he is, I just can't accept him any longer as a friend. I know that he took advantage of my generosity..."

"He treated you like shit!"

"All of which, as bad as it is, I'm prepared to put up with. I draw the line, though, when someone stops having respect for me as a friend, and stops showing any appreciation for what I'm doing."

"He was a fucking bastard, Brewin! We all knew it, except for you who couldn't see it. He used to joke with us about how he had you wrapped around his finger, and that as long as he apologised he could make you do whatever he wanted!"

I thought about Chopper's statement a little. As much as I had to be prepared to accept that I had been as blind as all that, I preferred to think that I was aware of what he was doing, but had decided to put up with it until now. That Cesyl had joked about it behind my back, something which I could fully envisage and believe, deepened my hurt and strengthened my resolve to distance myself from him. To this end, I repeated, "As I said, I don't hate him, I just can't accept him anymore as a friend of mine if he's going to treat me like that."

"Just so long as you don't go back to him and let him get away with it, or else he'll just keep doing it. Are you going to stick to your decision?"

I nodded, "Yeah, I hope so. It's been a decision that's been a long time coming. I don't regret the times that we have had, they were great times and he was my best friend. But now it's time I moved on from him, or else I'd be showing no respect for myself. The negative aspects of our friendship now outweigh the positive and unless he's prepared to change, which is his choice of course, I don't want him in my life anymore."

We had almost reached Apollo Bay by now, where we decided that we were going to rest until we had sobered up to make the two-hour drive back to Geelong. It would take Cesyl and Duncan eight hours to make the same trip to Apollo Bay on foot, only to miss the last bus back to Geelong, and have to end up staying overnight in a hotel.

"I guess also," Chopper began to speak, "that this is the end of my friendship with Cooper."

Cooper had recently broken off a ten to fifteen year-old friendship with both Chopper and Damien in anger for being mistreated and taken for granted. Cooper hadn't told them why he was pissed off, and said that if they didn't know then they couldn't have been good friends. As much as I tried to talk to 'both sides' about their differences and attempt reconciliation, it was something that didn't have much to do with me, and consequently something of which I didn't have much of an understanding. I had assumed, I guess, that eventually things would settle back down to what they had been. They'd be best of friends again with all forgotten.

But this was not the case.

"It has taken a while to accept," Chopper continued, "with us having been friends for so many years and never anything as big as this happening before. But I think it's finally sunk in, that from now on Cooper just won't be in my life anymore."

"Maybe he just needs a break, and then after a few months or so everything will be okay."

"Yeah... perhaps... but it really seems like this is it, this is the end."

My drunken mind and tired body were making it hard to be bothered doing anything except think of sleep. I couldn't carry on with the effort of being retrospective or analytical or constructively meaningful any more. I just lazily answered "Yeah," and left it at that. We discussed the topic a little more as we drove into Apollo Bay and looked for a secluded parking spot to sleep but the output of conversation wasn't great. Besides, I can't remember much more of what was said anyway.

Sleep.

I had hardly been there, when Chopper was waking me again.

"What time is it?" Were the first words I managed to formulate.

"Oh, about twelve, maybe one," he said.

Christ, it didn't feel like it, that would mean I'd been asleep four to five hours.

"I'm gunna go get something to eat man. D'you wanna come?" he asked.

I answered slowly, "Yeah, alright."

We staggered our dishevelled way across the road then, in dirty clothes and bare feet. We weren't so oblivious to things around us though, that we couldn't stop to admire a couple of fine ladies that passed us on the footpath.

Staggering into the milk bar I looked up at the wall clock opposite the doorway.

It was nine o'clock.

"Fucking hell, Chopper! It's only nine am!"

"Oh, sorry man. I seriously thought it was later than that."

I began to laugh. "We've only been asleep for a little over an hour for fuck's sake! Twelve or one you said!"

Putting his nicotine-stained hand to his unshaven face, he moaned, "I couldn't sleep in that car man, it was getting hot."

"Yeah it was, but getting up this early?"

Now it was a quarter to ten, and we were off again. We

were awake now and our bellies full. Lighting up our cigarettes, we decided that we might as well head back to Geelong but not onto Melbourne.

"Fuck man, these last couple of months have been crazy!" Chopper said.

"You got that right. I was talking to Cooper about it too. And he was saying that all these friendships breaking up etc. and people going in different directions was because he felt that some of us were growing up faster than others."

"Bloody Cooper, he would say something like that," he said angrily.

"I didn't quite agree with Cooper, I saw it as yeah we were growing up, all of us, but in different directions. It's twenty-one man. You know how I've talked to you before about how I believe life goes in sevens."

"Another of your Brewish theories."

"I mean of course this is a rough thing, but *generally* most of the biggest changes in your life I believe are in the year another seven turns over."

"But you have to be careful man," Chopper cautioned me, "and I don't want you to take offence at this, it may fit for you, and it may fit for me, but that doesn't mean that it works for everybody."

"Oh yes, of course! I only mean generally. And even then it's just a particular theory that I'm fond of at the moment. It has no real grounding at all, and I can't explain it scientifically; at least I haven't come up with an explanation for it yet. It's just a pattern that I've observed in my life and most of the lives of those around me."

"Well, as long as you know that."

We drove on towards Geelong. Talked a little. Thought mostly. And watched the scenery. The whole time Burton C Bell's immortal words, "They have tried to break you" echoed endlessly inside my head.

My thoughts. My attitude. My way of speaking. Did I seem arrogant and patronising? Perhaps I did. This is certainly the impression I often get. And yet I'm often inclined to agree with others and place belief in the ideas of others, and thus seem to be the opposite, gullible and impressionable.

I also thought a bit about my own behaviour, in particular towards Cesyl. And I realised that I suffered from the same problem Cooper did, and was guilty of the same thing he was, inexpressiveness.

I, like he, had kept things bottled up inside and had not addressed problems until I couldn't cope with them anymore. As a result we both had cut off friendships without giving the other a 'fair' chance, without resolving them before they reached such a climax.

But then I realised that I was doing it again. Living in self-doubt and criticism. Over-analysing myself and attempting to justify everything I did. I had taken this to an extreme and was quite sick of having to do it; or rather, feeling that I had to do it.

Maybe I'm being too harsh on myself, maybe I've been too harsh on others. Maybe I'm wrong. Maybe I'm a lot of things, but I know that one of these things I'm not is 'perfect'. I never truly could or will be; at least in the eyes of others. What I am though is me.

I let it pass, and Geelong only got closer.

And now. Like a lightning bolt that electrified through us and the car and our world and the world. Everything was different. I felt it. Chopper felt it too. Our world had changed. Things were as bad as they were ever going to be. We were descending no longer…

And all it had taken was two girls hitchhiking we had seen on the side of the road. Two girls, one of whom I thought I had recognised, both of whom we stopped and turned around to go pick up. Both of whom we missed out on as they climbed into another car. We realised our error. And subsequently the error of our lives.

Only Chopper and I truly know who said what, but it didn't matter; for either of us could have made either comment. For the first time in our friendship we thought as one, like twins, like kindred souls experiencing the same great revelation simultaneously.

"Fuck!" we cried in unison.

"I knew we should have picked them up!"

"We could have taken them both back to our place in Melbourne!"

"They were young, stupid and probably willing! We could have both had pussy for a week!"

"What were we thinking?"

"Our inhibitions prevented us from believing we had a chance, at last we could have given it a go and seen what would have happened!"

"*That's it! That's what we've been doing wrong all this time!* That experience symbolised our life and why we've been failing!"

"Opportunities! We've not been taking advantage of

opportunities, because we've not been believing in ourselves."

"Oh God! I can't believe this has happened. And it's just so simple! We've been missing it all along!"

"I've always said that's what you should do. Take advantage of opportunities. And this has just shown me my folly, and how it's done!"

"You've always said stuff like that, but it was like that's what you wanted to believe, not what you actually believed."

"I know."

"It's like I've always been so concerned with morals and how others see me, and being politically correct. But this has just shown us that it doesn't have anything to do with that."

"It's about taking advantage of opportunities. It's about doing what you want to do with your life. It's about freedom."

"It is!"

We were on our way to the station to drop Chopper off so he could catch the train back to Melbourne and I was to return to Geelong to see my mum who had arrived back today. But the restraints of reality exploded, burning away with it all the dilemmas that had choked our lives. Fuck that! We were going to Ballarat! On a whim and whirl! Crack open the beers! Let the highway roll on! Let life throw what it could at us, we would conquer all! We were free; we had control!

"I've never felt this happy in all my life!" Chopper boomed.

"It's a natural high, better than any drug!" I answered with a mad laugh.

And then began the song we sang together. It was just a simple tune really, the words didn't matter. Just a silly simple tune that emerged and expressed everything in soul. A tune we rolled and frolicked in as we laughed and bounced off each other into variations and elaborations of our answer to it all. Verse following verse in an eruption of improvised symmetry, creating movement, creating rhythm, and recreating life in all its wonder and fun.

"BERNEP BUM-BUM, BERNER-NER BUM-BUM;
BERNEP BUM-BUM, BERNER-NERNER BUM!"

I'M JUST CRUISING, OUT ON THE HIGHWAY;
LIFE IS MY OWN, I'LL LIVE IT MY WAY.

BERNAP BUM-BUM, BERNER-NER BUM-BUM;
BERNAP BUM-BUM, BERNER-NERNER BUM!

A BIRD'S A BIRD, AND A TREE'S A TREE;
YOU IS JUST YOU, AND ME IS JUST ME.

BERNAP BOM-BOM, BERNER-NER BOM-BOM;
BERNAP BOM-BOM, BERNER-NERER BOM!

AIN'T OUT TO HURT, NOT ME AND NOT YOU;
JUST OUT TO DO, WHAT I WANT TO DO.

BERNAP BOM-BOM, BERDU-DU BOM-BOM;
BERNAP BOM-BOM, BERDU-DUDU BOM!

IF EVER I'M DOWN, AND FOR HOPE I LONG;
I JUST SING THIS TUNE AND I CAN'T GO WRONG.

(This way to **THE INCOMPLETE** page 401)

BERNEP BUM-BUM, BERNER-NER BUM-BUM; (Ow!)
BERNEP BUM-BUM, BERNER-NERNER BUM! (Whoh!)

YOU LIVE YOUR LIFE, AND I'LL LIVE MINE;
OF YOUR LIES AND TRUTHS, I'VE GOT NO TIME.

BARDUP BAM-BAM, DARDAR-DAR BAM-BAM; (Bong!)
BARDUP BAM-BAM, CARDAR-DARDAR BAM! (Eeek!)

DON'T JUDGE, OPEN YOUR EYES AND SEE;
I'M NOT ANYBODY, I'M JUST FREE.

BOM-BOM BERNAP, BERNER-NER BOM-BOM (Bring
on the pussy!)
BOM-BOM BERNAP, BERNER-NERNER BOM! (Free
VBs!)

IF YOU EVER SEEK, YOUR JOURNEY'S END;
LOOK NO FURTHER, THIS IS IT MY FRIEND.

(This way to **THE VICTORIOUS** page 317)

BERNEP BUM-BUM, BERNER-NER BUM-BUM;
BERNEP BUM-BUM, BERNER-NERNER BUM!!!

*   *   *

And much later, when Chopper finally did go and I returned home to my anxious (!) mother, I saw something I had never seen before and will never forget:

Chopper was crying.

"I'm saved," he said...

(Turn now to **THE COMPLETE** page 417)

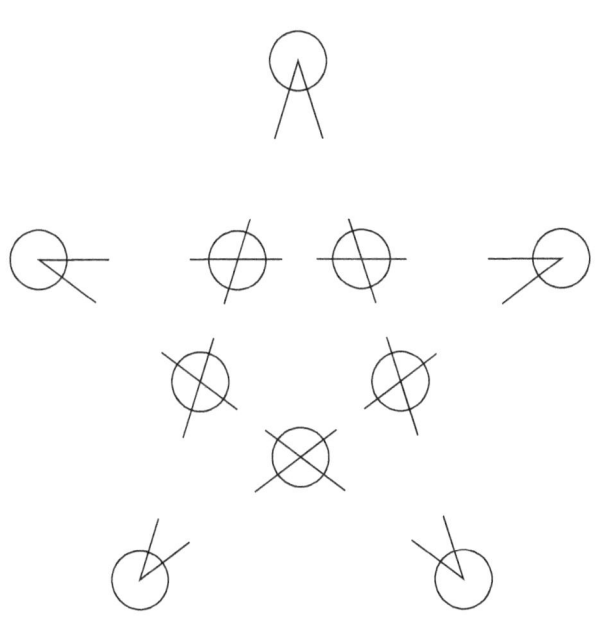

THE INCOMPLETE

THE INCOMPLETE

I have failed. I am lost. I am no longer.

I am nothing

Here I am again. Again I become. Again I try, I struggle, I fall, and again I weep with remorse, with pain, with loss.

Dreams become fractured, the mirror that reflects the person I may have been once, now no more.

Lord in me, of me, that is me.

Gone

Circles forever spiralling, paths forever turning on their end and spinning into their centre. Never maintained. Never restrained. Never claimed.

Yet never one

Help me, I pray. Emulating faith with desperation. Painting a portrait of hope with hopelessness. Drawing meanings of truth with lies. It was never meant to be this way, never should... never could.

Never will

Then a light shines forth, and my eyes are again open. It penetrates my consciousness, and bathes my soul in warmth. And then she says softly,

"Love is."

And then the stone my heart and mind once were, become as water again, and I am one once more.

Once and more...

*   *   *

Let us begin again then. With renewed vision. Let everything that was, be just that, and everything that will, be just this. Let us listen now to the words of another. Another that is you, that desires to speak to me. We enter the sphere of unity, where another waits to give us their words so that they may be ours.

In a round and radiant, yet incomplete, room a figure addresses us.

"Welcome. Let me tell of what you have come to learn from me at this part of your journey. But let me first tell you something of that which I am, and why I and you may be here.

"First. Take a look around you. Seriously," he says gesturing to us, "take a look around and see where you are. For the room you are in, is not the room I am in. Do you understand what I mean? Notice the design of the walls, notice the objects that fill the spaces, notice the sounds and smells that immerse you completely, notice the clothes you wear and the presence of others around you. Notice your feelings, your emotions and your thoughts.

"Are we noticing yet?" he says raising an eyebrow. "I think so. For notice these words reflect you and occupy part of your current consciousness.

"Now, I wonder if you can tell me something of what I am? Do you know? Perhaps you might, in fact you do. But let me tell you something of what I am, though this does not change what you see I am, unless you so choose, for I am also what you see.

"I am a mover. I have already moved your thoughts, feelings and emotions; however slightly; from where they were when this stage of your journey began, and from where they would have been had you not come here. Now I want to demonstrate to you how easy it is to do the same.

"Tell me something of what you are. Speak it aloud, repeat it... and notice. Notice a change? Do you notice a change, however slight, in your feelings, thoughts and emotions? Do it again and you may notice the difference you have induced even more. It does not matter if you elected not to do these things, the decision not to do, just as the decision to do, will have induced a change. A change you yourself induced.

"Now I am not you, this is obvious. But me being here with you, means that we can have an effect on each other, just as those around you can have an effect on you and you on them. Barriers of time and space make little difference, relative to the experience of the consciousness that we both share. For instance, that I am speaking the words to a listener such as you, has had an effect upon the words I speak. Were you not here to hear them then I might not have spoken them; this is an effect upon me that you have had.

"Now because any expectations of the nature of the effect I may have induced in you are based upon my own consciousness and experiences only, and not your consciousness and experiences, I may well be wrong (according to you) about my expectations. But despite this, I can still illustrate how not only your actions but also your consciousness (that you may come to realise are the same thing) have a direct effect on those around you, and they on you.

"Let me try to explain it this way. When you spoke something aloud of what you were (if you did) did you expect to see a change in those around you? (If there wasn't any around you at the time, this is a useful exercise to try later). Your expectations can guide your consciousness, and hence have an effect upon the perceptions you have of those around you.

"The expectation that you cannot have an effect upon others simply by a change in your own consciousness, if strong enough, creates exactly that effect. No change is observed because you did not expect such, in other words your consciousness did have an effect upon those around you to the extent that nothing happened! The reverse is also true if your expectation was strong enough that a change in your consciousness would induce a change in those around you, and a change in others would then be perceived.

"The other two cases, though in my experience less common, are of the expectation that one's consciousness can induce change in others and none is observed, and of the expectation that one's consciousness can't induce change in others and yet change is observed. But remember that just as you can induce change in others merely by the action of your consciousness, so can others induce change in you. Something contrary to our expectations, results in a change in our consciousness that is not the result of our expectations but the result of the consciousness of others that is guided by their expectations.

"And as one becomes increasingly sure of one's own beliefs, so one's expectations become stronger, directing one's consciousness more and more to observe the expectations one has.

"This means that someone convinced of their capacity to induce change in others, with increasing strength of expectation of this very effect, is likely to observe it more and more and thus becomes increasingly convinced of the truth of their beliefs. One who becomes increasingly convinced of their inability to induce change in others, likewise is likely to find increasing proof for this viewpoint as their expectations have a direct effect upon what they perceive.

"It is impossible to overstate the extent to which our consciousness has an effect upon the reality we experience. It shapes all our perceptions, beliefs and emotions on a fundamental level such that I find it fit to say that 'Imagination is your reality'.

"The extent to which you reject this and find cause to reject this, is precisely because of the very effect I am talking about. One finds 'wisdom' in the beliefs of others who are closest to their own, and rejects others as 'wrong' because of the extent to which their consciousness influences the way in which they perceive others and their beliefs.

"There is little point in me stressing this point any more, as those of you who were going to agree will have by now; and those of you who don't, probably never will because of the strength of your own expectations. My expectation that there is little point in stressing this further also serves to create this effect, which is why it is further futile.

"Having said that, I feel that we are getting somewhere. But where? Where is it that we are getting to? I hope for our sake that you know. And if you do not, have no fear for this only shields us. We seek to embrace, not hide or protect.

"I feel my thoughts becoming a little cloudy and I am reflected in you. I think it is time to open a window. Go over there, open that window that is before you now, and look out. Tell me what you see..."

It was beautiful. Sun-blessed golden wing tips crested majestic bronzed feathers in full bloom, like a richly embroidered Japanese fan. Eyes of purest emerald decorated an elegant head of soft amethyst whose purple caresses reached down to a supple torso that was a menagerie of dazzling colour and wonder. From this extended a brilliant plume of fiery magenta, and the slight but sturdy legs of what could be none other that the Si-ren. A true bird of paradise was what I had found.

"Well go on, you know you want to. Step outside and touch it," came a voice behind.

Carefully, oh so carefully, I eased myself through the window and out into the serene garden where perfection lay. Not wanting to scare it, not wanting to lose it, only to touch it, to breathe its presence.

Heaven on earth rested peacefully in a magical warm, olive grove where gentle light filtered down through ancient branches. A calming breeze blew through me and this natural sanctuary like a whisper stirring forgotten memories.

I crept barefoot through a lush carpet of sparkling dew and moss, engrossed in the deep earthy scents and textures of a place I had once known as home.

At the edge of its tranquil clearing, I was suddenly overcome by the desire to merely sit and watch, rather than be an intruder in this haven. Reluctantly, yet not daring disgrace, I contented myself to awe from a distance.

It turned to me, cooing sweetly in soothing tones. Humbled before this goddess of beauty, I was honoured that it should even notice me.

And then I thought, I felt, I might dare. I wanted, oh so badly, to touch it, to embrace it, to be one with its world and it with mine. My aching heart full of its beauty, I stepped into the dream, arms outstretched, wet with desire...

And then, startled, it took flight and was gone.

My world became dark and hopeless again.

"Open your eyes, brother, and see where you are."

Wearily I do and realise the dream is lost. Misery sets in. I'm back in the round and radiant room with the 'mover'.

"Do you know what that was?" he asks.

"Like nothing I have ever known or imagined," I answer with an infinite sadness.

"No. That was a memory, a memory of yours. That window you opened, was a window onto your past."

I stand now and face him, "That was my first experience of love, wasn't it?"

He corrects me, "That was your first experience of that kind of love. The kind that causes kings to give up their kingdoms, the kind that causes murderers to change their ways, the kind that causes the hopeless to find a new purpose to life."

Tiffany, my soul echoes. And with that comes the well of emotions, mostly painful, that were hidden beneath a thousand levels of denial. I had hurled myself through the seven heavens and nine hells for the love of her, and I suspect would do so again for the love of her.

"Look out that window again. What do you see now?"

Fearful of what I might see, expecting more pain to follow, I look.

I was searching. Searching an immense forest, for that which was no longer there to be found.

I was with a large company of friends, one of whom asked what I was looking for.

Feeling guilty about having to confess my obsession, I answered that I was searching for the Si-ren, that I had once seen here.

They laughed at me, all of them, and told me that my search was futile. The Si-ren would never be found, for it never existed.

But it does! It does! I insisted. It is somewhere here, we're so close! If we just keep looking, we'll find it.

They all laughed at me and I began to feel as if I hated them. My desire to find my idealised chimera drove me onwards and away from my friends who followed desperately trying to make me see reason.

We found many birds that were welcomed into our camp and one even ate out of my hand. The others said it fitted my description and must have been the one. But no, I said, it was much more beautiful than that, and I drove them all away and pushed on.

Days, weeks and years went on, and my friends became more and more frustrated with my efforts. But instead of admitting to my own stubbornness and relinquishing my dream, I merely became more secretive in my endeavours until eventually even I ceased to be aware of my persistence.

Beneath ever more layers of denial, the quest went on...

Tears in my eyes, I look away from the window.

"Take heart," he says to me, placing a sympathetic hand on my shoulder, "Everything has a negative and positive side to it, depending on how you perceive it. But it is not for me to comment on what you saw, it is for you to learn from. What do you feel it represented?"

I look up at him, my head feeling heavy. "It symbolised my search for love."

"Very good," he says, "And do you know what love is?"

I take a step back, having no idea what to say, or what he expects me to say. But then I begin to remember the feeling and a great spiritual warmth washes over me.

My head becomes clearer and lighter, and I answer, "Love is."

Is what the poorest man may have and the richest man may not.

Is beyond the minds of the greatest thinkers and beyond the plans of the greatest schemers.

Is the energy of life, the fabric of existence.

Is gravity that binds the universe.

Is the attraction between negative and positive.

Is unity, is everything.

Is Evermore, is God.

And yet it is always something else again, for it is not what it is and is what it is not.

The 'mover' speaks again, "I have one last thing to show you before you will again be on your journey from here. Something I think it important you see."

"What's that?"

"I'm going to show you your future..."

The 'mover' leads me to a window hidden behind a purple veil. It is dark on the other side, and at first I cannot make anything out. But then the vision becomes clearer, and I see myself, though years from now, sitting at a desk near the window writing, with my back turned.

I call out to myself writing on the other side, and look for a way to open the window. My future self writing does not hear my words, and I cannot see a way through to reach him. I want to ask him, 'What does my future hold? Will I achieve my dreams? Will I suffer? Will I find love?' but he is elsewhere, unreachable, in a world of his own.

And yet now I realise that by looking over his shoulder, and reading what he is writing, I might learn the answers to these very questions...

My future self continues writing, oblivious to my presence, and upon the pages before him I read:

A blank page stares up at me.
In its lines, I strain to see.
I try to speak my thoughts to this page,
And struggle to remain me...
Do I dare to feel again?

Has the seemingly endless torture of unrealised longing for a soul companion found the light of salvation at last? Do I dare to believe this?

I have become 'emotionally asleep' in progressively greater degrees ever since I first experienced the overwhelming and potentially crippling power of my own emotions; that being when I fell in love with Tiffany, a dream, a desire that was not to be. Better not to feel, not to care, not to aspire to have, than to be conscious of this need, to believe that I would find another. And so I became what my friends have seen me to be; the easygoing Brewin who was never fazed. And yet always beneath the veneer, the pain and longing lingered, suppressed ever deeper, a bottomless well of pity that I almost drowned in. And now I risk falling into that well again by rekindling hope. A paradox that in order to find idealised happiness I must face the danger of finding only misery once more...

*The last twenty-four hours have been as a dream that has brought me into contact with someone who has already 'swept me off my feet'. I know to admit this invites scorn and that it is reckless and potentially very damaging to the spirit of hope within me reignited. But I **want** to believe, and I seemingly can't staunch this rush of feeling, and I don't know where this leads. Yes, I think I must admit that this feeling is familiar and that I have previously called it 'love'. This is perhaps a shocking admission and it scares me greatly, for suddenly I have leapt to the edge of that well again and I don't know whether my judgement is sound enough to prevent me from plunging into its depths.*

Would fate, or whatever Gods/ spirits/ sentient force

that there is, deny me happiness again? I so dearly want to believe that after all the attempts, after all the myriad opportunities that have come to pass, this time will be different.

Twenty-four hours ago I had not even so much as kissed a girl for two years, since having left Kathryn of my own volition because of my own ideals that would seem to be more a curse than a boon. And yet many have tried to secure my affections, particularly Jacinta and Lana, whom I could not love despite their love for me, driving them into misery, which I too regret. For all this time I have waited and pretended I didn't care, wanting only to find someone whom I could share my existence with, and theirs with me.

> *So take my hand and render me blind.*
> *Hide me from the fear that grips my mind.*
> *I want to live, I want to be.*
> *No longer want to know nor want to see.*
> *A heart that knows is a heart that bleeds,*
> *A heart that feels is a heart that breeds.*
> *Let this life end and a new one begin.*
> *Let me enter the sphere of love to which I am kin.*
> *End this, end this now,*
> *Teach me to love, show me how.*
> *Willing to learn, don't want to burn,*
> *For destiny I yearn, my destiny I will earn.*

I feel I must end this passage now. I think it likely that I will not add to this for some time, as I fear the emotional consequences of such an exercise, as I have suffered before. Let this be an acknowledgment of this moment, of what I hope constitutes a new chapter in my life, one that will bring me the happiness I have sought for longer than I can remember. And only if so, will I acknowledge with any ease that this ever happened...

The veil falls back across the window and I turn to face the 'mover' once more. He makes to speak, but I interrupt him. "When do I write this? And what happens next? Do I find love?"

"I cannot provide answers to your questions for they cannot be known. The future is open and cannot be predicted, and yet that experience you just saw, is something you have already created."

"I see," I answer, disappointed.

"But really, this is your salvation, for it means that it's in your hands what happens. You write your own story; it is not fixed in stone.

"But I must leave you now to continue on your journey. If you seek to know where Andrew is now, you should move on to **THE DESCENDING** (page 383). If you seek an explanation for all of this, you should go to **THE CREATOR** (page 349). And if you're not sure where to go from here, let me suggest you turn to **THE UNCOMMITTED** (page 267)."

The choice as to what happens next is ours then...

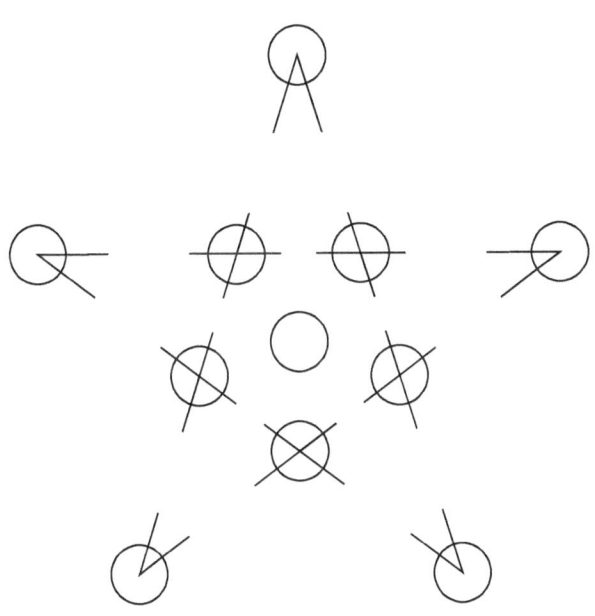

THE COMPLETE

THE COMPLETE

I entered a room and there he sat.

Smiling.

"Greetings," I said. "I have something to ask you."

"Ask it then," he said.

"I have nowhere left to go, I have no one left to turn to, I no longer know who I am, or what I am to do. They said that you were the one to seek, the fortress they call you, the one who would stand immune to all that existence could throw at you. I came to hear your words."

"I think it is time for you to begin again. To change the world that is yours and here's how you do it."

I bent forward, listening carefully and eager to catch every suggestion of meaning in the many expressions of his plastic and now elastic face.

"From within."

"What do you mean?" I asked, thinking that I did know and had already tried to do exactly that.

"It is important for you to understand that happiness, love, sorrow, despair, anger and security are all states of the mind, that are independent of the context that they arise from. This is to say, that in order to find heaven, or indeed hell, one cannot find it by looking for it in others, in possessions, or in fame or situations. It lies within. With the mind it is possible to make the brightest life the darkest, and the darkest life the brightest. Learn how to do this well, and you may never have to experience things such as regret, fear and sadness again."

"This would be what I would want."

"What you would want now, but I can assure you that once you understand how it is that these things come about, you will no longer fear experiencing them, and in fact you may find them enriching. For always beneath this 'veneer' of experience you will become aware of the unchanging soul within, the fortress that cannot be toppled."

"I still don't think I quite know what you mean. What is this fortress that you speak of?"

"Let me illustrate to you its strength. Come with me into my world and see where I have come from, and why I shall never be defeated. For I never seek to win."

*   *   *

I stood facing the interrogator. He must defeat me. He must show me what I was.

But he neither knew me nor was me.

"You're mad! Everyone says it. Everyone knows it. They see you as someone who no longer cares about anything, except yourself. Admit it."

"Yes."

"Hah! You admit that you are mad!"

"To you, yes."

"What do you mean 'to you'? You're either mad or you're not!"

"I expected more from you than a linear argument such as this. When you understand me from your point of view, perhaps I am. But this could well be the same conclusion I might reach if I were to understand you from my point of view, as opposed to attempting to understand another from the other's point of view."

The interrogator knew he was losing, he had to be better, and so he changed...

Now the interrogator became a (past) friend, intent on beating and toppling the fortress.

"You've changed!" claimed the interrogator. "You used to be such a good person, so full of compassion and care. Now look at you, you don't give a fuck about anyone except yourself!"

"You assume by my actions that I no longer care for my friends. I can understand your viewpoint but not agree with it."

"How can you say that? You don't give a shit about me! Or any of us! You're only there for us when it suits you!"

"Again I perceive that I can understand your reaction, but again I must disagree."

"How then? Explain to me how you can possibly disagree?"

"If you would listen, then I might bother."

"Yeah, I'm listening. Tell me!"

"Hah! Hah! Maybe you are listening with your ears, but little else. My words will mean nothing to you, whilst you continue to judge me and my actions like your perception is the ultimate truth."

"I am listening!"

"Okay, okay, I will try to explain to you, as I have done before. But I don't expect that it will do much, and indeed

I am beyond caring. I accept you as you, regardless of whether you accept me as me.

"Everyone has different experiences, different genes, and subsequently different beliefs and desires. Even our thought-patterns are distinctly different. This is why it is no good to attempt to make sense of something another does from one's own point of view. Because from one's own point of view, it doesn't make sense; but nor does one's own behaviour from the point of view of another. But despite this, most of us don't like to be seen as 'different' to others, as this usually results in misunderstanding and rejection. There is indeed strong social pressure towards homogeneity for this reason.

"An existing majority can easily perpetuate its beliefs and desires by conferring between each other and having one's own desires and beliefs reinforced in this way. For instance, you might well find that upon asking others, they agree with you, and therefore your judgement of me is strengthened. By all accountable means, this would appear to make your judgement certainly true now, if ever it was in doubt before. But this is not necessarily the case at all because of the social pressures of homogeneity that I explained before. When we consult another, we naturally 'choose' whom we consult, and this naturally results in us being far more likely to consult someone whom we know and trust than someone we do not. A criminal seeking confirmation of his/her beliefs will consult other criminals, a Christian other Christians, a parent other parents of the same outlook, etc. It is almost as if when we consult another, we are not seeking an objective evaluation, but rather that we receive support for our own viewpoint.

"I could deal with specifics, but I feel it would be pointless here and may be for some time to come. My actions are the result of my experience of the world, and yours the same. I have nothing further to say than this, and do not wish to entertain the possibility of arguing over semantics. If you don't understand now then I have no wish to expend further energy in the hope that you might. This is my choice, and it is nothing that you can force me to do without my choosing."

Beaten again, the interrogator changed once more, becoming an ex-girlfriend, one that I had once loved...

"I hate you! I hate everything about you! I used to think that you were so with it, so insightful and so gifted, but now I see how blinded I was. I see now how deluded you are."

"You once had respect for my view-point, probably because you understood it; and now you do not, probably because I could not return the love that you gave me."

"How can you be so cold?"

"Cold? Or honest?"

"You're just a remorseless liar!"

"To you maybe; but I am not you, and you are not me."

"You never cared for anyone but yourself!"

"If your objective is to make me admit that I am wrong, or to inflict hurt upon me that you perceive I have caused you, then you are wasting your time. To you what is cold and without care for others, to me is simply a belief that I should follow my own heart and not believe the words of others that try to erode my self-confidence. I do not lack care for you, or anyone else, but I will not sacrifice myself or be made to feel guilty for actions that I choose to undertake. I am as free to act, as you are."

"I've heard you say all this crap before. You just use it to hide behind and not have to admit the truth."

"If you insist on perceiving things in this way, I am not going to bother expending energy any longer to try to make you see any differently. However much I may care about and respect you, I will not allow your words to bring me down."

"You live in your own deluded world, like you're a god that can't be touched by anybody."

"God of myself perhaps, nothing more, or less."

"See you later then, you blind fool. Enjoy your fucked up kingdom!"

"See you later. I will look forward to a day when you can talk to me without hatred and anger, but will not despair if that day never comes."

"Don't worry. It won't!"

The interrogator tried one last time, this time as my mother...

"You've hurt me, your own mother. How could you do this to me?"

"Mum. I have no intention of hurting you and never have. You must understand that I cannot always be there for you when you need me, however much I may wish it to be otherwise, for I have my own life to lead and my own priorities which do not necessarily coincide with yours."

"You never come and see me. You never give me support. You only take from me. You've hurt me deeply."

"If you wish to continue seeing it in this way, then do so. But you must understand that this is not how I see it and not how I wish it to be. Most importantly you must understand that I will not allow you to use any form of blackmail over me in an attempt to make me feel responsible for how you feel. In the years to come you may understand my actions, but I feel it would be pointless to attempt to do so now, as you would probably not understand and, as in the past, it would do neither of us any good."

"Well, that really tops it off. You won't even try to explain to me why you are hurting me like this."

"I've tried before and it seems to have had little effect. I feel it would be pointless to try again now."

"Well, forget it then. Don't worry about ever coming to see your mother. I understand now; you don't care."

"Though that is not the way it is, if you insist on seeing it in this way, I will not accept responsibility for your perception. There may come a time when I shall try again to explain my actions to you, but that time is not now."

"Don't bother. You've hurt me too much. I don't think I could take any more hurt."

"In as much as I am sympathetic towards you for what you feel, I will not allow you to manipulate my feelings, or erode my own self-esteem. I am stronger than that, I will not be made to feel responsible for your feelings, however much you believe that I caused them, and however much others around you may confirm the same belief."

"I have..."

"I think that there is little point in continuing this conversation, as there seems little more to say. I am not without compassion for you, but I will not sacrifice myself for your sake."

"There is nothing more to say. I understand the way you feel. I'll try to cope. I know you don't care."

"I'll speak to you later, mum."

The fortress remained, as secure as ever.

*   *   *

The vision ended. I saw him differently now. And yet there was still a strength within him that I could not yet seem to comprehend. As if reading my thoughts, he answered.

"I, however I might try to be another, am I. Just as you, however you might try to be another, are you. The consequence of this is that however hard I might try to understand another from their point of view, it is still from my point of view; or more specifically it is still through the action of my consciousness that I understand another. In other words, it is still from my point of view, and not theirs at all. We only see things with our own eyes, we only hear things with our own ears, all thoughts we experience are our own, and the same for feelings that we may have. Though I might be able to assess what you see, hear, think or even feel, I still only evaluate what you see with what I see that you see, what you hear with what I hear that you hear, what you think with what I think you think, and what you feel with what I feel you feel. Which still means that this is my own world. For this reason you will never completely understand me, or I you. A result of this for me, is that I accept all others as what they are and try my best not to evaluate or discriminate against them. They are who they are and I will never truly understand what that is. This also means that I should not spend my life trying to get others to understand me, for this will never happen, except in the temporary sense that another might understand me (in a given situation) from their point of view.

"For this reason I will not endeavour to explain the fortress I have become any further. Judge me how you wish; it makes little difference to me. I hope despite this that you will find reason in at least some of what I have shown you, and that you are aware of this path as at least one possible means to reaching happiness and escaping the despair that you experience now."

"I hope so."

"If you choose to control it, you can. For fundamentally you *do* control your experience. Remember this and live with this knowledge, or belief as it may be, and you shall fare much better!"

"Thank you."

"Thank *you*! It's you, not me, to which you owe the greatest credit!"

*   *   *

I ascended through a vortex into the last of the eleven rooms. Yes, this was it. This was what I had been seeking. My journey's end at last.

The room in fact was empty, and dust-covered. Dust covered everything in grey. There were no features, no objects and no exits. Not many, if any, had come this way before. I looked around the room and realised that it was shaped as a dodecahedron, each of its twelve faces the shape of a pentagon.

I sat down cross-legged in the centre, searching my desires, thoughts and feelings for what I should do next.

...?

Truth, meaning and reality had ceased to have their place here. I was somewhere beyond in a way I cannot describe. Everything made perfect sense to me when I was there, but now that I am here, understanding fails me. That is to say, I cannot express any of this in words and something that can be expressed as such, is not what it is. The words you read are what I can recall, and my best efforts to describe something that is beyond beyondness. A blind man has more hope of understanding colour than I have of explaining this.

...,

From within came a voice. Actually it was not 'from', it was not 'within', it did not 'come', neither was it 'a', nor a 'voice'; yet given the tools of language that I have, that then seemed primitive in comparison, this was what happened.

THIS IS.

IT.

IT IS SIMPLE.

IT IS EASILY COMPREHENSIBLE TO ALL.

IT IS ONE, IT IS THERE FOR ALL, AND ALL ALREADY 'HAVE' IT.

IT WILL SET YOU 'FREE'...

Suffice to say, the room 'moved'. It 'became' and it 'went'.

And 'I' did too.

...!

I threw caution to the winds, I cast out all doubt and fear, in the purest 'knowing' that faith is, I fell to my knees and prayed.

"I believe."

And then all doorways were opened, for the last test had been passed.

The dust was 'cleared', and upon each of 'them' was written:

DO WHAT YOU WANT TO DO

BELIEVE WHAT YOU WANT TO BELIEVE

FEEL WHAT YOU WANT TO FEEL

And I knew that if nothing apart from these few words were ever told of my journey, it did not matter...

I am now given the choice to proceed onwards to The End, or to start the fifth circle over again if there is something I want to remember first.

The choice then is mine. Go on, or become ***THE WANDERER*** (page 249) once more.

What follows is my experience of what came after...
...and before, as it were.

I ascended finally into the ultimate, universal sphere. And man, what a party!

In room after room was the greatest collection of friends that had ever been in one place at any one time, clustered like the hives of a million, million bee colonies around the great hall of You Know What.

There were those who had been famous in life, and many more just as great and influential, who had not. Among them were wise seers, fabulous magicians, inspirational leaders, well-versed historians, the list went on *ad infinitum*. Here was the caring home-keeper, there the aboriginal warrior, over there the cunning thief, and there the pious priest. The forest druid, the insightful engineer, the gentle king and the delightful woman of the world. All in fact that had been and would be, were here. There were those who had lived for a thousand years as a single rock and those who had existed as a thousand species of insects. There were those who had been but a single bacterium, and those who had been the path of a single breath of air over the course of centuries. There were those whose existence had been a single feeling, sense or thought, whose lives did not go untold, and those whose consciousness had been of entire civilisations, species, or planets. There were those who had ventured into a life of pain and misery to experience what these qualities were; and those who had lived a life of luxury and material wealth for the exact same reason. There were those who had played the game of being the only enlightened one in the entire world to see what it was like, and those who experienced pure evil, emptiness or despair to understand its nature. There were those who studied the world from the viewpoint of mathematics, and those who did so from the viewpoint of psychology. There were those whose consciousness had been of a world without division of any form and others whose consciousness had been of a world without either love or God. There were those who had found that only one truth existed, and those who found that none at all existed. There were those whose consciousness had been one without thought, without feeling, or without physical sensations. There were those whose consciousness had been uniform between one and another, and those where time, hence memory, did not exist. There were those who spoke of ancient understanding via music, colour, deed, words or physical form. There were those who had played games of power, others of deceit, others of appearance, and others with truth, meaning or reality. There were those who had devised laws to explain the mechanics of imagination, emotion or time. There were those who had been the deities of differing religions, or the characters of folklore and fantasy. Every entity that had ever existed in conception, description or perception was here, and around stretching beyond the limits of being was every land, universe and reality ever imagined.

With every new idea, desire and action, on whatever place, level or being of existence, their number increased. They are all that is and will be, for they encompass time, consciousness and reality itself, and we are but the tiniest part of them, but no less important than any other for the uniqueness we represent.

It so was, that every other was the other, at another level of consciousness and reality. And they all met here and rejoiced in oneness regularly, before swapping identities and plunging anew into new journeys and games to remember, re-experience, relearn and again rejoice at the cosmos of being.

I could write an entire volume this size and larger, just trying to express a fraction of all the perceptions, emotions, thoughts and experiences encountered here on just a single visit. But it did not matter, for I knew that I, that we, that one, that all, would return here soon and 'be', and that our current 'level' of experience had been undertaken because I, we, one, all had chosen to.

At the centre of all this I found 'me', as I knew I would, being the creator of this journey. Not as I appear to you in your consciousness from reading of this journey or from meeting my physical persona, but the 'me' that I was.

That was when I realised that I was Evermore. That I was infinite yet finite, complete yet incomplete, ever-changing yet constant, comprehensible yet not, one yet many, separate yet unified, you yet me, God yet none, these things yet always something else, something more beyond description and current awareness. Further words here are futile, as I already understand me as me, and you, however I try, cannot for you are you. And though I will never understand you as you either, I am you. You, I, all, one is Evermore.

Evermore is Evermore, because it is.

(?, !)

I asked myself then, what is the truth?
As the wanderer on your journey you had read it:
DO WHAT YOU WANT TO DO
BELIEVE WHAT YOU WANT TO BELIEVE
FEEL WHAT YOU WANT TO FEEL
Through the words of Edwin you had heard it:
'YOU KNOW WHAT'
As one you know it:
'I'
These all express it, and by name I call it:
EVERMORE

I asked myself then, to explain it:
IT IS BEYOND EXPLANATION, FOR IT JUST IS. THOSE WHO TRY TO RESIST ALREADY ACT IT, THOSE WHO TRY TO REFUTE ALREADY KNOW IT, THOSE WHO TRY TO DENY ALREADY ARE IT. WHATEVER TRUTHS, MEANINGS, TERMS OR CONTEXTS ARE APPLIED TO IT, DO NOT CHANGE IT. IT JUST IS. AND WHAT IT IS TO AN OTHER, IS NOT WHAT IT IS TO ANOTHER OTHER, WHICH IS WHY IT IS EVERMORE.

I asked myself then, to describe it:
AS A STRAIGHT LINE IT IS A CIRCLE
AS A CIRCLE IT IS A SPIRAL

AS A SPIRAL IT IS A SPHERE
AS A SPHERE IT IS A SINGLE POINT
AS A COLLECTION OF POINTS IT IS A STRAIGHT
LINE
IT OCCUPIES ALL POINTS WITHIN IT AND SO IS
SOLID
ALL POINTS WITHIN IT HAVE NO VOLUME AND SO
IT IS EMPTY
IT IS NOT ANY OF THESE THINGS AS NOTHING
EXISTS OUTSIDE OF THESE THINGS, TO BE
THESE THINGS FROM
IT IS ALL REALITY AND POSSIBILITY
IT IS ALL PARADOX AND NOT
AS A PERCEPTION IT IS WHOLE YET EMPTY
AS AN EMOTION IT IS ALL YET NONE
AS A THOUGHT IT IS EVERYTHING YET NOTHING

I asked myself then, what its purpose is:
TO BE EVERMORE

I asked myself then, where it is going:
And to this, I laugh, "I don't know! Even if I did, I probably wouldn't tell you – that'd ruin the surprise! The ride itself is all the fun! And I can assure you, it's only just begun! Hah! Hah! Hah!"

I asked myself then, when it will end:
And to this, I laugh again, saying only:
"It won't!"

...HAH! HAH! HAH! HAH! HAH!

www.ingramcontent.com/pod-product-compliance
Lightning Source LLC
Chambersburg PA
CBHW071343020726
47502CB00001B/220

* 9 7 8 0 9 5 6 5 8 8 0 9 8 *